I0573191

William Shakespeare, Samuel Johnson, John Bell, George Steevens

The Dramatick Writings of Will. Shakspere

with the notes of all the various commentators - Vol. 4

William Shakespeare, Samuel Johnson, John Bell, George Steevens

The Dramatick Writings of Will. Shakspere
with the notes of all the various commentators - Vol. 4

ISBN/EAN: 9783337339760

Printed in Europe, USA, Canada, Australia, Japan

Cover: Foto ©Andreas Hilbeck / pixelio.de

More available books at **www.hansebooks.com**

THE

DRAMATICK WRITINGS

OF

WILL. SHAKSPERE,

With the Notes of all the various Commentators;

PRINTED COMPLETE FROM THE BEST EDITIONS OF

S A M. J O H N S O N and G E O. S T E E V E N S.

𝕮𝖔𝖑𝖚𝖒𝖊 𝖙𝖍𝖊 𝕱𝖔𝖚𝖗𝖙𝖍.

C O N T A I N I N G

MERRY WIVES of WINDSOR.
MUCH ADO ABOUT NOTHING.

L O N D O N:

Printed for, and under the Direction of,

JOHN BELL, 𝕭𝖗𝖎𝖙𝖎𝖘𝖍 𝕷𝖎𝖇𝖗𝖆𝖗𝖞, STRAND,

Bookseller to His Royal Highness the PRINCE of WALES.

M DCC LXXXVIII.

Bell's Edition.

MERRY WIVES of WINDSOR.

B Y

WILL. SHAKSPERE:

Printed Complete from the TEXT of

SAM. JOHNSON and GEO. STEEVENS,

And revised from the last Editions.

When Learning's triumph o'er her barb'rous foes
First rear'd the Stage, immortal *SHAKSPERE* rose;
Each change of many-colour'd life he drew,
Exhausted worlds, and then imagin'd new:
Existence saw him spurn her bounded reign,
And panting Time toil'd after him in vain:
His pow'rful strokes presiding Truth confess'd,
And unresisted Passion storm'd the breast.

DR. SAMUEL JOHNSON.

LONDON:

Printed for, and under the direction of,

JOHN BELL, British-Library, STRAND.

MDCCLXXXV.

OBSERVATIONS

ON THE Fable AND Composition OF THE
MERRY WIVES of WINDSOR.

OF this play there is a tradition preserved by Mr. Rowe, that it was written at the command of queen Elizabeth, who was so delighted with the character of Falstaff, that she wished it to be diffused through more plays; but suspecting that it might pall by continued uniformity, directed the poet to diversify his manner, by shewing him in love. No task is harder than that of writing to the ideas of another. Shakspere knew what the queen, if the story be true, seems not to have known, that by any real passion of tenderness, the selfish craft, the careless jollity, and the lazy luxury of Falstaff must have suffered so much abatement, that little of his former cast would have remained. Falstaff could not love, but by ceasing to be Falstaff. He could only counterfeit love, and his professions could be prompted, not by the hope of pleasure, but of money. Thus the poet approached as near as he could to the work enjoined him; yet having perhaps in the former plays completed his own idea, seems not to have been able to give Falstaff all his former power of entertainment.

This comedy is remarkable for the variety and number of the personages, who exhibit more characters appropriated and discriminated, than perhaps can be found in any other play.

Whether Shakspere was the first that produced upon the English stage the effect of language distorted and depraved by provincial or foreign pronunciation, I cannot certainly decide. This mode of forming ridiculous characters can confer praise only on him, who originally discovered it, for it re-

A ij

quires

quires not much of either wit or judgment: its success must be derived almost wholly from the player, but its power in a skilful mouth, even he that despises it, is unable to resist.

The conduct of this drama is deficient; the action begins and ends often before the conclusion, and the different parts might change places without inconvenience; but its general power, that power by which all works of genius shall finally be tried, is such, that perhaps it never yet had reader or spectator, who did not think it too soon at an end.   JOHNSON.

<hr>

Dramatis Perſonae.

MEN.

Sir JOHN FALSTAFF.
FENTON.
SHALLOW, *a Country Juſtice.*
SLENDER, *Cousin to Shallow.*
Mr. PAGE,   ⎱
Mr. FORD,   ⎰ *Two Gentlemen dwelling at Windsor.*
Sir HUGH EVANS, *a Welch Parson.*
Dr. CAIUS, *a French Doctor.*
Hoſt *of the Garter.*
BARDOLPH.
PISTOL.
NYM.
ROBIN, *Page to Falſtaff.*
WILLIAM PAGE, *a Boy, Son to Mr. Page.*
SIMPLE, *Servant to Slender.*
RUGBY, *Servant to Dr. Caius.*

WOMEN.

Mrs. PAGE.
Mrs. FORD.
Mrs. ANNE PAGE, *Daughter to Mr. Page, in love with Fenton.*
Mrs. QUICKLY, *Servant to Dr. Caius.*

Servants to PAGE, *Ford, &c.*

SCENE, *Windsor; and the Parts adjacent.*

MERRY WIVES of WINDSOR.

ACT I. SCENE I.

Before PAGE'S *House in Windsor.   Enter Justice* SHAL-
LOW, SLENDER, *and Sir* HUGH EVANS.

Shallow.

SIR Hugh, persuade me not: I will make a Star-
chamber matter of it : if he were twenty sir John
Falstaffs, he shall not abuse Robert Shallow,
esquire.

Slen. In the county of Gloster, justice of peace,
and *coram.*

Shal. Ay, cousin Slender, and *custalorum.*

Slen. Ay, and *ratalorum* too ; and a gentleman
born, master parson ; who writes himself *armigero;*
in any bill, warrant, quittance, or obligation, *armigero.*   11

Shal. Ay, that I do ; and have done any time these
three hundred years.

Slen.

Slen. All his successors, gone before him, have done't; and all his ancestors, that come after him, may : they may give the dozen white luces in their coat.

Shal. It is an old coat.

Eva. The dozen white louses do become an old coat well ; it agrees well, passant : it is a familiar beast to man, and signifies—love.   21

Shal. The luce is the fresh fish ; the salt fish is an old coat.

Slen. I may quarter, coz.

Shal. You may by marrying.

Eva. It is marring, indeed, if he quarter it.

Shal. Not a whit.

Eva. Yes, py'r-lady ; if he has a quarter of your coat, there is but three skirts for yourself, in my simple conjectures : but that is all one : If sir John Falstaff have committed disparagements unto you, I am of the church, and will be glad to do my benevolence, to make atonements and compromises between you.   34

Shal. The council shall hear it ; it is a riot.

Eva. It is not meet the council hear of a riot : there is no fear of Got in a riot : the council, look you, shall desire to hear the fear of Got, and not to hear a riot ; take your vizaments in that.

Shal. Ha ! o' my life, if I were young again, the sword should end it.   41

Eva. It is petter that friends is the sword, and end it : and there is also another device in my prain, which,

which, peradventure, prings goot discretions with it : there is Anne Page, which is daughter to master George Page, which is pretty virginity.

Slen. Mistress Anne Page ? she has brown hair, and speaks small like a woman. 48

Eva. It is that very person for all the 'orld, as just as you will desire ; and seven hundred pounds of monies, and gold, and silver, is her grandsire, upon his death's bed (Got deliver to a joyful resurrections !) give, when she is able to overtake seventeen years old : it were a goot motion, if we leave our pribbles and prabbles, and desire a marriage between master Abraham, and mistress Anne Page.

Slen. Did her grandsire leave her seven hundred pounds ?

Eva. Ay, and her father is make her a petter penny. 60

Slen. I know the young gentlewoman ; she has good gifts.

Eva. Seven hundred pounds, and possibilities, is good gifts.

Shal. Well, let us see honest master Page : is Falstaff there ?

Eva. Shall I tell you a lie ? I do despise a liar, as I do despise one that is false ; or, as I despise one that is not true. . The knight, sir John is there ; and, I beseech you, be ruled by your well-willers, I will peat the door [*Knocks*] for master Page, What, hoa! Got pless your house here ! 72

Enter

Enter PAGE.

Page. Who's there?

Eva. Here is Got's plessing, and your friend, and justice Shallow: and here is young master Slender; that, peradventures, shall tell you another tale, if matters grow to your likings.

Page. I am glad to see your worships well : I thank you for my venison, master Shallow.   79

Shal. Master Page, I am glad to see you ; Much good do it your good heart! I wish'd your venison better; it was ill kill'd :—How doth good mistress Page ?—and I thank you always with my heart, la; with my heart.

Page. Sir, I thank you.

Shal. Sir, I thank you ; by yea and no, I do.

Page. I am glad to see you, good master Slender.

Slen. How does your fallow greyhound, sir? I heard say, he was out-run on Cotsale.

Page. It could not be judg'd, sir.   90

Slen. You'll not confess, you'll not confess.

Shal. That he will not ;—'tis your fault, 'tis your fault :—'Tis a good dog.

Page. A cur, sir.

Shal. Sir, he's a good dog, and a fair dog; Can there be more said? he is good, and fair.—Is sir John Falstaff here?

Page. Sir, he is within ; and I would I could do a good office between you.

Eva.

Eva. It is spoke as a Christians ought to speak. 100

Shal. He hath wrong'd me, master Page.

Page. Sir, he doth in some sort confess it.

Shal. If it be confess'd, it is not redress'd ; is not that so, master Page ? He hath wrong'd me ;—indeed, he hath ;— at a word, he hath ;—believe me ;—Robert Shallow, esquire, saith, he is wrong'd.

Page. Here comes sir John.

Enter Sir JOHN FALSTAFF, BARDOLPH, NYM, *and* PISTOL.

Fal. Now, master Shallow ; you'll complain of me to the king ?

Shal. Knight, you have beaten my men, kill'd my deer, and broke open my lodge.   111

Fal. But not kiss'd your keeper's daughter ?

Shal. Tut, a pin ! this shall be answer'd.

Fal. I will answer it straight ;—I have done all this :—That is now answer'd.

Shal. The council shall know this.

Fal. 'Twere better for you, if 'twere known in council ; you'll be laugh'd at.

Eva. Pauca verba, sir John ; good worts.   119

Fal. Good worts ! good cabbage :—Slender, I broke your head ; What matter have you against me ?

Slen. Marry, sir, I have matter in my head against you ; and against your coney-catching rascals, Bardolph, Nym, and Pistol.

Bar. You Banbury cheese !

B

Slen.

Slen. Ay, it is no matter.

Pist. How now, Mephostophilus?

Slen. Ay, it is no matter.

Nym. Slice, I say! *pauca, pauca;* slice! that's my humour.   131

Slen. Where's Simple, my man?—can you tell, cousin?

Eva. Peace: I pray you! Now let us understand: There is three umpires in this matter, as I understand: that is—master Page, *fidelicet,* master Page; and there is myself, *fidelicet,* myself; and the three party is, lastly and finally, mine host of the Garter.

Page. We three, to hear it, and end it between them.   140

Eva. Fery goot: I will make a prief of it in my note-book; and we will afterwards 'ork upon the cause, with as great discreetly as we can.

Fal. Pistol,——

Pist. He hears with ears.

Eva. The tevil and his tam! what phrase is this, *He hears with ear?* Why, it is affectations.

Fal. Pistol, did you pick master Slender's purse?

Slen. Ay, by these gloves, did he (or I would I might never come in mine own great chamber again else), of seven groats in mill-sixpences, and two Edward shovel-boards, that cost me two shilling and two-pence a-piece of Yead Miller, by these gloves.

Fal. Is this true, Pistol?   155

Eva. No; it is false, if it is a pick-purse.

Pist.

Pist. Ha, thou mountain-foreigner!——Sir John,
    and master mine,
I combat challenge of this latten bilboe :
Word of denial in thy labra's here ;
Word of denial : froth and scum, thou ly'st.   160

Slen. By these gloves, then 'twas he.

Nym. Be avis'd, Sir, and pass good humours : I
will say, *marry trap*, with you, if you run the nuthook's humour on me ; that is the very note of it.

Slen. By this hat, then he in the red face had it :
for though I cannot remember what I did when you
made me drunk, yet I am not altogether an ass.

Fal. What say you, Scarlet and John ?

Bard. Why, sir, for my part, I say, the gentleman had drunk himself out of his five sentences.   170

Eva. It is his five senses : fie, what the ignorance
is !

Bard. And being fap, sir, was, as they say, cashier'd ; and so conclusions pass'd the careires.

Slen. Ay, you spoke in Latin then too ; but 'tis no
matter : I'll never be drunk whilst I live again, but
in honest, civil, godly company, for this trick : if I
be drunk, I'll be drunk with those that have the fear
of God, and not with drunken knaves.   179

Eva. So Got 'udge me, that is a virtuous mind.

Fal. You hear all these matters deny'd, gentlemen ; you hear it.

B ij

Enter

Enter Mistress Anne PAGE *with Wine;* Mistress FORD
and Mrs. PAGE *following.*

Page. Nay, daughter, carry the wine in ; we'll
drink within.   [*Exit* ANNE PAGE.

Slen. O heaven ! this is mistress Anne Page.

Page. How now, mistress Ford ?

Fal. Mistress Ford, by my troth, you are very
well met : by your leave, good mistress.

[*Kissing her.*

Page. Wife, bid these gentlemen welcome :—
Come, we have a hot venison pasty to dinner ; come,
gentlemen, I hope we shall drink down all un-
kindness.   192

[*Exeunt all but* SHAL. SLEND. *and* EVANS.

Slen. I had rather than forty shillings, I had my
book of songs and sonnets here :——

Enter SIMPLE.

How now, Simple ; where have you been ; I must
wait on myself, must I ? You have not the book of
riddles about you, have you ?

Sim. Bock of riddles ! why, did you not lend it to
Alice Shortcake npon Allhallowmas last, a fortnight
afore Michaelmas ?   200

Shal. Come, coz ; come, coz ; we stay for you.
A word with you, coz : marry, this, coz ; There is,
as 'twere, a tender, a kind of tender, made afar off
by sir Hugh here ;—Do you understand me ?

Slen.

Slen. Ay, sir, you shall find me reasonable; if it be so, I shall do that that is reason.

Shal. Nay, but understand me.

Slen. So I do, sir.

Eva. Give ear to his motions, master Slender: I will description the matter to you, if you be capacity of it.　　211

Slen. Nay, I will do, as my cousin Shallow says: I pray you, pardon me; he's a justice of peace in his country, simple though I stand here.

Eva. But that is not the question; the question is concerning your marriage.

Shal. Ay, there's the point, sir.

Eva. Marry, is it; the very point of it; to mis.tress Anne Page.

Slen. Why, if it be so, I will marry her, upon any reasonable demands.　　221

Eva. But can you affection the 'oman? let us command to know that of your mouth, or of your lips; for divers philosophers hold, that the lips is parcel of the mouth;—Therefore, precisely, can you carry your good-will to the maid?

Shal. Cousin Abraham Slender, can you love her?

Slen. I hope, sir,—I will do, as it shall become one that would do reason.

Eva. Nay, Got's lords and his ladies, you must speak possitable, if you can carry her your desires towards her.　　232

Shal. That you must: Will you, upon good dowry, marry her?

B iij

Slen.

Slen. I will do a greater thing than that, upon your request, cousin, in any reason.

Shal. Nay, conceive me, conceive me, sweet coz; what I do, is to pleasure you, coz: Can you love the maid? 239

Slen. I will marry her, sir, at your request; but if there be no great love in the beginning, yet heaven may decrease it upon better acquaintance, when we are marry'd, and have more occasion to know one another: I hope upon familiarity will grow more contempt: but if you say, *marry her*, I will marry her, that I am freely dissolved, and dissolutely.

Eva. It is a fery discretion answer; save the faul' is in the 'ort dissolutely: the 'ort is, according to our meaning, resolutely;—his meaning is good.

Shal. Ay, I think my cousin meant well. 250

Slen. Ay, or else I would I might be hanged, la.

Re-enter ANNE PAGE.

Shal. Here comes fair mistress Anne:—Would I were young for your sake, mistress Anne!

Anne. The dinner is on the table; my father desires your worship's company.

Shal. I will wait on him, fair mistress Anne.

Eva. Od's plessed will! I will not be absence at the grace. [*Ex.* SHAL. *and* EVANS.

Anne. Will't please your worship to come in, sir?

Slen. No, I thank you, forsooth, heartily; I am very well. 261

Anne. The dinner attends you, sir.

Slen.

Slen. I am not a-hungry, I thank you, forsooth:—
Go, sirrah, for all you are my man, go, wait upon
my cousin Shallow: [*Exit* Simp.] A justice of peace
sometime may be beholden to his friend for a man:
—I keep but three men and a boy yet, till my mother
be dead:. But what though: yet I live like a poor
gentleman born.

Anne. I may not go in without your worship: they
will not sit, till you come.   271

Slen. I'faith, I'll eat nothing: I thank you as much
as though I did.

Anne. I pray you, sir, walk in.

Slen. I had rather walk here, I thank you: I
bruis'd my shin the other day with playing at sword
and dagger with a master of fence, three veneys for
a dish of stew'd prunes; and, by my troth, I cannot abide the smell of hot meat since. Why do your
dogs bark so? be there bears i' the town?   280

Anne. I think, there are, sir; I heard them talk'd
of.

Slen. I love the sport well; but I shall as soon
quarrel at it, as any man in England:—You are
afraid, if you see the bear loose, are you not?

Anne. Ay, indeed, sir.

Slen. That's meat and drink to me now: I have
seen Sackerson loose, twenty times; and have taken
him by the chain: but, I warrant you, the women
have so cry'd and shriek'd at it, that it pass'd:—
but women, indeed, cannot abide 'em; they are very
ill-favour'd rough things.   292

Re-enter

Re-enter PAGE.

Page. Come, gentle master Slender, come; we stay for you.

Slen. I'll eat nothing, I thank you, sir.

Page. By cock and pye, you shall not choose, sir: come, come.

Slen. Nay, pray you lead the way.

Page. Come on sir.

Slen. Mistress Anne, yourself shall go first.   300

Anne. Not I, sir; pray you, keep on.

Slen. Truly, I will not go first; truly-la: I will not do you that wrong.

Anne. I pray you, sir.

Slen. I'll rather be unmannerly, than troublesome: you do yourself wrong, indeed-la.   [*Exeunt.*

SCENE II.

Enter EVANS and SIMPLE.

Eva. Go your ways, and ask of Dr. Caius' house, which is the way: and there dwells one mistress Quickly, which is in the manner of his nurse, or his dry nurse, or his cook, or his laundry, his washer, and his wringer.   311

Simp. Well, sir.

Eva. Nay, it is petter yet:—give her this letter; for it is a 'oman that altogether's acquaintance with mistress

mistress Anne Page; and the letter is, to desire and require her to solicit your master's desires to mistress Anne Page: I pray you, be gone; I will make an end of my dinner; there's pippins and cheese to come.   [*Exeunt severally.*

SCENE III.

The Garter Inn.   *Enter* FALSTAFF, HOST, BAR-DOLPH, NYM, PISTOL, *and* ROBIN.

Fal. Mine host of the Garter,—   320
Host. What says my bully-rook? speak scholarly, and wisely.
Fal. Truly mine host, I must turn away some of my followers.
Host. Discard, bully Hercules; cashier: let them wag; trot, trot.
Fal. I sit at ten pounds a week.
Host. Thou'rt an emperor, Cæsar, Keisar, and Pheezar. I will entertain Bardolph; he shall draw, he shall tap: said I well, bully Hector?   330
Fal. Do so, good mine host.
Host. I have spoke; let him follow: Let me see thee froth, and lime: I am at a word; follow.
                          [*Exit Host.*
Fal. Bardolph, follow him; a tapster is a good trade: An old cloak makes a new jerkin; a wither'd servingman, a fresh tapster: Go, adieu.
                          Bard.

Bard. It is a life that I have desir'd : I will thrive.

[*Exit* BARDOLPH.

Pist. O base Gongarian wight! wilt thou the spi-
got wield ?

Nym. He was gotten in drink : Is not the humour
conceited ? His mind is not heroic, and there's the
humour of it.   342

Fal. I am glad, I am so acquit of this tinderbox ;
his thefts were too open : his filching was like an un-
skilful singer, he kept not time.

Nym. The good humour is, to steal at a minute's
rest.

Pist. Convey, the wise it call : Steal ! foh ; a fico
for the phrase !

Fal. Well, sirs, I am almost out at heels.   350

Pist. Why then let kibes ensue.

Fal. There is no remedy ; I must coney-catch, I
must shift.

Pist. Young ravens must have food.

Fal. Which of you know Ford of this town ?

Pist. I ken the wight ; he is of substance good.

Fal. My honest lads, I will tell you what I am
about.

Pist. Two yards, and more.   359

Fal. No quips now, Pistol : Indeed, I am in the
waist two yards about : but I am now about no
waste ; I am about thrift. Briefly, I do mean to
make love to Ford's wife ; I spy entertainment in
her ; she discourses, she carves, she gives the leer
of invitation : I can construe the action of her familiar

liar stile ; and the hardest voice of her behaviour, to be English'd rightly, is, *I am sir John Falstaff's.*

Pist. He hath study'd her will, and translated her will; out of honesty into English.   369

Nym. The anchor is deep : Will that humour pass ?

Fal. Now, the report goes, she has all the rule of her husband's purse ; she hath a legion of angels.

Pist. As many devils entertain ; and, *To her, boy,* say I.

Nym. The humour rises ; it is good : humour me the angels.

Fal. I have writ me here a letter to her : and here another to Page's wife ; who even now gave me good eyes too, examin'd my parts with most judicious eyeliads : sometimes the beam of her view gilded my foot, sometimes my portly belly.   382

Pist. Then did the sun on dung-hill shine.

Nym. I thank thee for that humour.

Fal. O, she did so course-o'er my exteriors with such a greedy intention, that the appetite of her eye did seem to scorch me up like a burning-glass ! Here's another letter to her: she bears the purse too ; she is a region in Guiana, all gold and bounty.   I will be cheater to them both, and they shall be exchequers to me ; they shall be my East and West Indies, and I will trade to them both. Go, bear thou this letter to mistress Page ; and thou this to mistress Ford : we will thrive, lads, we will thrive.   395

Pist.

Pist. Shall I sir Pandarus of Troy become,
And by my side wear steel? then Lucifer take all!

Nym. I will run no base humour : here, take the
humour letter; I will keep the haviour of reputation.

Fal. Hold, sirrah, bear you these letters tightly;
Sail like my pinnace to these golden shores.   401
                              [*To* ROBIN.

Rogues, hence, avaunt! vanish like hail-stones, go;
Trudge, plod, away, o' the hoof; seek shelter,
        pack!
Falstaff will learn the humour of this age,
French thrift, you rogues; myself, and skirted page.
                      [*Exeunt* FALSTAFF *and Boy.*

Pist. Let vultures gripe thy guts! for gourd, and
        fullam holds;
And high and low beguiles the rich and poor :
Tester I'll have in pouch, when thou shalt lack,
Base Phrygian Turk!

Nym. I have operations in my head, which be humours of revenge.   411

Pist. Wilt thou revenge?

Nym. By welkin, and her star!

Pist. With wit, or steel?

Nym. With both the humours, I :
I will discuss the humour of this love to Ford.

Pist. And I to Page shall eke unfold,
        How Falstaff, varlet vile,
His dove will prove, his gold will hold,
        And his soft couch defile.   420
                              Nym.

Nym. My humour shall not cool: I will incense Ford to deal with poison : I will possess him with yellowness, for the revolt of mien is dangerous : that is my true humour.

Pist. Thou art the Mars of malecontents : I second thee ; troop on.   [*Exeunt.*

SCENE IV.

Dr. CAIUS's *House.*   *Enter Mrs.* QUICKLY, SIMPLE, *and* JOHN RUGBY.

Quic. What; John Rugby !—I pray thee, go to the casement, and see if you can see my master, master Doctor Caius, coming ; if he do, i'faith, and find any body in the house, here will be an old abusing of God's patience, and the king's English.

Rug. I'll go watch.   [*Exit* RUGBY.   432

Quic. Go ; and we'll have a posset for't soon at night, in faith, at the latter end of a sea-coal fire: An honest, willing, kind fellow, as ever servant shall come in house withal ; and, I warrant you, no tell-tale, nor no breed-bate : his worst fault is, that he is given to prayer ; he is something peevish that way : but no body but has his fault ;—but let that pass. Peter Simple, you say your name is ?   440

Sim. Ay, for fault of a better.

Quic. And master Slender's your master ?

Sim. Ay, forsooth.

C

Quic.

Quic. Does he not wear a great round beard, like a glover's paring-knife?

Sim. No forsooth: he hath but a little wee face, with a little yellow beard; a Cain-colour'd beard.

Quic. A softly-sprighted man, is he not?

Sim. Ay, forsooth: but he is as tall a man of his hands, as any is between this and his head; he hath fought with a warrener.   452

Quic. How say you?——oh, I should remember him; Does he not hold up his head, as it were? and strut in his gait?

Sim. Yes, indeed, does he.

Quic. Well, heaven send Anne Page no worse fortune! Tell master parson Evans, I will do what I can for your master: Anne is a good girl, and I wish——

Re-enter RUGBY.

Rug. Out, alas! here comes my master.   460

Quic. We shall all be shent: Run in here, good young man; go into this closet. [*Shuts* SIMPLE *in the closet.*] He will not stay long.—What, John Rugby! John, what, John, I say!—Go, John, go inquire for my master; I doubt, he be not well, that he comes not home:—*and down, down, a-down-a,* &c.

[*Sings.*

Enter Doctor CAIUS.

Caius. Vat is you sing? I do not like dese toys; Pray you, go and vetch me in my closet *un boitier*

verd;

verd; a box, a green-a box; Do intend vat I speak?
a green-a box.   470

Quic. Ay, forsooth, I'll fetch it you.
I am glad he went not in himself: if he had found
the young man, he would have been horn-mad.

> [*Aside.*

Caius. *Fe, fe, fe, fe! ma foi, il fait fort chaud.
Je m'en vai à la Cour,——la grande affaire.*

Quic. Is it this, Sir?

Caius. Ouy; mettez le au mon pocket; *Depéchez,*
quickly:—Vere is dat knave Rugby?

Quic. What, John Rugby! John!

Rug. Here, Sir.   480

Caius. You are John Rugby, and you are Jack
Rugby: Come, take-a your rapier, and come after
my heel to de court.

Rug. 'Tis ready, Sir, here in the porch.

Caius. By my trot, I tarry too long:——Od's me!
Qu'ay j'oublié? dere is some simples in my closet,
dat I vill not for the varld I shall leave behind.

Quic. Ay me! he'll find the young man there, and
be mad.

Caius. O diable, diable! vat is in my closet?—Vil-
laine, *Larron!* Rugby, my rapier.   491

> [*Pulls* SIMPLE *out of the Closet.*

Quic. Good master, be content.

Caius. Verefore shall I be content-a?

Quic. The young man is an honest man.

Caius. Vat shall de honest man do in my closet?
dere is no honest man dat shall come in my closet.

C i j

Quic.

Quic. I beseech you, be not so flegmatic; hear the truth of it. He came of an errand to me from parson Hugh.

Caius. Vell.   500

Sim. Ay, forsooth, to desire her to——

Quic. Peace, I pray you.

Caius. Peace-a your tongue :—Speak-a your tale.

Sim. To desire this honest gentlewoman, your maid, to speak a good word to mistress Anne Page for my master in the way of marriage.

Quic. This is all, indeed-la ; but I'll never put my finger in the fire, and need not.

Caius. Sir Hugh send-a you ?—Rugby, *baillez* me some paper: Tarry you a little while.   510

Quic. I am glad he is so quiet: if he had been thoroughly moved, you should have heard him so loud, and so melancholy ;—But notwithstanding, man, I'll do for your master what good I can: and the very yea and the no is, the French Doctor, my master,—I may call him my master, look you, for I keep his house; and I wash, wring, brew, bake, scour, dress meat and drink, make the beds, and do all myself.

Sim. 'Tis a great charge, to come under one body's hand.   520

Quic. Are you avis'd o' that? you shall find it a great charge : And to be up early, and down late ;—but notwithstanding (to tell you in your ear; I would have no words of it), my master himself is in love with mistress Anne Page ; but, notwithstanding

that,

that,——I know Anne's mind,——that's neither here
nor there.

Caius. You jack'nape ; give-a dis letter to sir
Hugh ; by gar, it is a shallenge : I vill cut his throat
in de park ; and I vill teach a scurvy jack-a-nape
priest to meddle or make :——you may be gone ; it
is not good you tarry here :——by gar, I will cut all
his two stones ; by gar, he shall not have a stone to
trow at his dog.   [*Exit* SIMPLE.

Quic. Alas, he speaks but for his friend.   535

Caius. It is no matter-a for dat :——do you not
tell-a me dat I shall have Anne Page for myself?——
by gar, I vill kill de jack priest; and I have appointed mine host of *de Jarterre* to measure our weapon :——by gar, I vill myself have Anne Page.   540

Quic. Sir, the maid loves you, and all shall be
well : we must give folks leave to prate : What, the
goujere !

Caius. Rugby, come to the court vit me ;——By
gar, if I have not Anne Page, I shall turn your
head out of door :——Follow my heels, Rugby.

[*Ex.* CAIUS *and* RUGBY.

Quic. You shall have An fools-head of your own.
No, I know Anne's mind for that : never a woman
in Windsor knows more of Anne's mind than I
do ; nor can do more than I do with her, I thank
heaven.   551

Fent. [*Within.*] Who's within there, ho ?

Quic. Who's there, I trow ? come near the house,
I pray you.

C iij

Enter

Enter Mr. FENTON.

Fent. How now, good woman; how dost thou?

Quic. The better that it pleases your good worship to ask.

Fent. What news? how does pretty mistress Anne?

Quic. In truth, Sir, and she is pretty, and honest, and gentle; and one that is your friend, I can tell you that by the way, I praise heaven for it.   561

Fent. Shall I do any good, thinkest thou? shall I not lose my suit?

Quic. Troth, sir, all is in his hands above: but notwithstanding, master Fenton, I'll be sworn on a book, she loves you :——Have not your worship a wart about your eye?

Fent. Yes, marry, have I; what of that?   568

Quic. Well, thereby hangs a tale;——good faith, it is such another Nan;——but I detest, an honest maid as ever broke bread :—We had an hour's talk of that wart;—I shall never laugh but in that maid's company!—But, indeed, she is given too much to allicolly and musing : But for you—Well—go to.

Fent. Well, I shall see her to-day : Hold, there's money for thee; let me have thy voice in my behalf : if thou seest her before me, commend me——

Quic. Will I? ay, faith, that we will : and I will tell your worship more of the wart, the next time we have confidence; and of other wooers.   580

Fent. Well, farewel; I am in great haste now.

[*Exit.*
Quic.

Quic. Farewel to your worship.—Truly, an honest gentleman; but Anne loves him not; I know Anne's mind as well as another does:—Out upon't! what have I forgot ?   [*Exit.*

ACT II.   SCENE I.

Before PAGE's *House.   Enter Mistress* PAGE *with a Letter.*

Mrs. Page.

WHAT, have I 'scap'd love-letters in the holy-day-time of my beauty, and am I now a subject for them? Let me see :

Ask me no reason why I love you; for though love use reason for his precisian, he admits him not for his counsellor : You are not young, no more am I; go to then, there's sympathy : you are merry, so am I; Ha! ha! then there's more sympathy : you love sack, and so do I; Would you desire better sympathy? let it suffice thee, mistress Page (at the least, if the love of a soldier can suffice), that I love thee; I will not say, pity me, 'tis not a soldier-like phrase; but I say, love me.   By me,   12

      Thine own true knight,
      By day or night,
      Or any kind of light,
      With all his might,
      For thee to fight.   John Falstaff.

                    What

What a Herod of Jewry is this?—O wicked, wicked world!—one that is well nigh worn to pieces with age, to shew himself a young gallant! What an un-weigh'd behaviour has this Flemish drunkard pick'd (with the devil's name) out of my conversation, that he dares in this manner assay me? Why, he hath not been thrice in my company!—What should I say to him?—I was then frugal of my mirth:—heaven forgive me!—Why, I'll exhibit a bill in the parliament for the putting down of men. How shall I be reveng'd on him? for reveng'd I will be, as sure as his guts are made of puddings.   29

Enter Mistress FORD.

Mrs. Ford. Mistress Page! trust me, I was going to your house.

Mrs. Page. And, trust me, I was coming to you. You look very ill.

Mrs. Ford. Nay, I'll ne'er believe that; I have to shew to the contrary.

Mrs. Page. 'Faith, but you do, in my mind.

Mrs. Ford. Well, I do then; yet, I say, I could shew you to the contrary: O, mistress Page, give me some counsel!

Mrs. Page. What's the matter, woman?   40

Mrs. Ford. O woman, if it were not for one trifling respect, I could come to such honour

Mrs. Page. Hang the trifle, woman; take the ho-nour: What is it?—dispense with trifles;—what is it?

Mrs.

Mrs. Ford. If I would but go to hell for an eternal moment, or so, I could be knighted.

Mrs. Page. What ?—thou liest !—Sir Alice Ford ! —These knights will hack ; and so thou shouldst not alter the article of thy gentry.   50

Mrs. Ford. We burn day-light !—here, read, read ; —perceive how I might be knighted.—I shall think the worse of fat men, as long as I have an eye to make difference of men's liking : And yet he would not swear ; prais'd women's modesty ; and gave such orderly and well-behav'd reproof to all uncomeliness, that I would have sworn his disposition would have gone to the truth of his words : but they do no more adhere, and keep place together, than the hundredth psalm to the tune of *Green Sleeves.* What tempest, I trow, threw this whale, with so many tuns of oil in his belly, ashore at Windsor ? How shall I be re-veng'd on him ? I think, the best way were to en-tertain him with hope, 'till the wicked fire of lust have melted him in his own grease.—Did you ever hear the like ?   66

Mrs. Page. Letter for letter ; but that the name of Page and Ford differs !—To thy great comfort in this mystery of ill opinions, here's the twin-brother of thy letter : but let thine inherit first ; for, I protest, mine never shall. I warrant, he hath a thousand of these letters, writ with blank space for different names (sure more), and these are of the second edition : He will print them out of doubt ; for he cares not what he puts into the press, when he would put us two.

I had

I had rather be a giantess, and lie under mount Pe-
lion.   Well, I will find you twenty lascivious turtles,
ere one chaste man.   78

Mrs. Ford. Why, this is the very same; the very
hand, the very words: What doth he think of us?

Mrs. Page. Nay, I know not: It makes me almost ready to wrangle with mine own honesty. I'll
entertain myself like one that I am not acquainted
withal; for, sure, unless he knew some strain in me,
that I know not myself, he would never have boarded me in this fury.

Mrs. Ford. Boarding, call you it? I'll be sure to
keep him above deck.   88

Mrs. Page. So will I; if he come under my hatch-
es, I'll never to sea again. Let's be reveng'd on him:
let's appoint him a meeting; give him a show of
comfort in his suit; and lead him on with a fine
baited delay, 'till he hath pawn'd his horses to mine
Host of the Carter.

Mrs. Ford. Nay, I will consent to act any villainy
against him, that may not sully the chariness of our
honesty. Oh, that my husband saw this letter! it
would give eternal food to his jealousy.

Mrs. Page. Why, look, where he comes; and my
good man too: he's as far from jealousy, as I am from
giving him cause; and that, I hope, is an unmea-
surable distance.   102

Mrs. Ford. You are the happier woman.

Mrs. Page. Let's consult together against this greasy
knight: Come hither.   [*They retire.*

Enter

Enter FORD *with* PISTOL, PAGE *with* NYM.

Ford. Well, I hope, it be not so.

Pist. Hope is a curtail-dog in some affairs :
Sir John affects thy wife.

Ford. Why, sir, my wife is not young.

Pist. He wooes both high and low, both rich and
  poor,   110
Both young and old, one with another, Ford ;
He loves thy gally-mawfry ; Ford, perpend.

Ford. Love my wife ?

Pist. With liver burning hot : Prevent, or go thou,
Like sir Actæon he, with Ring-wood at thy heels :—
O, odious is the name !

Ford. What name, sir ?

Pist. The horn, I say : Farewel.
Take heed ; have open eye ; for thieves do foot by
  night :
Take heed, ere summer comes, or cuckoo-birds do
  sing.—   120
Away, sir corporal Nym.——
Believe it, Page ; he speaks sense. [*Exit* PISTOL.

Ford. I will be patient ; I will find out this.

Nym. [*Speaking to* PAGE.] And this is true ; I like
not the humour of lying. He hath wrong'd me in
some humours : I should have borne the humour'd
letter to her ; but I have a sword, and it shall bite
upon my necessity. He loves your wife ; there's
the short and the long. My name is corporal Nym ;
I speak, and I avouch. 'Tis true :—my name is
           Nym,

Nym, and Falstaff loves your wife.—Adieu! I love
not the humour of bread and cheese; and there's the
humour of it. Adieu.   [*Exit* Nym.

Page. *The humour of it,* quoth a'! here's a fellow
frights humour out of its wits.   135

Ford. I will seek out Falstaff.

Page. I never heard such a drawling, affecting
rogue.

Ford. If I do find it, well.

Page. I will not believe such a Cataian, though
the priest o' the town commended him for a true
man.   142

Ford. 'Twas a good sensible fellow: Well.

Page. How now, Meg?

Mrs. Page. Whither go you, George?—Hark you.

Mrs. Ford. How now, sweet Frank, why art thou
melancholy?

Ford. I melancholy! I am not melancholy.—Get
you home, go.

Mrs. Ford. Faith, thou hast some crotchets in thy
head now.—Will you go, mistress Page? 151

Mrs. Page. Have with you.—You'll come to dinner, George?—Look, who comes yonder: she shall
be our messenger to this paltry knight.

       [*Aside to Mrs.* Ford.

Enter Mrs. Quickly.

Mrs. Ford. Trust me, I thought on her: she'll fit it.

Mrs. Page. You are come to see my daughter Anne?

          Quic.

Quic. Ay, forsooth; And, I pray, how does good mistress Anne?

Mrs. Page. Go in, with us, and see; we have an hour's talk with you.   160

  [*Ex. Mrs.* PAGE, *Mrs.* FORD, *and Mrs.* QUICKLY.

Page. How now, master Ford?

Ford. You heard what this knave told me; did you not?

Page. Yes; And you heard what the other told me?

Ford. Do you think there is truth in them?

Page. Hang 'em, slaves! I do not think the knight would offer it: but these, that accuse him in his intent towards our wives, are a yoke of his discarded men; very rogues, now they be out of service.

Ford. Were they his men?   170

Page. Marry, were they.

Ford. I like it never the better for that.—Does he lie at the Garter?

Page. Ay, marry, does he. If he should intend his voyage towards my wife, I would turn her loose to him; and what he gets more of her than sharp words, let it lie on my head.

Ford. I do not misdoubt my wife; but I would be loth to turn them together: A man may be too confident: I would have nothing lie on my head: I cannot be thus satisfied.   181

Page. Look, where my ranting host of the Garter comes: there is either liquor in his pate, or money in his purse, when he looks so merrily.—How, now, mine host?

D

Enter

Enter Host, and SHALLOW.

Host. How, now, bully-rook? thou'rt a gentleman: cavalero-justice, I say.

Shal. I follow, mine host, I follow.—Good even, and twenty, good master Page! Master Page, will you go with us? we have sport in hand.   190

Host. Tell him, cavalero-justice; tell him, bully-rook.

Shal. Sir, there is a fray to be fought, between sir Hugh the Welch priest, and Caius the French doctor.

Ford. Good mine host o' the Garter, a word with you.

Host. What say'st thou, bully-rook?

                       [*They go a little aside.*

Shal. [*To* PAGE.] Will you go with us to behold it? My merry host hath had the measuring of their weapons; and, I think, he hath appointed them contrary places: for, believe me, I hear, the parson is no jester. Hark, I will tell you what our sport shall be.

Host. Hast thou no suit against my knight, my guest-cavalier?

Ford. None, I protest: but I'll give you a pottle of burnt sack to give me recourse to him, and tell him, my name is Brook, only for a jest.   209

Host. My hand, bully: thou shalt have egress and regress; said I well? and thy name shall be Brook: It is a merry knight.—Will you go an-heirs?

Shal. Have with you, mine host.

Page. I have heard, the Frenchman hath good skill in his rapier.

Shal. Tut, sir, I could have told you more: In these times you stand on distance, your passes, stoccado's, and I know not what: 'tis the heart, master Page; 'tis here, 'tis here. I have seen the time, with my long sword, I would have made you four tall fellows skip like rats.   221

Host. Here, boys, here, here! shall we wag?

Page. Have with you:—I had rather hear them scold than fight.

        [*Exeunt Host,* SHALLOW, *and* PAGE.

Ford. Though Page be a secure fool, and stand so firmly on his wife's frailty, yet I cannot put off my opinion so easily: She was in his company at Page's house; and, what they made there, I know not. Well, I will look further into't: and I have a disguise to sound Falstaff: If I find her honest, I lose not my labour; if she be otherwise, 'tis labour well bestow'd.   [*Exit.*   232

SCENE II.

The Garter Inn.   Enter FALSTAFF *and* PISTOL.

Fal. I will not lend thee a penny.

Pist. Why, then the world's mine oyster, which I with sword will open.—I will retort the sum in equipage.

D ij

Fal.

Fal. Not a penny. I have been content, sir, you should lay my countenance to pawn : I have grated upon my good friends for three reprieves for you and your coach-fellow, Nym; or else you had look'd through the grate like a geminy of baboons. I am damn'd in hell, for swearing to gentlemen my friends, you were good soldiers, and tall fellows : and when mistress Bridget lost the handle of her fan, I took't upon mine honour, thou hadst it not.

Pist. Didst thou not share ? hadst thou not fifteen pence ?   247

Fal. Reason, you rogue, reason : Think'st thou, I'll endanger my soul *gratis?* At a word, hang no more about me, I am no gibbet for you :—go.—A short knife and a thong,—to your manor of Pickthatch, go.—You'll not bear a letter for me, you rogue! —you stand upon your honour!—Why, thou unconfinable baseness, it is as much as I can do, to keep the terms of my honour precise. I, I, I myself sometimes, leaving the fear of heaven on the left-hand, and hiding mine honour in my necessity, am fain to shuffle, to hedge, and to lurch; and yet you, rogue, will ensconce your rags, your cat-a-mountain looks, your red-lattice phrases, and your bold-beating oaths, under the shelter of your honour! You will not do it, you ?   262

Pist. I do relent; What wouldst thou more of man ?

Enter ROBIN.

Rob. Sir, here's a woman would speak with you.

Fal.

Fal. Let her approach.

Enter Mistress QUICKLY.

Quic. Give your worship good-morrow.

Fal. Good-morrow, good wife.

Quic. Not so, an't please your worship.

Fal. Good maid, then.

Quic. I'll be sworn; as my mother was, the first hour I was born. 271

Fal. I do believe the swearer: What with me?

Quic. Shall I vouchsafe your worship a word or two?

Fal. Two thousand, fair woman; and I'll vouchsafe thee the hearing.

Quic. There is one mistress Ford, sir;—I pray, come a little nearer this ways:—I myself dwell with master doctor Caius. 279

Fal. Well, on: Mistress Ford, you say,——

Quic. Your worship says very true: I pray your worship, come a little nearer this ways.

Fal. I warrant thee, nobody hears;—mine own people, mine own people.

Quic. Are they so? Heaven bless them, and make them his servants!

Fal. Well: mistress Ford;——what of her?

Quic. Why, sir, she's a good creature. Lord, lord! your worship's a wanton: Well, heaven forgive you, and all of us, I pray! 290

Fal. Mistress Ford;—come, mistress Ford,——

Quic. Marry, this is the short and the long of it;

D iij

you

you have brought her into such a canaries, as 'tis wonderful. The best courtier of them all, when the court lay at Windsor, could never have brought her to such a canary. Yet there has been knights, and lords, and gentlemen, with their coaches ; I warrant you, coach after coach, letter after letter, gift after gift ; smelling so sweetly (all musk), and so rusling, I warrant you, in silk and gold ; and in such alligant terms ; and in such wine and sugar of the best, and the fairest, that would have won any woman's heart; and, I warrant you, they could never get an eye-wink of her.—I had myself twenty angels given me this morning : but I defy all angels (in any such sort as they say), but in the way of honesty :—and, I warrant you, they could never get her so much as sip on a cup with the proudest of them all : and yet there has been earls, nay, which is more, pensioners ; but, I warrant you, all is one with her. 310

Fal. But what says she to me ? be brief, my good she Mercury.

Quic. Marry, she hath receiv'd your letter ; for the which she thanks you a thousand times : and she gives you to notify, that her husband will be absence from his house between ten and eleven.

Fal. Ten and eleven.

Quic. Ay, forsooth ; and then you may come and see the picture, she says, that you wot of ;—master Ford, her husband, will be from home. Alas ! the sweet woman leads an ill life with him ; he's a very jealousy man ; she leads a very frampold life with him,

him, good heart.

Fal. Ten and eleven : Woman, commend me to her; I will not fail her.

Quic. Why, you say well : But I have another messenger to your worship : Mistress Page has her hearty commendations to you too ;—and let me tell you in your ear, she's as fartuous a civil modest wife, and one (I tell you) that will not miss you morning nor evening prayer, as any is in Windsor, whoe'er be the other : and she bade me tell your worship, that her husband is seldom from home; but, she hopes, there will come a time. I never knew a woman so dote upon a man; surely, I think you have charms, la! yes, in truth.

Fal. Not I, I assure thee; setting the attraction of my good parts aside, I have no other charms.

Quic. Blessing on your heart for't!

Fal. But, I pray thee, tell me this : has Ford's wife, and Page's wife, acquainted each other how they love me?

Quic. That were a jest, indeed!—they have not so little grace, I hope :—that were a trick, indeed! But mistress Page would desire you to send her your little page, of all loves; her husband has a marvellous infection to the little page : and, truly, master Page is an honest man. Never a wife in Windsor leads a better life than she does; do what she will, say what she will, take all, pay all, go to bed when she list, rise when she list, all is as she will; and, truly, she deserves it; for if there be a kind woman in Windsor,

she

sle is one. You must send her your page ; no remedy.   354

Fal. Why, I will.

Quic. Nay, but do so then : and, look you, he may
come and go between you both ; and, in any case,
have a nay-word, that you may know one another's
mind, and the boy never need to understand any
thing ; for 'tis not good that children should know
any wickedness : old folks, you know, have discretion, as they say, and know the world.   362

Fal. Fare thee well ; commend me to them both :
there's my purse ; I am yet thy debtor.—Boy, go
along with this woman.—This news distracts me !

[*Exeunt* QUICKLY *and* ROBIN.

Pist. This pink is one of Cupid's carriers :—
Clap on more sails ; pursue ; up with your fights ;
Give fire ; she is my prize, or ocean whelm them all !

[*Exit* PISTOL.

Fal. Say'st thou so, old Jack ? go thy ways ; I'll
make more of thy old body than I have done. Will
they yet look after thee ? Wilt thou, after the expence
of so much money, be now a gainer ? Good body, I
thank thee : Let them say, 'tis grossly done, so it be
fairly done, no matter.   374

Enter BARDOLPH.

Bard. Sir John, there's one master Brook below
would fain speak with you, and be acquainted with
you ; and hath sent your worship a morning's draught
of sack.

Fal.

Fal. Brook, is his name?

Bard. Ay, sir.   380

Fal. Call him in; [*Exit* BARDOLPH.] Such Brooks
are welcome to me, that o'erflow such liquor.   Ah!
ha! mistress Ford and mistress Page, have I encom-
pass'd you? go to; *via!*

Re-enter BARDOLPH, *with* FORD *disguis'd.*

Ford. Bless you, sir.

Fal. And you, sir: Would you speak with me?

Ford. I make bold, to press with so little preparation upon you.

Fal. You're welcome; What's your will? Give us
leave, drawer.   [*Exit* BARDOLPH.

Ford. Sir, I am a gentleman that have spent much;
my name is Brook.   392

Fal. Good master Brook, I desire more acquaintance of you.

Ford. Good sir John, I sue for yours: not to
charge you; for I must let you understand, I think
myself in better plight for a lender than you are: the
which hath something embolden'd me to this unsea-
son'd intrusion; for they say, if money go before, all
ways do lie open.   400

Fal. Money is a good soldier, sir, and will on.

Ford. Troth, and I have a bag of money here
troubles me: if you will help me to bear it, sir John,
take all, or half, for easing me of the carriage.

Fal. Sir, I know not how I may deserve to be your
porter.

Ford.

Ford. I will tell you, sir, if you will give me the hearing.

Fal. Speak, good master Brook; I shall be glad to be your servant.   410

Ford. Sir, I hear you are a scholar,—I will be brief with you;—and you have been a man long known to me, though I had never so good means, as desire, to make myself acquainted with you. I shall discover a thing to you, wherein I must very much lay open mine own imperfection: but, good sir John, as you have one eye upon my follies, as you hear them unfolded, turn another into the register of your own; that I may pass with a reproof the easier, sith you yourself know, how easy it is to be such an offender.

Fal. Very well, sir; proceed.   421

Ford. There is a gentlewoman in this town, her husband's name is Ford.

Fal. Well, sir.

Ford. I have long lov'd her, and, I protest to you, bestow'd much on her; follow'd her with a doting observance; engross'd opportunities to meet her; fee'd every slight occasion, that could but niggardly give me sight of her; not only bought many presents to give her, but have given largely to many, to know what she would have given: briefly, I have pursued her, as love hath pursued me; which hath been, on the wing of all occasions. But whatsoever I have merited, either in my mind, or in my means, meed, I am sure, I have received none; unless experience be a jewel; that I have purchas'd at an infinite rate;

and

and that hath taught me to say this :   437

Love like a shadow flies, when substance love pursues;
Pursuing that that flies, and flying what pursues.

Fal. Have you receiv'd no promise of satisfaction
at her hands ?

Ford. Never.

Fal. Have you importun'd her to such a purpose ?

Ford. Never.

Fal. Of what quality was your love then ?

Ford. Like a fair house, built upon another man's
ground ; so that I have lost my edifice, by mistaking
the place where I erected it.

Fal. To what purpose have you unfolded this to
me ?   450

Ford. When I have told you that, I have told you
all. Some say, that, though she appear honest to me,
yet, in other places, she enlargeth her mirth so far,
that there is shrewd construction made of her. Now,
sir John, here is the heart of my purpose : You are a
gentleman of excellent breeding, admirable discourse,
of great admittance, authentic in your place and
person, generally allow'd for your many war-like,
court-like, and learned preparations.

Fal. O sir !   460

Ford. Believe it, for you know it :—There is money ;
spend it, spend it ; spend more ; spend all I have ;
only give me so much of your time in exchange of it,
as to lay an amiable siege to the honesty of this Ford's
                                                                                  wife :

wife: use your art of wooing, win her to consent to you; if any man may, you may as soon as any.

Fal. Would it apply well to the vehemence of your affection, that I should win what you would enjoy? methinks, you prescribe to yourself very preposterously.   470

Ford. O, understand my drift! she dwells so securely on the excellency of her honour, that the folly of my soul dares not present itself; she is too bright to be look'd against. Now, could I come to her with any detection in my hand, my desires had instance and argument to commend themselves; I could drive her then from the ward of her purity, her reputation, her marriage vow, and a thousand other her defences, which now are too too strongly embattled against me: What say you to't, sir John?   480

Fal. Master Brook, I will first make bold with your money; next, give me your hand; and last, as I am a gentleman, you shall, if you will, enjoy Ford's wife.

Ford. O good sir!

Fal. Master Brook, I say you shall.

Ford. Want no money, sir John, you shall want none.

Fal. Want no mistress Ford, master Brook, you shall want none. I shall be with her (I may tell you) by her own appointment; even as you came in to me, her assistant, or go-between, parted from me: I say, I shall be with her between ten and eleven; for at that time the jealous rascally knave, her husband,

will

will be forth. Come you to me at night; you shall
know how I speed.   495

Ford. I am blest in your acquaintance. Do you
know Ford, sir?

Fal. Hang him, poor cuckoldly knave! I know
him not:—yet I wrong him to call him poor; they
say, the jealous wittolly knave hath masses of money;
for the which, his wife seems to me well-favour'd. I
will use her as the key of the cuckoldly rogue's coffer; and there's my harvest-home.   503

Ford. I would you knew Ford, sir; that you might
avoid him, if you saw him.

Fal. Hang him, mechanical salt-butter rogue! I
will stare him out of his wits; I will awe him with
my cudgel; it shall hang like a meteor o'er the cuckold's horns: master Brook, thou shalt know, I will
predominate over the peasant, and thou shalt lie with
his wife.—Come to me soon at night:—Ford's a
knave, and I will aggravate his style; thou, master
Brook, shalt know him for knave and cuckold:—
come to me soon at night.   [*Exit.*

Ford. What a damn'd Epicurean rascal is this!—
My heart is ready to crack with impatience.—Who
says, this is improvident jealousy? my wife hath sent
to him, the hour is fix'd, the match is made: Would
any man have thought this?—See the hell of having a
false woman! my bed shall be abus'd, my coffers ran-
sack'd, my reputation gnawn at; and I shall not only
receive this villainous wrong, but stand under the
adoption of abominable terms, and by him that does

E

me

me this wrong. Terms! names!—Amaimon sounds
well; Lucifer, well; Barbason, well; yet they are
devils' additions, the names of fiends: but cuckold!
wittol! cuckold! the devil himself hath not such a
name. Page is an ass, a secure ass; he will trust his
wife, he will not be jealous: I will rather trust a
Fleming with my butter, parson Hugh the Welchman with my cheese, an Irishman with my aqua-vitæ
bottle, or a thief to walk my ambling gelding, than
my wife with herself: then she plots, then she rumi-
nates, then she devises; and what they think in their
hearts they may effect, they will break their hearts
but they will effect. Heaven be prais'd for my jealousy!—Eleven o'clock the hour;—I will prevent
this, detect my wife, be reveng'd on Falstaff, and
laugh at Page: I will about it;—better three hours
too soon, than a minute too late. Fie, fie, fie! cuckold! cuckold! cuckold!   [*Exit.*

SCENE III.

Windsor-Park.   Enter CAIUS *and* RUGBY.

Caius. Jack Rugby!
Rug. Sir.
Caius. Vat is de clock, Jack?
Rug. 'Tis past the hour, sir, that sir Hugh pro-
mis'd to meet.
Caius. By gar, he has save his soul, dat he is no
come; he has pray his Pible vell, dat he is no come:
                                                    by

by gar, Jack Rugby, he is dead already, if he be come.

Rug. He is wise, sir; he knew your worship would kill him, if he came.

Caius. By gar, de herring is no dead, so as I vill kill him. Take your rapier, Jack; I vill tell you how I vill kill him.

Rug. Alas, sir, I cannot fence.

Caius. Villan-a, take your rapier.

Rug. Forbear; here's company.

Enter Host, SHALLOW, SLENDER, *and* PAGE.

Host. 'Bless thee, bully doctor.

Shal. 'Save you, master doctor Caius.   560

Page. Now, good master doctor!

Slen. Give you good-morrow, sir.

Caius. Vat be all you, one, two, tree, four, come for?

Host. To see thee fight, to see thee foin, to see thee traverse, to see thee here, to see thee there; to see thee pass thy punto, thy stock, thy reverse, thy distance, thy montant. Is he dead, my Ethiopian? is he dead, my Francisco? ha, bully! What says my Æsculapius? my Galen? my heart of elder? ha! is he dead, bully Stale? is he dead?   571

Caius. By gar, he is de coward Jack priest of the vorld; he is not shew his face.

Host. Thou art a Castilian king, Urinal! Hector of Greece, my boy!

Caius. I pray you bear vitness that me have stay

six or seven, two, tree hours for him, and he is no
come.

Shal. He is the wiser man, master doctor : he is a
curer of souls, and you a curer of bodies ; if you
should fight, you go against the hair of your professions : is it not true, master Page?   582

Page. Master Shallow, you have yourself been a
great fighter, though now a man of peace.

Shal. Body-kins, master Page, though I now be
old, and of the peace, if I see a sword out, my finger
itches to make one : though we are justices, and doctors, and churchmen, master Page, we have some
salt of our youth in us ; we are the sons of women,
master Page.   590

Page. 'Tis true, master Shallow,

Shal. It will be found so, master Page. Master
doctor Caius, I am come to fetch you home. I am
sworn of the peace : you have shewn yourself a wise
physician, and sir Hugh hath shewn himself a wise
and patient churchman : you must go with me, master doctor.

Host. Pardon, guest justice :—A word, monsieur
mock-water.

Caius. Mock-vater ! vat is dat ?   6co

Host. Mock-water, in our English tongue, is valour, bully.

Caius. By gar, then I have as much mock-vater as
de Englishman : — Scurvy-jack-dog-priest ! by gar,
me vill cut his ears.

Host. He will clapper-claw thee tightly, bully.

Caius.

Caius. Clapper-de-claw! vat is dat?

Host. That is, he will make thee amends.

Caius. By gar, me do look, he shall clapper-de-claw me; for, by gar, me vill have it.   610

Host. And I will provoke him to't, or let him wag.

Caius. Me tank you for dat.

Host. And moreover, bully,—But first, master guest, and master Page, and eke cavalero Slender, go you through the town to Frogmore.   [*Aside to them.*

Page. Sir Hugh is there, is he?

Host. He is there: see what humour he is in; and I will bring the doctor about the fields; will it do well?

Shal. We will do it.   620

All. Adieu, good master doctor.

[*Exeunt* PAGE, SHALLOW, *and* SLENDER.

Caius. By gar, me vill kill de priest; for he speak for a jack-an-ape to Anne Page.

Host. Let him die: but, first, sheath thy impatience; throw cold water on thy choler: go about the fields with me through Frogmore; I will bring thee where mistress Anne Page is, at a farm-house a feasting; and thou shalt woo her: Cry'd game, said I well?   629

Caius. By gar, me tank you for dat: by gar, I love you; and I shall procure-a you de good guest, de earl, de knight, de lords, de gentlemen, my patients.

Host. For the which, I will be thy adversary toward Anne Page; said I well?

E iij

Caius.

Caius. By gar, 'tis good; vell said.

Host. Let us wag then.

Caius. Come at my heels, Jack Rugby. [*Exeunt.*

ACT III. SCENE I.

Frogmore. *Enter* EVANS *and* SIMPLE.

Evans.

I PRAY you now, good master Slender's serving-man, and friend Simple by your name, which way have you looked for master Caius, that calls himself *Doctor of Physick?*

Simp. Marry, sir, the Pitty-wary, the Park-ward, every way; old Windsor way, and every way but the town way.

Eva. I most fehemently desire you, you will also look that way.

Simp. I will, sir. 10

Eva. 'Pless my soul! how full of cholers I am, and trempling of mind!—I shall be glad, if he have deceiv'd me: how melancholies I am!—I will knog his urinals about his knave's costard, when I have good opportunities for the 'ork :—'pless my soul!

       [*Sings.*

> *By shallow rivers, to whose falls*
> *Melodious birds sing madrigals ;*
> *There will we make our peds of roses,*
> *And a thousand vragrant posies.*
>   *By shallow——* 20

       'Mercy

'Mercy on me! I have a great dispositions to cry.

> *Melodious birds sing madrigals;——*
> *When as I sat in Babylon——*
> *And a thousand vragrant posies.*
> *By shallow——*

Simp. Yonder he is coming, this way, sir Hugh.
Eva. He's welcome :——

> *By shallow rivers, to whose falls——*

Heaven prosper the right!—What weapons is he?
Simp. No weapons, sir: There comes my master, master Shallow, and another gentleman from Frogmore, over the stile, this way.   32
Eva. Pray you, give me my gown; or else keep it in your arms.

Enter PAGE, SHALLOW, and SLENDER.

Shal. How now, master parson? Good-morrow, good sir Hugh. Keep a gamester from the dice, and a good student from his book, and it is wonderful.
Slen. Ah sweet Anne Page!
Page. Save you, good sir Hugh!
Eva. 'Pless you from his mercy sake, all of you!
Shal. What! the sword and the word! do you study them both, master parson?   42
Page. And youthful still, in your doublet and hose, this raw rheumatick day?

Eva.

Eva. There is reasons and causes for it.

Page. We are come to you, to do a good office, master parson.

Eva. Fery well: What is it?

Page. Yonder is a most reverend gentleman, who belike, having receiv'd wrong by some person, is at most odds with his own gravity and patience, that ever you saw.

Shal. I have liv'd fourscore years, and upward; I never heard a man of his place, gravity, and learning, so wide of his own respect.

Eva. What is he?

Page. I think you know him; master doctor Caius, the renowned French physician.

Eva. Got's will, and his passion o' my heart! I had as lief you would tell me of a mess of porridge.

Page. Why?

Eva. He has no more knowledge in Hibocrates and Galen,—and he is a knave besides; a cowardly knave, as you would desires to be acquainted withal.

Page. I warrant you, he's the man should fight with him.

Slen. O, sweet Anne Page!

Enter HOST, CAIUS, *and* RUGBY.

Shal It appears so, by his weapons:—Keep them asunder;—here comes doctor Caius.

Page. Nay, good master parson, keep in your weapon.

Shal. So do you, good master doctor.

Host.

Host. Disarm them, and let them question ; let them keep their limbs whole, and hack our English.

Caius. I pray you, let-a me speak a word vit your ear : Verefore vill you not meet-a me ?

Eva. Pray you, use your patience : In good time.

Caius. By gar, you are de coward, de Jack dog, John ape.   79

Eva. Pray you, let us not be laughing-stogs to other men's humours; I desire you in friendship, and will one way or other make you amends :—I will knog your urinals about your knave's cogs-combs, for missing your meetings and appointments.

Caius. Diable!—Jack Rugby,—mine *Host de Jar-terre*, have I not stay for him, to kill him ? have I not, at de place I did appoint ?

Eva. As I am a Christians soul, now, look you, this is the place appointed; I'll be judgment by mine host of the Garter.   90

Host. Peace, I say, Gallia and Gaul, French and Welch, soul-curer and body-curer.

Caius. Ay, dat is very good ! excellent !

Host. Peace, I say; hear mine host of the Garter. Am I politick ? am I subtle ? am I a Machiavel ? Shall I lose my doctor ? no; he gives me the potions, and the motions. Shall I lose my parson ? my priest ? my sir Hugh ? no; he gives me the pro-verbs and the no-verbs.—Give me thy hand, terrestrial; so:—Give me thy hand, celestial ; so.—Boys of art, I have de-ceiv'd you both ; I have directed you to wrong places: your hearts are mighty, your skins are whole,

and

and let burnt sack be the issue.——Come, lay their swords to pawn:—Follow me, lad of peace; follow, follow, follow.

Shal. Trust me, a mad host.—Follow, gentlemen, follow.

Slen. O, sweet Anne Page!

[*Exeunt* SHAL. SLEN. PAGE, *and Host.*

Caius. Ha! do I perceive dat? have you make-a de sot of us? ha, ha!   110

Eva. This is well; he has made us his vlouting-stog.—I desire you, that we may be friends; and let us knog our prains together, to be revenge on this same scald, scurvy, cogging companion, the host of the Garter.

Caius. By gar, vit all my heart; he promise to bring me vere is Anne Page: by gar, he deceive me too.

Eva. Well, I will smite his noddles;—Pray you follow.

SCENE II.

The Street in Windsor.   Enter Mistress PAGE *and* ROBIN.

Mrs. Page. Nay, keep your way, little gallant; you were wont to be a follower, but now you are a leader: Whether had you rather, lead mine eyes, or eye your master's heels?

Rob.

Rob. I had rather, forsooth, go before you like a man, than follow him like a dwarf.

Mrs. Page. O, you are a flattering boy; now, I see, you'll be a courtier.

Enter FORD.

Ford. Well met, mistress Page : Whither go you?

Mrs. Page. Truly, sir, to see your wife; Is she at home? ¹³¹

Ford. Ay; and as idle as she may hang together, for want of company : I think, if your husbands were dead, you two would marry.

Mrs. Page. Be sure of that,—two other husbands.

Ford. Where had you this pretty weather-cock?

Mrs. Page. I cannot tell what the dickens his name is my husband had him of : What do you call your 'knight's name, sirrah?

Rob. Sir John Falstaff.

Ford. Sir John Falstaff!

Mrs. Page. He, he; I can never hit on's name. There is such a league between my good man and he! —Is your wife at home, indeed?

Ford. Indeed, she is.

Mrs. Page. By your leave, sir;—I am sick, 'till I see her.   [*Exeunt Mrs.* PAGE *and* ROBIN.

Ford. Has Page any brains? hath he any eyes? hath he any thinking? sure they sleep; he hath no use of them. Why, this boy will carry a letter twenty miles, as easy as a cannon will shoot point blank twelve score. He pieces-out his wife's inclination; he

gives

gives her folly motion, and advantage; and now she's going to my wife, and Falstaff's boy with her. A man may hear this shower sing in the wind!—and Falstaff's boy with her!——Good plots!—they are laid; and our revolted wives share damnation together. Well; I will take him, then torture my wife, pluck the borrow'd veil of modesty from the so seeming mistress Page, divulge Page himself for a secure and wilful Actæon; and to these violent proceedings all my neighbours shall cry aim. The clock gives me my cue, and my assurance bids me search; there I shall find Falstaff: I shall be rather prais'd for this, than mock'd; for it is as positive as the earth is firm, that Falstaff is there: I will go.   166

Enter PAGE, SHALLOW, SLENDER, *Host*, EVANS, *and* CAIUS.

Shal. Page, &c. Well met, master Ford.

Ford. Trust me, a good knot: I have good cheer at home; and, I pray you, all go with me.

Shal. I must excuse myself, master Ford.

Slen. And so must I, sir; we have appointed to dine with mistress Anne, and I would not break with her for more money than I'll speak of.

Shal. We have linger'd about a match between Anne Page and my cousin Slender, and this day we shall have our answer.

Slen. I hope, I have your good will, father Page.

Page. You have, master Slender; I stand wholly
                                                for

for you:—but my wife, master doctor, is for you altogether.   180

Caius. Ay, by gar; and de maid is love-a me; my
nursh-a Quickly tell me so mush.

Host. What say you to young master Fenton? he
capers, he dances, he has eyes of youth, he writes
verses, he speaks holy-day, he smells April and May:
he will carry't, he will carry't; 'tis in his buttons;
he will carry't.

Page. Not by my consent, I promise you. The
gentleman is of no having: he kept company with
the wild prince and Poins; he is of too high a region, he knows too much. No, he shall not knit a
knot in his fortunes with the finger of my substance :
if he take her, let him take her simply; the wealth
I have waits on my consent, and my consent goes not
that way.   195

Ford. I beseech you, heartily, some of you go home
with me to dinner : besides your cheer, you shall have
sport; I will shew you a monster.—Master doctor,
you shall go ;—so shall you, master Page ;—and you,
sir Hugh.   200

Shal. Well, fare you well :—we shall have the freer
wooing at master Page's.

Caius. Go home, John Rugby; I come anon.

Host. Farewel, my hearts: I will to my honest
knight Falstaff, and drink canary with him.

Ford. [*Aside*] I think, I shall drink in pipe-wine
first with him; I'll make him dance. Will you go,
gentles?

<table>
<tr><td>F</td><td style="text-align:right">*All.*</td></tr>
</table>

All. Have with you, to see this monster.

[*Exeunt.*

SCENE III.

FORD's *House.   Enter Mrs.* FORD, *Mrs.* PAGE, *and Servants with a Basket.*

Mrs. Ford. What, John! what, Robert!   210
Mrs. Page. Quickly, quickly; is the buck-basket—
Mrs. Ford. I warrant:——What, Robin, I say.
Mrs. Page. Come, come, come.
Mrs. Ford. Here, set it down.
Mrs. Page. Give your men the charge; we must be brief.

Mrs. Ford. Marry, as I told you before, John, and Robert, be ready here hard by in the brew-house; and when I suddenly call on you, come forth, and (without any pause or staggering) take this basket on your shoulders: that done, trudge with it in all haste, and carry it among the whitsters in Datchet mead, and there empty it in the muddy ditch, close by the Thames side.   224

Mrs. Page. You will do it?

Mrs. Ford. I have told them over and over; they lack no direction: Be gone, and come when you are call'd.   [*Exeunt Servants.*

Mrs. Page. Here comes little Robin.

Enter

Enter ROBIN.

Mrs. Ford. How now, my eyas-musket? what news with you? 231

Rob. My master sir John is come in at your back-door, mistress Ford; and requests your company.

Mrs. Page. You little Jack-a-lent, have you been true to us?

Rob. Ay, I'll be sworn : My master knows not of your being here; and hath threaten'd to put me into everlasting liberty, if I tell you of it; for, he swears, he'll turn me away. 239

Mrs. Page. Thou'rt a good boy; this secrecy of thine shall be a tailor to thee, and shall make thee a new doublet and hose.—I'll go hide me.

Mrs. Ford. Do so:—Go tell thy master, I am alone. Mistress Page, remember you your cue.

[*Exit* ROBIN.

Mrs. Page. I warrant thee ; if I do not aɛt it, hiss me. [*Exit Mrs.* PAGE.

Mrs. Ford. Go to then ;—we'll use this unwhole-some humidity, this gross watry pumpion ;—we'll teach him to know turtles from jays. 249

Enter FALSTAFF.

Fal. Have I caught thee, my heavenly jewel? Why, now let me die, for I have liv'd long enough ; this is the period of my ambition : O this blessed hour !

Mrs. Ford. O sweet sir John !

Fal. Mistress Ford, I cannot cog, I cannot prate,

F ij

mistress

mistress Ford. Now shall I sin in my wish : I would thy husband were dead ; I'll speak it before the best lord, I would make thee my lady.

Mrs. Ford. I your lady, sir John! alas, I should be a pitiful lady.   259

Fal. Let the court of France shew me such another ; I see how thine eye would emulate the diamond : Thou hast the right arched bent of the brow, that becomes the ship-tire, the tire-valiant, or any tire of Venetian admittance.

Mrs. Ford. A plain kerchief, sir John : my brows become nothing else ; nor that well neither.

Fal. Thou art a traitor to say so : thou would'st make an absolute courtier ; and the firm fixture of thy foot would give an excellent motion to thy gait, in a semi-circled farthingale. I see what thou wert, if fortune thy foe were not ; nature is thy friend : Come, thou canst not hide it.   272

Mrs. Ford. Believe me, there's no such thing in me.

Fal. What made me love thee ? let that persuade thee, there's something extraordinary in thee. Come, I cannot cog, and say, thou art this and that, like a many of these lisping haw-thorn buds, that come like women in men's apparel, and smell like Bucklers-bury in simple-time ; I cannot : but I love thee ; none but thee ; and thou deservest it.   281

Mrs. Ford. Do not betray me, sir ; I fear, you love mistress Page.

Fal. Thou might'st as well say, I love to walk by

the

the Counter-gate; which is as hateful to me as the reek of a lime-kiln.

Mrs. Ford. Well, heaven knows how I love you; and you shall one day find it.

Fal. Keep in that mind; I'll deserve it.

Mrs. Ford. Nay, I must tell you, so you do; or else I could not be in that mind.   291

Rob. [*Within*] Mistress Ford, mistress Ford! here's mistress Page at the door, sweating, and blowing, and looking wildly, and would needs speak with you presently.

Fal. She shall not see me; I will ensconce me behind the arras.

Mrs. Ford. Pray you, do so; she's a very tattling woman.——   [FALSTAFF *hides himself.*

Enter Mistress PAGE.

What's the matter? how now?   300

Mrs. Page. O mistress Ford, what have you done? you're sham'd, you are overthrown, you are undone for ever.

Mrs. Ford. What's the matter, good mistress Page?

Mrs. Page. O well-a-day, mistress Ford! having an honest man to your husband, to give him such cause of suspicion!

Mrs. Ford. What cause of suspicion?

Mrs. Page. What cause of suspicion?—Out upon you!—how am I mistook in you?   310

Mrs. Ford. Why, alas! what's the matter?

Mrs. Page. Your husband's coming hither, woman,

F iij   with

with all the officers in Windsor, to search for a gentleman, that, he says, is here now in the house, by your consent, to take an ill advantage of his absence: You are undone.

Mrs. Ford. Speak louder.—[*Aside*] 'Tis not so, I hope.

Mrs. Page. Pray heaven it be not so, that you have such a man here; but 'tis most certain your husband's coming with half Windsor at his heels, to search for such a one. I come before to tell you: If you know yourself clear, why I am glad of it: but if you have a friend here, convey, convey him out. Be not amaz'd; call all your senses to you; defend your reputation, or bid farewel to your good life for ever.

Mrs. Ford. What shall I do?—There is a gentleman, my dear friend; and I fear not mine own shame, so much as his peril: I had rather than a thousand pound, he were out of the house.   330

Mrs. Page. For shame, never stand *you had rather,* and *you had rather;* your husband's here at hand, bethink you of some conveyance: in the house you cannot hide him.—Oh, how have you deceived me!—Look, here is a basket; if he be of any reasonable stature, he may creep in here; and throw foul linen upon him, as if it were going to bucking: Or, it is whiting time, send him by your two men to Datchet mead.

Mrs. Ford. He's too big to go in there: What shall I do?   341

Re-enter

P.J. de Loutherbourg inv.t   P. Audinet sculp.t

Printed for J.Bell, British Library Strand London July n.th 1785.

Re-enter FALSTAFF.

Fal. Let me see't, let me see't! O let me see't! I'll in, I'll in;—follow your friend's counsel;—I'll in.

Mrs. Page. What! sir John Falstaff? Are these your letters, knight?

Fal. I love thee,—help me away: let me creep in here; I'll never——

  [*He goes into the Basket, they cover him with foul Linen.*

Mrs. Page. Help to cover your master, boy: Call your men, mistress Ford:—You dissembling knight!

Mrs. Ford. What, John, Robert, John! Go take up these clothes here, quickly; Where's the cowl-staff? look, how you drumble: carry them to the laundress in Datchet mead; quickly, come. 353

Enter FORD, PAGE, CAIUS, *and Sir* HUGH EVANS.

Ford. Pray you, come near: if I suspect without cause, why then make sport at me, then let me be your jest, I deserve it.—How now? whither bear you this?

Serv. To the laundress, forsooth.

Mrs. Ford. Why, what have you to do whither they bear it? you were best meddle with buck-washing.

Ford. Buck? I would I could wash myself of the buck! Buck, buck, buck? Ay, buck; I warrant you, buck; and of the season too, it shall appear. [*Exeunt Servants with the Basket.*] Gentlemen, I have dream'd to-night; I'll tell you my dream. Here, here, here

              be

be my keys : ascend my chambers, search, seek, find out : I'll warrant, we'll unkennel the fox :—Let me stop this way first :—So, now uncape.   368

Page. Good master Ford, be contented : you wrong yourself too much.

Ford. True, master Page.—Up, gentlemen ; you shall see sport anon : follow me, gentlemen.   [*Exit.*

Eva. This is fery fantastical humours, and jealousies.

Caius. By gar, 'tis no de fashion of France : it is not jealous in France.

Page. Nay, follow him, gentlemen ; see the issue of his search.   [*Exeunt.*

Mrs. Page. Is there not a double excellency in this ?

Mrs. Ford. I know not which pleases me better, that my husband is deceiv'd, or sir John.   381

Mrs. Page. What a taking was he in, when your husband ask'd who was in the basket!

Mrs. Ford. I am half afraid, he will have need of washing ; so throwing him into the water will do him a benefit.

Mrs. Page. Hang him, dishonest rascal! I would, all of the same strain were in the same distress.

Mrs. Ford. I think, my husband hath some special suspicion of Falstaff's being here ; for I never saw him so gross in his jealousy till now.   391

Mrs. Page. I will lay a plot to try that : And we will yet have more tricks with Falstaff : his dissolute disease will scarce obey this medicine.

Mrs. Ford. Shall we send that foolish carrion, mistress

tress Quickly, to him, and excuse his throwing into the water; and give him another hope, to betray him to another punishment?

Mrs. Page. We'll do it; let him be sent for to-morrow eight o'clock, to have amends.   400

Re-enter FORD, PAGE, *and the rest at a Distance.*

Ford. I cannot find him: may be the knave brag'd of that he could not compass.

Mrs. Page. Heard you that?

Mrs. Ford. I, I; peace :——You use me well, master Ford, do you?

Ford. Ay, I do so.

Mrs. Ford. Heaven make you better than your thoughts!

Ford. Amen.

Mrs. Page. You do yourself mighty wrong, master Ford.   411

Ford. Ay, ay; I must bear it.

Eva. If there be any pody in the house, and in the chambers, and in the coffers, and in the presses, heaven forgive my sins at the day of judgment!

Caius. By gar, nor I too; dere is no bodies.

Page. Fie, fie, master Ford! are you not asham'd? what spirit, what devil suggests this imagination? I would not have your distemper in this kind, for the wealth of Windsor-Castle.   420

Ford. 'Tis my fault, master Page: I suffer for it.

Eva. You suffer for a pad conscience : your wife is as honest a 'omans, as I will desires among five
thousand,

thousand, and five hundred too.

Caius. By gar, I see 'tis an honest woman.

Ford. Well;—I promis'd you a dinner :—Come, come, walk in the park : I pray you, pardon me; I will hereafter make known to you, why I have done this. Come, wife; come, mistress Page; I pray you pardon me; pray heartily, pardon me.   430

Page. Let's go in, gentlemen; but, trust me, we'll mock him. I do invite you to-morrow morning to my house to breakfast; after, we'll a birding together; I have a fine hawk for the bush : shall it be so?

Ford. Any thing.

Eva. If there is one, I shall make two in the company.

Caius. If there be one or two, I shall make-a de turd.

Eva. In your teeth :—for shame.   440

Ford. Pray you go, master Page.

Eva. I pray you now, remembrance to-morrow on the lousy knave, mine host.

Caius. Dat is good ; by gar, vit all my heart.

Eva. A lousy knave; to have his gibes, and his mockeries.   [*Exeunt.*

SCENE IV.

PAGE's *House. Enter* FENTON *and Mistress Anne* PAGE.

Fent. I see, I cannot get thy father's love ;
Therefore no more turn me to him, sweet Nan.

Anne.

Anne. Alas! how then?

Fent. Why, thou must be thyself.   450
He doth object, I am too great of birth;
And that, my state being gall'd with my expence,
I seek to heal it only by his wealth:
Besides these, other bars he lays before me,——
My riots past, my wild societies;
And tells me, 'tis a thing impossible
I should love thee, but as a property.

Anne. May be, he tells you true.

Fent. No, heaven so speed me in my time to come!
Albeit, I will confess, thy father's wealth   460
Was the first motive that I woo'd thee, Anne:
Yet, wooing thee, I found thee of more value
Than stamps in gold, or sums in sealed bags;
And 'tis the very riches of thyself
That now I aim at.

Anne. Gentle master Fenton,
Yet seek my father's love; still seek it, sir:
If opportunity and humblest suit
Cannot attain it, why then,——Hark you hither.

FENTON *and Mistress* ANNE *go apart.*

Enter SHALLOW, SLENDER, *and Mrs.* QUICKLY.

Shal. Break their talk, mistress Quickly; my kinsman shall speak for himself.   471

Slen. I'll make a shaft or a bolt on't: 'slid, 'tis but
venturing.

Shal. Be not dismay'd.

Slen.

Slen. No, she shall not dismay me : I care not for
that,—but that I am afeard.

Quic. Hark ye; master Slender would speak a word
with you.

Anne. I come to him.—This is my father's choice.
O, what a world of vile ill-favour'd faults   480
Look handsome in three hundred pounds a year!

[*Aside.*

Quic. And how does good master Fenton? Pray
you, a word with you.

Shal. She's coming; to her, coz. O boy, thou
hadst a father !

Slen. I had a father, mistress Anne ;—my uncle
can tell you good jests of him :—Pray you, uncle,
tell mistress Anne the jest, how my father stole two
geese out of a pen, good uncle.

Shal. Mistress Anne, my cousin loves you.   490

Slen. Ay, that I do ; as well as I love any woman
in Glocestershire.

Shal. He will maintain you like a gentlewoman.

Slen. Ay, that I will, come cut and long tail, under the degree of a 'squire.

Shal. He will make you a hundred and fifty pounds
jointure.

Anne. Good master Shallow, let him woo for himself.

Shal. Marry, I thank you for it ; I thank you for
that—good comfort. She calls you, coz : I'll leave
you.   501

Anne. Now, master Slender,

Slen. Now, good mistress Anne.

Anne.

Anne. What is your will?

Slen. My will? od's heartlings, that's a pretty jest,
indeed! I ne'er made my will yet, I thank heaven;
I am not such a sickly creature, I give heaven praise.

Anne. I mean, master Slender, what would you
with me?   509

Slen. Truly, for mine own part, I would little or
nothing with you: Your father, and my uncle, have
made motions: if it be my luck, so; if not, happy
man be his dole! They can tell you how things go,
better than I can: You may ask your father; here
he comes.

Enter PAGE, *and Mistress* PAGE.

Page. Now, master Slender:—Love him, daughter
        Anne.——
Why how now! what does master Fenton here?
You wrong me, sir, thus still to haunt my house:
I told you, sir, my daughter is dispos'd of.

Fent. Nay, master Page, be not impatient.   520

Mrs. Page. Good master Fenton, come not to my
        child.

Page. She is no match for you.

Fent. Sir, will you hear me?

Page. No, good master Fenton.
Come, master Shallow;—come, son Slender; in:—
Knowing my mind, you wrong me, master Fenton.
      [*Exeunt* PAGE, SHALLOW, *and* SLENDER.

Quic. Speak to mistress Page.

Fent. Good mistress Page, for that I love your
        daughter

G

In

In such a righteous fashion as I do,
Perforce, against all checks, rebukes, and manners,
I must advance the colours of my love,   531
And not retire: Let me have your good will.

Anne. Good mother, do not marry me to yon' fool.

Mrs. Page. I mean it not; I seek you a better hus-
    band.

Quic. That's my master, master doctor.

Anne. Alas, I had rather be set quick i' the earth,
And bowl'd to death with turnips.

Mrs. Page. Come, trouble not yourself: Good
    master Fenton,
I will not be your friend nor enemy :
My daughter will I question how she loves you,   540
And as I find her, so am I affected;
'Till then, farewel, sir :—She must needs go in.
Her father will be angry.

              [*Ex. Mrs.* PAGE *and* ANNE.

Fent. Farewel, gentle mistress; farewel, Nan.

Quic. This is my doing now;—Nay, said I, will
you cast away your child on a fool, and a physician ?
Look on master Fenton :—this is my doing.

Fent. I thank thee; and I pray thee, once to-night
give my sweet Nan this ring : There's for thy pains.

              [*Exit.*

Quic. Now heaven send thee good fortune! A kind
heart he hath : a woman would run through fire and
water for such a kind heart. But yet, I would my
master had mistress Anne; or I would master Slender
had her; or, in sooth, I would master Fenton had
              her :

her: I will do what I can for them all three! for so
I have promis'd, and I'll be as good as my word;
but speciously for master Fenton.   Well, I must of
another errand to Sir John Falstaff for my two mistresses; What a beast am I to slack it?   [*Exit.*

SCENE V.

The Garter Inn.   Enter FALSTAFF *and* BARDOLPH.

Fal. Bardolph, I say.—   560
Bard. Here, sir.
Fal. Go fetch me a quart of sack; put a toast in't.
[*Exit* BARD.] Have I liv'd to be carried in a basket,
like a barrow of butcher's offal; and to be thrown
into the Thames? Well; if I be serv'd such another
trick, I'll have my brains ta'en out, and butter'd, and
give them to a dog for a new year's gift. The rogues
slighted me into the river with as little remorse as
they would have drown'd a bitch's blind puppies,
fifteen i' the litter: and you may know by my size,
that I have a kind of alacrity in sinking; if the bottom were as deep as hell, I should down. I had
been drown'd, but that the shore was shelvy and shallow; a death that I abhor; for the water swells a
man; and what a thing should I have been, when I
had been swell'd! I should have been a mountain of
mummy.   577

Re-enter BARDOLPH, *with the Wine.*

Now, is the sack brew'd?

G i j

Bard.

Bard. Ay, sir: there's a woman below would speak with you.

Fal. Come, let me pour in some sack to the Thames water; for my belly's as cold, as if I had swallow'd snow-balls for pills to cool the reins. Call her in.

Bard. Come in, woman.   584

Enter Mrs. QUICKLY.

Quic. By your leave;—I cry you mercy:—Give your worship good morrow.

Fal. Take away these chalices: Go brew me a pottle of sack finely.

Bard. With eggs, sir?

Fal. Simple of itself; I'll no pullet-sperm in my brewage.—How now?   591

Quic. Marry, sir, I come to your worship from mistress Ford.

Fal. Mistress Ford! I have had ford enough: I was thrown into the ford; I have my belly full of ford.

Quic. Alas the day! good heart, that was not her fault: she does so take on with her men; they mistook their erection.

Fal. So did I mine, to build upon a foolish woman's promise.   601

Quic. Well, she laments, sir, for it, that it would yern your heart to see it. Her husband goes this morning a birding; she desires you once more to come to her between eight and nine: I must carry her word quickly: she'll make you amends, I warrant you.

Fal.

Fal. Well, I will visit her : Tell her so ; and bid her think, what a man is : let her consider his frailty, and then judge of my merit.

Quic. I will tell her. 610

Fal. Do so. Between nine and ten, say'st thou ?

Quic. Eight and nine, sir.

Fal. Well, be gone : I will not miss her.

Quic. Peace be with you, sir ! [*Exit.*

Fal. I marvel, I hear not of master Brook ; he sent me word to stay within : I like his money well. Oh, here he comes.

Enter FORD.

Ford. Bless you, sir !

Fal. Now, master Brook ? you come to know what hath pass'd between me and Ford's wife ? 620

Ford. That, indeed, sir John, is my business.

Fal. Master Brook, I will not lie to you ; I was at her house the hour she appointed me.

Ford. And you sped, sir ?

Fal. Very ill-favour'dly, master Brook.

Ford. How, sir ? Did she change her determination ?

Fal. No, master Brook : but the peaking cornuto her husband, master Brook, dwelling in a continual 'larum of jealousy, comes me in the instant of our encounter, after we had embrac'd, kiss'd, protested, and, as it were, spoke the prologue of our comedy ; and at his heels a rabble of his companions, thither provok'd and instigated by his distemper, and for- sooth, to search his house for his wife's love. 634

G i i j

Ford.

Ford. What, while you were there?

Fal. While I was there.

Ford. And did he search for you, and could not find you?

Fal. You shall hear. As good luck would have it, comes in one mistress Page; gives intelligence of Ford's approach; and, by her invention, and Ford's wife's distraction, they convey'd me into a buck-basket.

Ford. A buck-basket!   643

Fal. Yea, a buck-basket: ramm'd me in with foul shirts and smocks, socks, foul stockings, and greasy napkins; that, master Brook, there was the rankest compound of villanous smell, that ever offended nostril.

Ford. And how long lay you there?   649

Fal. Nay, you shall hear, master Brook, what I have suffer'd to bring this woman to evil for your good. Being thus cramm'd in the basket, a couple of Ford's knaves, his hinds, were call'd forth by their mistress, to carry me in the name of foul clothes to Datchet-lane: they took me on their shoulders; met the jealous knave their master in the door; who ask'd them once or twice, what they had in their basket: I quak'd for fear, lest the lunatic knave would have search'd it; but fate, ordaining he should be a cuckold, held his hand. Well; on went he for a search, and away went I for foul clothes. But mark the sequel, master Brook: I suffer'd the pangs of three several deaths: first, an intolerable fright, to be detected with a jealous rotten bell-weather: next, to be compass'd, like

a good

a good bilbo, in the circumference of a peck, hilt
to point, heel to head : and then, to be stopp'd in,
like a strong distillation, with stinking clothes that
fretted in their own grease : think of that,—a man
of my kidney—think of that ; that am as subject to
heat, as butter; a man of continual dissolution and
thaw ; it was a miracle, to 'scape suffocation. And in
the height of this bath, when I was more than half
stew'd in grease, like a Dutch dish, to be thrown into
the Thames, and cool'd, glowing hot, in that surge,
like a horse-shoe; think of that—hissing hot—think
of that, master Brook.   676

Ford. In good sadness, sir, I am sorry that for my
sake you have suffer'd all this.   My suit is then desperate; you'll undertake her no more ?

Fal. Master Brook, I will be thrown into Ætna, as
I have been into Thames, ere I will leave her thus.
Her husband is this morning gone a birding : I have
receiv'd from her another embassy of meeting; 'twixt
eight and nine is the hour, master Brook.   684

Ford. 'Tis past eight already, sir.

Fal. Is it ? I will then address me to my appointment.   Come to me at your convenient leisure, and
you shall know how I speed ; and the conclusion shall
be crown'd with your enjoying her : Adieu. You shall
have her, master Brook ; master Brook, you shall
cuckold Ford.   [*Exit.*   691

Ford. Hum! ha! is this a vision? is this a dream ?
do I sleep? master Ford, awake; awake, master Ford;
there's a hole made in your best coat, master Ford.

                                              This

This 'tis to be married! this 'tis to have linen, and buck-baskets!—Well, I will proclaim myself what I am : I will now take the lecher; he is at my house, he cannot 'scape me ; 'tis impossible he should ; he cannot creep into a half-penny purse, nor into a pepper-box : but, lest the devil that guides him should aid him, I will search impossible places. Though what I am I cannot avoid, yet to be what I would not, shall not make me tame : if I have horns to make one mad, let the proverb go with me, I'll be horn-mad.   [*Exit.*]   705

ACT IV. SCENE I.

PAGE'S *House.*   *Enter Mrs.* PAGE, *Mrs.* QUICKLY, *and* WILLIAM.

Mrs. Page.

Is he at master Ford's already, think'st thou?

Quic. Sure, he is by this ; or will be presently ; but truly, he is very courageous mad, about his throwing into the water. Mistress Ford desires you to come suddenly.

Mrs. Page. I'll be with her by and by ; I'll but bring my young man here to school : Look, where his master comes ; 'tis a playing-day, I see.

                         Enter

Enter Sir HUGH EVANS.

How now, sir Hugh? no school to-day?   9

Eva. No; master Slender is let the boys leave to play.

Quic. Blessing of his heart!

Mrs. Page. Sir Hugh, my husband says, my son profits nothing in the world at his book; I pray you, ask him some questions in his accidence.

Eva. Come hither, William;—hold up your head; come.

Mrs. Page. Come on, sirrah; hold up your head; answer your master, be not afraid.

Eva. William, how many numbers is in nouns?

Will. Two.   21

Quic. Truly I thought there had been one number more; because they say, od's nouns.

Eva. Peace your tatlings. What is *fair*, William?

Will. Pulcher.

Quic. Poulcats! there are fairer things than poulcats, sure.

Eva. You are a very simplicity 'oman; I pray you, peace. What is *Lapis*, William?

Will. A stone.   30

Eva. And what is a stone, William?

Will. A pebble,

Eva. No, it is *Lapis*; I pray you, remember in your prain.

Will. Lapis.

Eva.

Eva. That is a good William: What is he, William, that does lend articles?

Will. Articles are borrow'd of the pronoun; and be thus declin'd, *Singulariter, nominativo, hic, hæc, hoc.*   40

Eva. *Nominativo, hig, hag, hog;*—pray you, mark: *genitivo, hujus:* Well, what is your *accusative case?*

Will. *Accusative, hinc.*

Eva. I pray you, have your remembrance, child; *Accusativo, hung, hang, hog.*

Quic. Hang hog is Latin for bacon, I warrant you.

Eva. Leave your prabbles, 'oman. What is the focative case, William?

Will. O—*vocativo,* O.

Eva. Remember, William, focative is, *caret.*   50

Quic. And that's a good root.

Eva. 'Oman, forbear.

Mrs. Page. Peace.

Eva. What is your *genitive case plural,* William?

Will. *Genitive case?*

Eva. Ay.

Will. *Genitive, horum, harum, horum.*

Quic. 'Vengeance of *Giney's* case! fie on her!—never name her, child, if she be a whore.

Eva. For shame, 'oman.   60

Quic. You do ill to teach the child such words: he teaches him to hick and to hack, which they'll do fast enough of themselves; and to call horum:—fie upon you!

Eva. 'Oman art thou lunatics? hast thou no understanding

standing for thy cases, and the numbers of the gen-
ders? thou art a foolish Christian creatures, as I,
would desires.

Mrs. Page. Pr'ythee, hold thy peace.   69

Eva. Shew me now, William, some declensions of
your pronouns.

Will. Forsooth, I have forgot.

Eva. It is *ki*, *kæ*, *cod*; if you forget your *kies*,
your *kæs*, and your *cods*, you must be preeches. Go
your ways and play, go.

Mrs. Page. He is a better scholar, than I thought
he was.

Eva. He is a good sprag memory. Farewel, mistress Page.   79

Mrs. Page. Adieu, good sir Hugh. Get you home,
boy.—Come, we stay too long.   [*Exeunt.*

SCENE II.

FORD's *House.   Enter* FALSTAFF, *and Mrs.* FORD.

Fal. Mistress Ford, your sorrow hath eaten up my
sufferance : I see, you are obsequious in your love,
and I profess requital to a hair's breadth; not only,
mistress Ford, in the simple office of love, but in all
the accoutrement, complement, and ceremony of it.
But are you sure of your husband now?

Mrs. Ford. He's a birding, sweet sir John.

Mrs.

Mrs. Page. [*Within.*] What hoa, gossip Ford ! what hoa!   90

Mrs. Ford. Step into the chamber, sir John.

          [*Exit* FALSTAFF.

Enter Mrs. PAGE.

Mrs. Page. How now, sweetheart ? who's at home besides yourself?

Mrs. Ford. Why, none but mine own people.

Mrs. Page. Indeed ?

Mrs. Ford. No, certainly—Speak louder. [*Aside.*

Mrs. Page. Truly, 1 am so glad you have nobody here.

Mrs. Ford. Why?   99

Mrs. Page. Why, woman, your husband is in his old lunes again : he so takes on yonder with my husband ; so rails against all married mankind ; so curses all Eve's daughters, of what complexion so-ever; and so buffets himself on the forehead, crying, *Peer-out, peer-out !* that any madness, I ever yet beheld, seem'd but tameness, civility, and patience, to this distemper he is in now : I am glad the fat knight is not here.

Mrs. Ford. Why, does he talk of him ?   109

Mrs. Page. Of none but him ; and swears, he was carried out, the last time he search'd for him, in a basket : protests to my husband, he is now here ; and hath drawn him and the rest of their company from their sport, to make another experiment of his sus-

             picion :

picion: but I am glad the knight is not here; now he shall see his own foolery.

Mrs. Ford. How near is he, mistress Page?

Mrs. Page. Hard by; at street end; he will be here anon.

Mrs. Ford. I am undone!—the knight is here. 120

Mrs. Page. Why, then thou art utterly sham'd, and he's but a dead man. What a woman are you?—Away with him, away with him; better shame than murder.

Mrs. Ford. Which way should he go? how should I bestow him? Shall I put him into the basket again?

Enter FALSTAFF.

Fal. No, I'll come no more i' the basket: May I not go out, ere he come?   128

Mrs. Page. Alas, three of master Ford's brothers watch the door with pistols, that none should issue out; otherwise you might slip away ere he came.—But what make you here?

Fal. What shall I do? I'll creep up into the chimney.

Mrs. Ford. There they always use to discharge their birding-pieces: creep into the kiln-hole.

Fal. Where is it?

Mrs. Ford. He will seek there on my word. Neither press, coffer, chest, trunk, well, vault, but he hath an abstract for the remembrance of such places, and goes to them by his note: There is no hiding you in the house.   142

H

Fal.

Fal. I'll go out then.

Mrs. Ford. If you go out in your own semblance, you die, sir John; unless you go out disguis'd—— How might we disguise him?

Mrs. Page. Alas the day, I know not. There is no woman's gown big enough for him; otherwise, he might put on a hat, a muffler, and a kerchief, and so escape.   150.

Fal. Good hearts, devise something: any extremity, rather than a mischief.

Mrs. Ford. My maid's aunt, the fat woman of Brentford, has a gown above.

Mrs. Page. On my word, it will serve him; she's as big as he is: and there's her thrum hat, and her muffler too: Run up, sir John.

Mrs. Ford. Go, go, sweet sir John: mistress Page, and I, will look some linen for your head.   159

Mrs. Page. Quick, quick; we'll come dress you straight: put on the gown the while.

[*Exit* FALSTAFF.

Mrs. Ford. I would, my husband would meet him in this shape; he cannot abide the old woman of Brentford; he swears, she's a witch; forbade her my house, and hath threatened to beat her.

Mrs. Page. Heaven guide him to thy husband's cudgel; and the devil guide his cudgel afterwards!

Mrs. Ford. But is my husband coming?

Mrs. Page. Ay, in good sadness, is he; and talks of the basket too, howsoever he hath had in-telligence.   171.

Mrs.

Mrs. Ford. We'll try that; for I'll appoint my men to carry the basket again, to meet him at the door with it, as they did last time.

Mrs. Page. Nay, but he'll be here presently: let's go dress him like the witch of Brentford.

Mrs. Ford. I'll first direct my men what they shall do with the basket. Go up, I'll bring linen for him straight.

Mrs. Page. Hang him, dishonest varlet! we cannot misuse him enough.   181
We'll leave a proof, by that which we will do,
Wives may be merry, and yet honest too:
We do not act, that often jest and laugh;
'Tis old but true, *Still swine eat all the draugh.*

Mrs. Ford. Go, sirs, take the basket again on your shoulders; your master is hard at door; if he bid you set it down, obey him: quickly, dispatch.

          [*Exeunt Mrs.* PAGE, *and Mrs.* FORD.

Enter Servants with the Basket.

1 *Serv.* Come, come, take up.

2 *Serv.* Pray heaven, it be not full of the knight again.   191

1 *Serv.* I hope not; I had as lief bear so much lead.

Enter FORD, SHALLOW, PAGE, CAIUS, *and Sir*
HUGH EVANS.

Ford. Ay, but if it prove true, master Page, have you any way then to unfool me again?—Set down the

                H ij   basket,

basket, villain :—Somebody call my wife :—Youth in a basket !—Oh, you panderly rascals! there's a knot, a gang, a pack, a conspiracy against me : Now shall the devil be sham'd. What! wife, I say! come, come forth ; behold what honest clothes you send forth to bleaching. 201

Page. Why, this passes ! Master Ford, you are not to go loose any longer; you must be pinion'd.

Eva. Why, this is lunatics! this is mad as a mad dog!

Shal. Indeed, master Ford, this is not well; indeed.

Enter Mrs. FORD.

Ford. So say I too, sir.—Come hither, mistress Ford ;—mistress Ford, the honest woman, the modest wife, the virtuous creature, that hath the jealous fool to her husband!—I suspect without cause, mistress, do I ? 211

Mrs. Ford. Heaven be my witness, you do, if you suspect me in any dishonesty.

Ford. Well said, brazen-face; hold it out.—Come forth, sirrah.   [*Pulls the Clothes out of the Basket.*

Page. This passes.

Mrs. Ford. Are you not asham'd? let the clothes alone.

Ford. I shall find you anon.

Eva. 'Tis unreasonable! Will you take up your wife's clothes ? come away. 221

Ford. Empty the basket, I say.

Mrs. Ford. Why, man, why,——

Ford.

Ford. Master Page, as I am a man, there was one convey'd out of my house yesterday in this basket; Why may not he be there again? In my house I am sure he is: my intelligence is true; my jealousy is reasonable: Pluck me out all the linen.

Mrs. Ford. If you find a man there, he shall die a flea's death.   230

Page. Here's no man.

Shal. By my fidelity, this is not well, master Ford; this wrongs you.

Eva. Master Ford, you must pray, and not follow the imaginations of your own heart: this is jealousies.

Ford. Well, he's not here I seek for.

Page. No, nor no where else but in your brain.

Ford. Help to search my house this one time: if I find not what I seek, shew no colour for my extremity, let me for ever be your table-sport; let them say of me, As jealous as Ford, that search'd a hollow wall-nut for his wife's leman.   Satisfy me once more, once more search with me.   243

Mrs. Ford. What hoa, mistress Page! come you, and the old woman down; my husband will come into the chamber.

Ford. Old woman! what old woman's that?

Mrs. Ford. Why it is my maid's aunt of Brentford.   249

Ford. A witch, a quean, an old cozening quean! Have I not forbid her my house? She comes of errands, does she? We are simple men; we do not know what's brought to pass under the profession of

fortune-

fortune-telling. She works by charms, by spells, by
the figure, and such daubery, as this is: beyond our
element : we know nothing.——Come down, you
witch ; you hag you, come down, I say.

Mrs. Ford. Nay, good, sweet husband ;—good gentlemen, let him not strike the old woman.   259

Enter FALSTAFF *in Women's Clothes, led by Mrs.* PAGE.

Mrs. Page, Come, mother Prat, come, give me
your hand.

Ford. I'll prat her :—Out of my doors, you witch!
[*Beats him.*] you hag, you baggage, you poulcat,
you ronyon! out! out! I'll conjure you, I'll fortune-
tell you.   [*Exit* FALSTAFF.

Mrs. Page. Are you not asham'd ? I think, you
have kill'd the poor woman.

Mrs. Ford. Nay, he will do it :—'Tis a goodly credit for you.

Ford. -Hang her, witch !   270

Eva. By yea and no, I think, the 'oman is a witch
indeed : I like not when a 'omans has a great peard ;
I spy a great peard under his muffler.

Ford. Will you follow, gentlemen ? I beseech you,
follow ; see but the issue of my jealousy : if I cry
out thus upon no trail, never trust me when I open
again.

Page. Let's obey his humour a little further :
Come, gentlemen.   [*Exeunt.*

Mrs. Page. Trust me, he beat him most pitifully. '

Mrs.

Mrs. Ford. Nay, by the mass, that he did not ; he beat him most unpitifully, methought.

Mrs. Page. I'll have the cudgel hallow'd, and hung o'er the altar ; it hath done meritorious service.

Mrs. Ford. What think you ? may we, with the warrant of woman-hood, and the witness of a good conscience, pursue him with any further revenge ?

Mrs. Page. The spirit of wantonness is, sure, scar'd out of him ; if the devil have him not in fee-simple, with fine and recovery, he will never, I think, in the way of waste, attempt us again.   291

Mrs. Ford. Shall we tell our husbands how we have served him ?

Mrs. Page. Yea, by all means ; if it be but to scrape the figures out of your husband's brains. If they can find in their hearts, the poor unvirtuous fat knight shall be any further afflicted, we two will be still the ministers.

Mrs. Ford. I'll warrant, they'll have him publickly sham'd : and, methinks, there would be no period to the jest, should he not be publickly sham'd.   301

Mrs. Page. Come, to the forge with it then, shape it : I would not have things cool.   [*Exeunt.*

SCENE III.

The Garter Inn.   Enter Host and BARDOLPH.

Bard. Sir, the Germans desire to have three of your horses : the duke himself will be to-morrow at court, and they are going to meet him.

Host.

Host. What duke should that be, comes so secretly?
I hear not of him in the court: let me speak with the
gentlemen; they speak English?

Bard. Sir, I'll call them to you.   310

Host. They shall have my horses; but I'll make
them pay, I'll sauce them: they have had my houses
a week at command; I have turn'd away my other
guests: they must come off; I'll sauce them; come.

[*Exeunt.*

SCENE IV.

FORD'S *House.   Enter* PAGE, FORD, *Mrs.* PAGE,
Mrs. FORD, *and Sir* HUGH EVANS.

Eva. 'Tis one of the best discretions of a 'omans
as ever I did look upon.

Page. And did he send you both these letters at an
instant?

Mrs. Page. Within a quarter of an hour.

Ford. Pardon me, wife: Henceforth do what thou
     wilt;   320
I rather will suspect the sun with cold,
Than thee with wantonness: now doth thy honour
     stand,
In him that was of late an heretick,
As firm as faith.

Page. 'Tis well, 'tis well; no more.
Be not as extreme in submission,
     As in offence;

                                        But

But let our plot go forward : let our wives
Yet once again, to make us public sport,
Appoint a meeting with this old fat fellow,   330
Where we may take him, and disgrace him for it.
 Ford. There is no better way than that they
  spoke of.
 Page. How! to send him word they'll meet him in
  the park
At midnight! fie, fie ; he will never come.
 Eva. You say, he hath been thrown into the rivers ;
and hath been grievously peaten, as an old 'oman :
methinks, there should be terrors in him, that he
should not come ; methinks, his flesh is punish'd, he
shall have no desires.
 Page. So think I too.   340
 Mrs. Ford. Devise but how you'll use him when he
  comes,
And let us two devise to bring him hither.
 Mrs. Page. There is an old tale goes, that Herne
  the hunter,
Sometime a keeper here in Windsor forest,
Doth all the winter time, at still midnight,
Walk round about an oak, with great ragg'd horns ;
And there he blasts the tree, and takes the cattle ;
And makes milch-kine yield blood, and shakes a
  chain
In a most hideous and dreadful manner :
You have heard of such a spirit ; and well you
  know,   350
The superstitious idle-headed eld

Receiv'd,

Recciv'd, and did deliver to our age,
This tale of Herne the hunter for a truth.

    Page. Why, yet there want not many, that **do**
      fear
In deep of night to walk by this Herne's oak:
But what of this?

    Mrs. Ford. Marry, this is our device;——
That Falstaff at that oak shall meet with us.
We'll send him word to meet us in the field,
Disguis'd like Herne, with huge horns on his
      head.   360

    Page. Well, let it not be doubted but he'll come,
And in this shape; When you have brought him
      thither,
What shall be done with him? what is your plot?

    Mrs. Page. That likewise we have thought upon,
      and thus:
Nan Page my daughter, and my little son,
And three or four more of their growth, we'll dress
Like urchins, ouphes, and fairies, green and white,
With rounds of waxen tapers on their heads,
And rattles in their hands; upon a sudden,
As Falstaff, she, and I, are newly met,   370
Let them from forth a saw-pit rush at once
With some diffused song: upon their sight,
We two in great amazedness will fly:
Then let them all encircle him about,
And, fairy-like, to-pinch the unclean knight;
And ask him, why, that hour of fairy revel,
In their so sacred paths he dares to tread

                                    In

In shape prophane?

Mrs. Ford. And till he tell the truth,
Let the supposed fairies pinch him sound,   380
And burn him with their tapers.

Mrs. Page. The truth being known,
We'll all present ourselves; dis-horn the spirit,
And mock him home to Windsor.

Ford. The children must
Be practis'd well to this, or they'll ne'er do't.

Eva. I will teach the children their behaviours;
and I will be like a jack-an-apes also, to burn the
knight with my taber.

Ford. This will be excellent. I'll go buy them
vizards.   391

Mrs. Page. My Nan shall be the queen of all the
          fairies,
Finely attired in a robe of white.

Page. That silk will I go buy; and, in that time
Shall master Slender steal my Nan away,   [*Aside.*
And marry her at Eton.——Go, send to Falstaff
          straight.

Ford. Nay, I'll to him again in the name of
          Brook:
He'll tell me all his purpose. Sure, he'll come.

Mrs. Page. Fear not you that: Go get us pro-
          perties
And tricking for our fairies.   400

Eva. Let us about it: It is admirable pleasures,
and fery honest knaveries.

[Ex. PAGE, FORD, and EVANS.
Mrs.

Mrs. Page. Go, mistress Ford,
Send Quickly to sir John, to know his mind.

      [*Exit Mrs.* FORD.

I'll to the doctor; he hath my good will,
And none but he, to marry with Nan Page.
That Slender, though well landed, is an ideot;
And he my husband best of all affects:
The doctor is well money'd, and his friends
Potent at court: he, none but he shall have
  her,   410
Though twenty thousand worthier come to crave her.

          [*Exit.*

SCENE V.

The Garter Inn. Enter Host and SIMPLE.

Host. What would'st thou have, boor? what, thick-skin? speak, breathe, discuss; brief, short, quick, snap.

Simp. Marry, sir, I come to speak with sir John Falstaff from master Slender.

Host. There's his chamber, his house, his castle, his standing-bed, and truckle-bed; 'tis painted about with the story of the prodigal, fresh and new: Go, knock and call; he'll speak like an *Anthropophaginian* unto thee: Knock, I say.   421

Simp. There's an old woman, a fat woman gone up into his chamber; I'll be so bold as stay, sir, 'till she come down: I come to speak with her, indeed.

          Host.

Host. Ha! a fat woman! the knight may be robb'd;
I'll call.——Bully knight! Bully sir John! speak
from thy lungs military: Art thou there? it is thine
host, thine Ephesian, calls.

FALSTAFF *above.*

Fal. How now, mine host?

Host. Here's a Bohemian-Tartar tarries the coming down of thy fat woman: Let her descend, bully,
let her descend; my chambers are honourable: Fie!
privacy? fie!   433

Enter FALSTAFF.

Fal. There was, mine host, an old fat woman even
now with me; but she's gone.

Simp. Pray you, sir, was't not the wise woman of
Brentford?

Fal. Ay, marry was it, mussel-shell; What would
you with her?

Simp. My master, sir, master Slender sent to her,
seeing her go through the street, to know, sir, whether one Nym, sir, that beguil'd him of a chain, had
the chain, or no.   443

Fal. I spake with the old woman about it.

Simp. And what says she, I pray, sir?

Fal. Marry, she says, that the very same man, that
beguil'd master Slender of his chain, cozen'd him of
it.

Simp. I would I could have spoken with the wo-

I

man

man herself; I had other things to have spoken with
her too, from him.   451

 Fal. What are they? let us know.

 Host. Ay, come; quick.

 Simp. I may not conceal them, sir.

 Fal. Conceal them, or thou dy'st.

 Simp. Why, sir, they were nothing but about mistress Anne Page; to know, if it were my master's
fortune to have her, or no.

 Fal. 'Tis, 'tis his fortune.

 Simp. What, sir?   460

 Fal. To have her—or no : Go; say the woman
told me so.

 Simp. May I be so bold to say so, sir?

 Fal. Ay, sir Tike; like who more bold.

 Simp. I thank your worship : I shall make my
master glad with these tidings.   [*Exit* SIMP.

 Host. Thou art clerkly, thou art clerkly, sir John :
Was there a wise woman with thee ?

 Fal. Ay, that there was, mine host; one, that
hath taught me more wit than ever I learn'd before in
my life : and I paid nothing for it neither, but was
paid for my learning.   472

Enter BARDOLPH.

 Bard. Out, alas, sir! cozenage! meer cozenage!

 Host. Where be my horses? speak well of them,
varletto.

 Bard. Run away with the cozeners : for so soon as
I came beyond Eton, they threw me off, from behind

hind one of them, in a slough of mire; and set spurs,
and away, like three German devils, three Doctor
Faustus's.   480

Host. They are gone but to meet the duke, villain:
do not say, they are fled; Germans are honest men.

Enter Sir HUGH EVANS.

Eva. Where is mine host?

Host. What is the matter, sir?

Eva. Have a care of your entertainments: there is
a friend of mine come to town, tells me, there is
three couzin-germans, that hath cozen'd all the hosts
of Readings, of Maidenhead, of Colebrooke, of
horses and money. I tell you for good will, look
you: you are wise, and full of gibes and vlouting-
stogs; and 'tis not convenient you should be cozen'd:
Fare you well.   [*Exit.*]   492

Enter CAIUS.

Caius. Vere is mine *Host de Jarterre?*

Host. Here, master doctor, in perplexity, and
doubtful dilemma.

Caius. I cannot tell vat is dat: But it is tell-a-me,
dat you make a grand preparation for a duke *de Ja-
many:* by my trot, dere is no duke, dat the court is
know, to come: I tell you for good vill: adieu.

[*Exit.*

Host. Hue and cry, villain, go! assist me, knight;
I am undone:—fly, run, hue and cry, villain! I am
undone!   [*Exit.*]   502

I i j   *Fal.*

Fal. I would all the world might be cozen'd; for I have been cozen'd, and beaten too. If it should come to the ear of the court, how I have been trans-form'd, and how my transformation hath been wash'd and cudgel'd, they would melt me out of my fat, drop by drop, and liquor fishermen's boots with me; I warrant they would whip me with their fine wits, till I were as crest-faln as a dry'd pear. I never prosper'd since I forswore myself at *Primero.* Well, if my wind were but long enough to say my prayers, I would repent.——   513

Enter Mistress QUICKLY.

Now, whence come you?

Quic. From the two parties, forsooth.

Fal. The devil take one party, and his dam the other, and so they shall be both bestow'd! I have suf-fer'd more for their sakes, more, than the villanous inconstancy of man's disposition is able to bear.

Quic. And have not they suffer'd? yes, I warrant, speciously one of them; mistress Ford, good heart, is beaten black and blue, that you cannot see a white spot about her.   523

Fal. What tell'st thou me of black and blue; I was beaten myself into all the colours of the rainbow; and I was like to be apprehended for the witch of Brent-ford; but that my admirable dexterity of wit, coun-terfeiting the action of an old woman, deliver'd me, the knave constable had set me i' the stocks, i' the common stocks, for a witch.   530

Quic.

Rhandez del.   Grignion sculp.

Mr HENDERSON in FALSTAFF.

Master, is a letter will say somewhat.

Printed for John Bell British Library Strand London, Jan.r 12. 1784.

Quic. Sir, let me speak with you in your chamber: you shall hear how things go; and, I warrant, to your content. Here is a letter will say somewhat. Good hearts, what ado is here to bring you together! sure, one of you does not serve heaven well, that you are so cross'd.

Fal. Come up into my chamber.　　[*Exeunt.*

SCENE VI.

Enter FENTON *and Host.*

Host. Master Fenton, talk not to me; my mind is
　　heavy, I will give over all.

Fent. Yet hear me speak : Assist me in my
　　purpose,
And, as I am a gentleman, I'll give thee　　540
A hundred pound in gold, more than your loss.

Host. I will hear you, master Fenton; and I will,
at the least keep your counsel.

Fent. From time to time I have acquainted you
With the dear love I bear to fair Anne Page;
Who, mutually, hath answer'd my affection
(So far forth as herself might be her chuser)
Even to my wish : I have a letter from her
Of such contents as you will wonder at;
The mirth whereof's so larded with my matter,　　550
That neither, singly, can be manifested,
Without the shew of both : Fat sir John Falstaff

Hath a great scene ; the image of the jest

      [*Shewing a Letter.*

I'll shew you here at large.   Hark, good mine host :
To-night at Herne's oak, just 'twixt twelve and one,
Must my sweet Nan present the fairy queen ;
The purpose why, is here ; in which disguise,
While other jests are something rank on foot,
Her father hath commanded her to slip
Away with Slender, and with him at Eton   560
Immediately to marry : she hath consented : now,
   sir,
Her mother, even strong against that match,
And firm for doctor Caius, hath appointed
That he shall likewise shuffle her away,
While other sports are tasking of their minds,
And at the deanery, where a priest attends,
Straight marry her : to this her mother's plot
She, seemingly obedient, likewise hath
Made promise to the doctor :—Now, thus it rests ;
Her father means she shall be all in white ; 570
And in that habit, when Slender sees his time
To take her by the hand, and bid her go,
She shall go with him :—her mother hath intended,
The better to devote her to the doctor
(For they must all be mask'd and vizarded),
That, quaint in green, she shall be loose enrob'd,
With ribbands pendant, flaring 'bout her head ;
And when the doctor spies his vantage ripe,
To pinch her by the hand, and, on that token,
The maid hath given consent to go with him. 580
       Host.

Host. Which means she to deceive ? father or mo-
    ther ?

Fent. Both, my good host, to go along with me :
And here it rests,—that you'll procure the vicar
To stay for me at church, 'twixt twelve and one,
And, in the lawful name of marrying,
To give our hearts united ceremony.

Host. Well, husband your device ; I'll to the
    vicar :
Bring you the maid, you shall not lack a priest.

Fent. So shall I evermore be bound to thee ;
Besides, I'll make a present recompence.   590
                      [*Exeunt.*

ACT V.   SCENE I.

Enter FALSTAFF *and Mrs.* QUICKLY.

Falstaff.

PR'YTHEE, no more pratling ;—go.—I'll hold :
This is the third time ; I hope, good luck lies in odd
numbers. Away, go ; they say, there is divinity in
odd numbers, either in nativity, chance, or death.—
Away.

Quic. I'll provide you a chain ; and I'll do what I
can to get you a pair of horns.
                    [*Exit Mrs.* QUICKLY.
                          Fal.

Fal. Away, I say ; time wears : hold up your head, and mince.   9

Enter FORD.

How now, master Brook ? Master Brook, the matter will be known to-night, or never.   Be you in the Park about midnight, at Herne's oak, and you shall see wonders.

Ford. Went you not to her yesterday, sir, as you told me you had appointed ?   15

Fal. I went to her, master Brook, as you see, like a poor old man : but I came from her, master Brook, like a poor old woman.   That same knave, Ford her husband, hath the finest mad devil of jealousy in him, master Brook, that ever govern'd frenzy.   I will tell you.—He beat me grievously, in the shape of a woman ; for in the shape of man, master Brook, I fear not Goliah with a weaver's beam ; because I know also, life is a shuttle.   I am in haste; go along with me; I'll tell you all, master Brook.   Since I pluck'd geese, play'd truant, and whipp'd top, I knew not what 'twas to be beaten, till lately.   Follow me: I'll tell you strange things of this knave Ford ; on whom to-night I will be reveng'd, and I will deliver his wife into your hand.—Follow : Strange things in hand, master Brook ! follow.——   31

[*Exeunt.*

SCENE

SCENE II.

Windsor Park. Enter PAGE, SHALLOW, *and* SLENDER.

Page. Come, come; we'll couch i' the castle-ditch,
till we see the light of our fairies.—Remember, son
Slender, my daughter.

Slen. Ay, foisooth ; I have spoke with her, and
we have a nay-word how to know one another. I
come to her in white, and cry, *mum* ; she cries, *budget* ;
and by that we know one another.

Shal. That's good too ; But what needs either your
mum, or her *budget?* the white will decipher her well
enough.—It hath struck ten o'clock.   41

Page. The night is dark ; light and spirits will become it well.   Heaven prosper our sport ! No man
means evil but the devil, and we shall know him by
his horns.   Let's away ; follow me.   [*Exeunt.*

SCENE III.

Enter Mistress PAGE, *Mistress* FORD, *and Dr.* CAIUS.

Mrs. Page. Master doctor, my daughter is in green :
when you see your time, take her by the hand, away
with her to the deanery, and dispatch it quickly : Go
before into the park ; we two must go together.   49

Caius. I know vat I have to do ; Adieu.   [*Exit.*

Mrs. Page. Fare you well, sir.   My husband will
not rejoice so much at the abuse of Falstaff, as he
                                          will

will chafe at the doctor's marrying my daughter : but
'tis no matter ; better a little chiding, than a great
deal of heart-break.

Mrs. Ford. Where is Nan now, and her troop of
fairies ? and the Welch devil Evans?

Mrs. Page. They are all couch'd in a pit hard by
Herne's oak, with obscur'd lights ; which, at the very
instant of Falstaff's and our meeting, they will at once
display to the night.   61

Mrs. Ford. That cannot chuse but amaze him.

Mrs. Page. If he be not amaz'd, he will be mock'd;
if he be amaz'd, he will every way be mock'd.

Mrs. Ford. We'll betray him finely.

Mrs. Page. Against such lewdsters, and their
          lechery,
Those that betray them do no treachery.

Mrs. Ford. The hour draws on ; To the oak, to the
oak !   [*Exeunt.*]   69

SCENE IV.

Enter Sir HUGH EVANS, *and Fairies.*

Eva. Trib, trib, fairies ; come ; and remember
your parts : be pold, I pray you ; follow me into the
pit ; and when I give the watch-'ords, do as I pid
you ; Come, come ; trib, trib.   [*Exeunt.*

SCENE

SCENE V.

Enter FALSTAFF *with a Buck's Head on.*

Fal. The Windsor bell hath struck twelve; the minute draws on : Now, the hot-blooded gods assist me !—Remember, Jove, thou wast a bull for thy Europa ; love set on thy horns.—Oh powerful love ! that, in some respects, makes a beast a man ; in some other, a man a beast.—You were also, Jupiter, a swan, for the love of Leda ;—Oh, omnipotent love ! how near the god drew to the complexion of a goose ?—A fault done first in the form of a beast ;——O Jove, a beastly fault !—and then another fault in the semblance of a fowl ;—think on't, Jove ; a foul fault.— When gods have hot backs, what shall poor men do ? For me, I am here a Windsor stag ; and the fattest, I think, i' the forest : Send me a cool rut-time, Jove, or who can blame me to piss my tallow ? Who comes here ? my doe ?   89

Enter Mistress FORD *and Mistress* PAGE.

Mrs. Ford. Sir John ? art thou there, my deer ? my male deer ?

Fal. My doe with the black scut ?—Let the sky rain potatoes ; let it thunder to the tune of *Green Sleeves* ; hail kissing-comfits, and snow eringoes ; let there come a tempest of provocation, I will shelter me here.

Mrs. Ford. Mistress Page is come with me, sweetheart.   97

Fal.

Fal. Divide me like a bribe-buck, each a haunch :
I will keep my sides to myself, my shoulders for the
fellow of this walk, and my horns I bequeath your
husbands.   Am I a woodman ? ha ! Speak I like
Herne the hunter ?—Why, now is Cupid a child of
conscience : he makes restitution.   As I am a true
spirit, welcome !   [*Noise within.*

Mrs. Page. Alas ! what noise ?

Mrs. Ford. Heaven forgive our sins !

Fal. What shall this be ?

Mrs. Ford. }
Mrs. Page. } Away, away.

                              [*The Women run out.*

Fal. I think the devil will not have me damn'd, lest
the oil that is in me should set hell on fire ; he never
would else cross me thus.   111

Enter Sir HUGH *like a Satyr* ; QUICKLY, *and others,
dress'd like Fairies, with Tapers.*

Quic. Fairies, black, grey, green, and white,
You moon-shine revellers, and shades of night,
You orphan-heirs of fixed destiny,
Attend your office, and your quality.——
Crier Hobgoblin, make the fairy o-yes.

Eva. Elves, list your names ; silence, you airy
        toys.

Cricket, to Windsor chimneys shalt thou leap :
Where fires thou find'st unrak'd, and hearths un-
        swept,

                    2   There

There pinch the maids as blue as bilberry :   120
Our radiant queen hates sluts, and sluttery.

 Fal. They are fairies; he that speaks to them,
   shall die;
I'll wink and couch ; No man their works must eye.
       [*Lies down upon his Face.*

 Eva. Where's *Bede ?*—Go you, and where you
   find a maid,
That, ere she sleep, hath thrice her prayers said,
Rein up the organs of her fantasy ;
Sleep she as sound as careless infancy :
But those as sleep, and think not on their sins,
Pinch them, arms, legs, backs, shoulders, sides,
   and shins.

 Quic. About, about ;   130
Search Windsor castle, elves, within and out :
Strew good luck, ouphes, on every sacred room ;
That it may stand till the perpetual doom,
In state as wholsome, as in state 'tis fit ;
Worthy the owner, and the owner it.
The several chairs of order look you scour
With juice of balm, and every precious flower :
Each fair instalment coat, and several crest,
With loyal blazon, evermore be blest !
And nightly, meadow-fairies, look, you sing,   140
Like to the Garter's compass, in a ring :
The expressure that it bears, green let it be,
More fertile-fresh than all the field to see ;
And, *Hony Soit Qui Mal y Pense,* write,
In emerald tufts, flowers purple, blue, and white ;

K

Like

Like saphire, pearl, and rich embroidery,
Buckled below fair knight-hood's bending knee ;
Fairies use flowers for their charactery.
Away ; disperse : But, till 'tis one o'clock,
Our dance of custom, round about the oak   150
Of Herne the hunter, let us not forget.

 Eva. Pray you, lock hand in hand ; yourselves in
    order set :
And twenty glow-worms shall our lanterns be,
To guide our measure round about the tree.
But, stay ; I smell a man of middle earth.

 Fal. Heavens defend me from that Welch fairy !
Lest he transform me to a piece of cheese !

 Eva. Vile worm, thou wast o'er-look'd even in thy
    birth.

 Quic. With trial-fire touch me his finger-end :
If he be chaste, the flame will back descend,   160
And turn him to no pain ; but if he start,
It is the flesh of a corrupted heart.

 Eva. A trial, come.——
    [*They burn him with their Tapers and pinch him.*
Come, will this wood take fire ?

 Fal. Oh, oh, oh !

 Quic. Corrupt, corrupt, and tainted in desire !—
About him, fairies ; sing a scornful rhime :
And, as you trip, still pinch him to your time.

 Eva. It is right ; indeed, he is full of lecheries
and iniquity.   470

          The

The S O N G.

Fie on sinful phantasy!
Fie on lust and luxury!
Lust is but a bloody fire,
Kindled with unchaste desire,
Fed in heart; whose flames aspire,
As thoughts do blow them, higher and higher.
Pinch him, fairies, mutually;
Pinch him for his villain'y;

Pinch him, and burn him, and turn him about,
'Till candles, and star-light, and moon-shine be out.   180

During this Song, they pinch him. Dr. CAIUS *comes one way, and steals away a Fairy in green;* SLENDER *another way, and he takes away a Fairy in white; and* FENTON *comes, and steals away Mrs.* ANNE PAGE. *A Noise of Hunting is made within. All the Fairies run away.* FALSTAFF *pulls off his Buck's Head, and rises.*

Enter PAGE, FORD, *&c. They lay hold on him.*

Page. Nay, do not fly : I think, we have watch'd you now ;

Will none but Herne the hunter, serve your turn ?

Mrs. Page. I pray you, come; hold up the jest no higher :—

Now, good sir John, how like you Windsor wives ?
See you these, husband ? do not these fair yokes
Become the forest better than the town ?

Ford. Now, sir, who's a cuckold now ?—Master Brook, Falstaff's a knave, a cuckoldly knave ; here are his horns, master Brook : And, master Brook, he

K ij   *hath*

hath enjoyed nothing of Ford's but his buck-basket, his cudgel, and twenty pounds of money ; which must be paid to master Brook ; his horses are arrested for it, master Brook.   193

Mrs. Ford. Sir John, we have had ill luck ; we could never meet. I will never take you for my love again, but I will always count you my deer.

Fal. I do begin to perceive that I am made an ass.

Ford. Ay, and an ox too ; both the proofs are extant.   200

Fal. And these are not fairies ? I was three or four times in the thought they were not fairies : and yet the guiltiness of my mind, the sudden surprise of my powers, drove the grossness of the foppery into a re-ceiv'd belief, in despight of the teeth of all rhime and reason, that they were fairies. See now, how wit may be made a Jack-a-lent, when 'tis upon ill em-ployment !

Eva. Sir John Falstaff, serve Got, and leave your desires, and fairies will not pinse you.   210

Ford. Well said, fairy Hugh.

Eva. And leave your jealousies also, I pray you.

Ford. I will never mistrust my wife again, till thou art able to woo her in good English.

Fal. Have I laid my brain in the sun, and dried it, that it wants matter to prevent so gross o'er-reaching as this ? Am I ridden with a Welch goat too ? shall I have a coxcomb of frize ? 'tis time I were chok'd with a piece of toasted cheese.   219

Eva. Seese is not good to give putter ; your pelly is all putter.   *Fal.*

Fal. Seese and putter! have I liv'd to stand in the taunt of one that makes fritters of English? this is enough to be the decay of lust and late-walking, through the realm.

Mrs. Page. Why, sir John, do you think, though we would have thrust virtue out of our hearts by the head and shoulders, and have given ourselves without scruple to hell, that ever the devil could have made you our delight?   230

Ford. What, a hodge-pudding? a bag of flax?

Mrs. Page. A puff'd man?

Page. Old, cold, wither'd, and of intolerable entrails?

Ford. And one that is as slanderous as Satan?

Page. And as poor as Job?

Ford. And as wicked as his wife?

Eva. And given to fornications, and to taverns, and sacks, and wines, and metheglins, and to drinkings, and swearings, and starings, pribbles and prabbles?

Fal. Well, I am your theme; you have the start of me; I am dejected; I am not able to answer the Welch flannel; ignorance itself is a plummet o'er me: use me as you will.   244

Ford. Marry, sir, we'll bring you to Windsor, to one master Brook, that you cozen'd of money, to whom you should have been a pandar: over and above that you have suffer'd, I think, to repay that money will be a biting affliction.

Mrs. Ford. Nay, husband, let that go to make amends:
Forgive that sum, and so we'll all be friends.   251

Ford.

Ford. Well, here's my hand; all's forgiven at last.

Page. Yet be cheerful, knight: thou shalt eat a posset to-night at my house; where I will desire thee to laugh at my wife, that now laughs at thee: Tell her, master Slender hath married her daughter.

Mrs. Page. Doctors doubt that; if Anne Page be my daughter, she is, by this, doctor Caius' wife.

[*Aside.*

Enter SLENDER.

Slen. Whoo, ho! ho! father Page!

Page. Son! how now? how now, son? have you dispatch'd?   261

Slen. Dispatch'd!—I'll make the best in Gloucestershire know on't; would I were hang'd, la, else.

Page. Of what, son?

Slen. I came yonder at Eton to marry mistress Anne Page, and she's a great lubberly boy: If it had not been i' the church, I would have swing'd him, or he should have swing'd me. If I did not think it had been Anne Page, would I might never stir, and 'tis a post-master's boy.   270

Page. Upon my life then you took the wrong.

Slen. What need you tell me that? I think so, when I took a boy for a girl: If I had been married to him, for all he was in woman's apparel, I would not have had him.

Page. Why, this is your own folly; Did not I tell you, how you should know my daughter by her garments?

Slen. I went to her in white, and cry'd, *mum,* and

she

she cry'd *budget*, as Anne and I had appointed; and
yet it was not Anne, but a post-master's boy.   281

Eva. Jeshu! Master Slender, cannot you see but
marry boys?

Page. O, I am vex'd at heart: What shall I do?

Mrs. Page. Good George, be not angry: I knew
of your purpose; turn'd my daughter into green;
and, indeed, she is now with the doctor at the deanery,
and there married.

Enter CAIUS.

Caius. Vere is mistress Page? By gar, I am cozen'd;
I ha' married *un garçon*, a boy; *un paisan*, by gar, a
boy; it is not Anne Page: by gar, I am cozen'd. 291

Mrs. Page. Why, did you not take her in green?

Caius. Ay, be gar, and 'tis a boy: be gar, I'll raise
all Windsor.   [*Exit* CAIUS.

Ford. This is strange: Who hath got the right Anne?

Page. My heart misgives me: Here comes master
Fenton.

Enter FENTON, *and* ANNE PAGE.

How now, master Fenton?

Anne. Pardon, good father! good my mother, pardon!   300

Page. Now, mistress? how chance you went not
with master Slender?

Mrs. Page. Why went you not with master doctor,
maid?

Fent. You do amaze her; Hear the truth of it.
You would have married her most shamefully,

Where

Where there was no proportion held in love.
The truth is, She and I, long since contracted,
Are now so sure, that nothing can dissolve us.
The offence is holy, that she hath committed: 310
And this deceit loses the name of craft,
Of disobedience, or unduteous title ;
Since therein she doth evitate and shun
A thousand irreligious cursed hours,
Which forced marriage would have brought upon
  her.
 Ford. Stand not amaz'd : here is no remedy :——
In love, the heavens themselves do guide the state;
Money buys lands, and wives are sold by fate.
 Fal. I am glad, though you have ta'en a special
stand to strike at me, that your arrow hath glanc'd.
 Page. Well, what remedy ? Fenton, heaven give
  thee joy !   321
What cannot be eschew'd, must be embrac'd.
 Eva. I will dance and eat plums at your wedding.
 Fal. When night-dogs run, all sorts of deer are
chac'd.
 Mrs. **Page.** Well, I will muse no further :—Master
  Fenton,
Heaven give you many, many merry days!——
Good husband, let us every one go home,
And laugh this sport o'er by a country fire ;
Sir John and all.   330
 Ford. Let it be so :——Sir John,
To master Brook you yet shall hold your word ;
For he, to-night, shall lye with mistress Ford.
       [*Exeunt omnes.*

THE END.

ANNOTATIONS

BY

SAM. JOHNSON & GEO. STEEVENS,

AND

THE VARIOUS COMMENTATORS,

UPON

MERRY WIVES OF WINDSOR,

WRITTEN BY

WILL. SHAKSPERE.

———*SIC ITUR AD ASTRA.*

VIRG.

LONDON:

Printed for, and under the Direction of,

JOHN BELL, British-Library, STRAND,

Bookseller to His Royal Highness the PRINCE of WALES.

M DCC LXXXVII.

ANNOTATIONS

UPON

MERRY WIVES OF WINDSOR,

MERRY WIVES.] A FEW of the incidents in this comedy might have been taken from some old translation
of *Il Pecorone* by Giovanni Fiorentino. I have lately
met with the same story in a very contemptible performance, intituled, *The fortunate, deceived, and the unfortu-
nate Lovers.* Of this book, as I am told, there are several
impressions; but that in which I read it, was published
in 1632, quarto. A something similar story occurs in
Piacevoli Notti di Straparola, Nott. 4 Fav. 4

This comedy was first entered at Stationers' Hall,
Jan. 18, 1601, by John Busby. STEEVENS.

This play should be read between *K. Henry IV.* and
K. Henry V. JOHNSON.

A passage in the first sketch of the *Merry Wives of
Windsor*, shews, I think, that it ought to be read between *the First* and *the Second Part of K. Henry IV.* in

A ij

the

the latter of which young Henry becomes king. In the last act, Falstaff says :

> " Herne the hunter, quoth you? am I a ghost?
> " 'Sblood the fairies hath made a ghost of me.
> " What hunting at this time of night!
> " I'll lay my life the mad *prince of Wales*
> " Is stealing his father's deare."

And in the play, as it now appears, Mr. Page, dis-countenances the addresses of Fenton to his daughter, because he keeps company with the wild *prince*, and with Poins.

The Fishwife's Tale of Brentford in WESTWARD FOR SMELTS, a book which Shakspere appears to have read (having borrowed from it part of the fable of *Cymbeline*), probably led him to lay the scene of Falstaff's love-adventures at *Windsor*. It begins thus : " In *Windsor* not long agoe dwelt a sumpter-man, who had to wife a verie faire but wanton creature, over whom, not without cause, he was something *jealous*; yet had he never any proof of her inconstancy."

MALONE.

The adventures of *Falstaff* in this play seem to have been taken from the story of the *Lovers of Pisa*, in an old piece, called " *Tarleton's News out of Purgatorie.*"

Mr. Warton observes, in a note to the last *Oxford* edition, that the play was probably not written, as we now have it, before 1607, at the earliest. I agree with my very ingenious friend in this supposition; but yet the argument here produced for it may not be conclu-sive. *Slender* observes to master *Page,* that his *greyhound*

was

was out-run on Cotsole [*Cotswold-Hills* in *Gloucestershire*];
and Mr. Warton thinks, that the *games*, established
there by Capt. Dover in the beginning of K. James's
reign, are alluded to.—But perhaps, though the Captain be celebrated in the *Annalia Dubrensia* as the *founder* of them, he might be the *reviver* only, or some
way contribute to make them more famous; for in the
Second Part of Henry IV. 1600, justice *Shallow* reckons
among the *Swinge-bucklers* "*Will Squeel, a Cotsole man.*"

In the first edition of the imperfect play, *sir Hugh
Evans* is called, on the title page, the *Welch Knight*;
and yet there are some persons who still affect to believe, that all our author's plays were originally published by *himself*.   FARMER.

Dr. Farmer's opinion is well supported by " An
eclogue on the noble assemblies *revived* on Cotswold
Hills, by Mr. Robert Dover." See Randolph's Poems,
printed at Oxford, 4to. 1638, p. 114.   The hills of
Cotswold, in *Gloucestershire*, are mentioned in *K. Rich.
II.* act ii. sc. iii. and by Drayton, in his *Polyolbion*
song 14.   STEEVENS

WINDSOR.] *The Merry Wives of Windsor.*] Queen Elizabeth was so well pleased with the admirable character of Falstaff in the *The Two Parts of Henry IV.* that,
as Mr. Rowe informs us, she commanded Shakspere
to continue it for one play more, and to shew him in
love.   To this command we owe *The Merry Wives of
Windsor:* which Mr. Gildon says, he was very well
assured our author finished in a fortnight.   But this
must be meant only of the first imperfect sketch of

A ij

this

this comedy; an old quarto edition which I have seen, printed in 1602, says, in the title page——*As it hath been divers times acted both before her majesty and elsewhere.*

Pope. Theobald.

Mr. Gildon has likewise told us, that " our author's house at Stratford bordered on the church-yard, and that he wrote the scene of the Ghost in *Hamlet* there; but neither for this, nor the assertion that the play before us was written in a fortnight (which was first mentioned by Mr. Dennis in his preface to the *Comical Gallant,* 1702), does he quote any authority. Stories of this kind, not related till a century after an author's death, stand on a very weak foundation.   Malone.

ACT I.

Line 1. *Sir Hugh,*] This is the first, of sundry instances in our poet, where a *parson* is called *sir.* Upon which it may be observed, that anciently it was the common designation both of one in holy orders and a knight. Fuller somewhere in his Church History says, that anciently there were more *sirs* than *knights;* and so lately as temp. W. and Mar. in a deposition in the Exchequer in a case of tythes, the witness speaking of the curate, whom he remembered, styles him *sir Giles.* Vide Gibson's View of the State of the Churches of Door, Home-Lacy, &c. page 36.

Sir J. Hawkins.

1. *——a Star-chamber matter of it:*] Ben Jonson, intimates, that the *Star-chamber* had a right to take cognizance of such matters. See *The Magnetic Lady*, act iii. sc. iv.

"There is a court above, of the *Star-chamber*,

"To punish *routs* and *riots*."   STEEVENS.

7. *custalorum.*] This is, I suppose, intended for a corruption of *Custos Rotulorum*. The mistake was hardly designed by the author, who, though he gives Shallow folly enough, makes him rather pedantic than illiterate. If we read:

Shal. *Ay, cousin Slender, and* Custos Rotulorum.

It follows naturally:

Slen. *Ay, and* Ratolorum *too.*   JOHNSON.

"Ay, cousin *Slender*, and *custalorum.*]

I think with Dr. Johnson, that this blunder could scarcely be intended. *Shallow*, we know, had been bred to the law at *Clement's-Inn*—But I would rather read *custos* only; then *Slender* adds naturally, "Ay, and *ratolorum* too." He had heard the words *custos rotulorum*, and supposes them to mean different offices.

FARMER.

12. *Ay, that I do;——*] We should read:

Ay, that *we* do.

This emendation was suggested to me by Dr. Farmer.

STEEVENS.

22. *The luce, &c.*] Shakspere, by hinting that the arms of the Shallows and the Lucys were the same, shews he could not forget his old friend sir Thomas Lucy, pointing at him under the character of justice Shallow. But to put the matter out of all doubt, Shak-

spere

spere has here given us a distinguishing mark, whereby it appears that sir Thomas was the very person represented by Shallow. To set blundering parson Evans right, Shallow tells him, the *luce* is not the *louse*, but the *fresh fish*, or pike, the salt fish (indeed) is *an old coat.* The plain English of which is (if I am not greatly mistaken), the family of the Charlcotts had for their arms a *salt fish* originally; but when William, son of Walker de Charlcott, assumed the name of Lucy, in the time of Henry III. he took the arms of the Lucys. This is not at all improbable; for we find, when Maud Lucy bequeathed her estates to the Percys, it was upon condition they joined her arms with their own. Says Dugdale, " it is likely William de Charlcott took the name of Lucy to oblige his mother." And I say further, it is likely he took the arms of the Lucy's at the same time.   SMITH.

May it not be asked Mr. Smith, on the supposition that it was usual to salt the *luce* or *pike* (which however, I believe, was never heard of before) in what manner it could be inferred from the *painted fish* in the emblazoned arms, that it was not *fresh*, but *salted?* HENLEY.

The luce is the fresh fish, the salt fish is an old coat.]

I am not satisfied with any thing that has been offered on this difficult passage. All that Mr. Smith tells is a mere *gratis dictum.* I cannot find that *salt fish* were ever really borne in heraldry. I fancy the latter part of the speech should **be** given to sir *Hugh*, who is at cross purposes with the *Justice. Shallow* had said just before, the coat is an old one; and now, that it is the luce, the fresh fish.—No, replies the parson, it can-

not

not be *old* and *fresh* too—"the *salt fish* is an *old coat*." I give this with rather the more confidence, as a similar mistake has happened a little lower in the scene.— " *Slice*, I say!" cries out Corporal *Nym*, " *Pauca, pauca: Slice*, that's my humour." There can be no doubt, but *pauca, pauca* should be spoken by *Evans*.

Again, a little before this, the copies give us :

Slender. You'll not confess, you'll not confess.

Shallow. That he will not—'tis your fault, 'tis fault —'tis a good dog.

Surely it should be thus :

Shallow. You'll not confess, you'll not confess.

Slender. That he will not.

Shallow. 'Tis your fault, 'tis your fault, &c.

This fugitive scrap of Latin, *pauca*, &c. is used in several old pieces, by characters, who have no more of literature about them, than *Nym*. So *Skinke*, in *Look about you*, 1600 :

" But *pauca Verba, Skinke*."

Again, in *Every Man in his Humour*, where it is called *benchers phrase*. STEEVENS.

Shakspere seems to frolick here in his heraldry, with a design not to be easily understood. In Leland's Collectanea, vol. I. p. ii. p. 615. the arms of *Geffrey de Lucy* are " de goules *poudre* a croisil dor a treis luz dor." Can the poet mean to quibble upon the word *poudré*, that is, *powdered*, which signifies *salted*; or strewed and sprinkled with any thing? In *Measure for Measure*, Lucio says——

" Ever your fresh whore and your *powder'd* bawd." TOLLET.

The

The *luce* is a *pike* or *jak :*

 " Ful many a fair partrich hadde he in mewe,

 " And many a breme, and many a *luce* in stewe."

In Ferne's *Blazon of Gentry*, 1586, quarto, the arms of the Lucy family are represented as an instance, that " signs of the coat should something agree with the name. It is the coat of Geffrey Lord Lucy. He did bear Gules, three *lucies* hariant, Argent."

Mr. William Oldys, (Norroy King at Arms, and well known from the share he had in compiling the *Biographica Britannica)* among the collections which he left for a *Life of Shakspere*, observes, that——" there was a v ry aged gentleman living in the neighbourhood of Stratford, (where he died fifty years since) who had not only heard, from several old people in that town, of Shakspere's transgression, but could remember the first stanza of that bitter ballad, which, repeating to one of his acquaintance, he preserved it in writing; and here it is, neither better nor worse, but faithfully transcribed from the copy which his relation very courteously communicated to me."

 " A parliament member, a justice of peace,

 " At home a poor scare-crow, at London an asse,

 " If lowsie is Lucy, as some volke miscalle it,

 " Then Lucy is lowsie whatever befall it :

  " He thinks himself greate,

  " Yet an asse in his state,

 " We allowe by his ears but with asses to mate,

  " If Lucy is lowsie, as some volke miscalle it,

 " Sing lowsie Lucy, whatever befall it."

Contemptible as this performance must now appear,

at the time when it was written it might have had
sufficient power to irritate a vain, weak, and vindic-
tive migistrate; especially as it was affixed to several
of his park-gates, and consequently published among
his neighbours.—It may be remarked likewise, that
the jingle on which it turns, occurs in the first scene
of the *Merry Wives of Windsor.*

I may add, that the veracity of the late Mr. Oldys
has never yet been impeached; and it is not very probable that a ballad should be forged, from which an
undiscovered wag could derive no triumph over anti-
quarian credulity. STEEVENS.

35. *The council shall hear it; it is a riot.*] He alludes
to a statute made in the reign of K. Henry IV. (13,
chap. 7.) by which it is enacted, "That the justices,
" three, or two of them, and the sheriff, shall certify
" before the king, and his counselle, all the deeds
" and circumstances thereof (namely the *riot*); which
" certification should be of the like force as the pre-
" sentment of twelve: upon which certificate the tres-
" passers and offenders shall be put to answer, and
" they which be found guilty shall be punished, ac-
" cording to the discretion of the kinge and counselle."
GREY.

By *the council* is only meant the court of star-chamber, composed chiefly of the king's council sitting in
Camera stellata, which took cognizance of atrocious
riots. In the old 4to, " the council shall know it,"
follows immediately after " I'll make a star-chamber
matter of it." BLACKSTONE.

So,

So, in sir John Harrington's *Epigrams*, 1618:

    " No marvel men of such a sumptuous dyet

    " Were brought into the *Star-chamber* for a riot."

MALONE.

39.   ——*your* vizaments *in that.*] *Advisement* is now an obselete word. I meet with it in the ancient morality of *Every Man:*

    " That I may amend me with good *advysement.*"
Again :

    " I shall smite without any *advysement.*"
Again :

    " To go with good *advysements* and delyberacyon."
It is often used by Spenser in his *Faery Queene.* So, b. ii. c. 9:

    " Perhaps my succour and *advizement* meete."

STEEVENS.

45.   ——*which is daughter to Master Thomas Page,*] The whole set of editions have negligently blundered one after another in Page's Christian name in this place; though Mrs. Page calls him George afterwards in at least six several passages.   THEOBALD.

48.   ——*speaks* SMALL *like a woman.*] This is from the edition of 1623, and is the true reading. Thus *Lear* speaking of *Cordelia,*

    " ——Her *voice* was ever soft,

    " *Gentle* and *low:*—an excellent thing in woman."

STEEVENS.

In *The Midsummer Night's dream,* Quince tells Flute, who objects to playing a woman's part, " You shall

play

play it in a mask, and you may speak as *small* as you will."   MALONE.

57. Slend. *Did her grandsire, &c.*
And afterwards,———

" *I know the young gentlewoman, &c.*] These two speeches are in the old copy given by mistake to *Slender.* From the foregoing words it appears that *Shallow* is the person here addressed by sir Hugh, and that they both belong to him. On a marriage being proposed for his kinsman, he very naturally inquires concerning the lady's fortune. *Slender* should seem not to know what they are talking about; (except that he just hears the name of Anne Page, and breaks out into a foolish elogium on her:) for in a subsequent part of the scene, Shallow says to him:—
" Coz, there is, as it were, a tender, a kind of tender made afar off by Sir Hugh here, do you understand me." The tender, therefore, we see had been made to Shallow and not to Slender, the former of which names should, on that account, be prefixed to the two speeches before us.

In this play, as exhibited in the first folio, many of the speeches are given to characters to whom they do not belong. Printers, to save themselves trouble, keep the names of the speakers in each scene ready composed, and are, in consequence, very liable to mistakes when two names begin (as in the present instance) with the same letter.

This change was suggested by one of the modern editors.

83. ——*I thank you always*——] Here and in the next speech of Shallow, the 4to, 1619, reads *love,* which perhaps, as Dr. Farmer observes, is right.

STEEVENS.

88. *How does your fallow greyhound, sir? I heard say, he was out-run on* Cotsale.] He means *Cotswold* in *Gloucestershire.* In the beginning of the reign of James the First, by permission of the king, one Dover, a publick-spirited attorney of Barton on the Heath, in Warwickshire, instituted on the hills of *Cotswold* an annual celebration of games, consisting of rural sports and exercises. These he constantly conducted in person, well mounted, and accoutred in a suit of his majesty's old clothes; and they were frequented above forty years by the nobility and gentry for sixty miles round, till the grand rebellion abolished every liberal establishment. I have seen a very scarce book, entitled, "*Annalia Dubrensia. Upon the yearly celebration of Mr. Robert Dover's Olympick games upon Cotswold hills,*" &c. *London,* 1636, 4to. There are recommendatory verses prefixed, written by Drayton, Jonson, Randolph, and many others, the most eminent wits of the times. The games, as appears by a curious frontispiece, were chiefly, wrestling, leaping, pitching the bar, handling the pike, dancing of women, various kinds of hunting, and particularly coursing the hare with greyhounds. Hence also we see the meaning of another passage, where Falstaff, or Shallow, calls a stout fellow a *Cotswold-man.* But from what is here said, an inference of another kind may be drawn, respecting the

the age of the play. A meager and imperfect sketch of this comedy was printed in 1602. Afterwards Shakspere new-wrote it entirely. This allusion therefore to *Cotswold* games, not founded till the reign of James the First, ascertains a period of time beyond which our author must have made the additions to this original rough draught, or, in other words, composed the present comedy. James the First came to the crown in the year 1603. And we will suppose that two or three more years at least must have passed before these games could have been effectually established. I would therefore, at the earliest, date this play about the year 1607. It is not generally known, at least it has not been observed by the modern editors, that the first edition of the *Merry Wives* in its present state, is in the valuable folio, printed 1623. From whence the quarto of the same play, dated 1630, was evidently copied. The two earlier quartos, 1602 and 1619, only exhibit this comedy as it was originally written, and are so far curious, as they contain Shakspere's first conceptions in forming a drama, which is the most complete specimen of his comick powers. WARTON.

The *Cotswold-hills* in *Gloucestershire* are a large tract of downs, famous for their fine turf, and therefore excellent for coursing. I believe there is no village of that name. BLACKSTONE.

111. ——*and broke open my lodge.*] This probably alludes to some real incident, at that time well known. JOHNSON.

So probably Falstaff's answer. FARMER.

117. *'Twere better for you, if 'twere known in council;
you'll be laugh'd at.*] This is quite in Falstaff's insolent
sneering manner. " It would be much better, indeed,
to have it known in the council, where you would
only be laughed at.   REMARKS.

120. *Good* worts! *good cabbage:——*] *Worts* was
the ancient name of all the cabbage kind. So in Beaumont and Fletcher's *Valentinian :*

" Planting of *worts* and onions, any thing."
                                             STEEVENS.

124. *——coney-catching rascals,——*] A *coney-catcher*
was, in the time of Elizabeth, a common name for a
cheat or sharper.   Green, one of the first among us
who made a trade of writing pamphlets, published *A
Detection of the Frauds and Tricks of Coney-catchers and
Couzeners.*   JOHNSON.

So in Decker's *Satiromastix :*

" Thou shalt not *coney-catch* me for five pounds."
                                             STEEVENS.

Your *coney-catching* rascals, Bardolph, Nym, and
Pistol.] In the early quarto, Slender, speaking of the
same transaction, adds,

" They carried me to the tavern, and made me
         drunk, and afterwards pick'd my pocket."
These words surely deserve a place in the text, being
necessary to introduce what Falstaff says afterwards :

" Pistol, did you pick Master Slender's purse ?"
a circumstance, of which, as the play is exhibited in
the folio, he could have no knowledge.   MALONE.

126. *You Banbury cheese!*] This is said in allusion

to the thin carcase of Slender. The same thought occurs in *Jack Drum's Entertainment*, 1601 :

> " Put off your clothes, and you are like a *Banbury-*
> *cheese*——nothing but paring."

So Heywood, in his collection of epigrams :

> " I never saw *Banbury-cheese thick enough.*"

STEEVENS.

128. *How now, Mephostophilus?*] This is the name
of a spirit or familiar, in the old story book of *Sir
John Faustus*, or *John Faust:* to whom our author afterwards alludes. That it was a cant phrase of abuse,
appears from the old comedy cited above, called *A
pleasant Comedy of the Gentle Craft*, Signat. H. 3.

> " Away you *Islington* whitepot, hence you hopper-arse,
> you barley-pudding full of maggots, you broiled carbo-
> nado, avaunt, avaunt *Mephostophilus.*"

In the same vein, *Bardolph* here also calls *Slender,*

> " You *Banbury* cheese."   WARTON.

130. ——*that's my humour.*] So in the ancient MS.
play, entitled, *The Second Maiden's Tragedy:*

> " ——I love not to disquiet ghosts, sir,
> " Of any people living ; *that's my humour*, sir."

STEEVENS.

146. ——*what phrase is this,*] Sir Hugh is justified
in his censure of this passage by Pecham, who in his
Garden of Eloquence, 1577, places this very mode of
expression under the article *Pleonasmus.* HENDERSON.

151. ——*mill'd-sixpences,*——] It appears from a
passage in sir W. Davenant's *News from Plimouth*, that

. B iij these

these *mill'd-sixpences* were used by way of counters to cast up money :

    "———A few *mill'd sixpencies* with which

    " My purser casts accompts."   STEEVENS.

    152.   *Edward Shovel-boards,*———]   One of these pieces of metal is mentioned in Middleton's comedy of *The Roaring Girl,* 1611 :

    "Away slid I my man, like a *shovel-board shilling,*"&c.

                             STEEVENS.

" *Edward Shovel-boards,*" were the broad shillings of Edw. VI.

Taylor the water-poet, in his *Travel of Twelve-pence,* makes him complain :

    "———the unthrift every day

    " With my face downwards do at *shoave-board*
         play ;

    " That had I had a beard, you may suppose,

    " They had worne it off, as they have done my
         nose."

And in a note he tells us :

    " Edw. shillings for the most part are used at *shoave-*
         board."   FARMER.

The following extract, for the notice of which I am indebted to Dr. Farmer, will shew further the species of coin mentioned in the text : " I must here take notice before I entirely quit the subject of these last-mentioned shillings, that I have also seen some other pieces of good silver, greatly resembling the same, and of the same date 1547, that have been so much thicker as to weigh about *half an ounce,* together with

some

some others that have weighed an ounce." *Folke's Table of English silver coins*, p. 32. The former of these were probably what cost Master Slender two shillings and two-pence a piece.   REED.

158.   ——*latten bilboe:*] Pistol, seeing Slender such a slim, puny wight, would intimate, that he is as thin as a plate of that compound metal, which is called *latten:* and which was, as we are told, the old *orichale.* Monsieur Dacier, upon this verse in Horace's epistle *de Arte Poëtica,*

"Tibia non ut nunc *orichalco.*" &c.

says, *C'est une espece de cuivre de montagne, comme somme son mesme le temoigne; c'est ce que nous appellons aujourd'* *huy du* leton.   "It is a sort of mountain-copper, as its very name imports, and which we at this time of day call *latten.*"   THEOBALD.

After all this display of learning in Mr. Theobald's note, I believe our poet had a much more obvious meaning.   *Latten* may signify no more than *as thin as a lath.* The words in some counties is still pronounced as if there was *h* in it: and Ray in his Dictionary of North Country Words, affirms it to be spelt *lat* in the north of England.

Falstaff threatens, in another play, to drive prince Henry out of his kingdom with *a daggar of lath.* A *latten bilboe* means therefore, I believe, no more than *a blade as thin as a lath—a vice's dagger.*

Theobald, however, is right in his assertion that *latten* was a metal.   So Turbervile, in his Book of Falconry, 1575: "—you must set her *latten* bason, or
                                        a vessel

a vessel of stone or earth." Again, in *Old Fortunatus*, 1600: " Whether it were lead or *lattin* that hasp'd down those winking casements, I know not." Again, in the old metrical Romance of *Syr Bevis of Hampton*, b. l. no date:

" Windowes of *latin* were set with glasse."
Latten is still a common word for *tin* in the North.

STEEVENS.

I believe Theobald has given the true sense of *latten*, though he is wrong in supposing, that the allusion is to Slender's *thinness*. It is rather to his *softness* or *weakness*.   TYRWHITT.

Lattin properly so called, is *tinned iron*, which not only serves for the ordinary utensils of a kitchen, but is also used for play-house daggers, &c.   HENLEY.

159.   *Word of denial in* thy *labra's here*;] I suppose it should rather be read:

Word of denial in my *labra's* hear;
that is, *hear* the word of denial in my *lips. Thou ly'st.*

JOHNSON.

We often talk of giving the lie in a man's *teeth*, or in his *throat*. Pistol chooses to throw the world of denial in the *lips* of his adversary, and is supposed to point to them as he speaks.   STEEVENS.

I incline strongly to Dr. Johnson's emendation. There are few words in the old copies more frequently misrepresented than the word *hear*.   MALONE.

Labra's ought to be printed *labras*.   * * *

163.   ——*marry trap,*——] When a man was
caught

caught in his own stratagem, I suppose the exclamation of insult was *marry, trap!*   JOHNSON.

164. ——nuthook's *humour*——] Read, *pass the nuthook's humour.* *Nuthook* was a term of reproach in the vulgar way, and in cant strain. In *The Second Part of Henry IV.* Dol Tearsheet says to the beadle, *Nuthook, Nuthook, you lie.* Probably it was a name given to a baliff or catchpole, very odious to the common people.
                                                HANMER.

Nuthook is the reading of the folio, and the third quarto. The second quarto reads, *base* humour.

If you run the Nuthook's humour on me, is in plain English, *if you say I am a Thief.* Enough is said on the subject of *hooking moveables out at windows,* in a note on *K. Henry IV.*   STEEVENS.

168. ——*Scarlet and John?*] The names of two of Robin Hood's companions; but the humour consists in the allusion to Bardolph's *red face;* concerning which, see *The Second Part of Henry IV.*
                                            WARBURTON.

173. *And being* fap,——] I know not the exact meaning of this cant word, neither have I met with it in any of our old dramatick pieces, which have often proved the best comments on Shakspere's vulgarisms.

Dr. Farmer, indeed observes that *to fib* is to *beat;* so that *fap* may mean *being beaten,* and *cashired, turned out of company.*   STEEVENS.

The word *fap,* is probably made from *vappa,* a drunken fellow, or a good for nothing fellow, whose virtues all are exhaled. Slender in his answer seems to
                                                under-

understand that Bardolph had made use of a Latin word.

    Slen. Ay, you spake in Latin then too;" as Pistol had just before.   S. W.

    194. ——my book of *songs* and *sonnets* here :] Slender very probably means the poems of Lord Surrey and others, which were extremely popular in the age of Queen Elizabeth. They were printed in 1567, with this title : *Songs and Sonnets,* written by the right honourable Lord Henry Howard, late Earl of Surrey, and others.

Slender laments that he has not this fashionable book about him, supposing that it would have assisted him in his address to Anne Page.   MALONE.

    196. ——*the book of riddles!*] This appears to have been a popular book, and is enumerated with others in *The English Courtier, and Country Gentleman.* bl. let 4to. 1586, Sign. H 4. See quotation in note to *Much ado about Nothing.*   REED.

    224. ——*the lips is a parcel of the mouth;*——] Thus the old copies.   The modern editors read :

    " ——parcel of the *mind.*"

To be a *parcel* of any thing is an expresson that often occurs in the old plays.   So in Decker's *Satiromastix :*

    " And make damnation *parcel* of your oath." Again, in *Tamburlaine,* 1590 :

    " To make it *parcel* of my empery." This passage, however, might have been designed as a ridicule on another, in John Lylly's *Midas,* 1592 :

    " *Pet.*

"*Pet.* What lips hath she?

"*Li.* Tush! *Lips are no part of the head*, only made for *a double leaf door for the mouth.*　　STEEVENS.

277. ——*a master of fence,*——] *Master of defence,* on this occasion, does not simply mean a professor of the art of fencing, but a person who had taken his *master's degree* in it,　I learn from one of the Sloanian MSS (now in the British Museum, No. 2530, xxvi. D.) which seems to be the fragment of a rigister formerly belonging to some of our schools where the "Noble Science of Defence" was taught, from the year 1568 to 1583, that in this art there are three degrees, viz. a *master's,* a provest's, and a scholar's. For each of these a prize is played, as exercises are kept in universities for similar purposes. The weapons they used were the axe, the pike, rapier, and target, rapier and cloke, two swords, the two-hand sword, the bastard sword, the dagger and staff, the sword and buckler, the rapier and dagger, &c. The places where they exercised were commonly theatres, halls, or other enclosures sufficient to contain a number of spectators, as Ealy-Place, in Holborn; the Bell Savage, Ludgate-Hill; the Curtain in Hollywell; the Gray Friars, within Newgate; Hampton Court; the Bull in Bishopsgate-Street; the Clink, Duke's-Place, Salisbury-Court; Bridewell; the Artillery-Garden, &c. &c. &c. Among those who distinguished themselves in this science, I find Tarlton the Comedian, who "was allowed a master," the 23d of October, 1587 [I suppose, either as grand compounder, or mandamus],

he

he being " ordinary grome of her majesties chamber,"
and Robert Greene, who " plaide his master's prize
at Leadenhall with three weapons," &c. The book
from which these extracts are made is a singular cu-
riosity, as it contains the oaths, customs, regulations,
prizes, summonses, &c. of this once fashionable society. *K. Henry VIII. K. Edward VI. Philip* and *Mary,*
Q. Elizabeth, were frequently spectators of their skill
and activity.   STEEVENS.

277. ———*three* veneys *for a dish,* &c.] *i. e.* three
venues, French. Three different set-to's, *bouts,* a technical term. So in Beaumont and Fletcher's *Philaster:*
—" thou wouldst be loth to play half dozen *venies* at
Wasters with a good fellow for a broken head."
Again, in *The Two Maids of More-clacke,* 1609: " This
was a pass, 'twas fencer's play, and for after *veny,*
let me use my skill." So in *The famous Hist.* &c.
of Capt. Tho. Stukely, 1605:——" for forfeits and *ven-*
neys, given upon a wager at the ninth button of your
doublet."

Again, in the MSS mentioned in the preceding
note, " and at any prize whether it be maister's prize,
&c. whosoever doth strike his blowe and close with
all, the prizer cannot strike his blowe after agayne
shall wynne no game for any *veneye* so given although
it should break the prizer's head."   STEEVENS.

287. *That's meat and drink to me now:*——] Deckar
has this proverbal phrase in *Satiromastix:* " Yes faith,
'tis *meat and drink to me.*"   WHALLEY.

288.

288. ——*Sackerson*——] *Sackerson* is likewise the name of a bear in the old comedy of *Sir Giles Goosecap*.

STEEVENS.

Sacarson was the name of a bear that was exhibited in our author's time at Paris Garden. See an old collection of *Epigrams* [by Sir John Davis] printed at Middlebourgh (without date, but in or before 1598):

" Publius, a student of the common law,

" To *Paris garden* doth himself withdraw;——

" ——Leaving old Ployden, Dyer, and Broke alone,

" To see old *Harry Hunkes* and *Sacarson*."

MALONE.

290. ——*that it pass'd:*——] *It pass'd*, or *this passes*, was a way of speaking customary heretofore, to signify the *excess*, or *extraordinary degree* of any thing. The sentence completed would be, *This passes all expression*, or perhaps, *This passes all things*. We still use *passing well, passing strange*.   WARBURTON

296. *By cock and pye,*——] See a note on act v. sc. 1. *Henry IV.*   STEEVENS.

321. ——*Bully-rook.*] This seems to have been the reading of some editions: in others it is a bully-rock. Mr. Steevens's explanation of it as alluding to chess-men is right. But Shakspere might possibly have given it bully-rock, as *rock* is the true name of these men, which is softened or corrupted into *rook*. There is seemingly more humour in bully-rock.

WHALLEY.

C   288.

328. ——Keisar,——] The preface to Stowe's Chronicle observes, that the Germans use the K for C, pronouncing *Keysar* for *Cæsar*, their general word for an emperor.　　　　　　　　　　Tollet.

335. ——*a wither'd servingman, a fresh tapster :*] This not improbably a parody on the old proverb— " A broken apothecary, a new doctor." See Ray's Proverbs, 3d edit. p. 2.　　　　　　　Steevens.

338. *O base Gongarian wight!* &c.] This is a parody on a line taken from on of the old bombast plays, beginning,

　　" O base *Gongarian*, wilt thou the distaff wield ?"
I had marked the passage down, but forgot to note the play.

The folio reads *Hungarian.*

Hungarian is likewise a cant term. So in the *Merry Devil of Edmonton*, 1626, the merry Host says,

" I have knights and colonels in my house, and must tend the *Hungarians*." Again :

" Come ye *Hungarian* pilchers."
Again, in *Westward Hoe*, 1607 :

" Play you louzy *Hungarians*."

Again, in *News from Hell, wrought by the Devil's Carrier*, by Thomas Decker, 1606: " ——the leane-jaw'd *Hungarian* would not lay out a penny.pot of sack for himself."　　　　　　　　　　Steevens.

The *Hungarians*, when infidels, over-ran Germany and France, and would have invaded England, if they could have come to it. See Stowe, in the year 930,
and

and Holinshed's invasion of Ireland, p. 56. Hence their name might become a proverb of baseness. Stowe's Chronicle, in the year 1492, and Leland's Collectanea, vol. i. p. 610, spell it *Hongarian* (which might be misprinted *Gongarian*); and this is right according to their own etymology. *Hongyars i. e.* domus suæ strenui defensores.   TOLLET.

The word is *Gongarian* in the first edition, and should be continued, the better to fix the allusion.

FARMER.

342.   ——*humour of it.*] This speech is partly taken from the corrected copy, and partly from the slight sketch in 1602. I mention it, that those who do not find it in either of the common old editions, may not suspect it to be spurious.   STEEVENS.

346.   ——*at a* minute's *rest.*] Our author probably wrote :

——*at a* minim's *rest.*   LANGTON.

This conjecture seems confirmed by a passage in *Romeo and Juliet :*

" ——*rests his* minim," &c.

It may however mean, that, like a skilful harquebuzier, he takes a good aim, though he has rested his piece for a minute only. So in Daniel's *Civil Wars,* &c. b. vi.

" To *set up's rest* to venture now for all."

STEEVENS.

At a minute's *rest.*] A *minim* was anciently, as the term imports, the shortest note in musick. Its

C ij   measure

measure was afterwards, as it is now, as long as while two may be moderately counted. In *Romeo and Juliet*, act ii. Mercutio says of Tibalt, that in fighting he rests his *minim*, one, two, and the third in your bosom. A minute contains sixty seconds, and is a long time for an action supposed to be instantaneous. Nym means to say, that the perfection of stealing is to do it in the shortest time possible.

SIR J. HAWKINS.

Nym, I think, means to say, '*Tis true ; Bardolph did not keep time, did not steal at the critical and exact season when he would probably be least observed. The true method is, to steal just at the instant when watchfulness is off its guard,* and reposes but for a moment.

The reading proposed by Mr. Langton certainly corresponds more exactly with the preceding speech ; but Shakspere scarcely ever pursues his metaphors far.

MALONE.

348.   Convey, *the wise it call :———*]
So in the old morality of *Hycke Scorner*, bl. l. no date :

>   " Syr, the horesones could not *convaye* clene ;
>   " For an they could have carried by craft as I
>   can," &c.   STEEVENS.

354.   *Young ravens must have food.*] An adage. See Ray's *Proverbs*.   STEEVENS.

361.   *———about no waste ;———*]
I find the same play on words in Heywood's *Epigrams*, 1562 :

" Where

  “ Where am I least, husband ? quoth he, in the
   waist ;
  “ Which cometh of this, thou art vengeance strait
   lac'd.
  “ Where am I biggest, wife ? in the *waste,* quoth
   she,
  “ For all is *waste* in you, as far as I see.''
And again, in *The Wedding,* a comedy by Shirley, 1629:
  “ He's a great man indeed ;
  “ Something given to the *wast,* for he lives within
   reasonable compass.'' STEEVENS.

 364. —*she* carves—] It should be remembered,
that anciently the young of both sexes were instructed
in *carving,* as a necessary accomplishment. In 1508,
Wynkyn de Worde published “ A Boke of *Kerving.*''
So in *Love's Labour Lost,* Biron says of Boyet, the
French courtier : “ —He can *carve* too, and lisp.''
          STEEVENS.

 370. *The* anchor *is deep; Will that humour pass ?*] I
see not what relation *the anchor* has to *translation.* Perhaps we may read, *the* author *is deep;* or perhaps the
line is out of its place, and should be inserted lower
after Falstaff has said,
 “ Sail like my pinnace to these golden shores.''
It may be observed, that in the tracts of that time
anchor and *author* could hardly be distinguished.
          JOHNSON.

 The *anchor* is deep :] Dr. Johnson very acutely proposes “ the *author* is deep.'' He reads with the first
copy, “ he hath study'd her *well.*''—And from this
     C iij   equivo-

equivocal word, Nym catches the idea of *deepness*. But it is almost impossible to ascertain the diction of this whimsical character: and I meet with a phrase in *Fenner's Comptor's Commonwealth*, 1617, which perhaps may support the old reading, " Master *Decker's Bellman of London*, hath set forth the vices of the time so lively, that it is impossible the *anchor* of any other man's braine can sound the sea of a more deepe and dreadful mis-cheefe."   FARMER.

——studied her *will*, and translated her *will*——is the reading of the first folio, 1623. The contested part of the passage may mean, *His hopes are well founded*. So in the *Knight of the Burning Pestle*, by Beaumont and Fletcher:

   " Now my latest *hope*
   " Forsake me not, but fling thy *anchor* out,
   " And let it hold."

In the year 1558 a ballad, intitutled " Hold the *ancer* fast." is entered on the books of the Stationers Company.

Translation is not used in its common acceptation, but means to *explain*, as one language is explained by another.   So in *Hamlet:*

   " ——these profound heaves
   " You must *translate*, 'tis fit we understand them."
Again, in *Troilus* and *Cressida:*
   " Did in great Ilion thus *translate* him to me."
             STEEVENS.

  374.   *As many devils entertain, &c.*] The old quarto reads:

             " As

" As many devils *attend her!*" &c.   STEEVENS.

I would read with the quarto—*As many devils attend her! i. e.* let as many devils attend her. MUSGRAVE.

378.   ——*and here another to Page's wife; who even now gave me good eyes too, examined my parts with the most judicious eyelids: sometimes* the beam of her view gilded *my foot, sometimes my portly belly.*]   So, in our author's 20th sonnet :

 " *An eye* more bright than theirs, less false in
  rolling,
 " *Gilding* the object whereupon it gazeth."

MALONE.

381.   ——*eyelids :*——]   This word is differently spelt in all the copies. I suppose we should write *oëillades,* French.   STEEVENS.

383.   *Then did the sun on dunghill shine.*] So in Lilly's *Euphues,* 1581 :

 " The sun shineth upon a dunghill.'   T. H. W.

384.   ——*that humour.*]   What distinguishes the language of Nym from that of the other attendants on Falstaff, is the constant repetition of this phrase. In the time of Shakspere such an affectation seems to have been sufficient to mark a character. In *Sir Giles Goose-cap,* a play of which I have no earlier edition than that of 1606, the same peculiarity is mentioned in the hero of the piece :

 " ——his only reason for every thing is, that *we are all mortal;* then hath he another pretty phrase too, and that is, he will *tickle the vanity* of every thing."

STEEVENS.

5

385.

385.   *O, she did so course-o'er my exteriors——*] So in *Cupid's Whirligig,* 1607:

> "——with a gredie eye feedes on my exteryors."
>
>   HENDERSON.

386.   *——intention,——*] *i. e.* eagerness of desire.

                                  STEEVENS.

389.   *——she is a region in Guiana, all gold and bounty.*]' If the tradition be true (as I doubt not but it is) of this play being wrote at queen Elizabeth's command, this passage, perhaps, may furnish a probable conjecture that it could not appear till after the year 1598.   The mention of Guiana, then so lately discovered to the English, was a very handsome compliment to sir Walter Raleigh, who did not begin his expedition to South America till 1535, and returned from it in 1596, with an advantageous account of the great wealth of Guiana.   Such an address of the poet was likely, I imagine, to have a proper impression on the people, when the intelligence of such a golden country was fresh in their minds, and gave them expectatations of immense gain.   THEOBALD.

390.   *I will be* cheater *to them both, and they shall be* exchequers *to me;——*]   The same joke is intended here, as in the *The Second Part of Henry the Fourth,* act ii.

> "——I will bar no honest man my house, nor no
>   *cheater.*"——

By which is meant *Escheatour,* an officer in the Exchequer, in no good repute with the common people.

                                  WARBURTON.

                                       400.

400. ———*tear you these letters* tightly;] *i. e.* cleverly, alertly. So in *Antony and Cleopatra.* Antony, putting on his armour, says,

> " My queen's a squire
> " More *tight* at this than thou."

Tightly is the reading of the early quarto, and of the first folio, the only authentick ancient copy of this play as enlarged by the author. *Rightly* is the arbitrary reading of the quarto 1630, and of the folio 1632:

MALONE.

No phrase is so common in the eastern counties of this kingdom, and particularly in Suffolk, as *good tightly*, for *briskly and effectually.*   HENLEY.

401. ———*my* pinnace———] A pinnace seems anciently to have signified a small vessel, or sloop, attending on a larger.
So in Rowley's *When you see me you know me*, 1613:

> " ———was lately sent
> " With threescore sail of ships and *pinnaces.*"

Again, in *Muleasses the Turk*, 1610:

> " Our life is but a sailing to our death
> " Thro' the world's ocean : it makes no matter
>   then,
> " Whether we put into the world's vast sea
> " Shipp'd in a *pinnace* or an argosy."

At present it signifies only a man of war's boat.

STEEVENS.

404. ———*the* humour *of* this *age*,] Thus the 4to, 1619: The folio reads—the *honor* of *the* age.

STEEVENS.

406.

406.   *Let vultures gripe thy guts!——*] This hemistich is a burlesque on a passage in *Tamburlaine, or The Scythian Shepherd,* of which play a more particular account is given in one of the notes to *Henry the IV.* p. ii. act ii. sc. iv.   STEEVENS.

406.   *——for* gourd, *and* fullam *holds;*

   And high *and* low *beguiles the rich and poor:*] *Fullam* is a cant term for false dice, *high* and *low.* Torriano, in his Italian dictionary, interprets *Pise* by *false dice, high and low men, high fullams and low fullams.* Jonson, in his *Every Man out of his Humour,* quibbles upon this cant term: " *Who, he serve? He keeps* high men and low men, *he has a fair living at* fullam."—As for *gourd,* or rather *gord,* it was another instrument of gaming, as appears from Beaumont and Fletcher's *Scornful Lady:* · "——*and thy dry bones can reach at nothing now, but* gords *or* inne-pins." WARBURTON.

   In the *London Prodigal* I find the following enumeration of false dice.——" I bequeath two bale of false dice, videlicet, *high men* and *low men, fulloms,* stop cater-traies, and other bones of function." STEEVENS,

   410.   *I have operations* in my head,——] The words in Roman, which are omitted in the folio, were recovered from the early quarto.   MALONE.

   416.   *I will discuss the humour of this love to Ford.*] The very reverse of this happens. See act ii. where *Nym* makes the discovery to *Page,* and not to *Ford,* as here promised; and *Pistol,* on the other hand, to *Ford,* and not to *Page.* Shakspere is frequently guilty of these little forgetfulnesses.   STEEVENS.

Though

Though Shakspere is sometimes forgetful, it appears from the first copy of this play that the editors of the folio alone are answerable for the present inaccuracy. In the early quarto *Nym* declares, he will make the discovery to *Page*; and *Pistol* says, " And I to *Ford* will likewise tell," &c.   And so without doubt these speeches ought to be printed.   MALONE.

423.   *yellowness,*——] *Yellowness* is jealousy.
                                    JOHNSON.

So, in *Law Tricks*, &c. 1608:
   " If you have me you must not put on *yellow*."
Again, in *The Arraignment of Paris*, 1584:
   " ——Flora well, perdie,
   " Did paint her *yellow* for her *jealousy*."
                                    STEEVENS.

423.   ——*the revolt of mien*——] *The revolt of mine* is the old reading.   *Revolt of mien*, is *change of countenance*, one of the effects he has just been ascribing to jealousy.   STEEVENS.

This, Mr. Steevens truly observes to be the old reading, and it is authority enough for *the revolt of mien* in modern orthography. " Know you that fellow that walketh there?" says Eliot, 1593—" he is alchymist by his *mien*, and hath multiplied all to moonshine."
                                    FARMER.

434.   ——*at the latter end*, &c.] *i. e.* when my master is in bed.   JOHNSON.

437.   ——*no breed bate:*——] *Bate* is an obsolete word signifying strife, contention.   So, in the Coun-
                                    tess

tess of Pembroke's *Antonius,* 1530:

  " Shall ever civil *bate*

  " Gnaw and devour our state!"

Again, in *Acolastus,* a comedy, 1540:

  " We shall not fall at *bate,* or stryve for this

   matter.'"

Stanyhurst, in his translation of Virgil, 1582, calls
Erinnys a *make bate.*   STEEVENS.

 438. *He's somewhat* peevish *that way:*] I believe this
is one of Dame Quickly's blunders, and she means
precise.   MALONE.

 ——*peevish*] *Peevish* is foolish. So in *Cymbeline,*
act ii.

  " ——he's strange and *peevish.*" STEEVENS.

 446. ——*a little* wee *face,*——] *Wee,* in the northern dialect, signifies very little. Thus in the Scottish
proverb, that apologizes for a little woman's marriage
with a big man: " —A *wee* mouse will creep under a
mickle cornstack.   COLLINS.

 So in Heywood's *Fair Maid of the West,* com. 1631:
" He was nothing so tall as I, but a little *wee* man, and
somewhat hutch-back." Again, in *The Wisdom of Doctor Dodypoll,* 1600:

  " Some two miles, and a *wee* bit, Sir."

Wee is derived from *wenig.* Dutch. On the authority
of the 4to, 1619, we might be led to read *whey*-face:
" —Somewhat of a weakly man, and has as it were a
whay-coloured beard." *Macbeth* calls one of the mes-
sengers *Whey*-face.   STEEVENS.

 Little wee is certainly the right reading; it implies
           some-

something extremely diminutive, and is a very common vulgar idiom in the North.   *Wee* alone has only
the signification of *little*.   Thus *Cleiveland:*

   " A Yorkshire *wee bitt*, longer than a mile."
The proverb is a mile and a *wee bit; i. e.* about a league
and a half.   REMARKS.

   447.   ——*a* Cain-*colour'd beard.*]   Cain and Judas,
in the tapestries and pictures of old, were represented
with *yellow* beards.   THEOBALD.

   Theobald's conjecture may be countenanced by a
parrallel expression in an old play called *Blurt Master
Constable*, or, *The Spaniard's Night-Walk*, 1602:

   " ——over all,

   " A goodly, long, thick, *Abraham-coloured* beard."
Again, in *Soliman and Perseda*, 1599, Basilisco says:

   " ——where is the eldest son of Priam,

   " That *Abraham-colour'd* Trojan ?"——
I am not however certain, but that *Abraham* may be a
corruption of *Auburn*.   Again, in *The Spanish Tragedy*,
1605:

   " And let their beards be of *Judas* his own *colour*."
Again, in *A Christian turn'd Turk*, 1612:

   " That's he in the *Judas* beard."——
Again, in the *Insatiate Countess*, 1613:

   " I ever thought by his *red beard* he would prove
           a *Judas*."
In an age, when but a small part of the nation could
read, ideas were frequently borrowed from presenta-
tions in painting or tapestry.   A *cane*-coloured beard,
however, might signify a beard of the colour of *cane*,

D

i. e.

i. e. a sickly yellow; for *straw*-coloured beards are mentioned in the *Midsummer Night's Dream.*   STEEVENS.

The new edition of Leland's *Collectanea*, vol. v. p.
295, asserts, that painters constantly represented *Judas*
the traytor with a *red head.* Dr. Plot's *Oxfordshire*, p.
153, says the same.   This conceit is thought to have
arrisen in England, from our ancient grudge to the
red-haired Danes.   TOLLET.

See my quotation in *K. Henry VIII.* act. v.

                                          STEEVENS.

450.   ——*as* tall *a man of his hands,*——] Perhaps
this is an allusion to the jockey measure, *so many hands
high,* used by grooms when speaking of horses. *Tall,*
in our author's time, signified not only height of stature, but stoutness of body.   The ambiguity of the
phrase seems intended.   PERCY.

Whatever be the origin of this phrase, is very ancient, being used by Gower:

    " A worthie knight was *of his honde,*
    " There was none suche in all the londe."

        De Confessione Amantis, lib. v. fol. 118. b.
                                          STEEVENS.

461.   ——we shall be *shent*————] *i. e.* Scolded,
roughly treated.   So in the old *Interlude of Nature,*
bl. l. no date :

    " ——I can tell thee one thyng,
    " In fayth you wyll be *shent.*"   STEEVENS.

466   ——*and down, down, a-down-a,* &c.] To deceive her master, she sings as if at her work.

                                 SIR J HAWKINS.
                                          This

This appears to have been the burden of some song then well known. In *Every Woman in her Humour,* 1609, sign. E. 1. one of the characters says, " Hey good boies i'faith now a three man's song, *or the old downe a downe.*" REED.

467. Enter Doctor *Caius.*] It has been thought strange, that our author should take the name of *Caius* for his Frenchman in this comedy; but Shakspere was little acquainted with literary history; and without doubt, from this unusual name, supposed him to have been a foreign quack. Add to this, that the doctor was handed down as a kind of Rosicrucian: Mr. Ames had in MS. one of the " *Secret Writings of Dr. Caius.*" FARMER.

This character of *Dr. Caius* might have been drawn from the life; as in *Jacke of Dover's Quest of Enquirie,* 1604 (perhaps a republication), a story called *The Foole of Winsor* begins thus " Upon a time there was in *Winsor* a certain simple *outlandish doctor of phisicke* belonging to the deane," &c. STEEVENS.

468. ——*un boitier verd;*——] *Boitier* in French signifies a case of surgeon's instruments. GREY.

I believe it rather means a *box of salve,* or case to hold *simples,* for which Caius professes to seek. The same word, somewhat curtailed, is used by Chaucer, in the *Pardoneres Prologue,* v. 12241:

" And every *boist* full of thy letuarie."

Again, in the *Skynner's Play,* in the Chester Collection of Mysteries. MS. Harl. p. 149, Mary Magdalen says:

D ij

" To

" To balme his bodye that is so brighte,

" *Boist* here have I brought."   STEEVENS.

43.   ——What, the *goujere!*] So in *K. Lear:*

" The *goujeers* shall devour them."

The *goujere*; i. e. *morbus Gallicus.* See Hanmer's note, *K. Lear*, act v.   STEEVENS.

457.   *You shall have an fool's-head*——]Mrs. Quickly, I believe, intends a quibble between *ann*, sounded broad, and *one*, which was formerly sometimes pronounced *on.* In the Scottish dialect *one* is written, and I suppose pronounced, *ane.*

In 1603, was published *Ane* verie excellent and delectable treatise intitulit *Philotus*, &c.

In act ii. sc. i. of this play, *an* seems to have been misprinted for *one:*

" What *an* unweigh'd behaviour," &c.
The mistake there probably arose from the similarity of the sounds.   MALONE.

570.   ——*but I detest, an honest maid as ever broke bread.*]   Dame Quickly means to say ——*I protest.*
          MALONE.

ACT II.

Line 4. ——*THOUGH love use reason for his precisian, he admits him not for his counsellor:*——]   This is obscure: but the meaning is, *though love permit reason to*

ell

tell what is fit to be done, he seldom follows its advice.—By *precisian*, is meant one who pretends to a more than ordinary degree of virtue and sanctity. On which account they gave this name to the Puritans of that time. So Osborne—"*Conform their mode, words, and looks to these* PRECISIANS." And Maine, in his *City Match :*

"——I did commend
" A great PRECISIAN to her for her woman."
                              WARBURTON.

——*precisian,*——] Of this word I do not see any meaning that is very apposite to the present intention. Perhaps Falstaff said, *Though love use reason as his* physician, *he admits him not for his counsellor.* This will be plain sense. Ask not the *reason* of my love; the business of *reason* is not to assist love, but to *cure* it. There may however be this meaning in the present reading, *Though love,* when he would submit to regulation, may *use reason as his precisian,* or director in nice cases, yet when he is only eager to attain his end, he takes not reason for his *counsellor.*
                              JOHNSON.

Dr. Johnson wishes to read *physician;* and this conjecture becomes almost a certainty from a line in our author's 147th sonnet,

" My reason the *physician* to my love," &c.
                              FARMER.

The character of a *precisian* seems to have been very generally ridiculed in the time of Shakspere. So in the *Malcontent,* 1604: "You must take her in the right

vein then : as, when the sign is in Pisces, a fishmon-
ger's wife is very sociable : in Cancer, a *precisian's*
wife is very flexible." Again, *Dr. Faustus,* 1604 :

"I will set my countenance like a *precisian.*"
Again, in Ben Jonson's *Case is alter'd,* 1609 :

"It is *precisianism* to alter that,

"With austere judgment, which is given by na-
        ture."   STEEVENS.

If *physician* be the right reading, the meaning may
be this : A lover, uncertain as yet of success, never
takes reason for his counsellor, but, when desperate,
applies to him as his physician.   MUSGRAVE.

13.   *Thine own true knight,*

By day or night.]   This expression, which is
ludicrously employed by Falstaff, anciently meant, *at
all times.*   So, in the third book of Gower, *De Confessione Amantis :*

"The sonne cleped was Machayre,

"The daughter eke Canace hight,

"*By daie bothe and eke by night.*"
Loud and still, was another phrase of the same meaning.

        STEEVENS.

20.   *What* an *unweigh'd behaviour,* &c.]   Thus the
folio and 4to. 1630. It has been suggested to me, that
we should read, *one.*   STEEVENS.

21.   ——*Flemish drunkard*——]   It is not without
reason that this term of reproach is here used.   Sir
John Smythe in *Certain Discourses,* &c. 4to. 1590, says,
that the habit of drinking to excess was introduced
into England from the Low Countries, "by some of
        "our

" our such men of warre within these very few years,
" whereof it is come to passe that now-a-days there
" are very fewe feastes where our said men of warre
" are present, but that they do invite and procure all
" the companie, of what calling soever they be, to
" carowsing and quaffing; and, because they will not
" be denied their challenges, they, with many new
" conges, ceremonies, and reverences, drinke to the
" health and prosperitie of princes; to the health of
" counsellors, and unto the health of their greatest
" friends both at home and abroad; in which exercise
" they never cease till they be dead drunke, or, as the
" *Flemings* say, *Doot dronken.* He adds, " And this
" aforesaid detestable vice hath within these sixe or
" seven yeares taken wonderful roote amongest our
" English Nation, that in times past was wont to be of
" all other nations of Christendome one of the so-
" berest."   REED.

25. ——*I was then frugal of my mirth:*] By break-
ing this speech into exclamations, the text may stand;
but I once thought it must be read, If *I was* not *then
frugal of my mirth.*   JOHNSON.

48. *What ?—thou liest !—Sir Alice Ford !—These
knights will* HACK; *and so thou shouldst not alter the article of thy gentry.*] Hanmer says, to *hack,* means to
hackney, or prostitute. I suppose he means—*These
knights will degrade themselves, so that she will* acquire no
honour by being connected with them. Perhaps the
passage has been hitherto entirely misunderstood. To
hack, is an expression used in the ridiculous scene between

tween Quickly, Evans, and the boy; and signifies, *to do mischief.* The sense of this passage may therefore be, these knights are a riotous, dissolute sort of people, and on that account thou should'st not wish to be of the number.

It is not, however, impossible that Shakspere meant by—*these knights will hack*—these knights will soon become *hackney'd* characters.—So many knights were made about the time this play was amplified (for the passage is neither in the copy 1602, nor 1619) that such a stroke of satire might not have been unjustly thrown in. In *Hans Beer Pot's Invisible Comedy*, 1618, is a long piece of ridicule on the same occurrence :

> " 'Twas strange to see what *knighthood* once would
>   do :
> " Stir great men up to lead a martial life——
> " To gain this honour and this dignity.——
> " But now, alas! 'tis grown ridiculous ;
> " Since bought with money, sold for basest prize,
> " That some refuse it who are counted wise."

Steevens.

These knights will *hack* (that is, become cheap and vulgar), and therefore she advises her friend not to sully her gentry by becoming one. The whole of this discourse about knighthood is added since the first edition of this play; and therefore I suspect this is an oblique reflection on the prodigality of James I. in bestowing these honours, and in erecting in 1611 a new order of knighthood, called Baronets; which few of the ancient gentry would condescend to accept. See

sir

sir Hugh Spelman's epigram on them, *Gloss.* p. 76, which ends thus:

"——dum cauponare recusant
" Ex vera geniti nobilitate viri;
" Interea e caulis hic prorepit, ille tabernis,
    " Et modo fit dominus, qui modo servus erat."

See another stroke at them in *Othello.* act iii.

To *hick* and to *hack*, in Mrs. Quickley's language, signifies to *stammer* or *hesitate*, as boys do in saying ther lessons.   BLACKSTONE.

Between the time of King James's arrival at Berwick in April 1603, and the 20th of May, he made two hundred and thirty-seven knights; and, in the July following, between three and four hundred. It is highly probable that the play before us was enlarged in that or the subsequent year, when this stroke of satire must have been highly relished by the audience. That the order of *Baronets* was pointed at here, is, I think, highly improbable.   MALONE.

51. *We burn day-light!——*] *i. e.* we have more proof than we want. The same proverbial phrase occurs in the *Spanish Tragedy:*

Hier. " Light me your torches."

Pedro. " Then *we burn day-light.*"

So in *Romeo and Juliet*, Mercutio uses the same expression, and then explains it:

" *We waste our lights in vain like lamps by day.*"
                                STEEVENS

I think, the meaning rather is, we are wasting time in idle talk, when we ought to read the letter: re-
                                        sembling

sembling those who waste candles by burning them in the day-time.   MALONE.

60. ——*Green Sleeves.*] This song was entered on the books of the Stationer's Company in September 1580: "Licensed unto Richard Jones, a newe northern dittye of the lady *Green Sleeves.*" Again, "Licensed unto Edward White, a ballad, beinge the lady *Greene Sleeves*, answered to Jenkyn hir friend." Again, in the same month and year: "*Green Sleeves* moralized to the Scripture," &c. Again to Edward White:

"*Green Sleeves* and countenaunce.

"In countenaunce is *Green Sleeves.*" STEEVENS.

75. ——*press*——] *Press* is used ambiguously, for a *press* to print, and a *press* to squeeze.   JOHNSON.

84. ——*some strain in me,*] Thus the old copies. The modern editors read,

"some *stain* in me,"

but, I think, unnecessarily. A similar expression occurs in *The Winter's Tale:*

"With what encounter so uncurrent, have I

"*Strain'd* to appear thus?"

And again in *Timon:*

"——a noble nature

"May catch a *wrench.*"   STEEVENS.

96. ——the *chariness* of our honesty.] *i. e.* the *caution* which ought to attend on it.   STEEVENS.

97. *Oh,* that *my husband saw this letter!*] Surely Mrs. Ford does not wish to excite the jealousy, of which she complains. I think we should read—Oh, *if* my husband, &c. and thus the copy, 1619: "Oh lord,

lord, *if* my husband should see the letter! i' faith, this would even give edge to his jealousie." STEEVENS.

107. ——*curtail-dog*——] *i. e.* a dog that misses his game. The tail is counted necessary to the agility of a greyhound. JOHNSON.

112. ——*gally-mawfry;*——]*i. e.* A medley. So in the *Winter's Tale:* "They have a dance, which the wenches say is a *gallimaufry* of gambols." Pistol ludicrously uses it for a woman. Thus, in *A Woman never vex'd,* 1632:

"Let us show ourselves gallants or *galli-maufries.*"
STEEVENS.

The folio reads:

"*He loves* the *gallymaufry*——"
which may be right.—He loves a medley; all sorts of women, high and low, &c.

Ford's reply——*love my wife*——may refer to what Pistol had said before:

"*Sir John affects thy wife.*" MALONE.

I am not induced by this reasoning to follow the folio. STEEVENS.

112. ——Ford, *perpend.*]This is perhaps a ridicule on a passage in the old comedy of *Cambyses:*

"My sapient words I say *perpend.*"
Again:

"My queen *perpend* what I pronounce."
Shakspere has put the same word into the mouth of Polonius. STEEVENS.

120. ——*cuckoo birds do sing.*] Such is the reading of the folio, and the quarto 1630. The quartos 1602, and 1619, read:

"——*when*

" ———*when cuckoo-birds* appear."   STEEVENS.

121.   *Away, sir corporal Nym.* ———

     Believe it, Page; he speaks sense.] Nym, I be-lieve, is out of place, and we should read thus:

     Away, sir corporal.

Nym. *Believe it, Page; he speaks sense.*   JOHNSON.

Perhaps Dr. Johnson is mistaken in his conjecture. He seems not to have been aware of the manner in which the author meant this scene should be repre-sented. Ford and Pistol, Page and Nym, enter in pairs, each pair in separate conversation: and while Pistol is informing Ford of Falstaff's design upon his wife, Nym is, during that time, talking *aside* to Page, and giving information of the like plot against *him.*——When Pistol has finished, he calls out to Nym to come *away*; but seeing that he and Page are still in close debate, he goes off alone, first assuring Page, he may depend on the truth of Nym's story. *Believe it, Page.* Nym then proceeds to tell the remainder of his tale out aloud. *And this is true,* &c. A little further on in this scene, Ford says to Page, *You heard what this knave* (i e. Pistol) *told me.* Page replies, *Yes, and you heard what the other* (i. e. Nym) *told me.*   STEEVENS.

122.   *Believe it, Page; he speaks sense.*] Thus has the passage been hitherto printed, says Dr. Farmer; but surely we should read, as it now stands in the text. *Believe it Page, he speaks,* means no more than ———*Page, believe what he says.* This sense is expressed not only in the manner peculiar to *Pistol,* but to the grammar of the times.   STEEVENS.

127.

127. ——*I have a sword, and it shall bite upon my necessity.—He loves your wife, &c.*] Nym, to gain credit, says, that he is above the mean office of carrying love-letters; he has nobler means of living; *he has a sword, and upon his necessity,* i. e. *when his need drives him to unlawful expedients,* his sword *shall bite.*   JOHNSON.

134. *The humour of it,——*] The following epigram taken from an old collection without date, but apparently printed before the year 1600, will best account for Nym's frequent repetition of the word *humour*   Epig. 27.

Aske HUMOUR what a feather he doth weare,
It is his *humour* (by the Lord) he'll sweare.
Or what he doth with such a horse-taile locke;
Or why upon a whore he spends his stocke?
He hath a *humour* doth determine so.
Why in the stop-throte fashion he doth goe,
With scarfe about his necke, hat without band?
It is his *humour.*   Sweet sir, understand
What cause his purse is so extreame distrest
That oftentimes is scarcely penny-blest?
Only a *humour.*   If you question why
His tongue is ne'er unfurnish'd with a lye?
It is his *humour* too he doth protest.
Or why with serjeants he is so opprest,
That like to ghosts they haunt him ev'rie day?
A rascal *humour* doth not love to pay.
Object why bootes and spurres are still in season?
His *humour* answers: *humour* is his reason.
If you perceive his wits in wetting shrunke,
It cometh of a *humour* to be drunke.

E

When

When you behold his lookes pale, thin, and poore,
Th' occasion is, his *humour* and a whoore.
And every thing that he doth undertake,
It is a veine, for senceless *humour's* sake.

STEEVENS.

140.   *I will not believe such a Cataian,*——] That by a *Cataian* some kind of *sharper* was meant, I infer from the following passage in *Love and Honour*, a play by sir W. Davenant, 1649:

" Hang him, bold *Cataian*, he indites finely,
" And will live as well by sending short epistles,
" Or by the sad *whisper* at your *gamester's* ear,
" When the great By is drawn,
" As any *distrest gallant* of them all."

Cathaia is mentioned in the *Tamer Tamed*, of Beaumont and Fletcher:

" I'll wish you in the Indies, or *Cathaia*."

The tricks of the *Cataians* are hinted at in one of the old black letter histories of that country; and again in a dramatic performance, called the *Pedler's Pro-phecy*, 1595:

" ———in the *east part of Inde*,
" Through seas and floods, they work all *thievish*."

Mr. Malone observes, that in a book of Shakspere's age, entitled, *A brief Description of the whole World*, " —the people of China are (said to be) very *politick* and *crafty*, and in respect thereof contemning the wits of others; using a proverb, That all other nations do see but with one eye, but they with two."   STEEVENS.

143.   *'Twas a good sensible fellow:*——] This, and the
two

two preceding speeches of Ford, are spoken to himself, and have no connection with the sentiments of
Page, who is likewise making his comment on what
had passed, without attention to Ford.   STEEVENS.

187.   ——*cavalero* justice,] So in *The Stately Moral
of three Ladies of London*, 1590:

"Then know, Castilian *cavalieros*, this."
There is a book printed in 1599, called, *A countercuffe
given to Martin Junior; by the venturous, hardie, and renowned Pasquil of Englande*, CAVALLIERO. STEEVENS.

209.   ——*and tell him, my name is Brook,*——] Thus
both the old quartos; and thus most certainly the
poet wrote. We need no better evidence than the pun
that Falstaff anon makes on the name, when Brook
sends him some burnt sack.

"*Such* Brooks *are welcome to me, that overflow with
such liquor.*"
The players, in their editions, altered the name to
Broom.   THEOBALD.

211.   ——*said I well?*] The learned editor of the
Canterbury Tales of Chaucer, in 4 vols. 8vo. 1775, observes, that this phrase is given to the *host* in the *Par-
donere's Prologue :*

"*Said I not well?* I cannot speke in terme :"
v. 12246. and adds, "it may be sufficient with the
other circumstances of general resemblance, to make
us believe that Shakspere, when he drew the character, had not forgotten his Chaucer." The same
gentleman has since informed me, that the passage is

E ij

not

not found in any of the ancient printed editions, but only in the MSS.   STEEVENS.

212. ——*Will you go* AN-HEIRS?] This nonsense is spoken to Shallow. We should read, *Will you go* ON HERIS? *i. e.* Will you go on, master? *Heris,* an old Scotch word for master.   WARBURTON.

The merry Host has already saluted them separately by titles of distinction; he therefore probably now addresses them collectively by a general one,

"——*Will you go on,* heroes?"

or, as probably,

"——*Will you go on,* hearts?"

He calls Dr. Caius *Heart of Elder;* and adds, in a subsequent scene of this play, *Farewell my hearts.* Again, in the *Midsummer Night's Dream,* Bottom says,

"Where are these *hearts?*"

My brave hearts, or *my bold hearts,* is a common word of encouragement. A *heart of gold* expresses the more soft and amiable qualities, the *Mores aurei* of Horace; and a *heart of oak* is a frequent encomium of rugged honesty.   STEEVENS.

Will you go *an-heirs?*] Perhaps we should read, "Will you go and *hear us?*" So in the next page,

"I had rather *hear them* scold than fight."

MALONE.

213. *Have with you, mine host.*] This speech is given in all the editions to *Shallow*; but it belongs, I think, to *Ford,* to whom the host addresses himself when he says:

"*Will you go and hear us?*"

It

It is not likely he should address himself to *Shallow*, because *Shallow* and he had already concerted the scheme, and agreed to go together; and accordingly, *Shallow* says, a little before to *Page*,

" Will you go with *us* to behold it ?

The former speech of *Ford—None I protest*, &c. is given in like manner, in the first folio, to *Shallow*, instead of *Ford:* The editors corrected the one, but over-looked the other.   MALONE.

214.   *I have heard, the Frenchman hath good skill in his rapier.*] In the old quarto, here follows these words:

" *Shal.* I tell you what, master Page; I believe the doctor is no jester, he'll lay it on ; for though we be justices, and doctors, and churchmen, yet we are the sons of women, master Page.

" *Page.* True, master Shallow.

" *Shal.* It will be found so, master Page.

" *Page.* Master Shallow, you yourself, have been a great fighter, now a man of peace."

Part of this dialogue is found afterwards in the third scene of the present act; but it seems more proper here, to introduce what *Shallow* says of the prowess of his youth.   MALONE.

220.   *my long sword,——*] Before the introduction of rapiers, the swords in use were of an enormous length, and sometimes raised with both hands. *Shallow*, with an old man's vanity, censures the innovation by which lighter weapons were introduced, tells what he could once have done with his *long-sword*, and ridicules the terms and rules of the rapier.   JOHNSON.

The *two-handed* sword is mentioned in the ancient
Interlude of Nature, bl. l. no date :

    " Somtyme he serveth me at borde,

    " Somtyme he bereth my *two-hand* sword."
See a note to the *First Part of K. Henry IV.* act ii.

                                        STEEVENS.

Dr. Johnson's explanation of the *long-sword* is certainly right; for the early quarto reads my *two-hand*
sword; so that they appear to have been synonymous.

Carleton, in his *Thankful Rembrance of God's Mercy,*
1625, speaking of the treachery of one Rowland York,
in betraying the town of Deventer to the Spaniards in
1587, says; " he was a Londoner, famous among the
cutters in his time, for bringing a new kind of fight—
to run the point of a *rapier* into a man's body.   This
manner of fight *he* brought *first* into *England,* with great
admiration of his audaciousnes: when in England before that time, the use was, with little bucklers, and
with broad swords, to strike and not to thrust; and it
was accounted unmanly to strike under the girdle."

                                        MALONE.

221.   ——tall *fellows*——] The old quartos read—
tall *fencers.*   STEEVENS.

226.   ——stand *so firmly on his wife's frailty,*——]
To *stand on any thing,* does signify *to insist on it.* So in
Heywood's *Rape of Lucrece,* 1630 : " All captains, and
stand upon the honesty of your wives."   Again in
Warner's *Albion's England,* 1602, book 6. chap. 30.

    " For stoutly *on their honesties* do wylie harlots
        stand."

                                        The

The *jealous Ford* is the speaker, and all *chastity* in women appears to him as a *frailty*.   He supposes *Page*
therefore to insist on that *virtue* as steady, which he
himself suspects to be without foundation. STEEVENS.

234.   ——*the world's mine oyster*, &c.] Dr. Grey
supposes Shakspere to allude to an old proverb,
" ——The mayor of Northampton opens *oysters* with
with his dagger."——*i. e.* to keep them at a sufficient
distance from his nose, that town being fourscore
miles from the sea.   STEEVENS.

235.   ——*I will retort the sum in equipage.*] This is
added from the old quarto of 1619, and means, I wil
pay you again in stolen goods.   WARBURTON.

I rather believe he means, that he will pay him by
waiting on him for nothing.   So in *Love's Pilgrimage,*
by Beaumont and Fletcher:

" And boy, be you my guide,
" For I will make a full descent in *equipage.*"
That *equipage* ever meant *stolen goods,* I am yet to learn.
                                    STEEVENS.

Dr. Warburton may be right; for I find *equipage*
was one of the cant words of the time.   *In Davies'*
Papers Complaint, (a poem which has erroneously been
ascribed to *Donne)* we have several of them:

" Embellish, blandishment, and *equipage.*"
Which words, he tells us in the margin, *overmuch sa-*
vour of witlesse affectation.   FARMER.

240.   *your* coach-fellow, *Nym*;——] Thus the old
copies.   *Coach-fellow* has an obvious meaning, but the
modern editors read, *couch-fellow.* The following passage

sage from B. Jonson's *Cynthia's Revels* may justify the reading I have chosen: "—'Tis the swaggering *coach-horse* Anaides, that *draws with him* there." Again, in *Monsieur D'Olive*, 1606: " Are you he, my Page here makes choice of, to be his fellow *coach-horse!*" Again, in *a True Narrative of the entertainment of his Royal Majestie, from the time of his departure from Edinburgh, till his receiving in London, &c.* 1603: " ——Base pilfering theefe was taken who plaid the cutpurse in the court: his fellow was ill mist, for no doubt he had a walking mate: they drew together like *coach-horses*, and it is a pitie they did not hang together." Again, in *Every Woman in her Humour*, 1609:

"For wit, ye may be *coach'd* together."

Again, in 10th B. of *Chapman's Translation of Homer:*

"——their chariot horse, as they *coach-fellows*
          were."   STEEVENS.

243. ——*and* tall *fellows :*——] A *tall fellow*, in the time of our author, meant, *a stout, bold, or courageous person.* In *A Discourse on Usury*, by Dr. Wilson, 1584, he says, " Here in England, he that can rob a man by the high way, is called a *tall fellow.*" Lord Bacon says, " that bishop Fox caused his castle of Norham to be fortified, and manned it likewise with a very great number of *tall soldiers.*"   STEEVENS.

244. ——*lost the handle of her fan,*——] It should be remembered that *fans*, in our author's time, were more costly than they are at present, as well as of a different construction. They consisted of ostrich feathers (or others of equal length and flexibility), which
                              were

SPECIMENS of FANS.

from the Drawings of Titian & Cesare Vecelli
as referred to in the Notes on the Merry Wives of Windsor.

London Printed for John Bell British Library Strand Dec.r 23.d 1786.

were stuck into handles. The richer sort of these were composed of gold, silver, or ivory of curious workmanship. One of them is mentioned in *The Fleire*, Com. 1610: " —she hath a fan with a *short silver handle*, about the length of a barber's syringe." Again, in *Love and Honour*, by sir W. Davenant, 1649: " All your plate, Vaso, is the *silver handle* of your old prisoner's *fan*."

In the frontispiece to a play, called *Englishmen for my Money*, or *A pleasant Comedy of a Woman will have her Will*, 1616, is a portrait of a lady with one of these fans, which, after all, may prove the best commentary on the passage.   Three other specimens are taken from the *Habiti Antichi et Moderni di tutto il Mondo*, published at Venice, 1598, from the drawings of *Titian*, and *Cesare Vecelli*, his brother.   This fashion was perhaps imported from Italy, together with many others in the reign of King Henry VIII. if not in that of King Richard II.   STEEVENS.

Thus also Marston, in the *Scourge of Villainie*, lib. iii. sat. 8.

  " ———Another he
 " Her *silver-handled* fan would gladly be."
And in other places. And bishop Hall, in his *Satires*, published 1597, lib. v. sat. 4.

  " Whiles one piece pays her idle waiting manne,
  " Or buys a hoode, or *silver-handled* fanne."

          WARTON.

It appears from *Marston's Satires*, that the sum of 40l. was sometimes given for a fan in the time of queen Elizabeth.   MALONE.

           " While

In the Sidney papers, published by *Collins*, a fan is presented to queen Elizabeth for a new year's gift, the handle of which was studded with diamonds.

WARTON.

A repesentation of the *fan* here mentioned by Mr. Warton, together with the others by *Titian* and his *brother*, to which Mr. Steeven's refers are here given from a print of them in the NOTES *subjoined to the* HISTORY *of* VATHOK.   J. B.

251.   ———*A short knife and a* thong:———] So Lear:
      " When cutpurses come not to *thongs.*"

WARBURTON.

Part of the employment given by Drayton, in *The Mooncalf,* to the *Baboon,* seems the same with this recommended by Falstaff:

      " *He like a gypsy oftentimes would go,*
      " *All kinds of gibberish he hath learn'd to know:*
      " *And with a stick, a short string, and a noose,*
      " *Would show the people tricks at fast and loose.*"

Theobald has *throng* instead of *thong.* The latter seems right.   LANGTON.

      Both the folio and quarto read *throng.*   MALONE.

      Greene, in his *Life of Ned Browne,* 1592, says: " I had no other fence but my *short knife,* and a paire of *purse-strings.*"   STEEVENS.

      See a note on *Antony and Cleopatra,* that explains the trick of *fast and loose.*   SIR J. HAWKINS.

      251.   ———*Pickt - hatch,*———] A noted place for thieves and pick-pockets.   THEOBALD.

Pict-

Piɛ̌t-hatch is frequently mentioned by contemporary writers. So, in Ben Jonson's *Every Man in his Humour:*

" From the Bordello it might come as well,
" The Spital, or *Piɛ̌t-hatch*."

Again, in Randolph's *Muses Looking-glass,* 1638:

" ———the lordship of *Turnbull* so
" Which with my *Piɛ̌t-hatch*, Grange, and Shoreditch farm," &c.

Piɛ̌t-hatch was in *Turnbull-street:*

" ———your whore doth live
" In Piɛ̌t-hatch, *Turnbull-street*."

Amends for Ladies, a Comedy by N. Field, 1639. The derivation of the word *Piɛ̌t-hatch* may perhaps be discovered from the following passage in *Cupid's Whir-ligig*, 1607: " ———Set some *picks* upon your *hatch*, and I pray, profess to keep a bawdy-house." Perhaps the unseasonable and obstreperous irruptions of the gallants of that age might render such a precaution necessary. So, in *Pericles P. of Tyre*, 1609: " ——If in our youths we could *pick* up some pretty estate, 'twere not amiss to keep our door *hatch'd*," &c.

STEEVENS.

This was a cant name of some part of the town noted for bawdy-houses; as appears from the following passage in Marston's *Scourge for Villanie,* lib. iii. sat. 11:

" ———Looke, who yon doth go?
" The meager letcher lewd Luxurio.——
" No newe edition of drabbes come out,
" But seene and allow'd by Luxurio's snout.

" Did

" Did ever any man ere hear him talke
" But of *Pick-hatch,* or of some Shoreditch balke,
" Aretine's filth," &c.

Sir Thomas Hanmer says, that this was " a noted harbour for thieves and pickpockets," who certainly were proper companions for a man of Pistol's profession. But Falstaff here more immediately means to ridicule another of his friend's vices; and there is some humour in calling Pistol's favourite brothel, his manor of *Pickt-hatch.* Marston has another allusion to *Pickt-hatch* or *Pick-hatch,* which confirms this illustration:

" ———His old cynicke dad
" Hath forc't 'hem cleane forsake his *Pick-hatch*
         drab." Lib. i. sat. 3.   WARTON.

259. ———*ensconce* your rags, &c.] A *sconce* is a petty fortification. To *ensconce,* therefore, is to protect as with a fort. The word occurs again in *K. Henry IV. Part I.*   STEEVENS.

260. ———*red lattice phrases,*———] Your ale-house conversation.   JOHNSON.

Red lattice at the doors and windows, were formerly the external denotements of an ale-house So, in *A Fine Companion,* one of Shackerley Marmion's plays: ———" A waterman's widow at the sign of the *red lattice* in Southwark." Again, in *Arden of Feversham,* 1592:

" ———his sign pulled down, and his *lattice* born
         away."

Again, in the *Miseries of enforc'd Marriage,* 1607:

" ———'tis

    " ——'tis treason to the *red lattice*, enemy to
        the sign-post."

Hence the present *chequers*. Perhaps the reader will express some surprize, when he is told that shops, with the sign of the *chequers*, were common among the Romans. See a view of the left hand street of Pompeii, (No. 9.) presented by Sir William Hamilton (together with several others, equally curious), to the *Antiquary Society*.   STEEVENS.

    ——*your* red lattice *phrases*.] Again, more appositely, in *A Strapado for the Divell*, by R. Braithwaite, 1615: " To the true discoverer of secrets, Monsieur *Bacchus*,—Master gunner of the pottle-pot ordnance, prime founder of *red lattices*, &c.   MALONE.

    293. ——*canaries*.] This is the name of a brisk light dance, and is therefore properly enough used in low language for any hurry or perturbation.

                        JOHNSON.

So Nash, in *Pierce Pennyless his Supplication*, 1595, says : " A merchant's wife jets it as gingerly, as if she were dancing the *canaries*." It is highly probable, however, that *canaries* is only a mistake of Mrs. Quickly's for *quandaries* ; and yet the Clown, in *As You Like it*, says, " we that are true lovers run into strange *capers*."   STEEVENS.

    309. ——*earls, nay, which is more, pensioners ;*——] This may be illustrated by a passage in Gervase Holles's *Life of the First Earl of Clare. Biog. Brit.* Art. HOLLES. " I have heard the earl of Clare say, that when he was *pensioner* to the queen, he did not

            F   know

know a worse man of the whole band than himself; and that all the world knew he had then an inheritance of 4000l. a year."   TYRWHITT.

Barrett, in his *Alvearie,* or Quadruple Dictionary, 1580, says, that a *pensioner* was " a gentleman about his prince alwaie redie, with his speare."   STEEVENS.

" In the month of December, 1539," says Stowe. [Annals, p. 973. edit. 1605], "were appointed to wait on the king's person fifty gentlemen, called *pensioners,* or spears, like as they were in the first yeare of the king; unto whom was assigned the summe of fiftie pounds yearly for the mayntenance of themselves, and every man two horses, or one horse and a gelding of service."

Their dress was remarkably splendid, and therefore likely to strike Mrs. Quickly —Hence, in *A Midsummer Night's Dream,* our author selected from all the tribes of flowers, the *golden-coated* cowslips for *pensioners* to the Fairy Queen.

" The cowslips tall, her *pensioners* be ;

" In their *gold coats* spots you may see," &c.

MALONE.

319.   —you *wot* of;——] To *wot* is to know. Obsolete.   So in *K. Henry VIII.*

"——*Wot* you what I found?"   STEEVENS.

322.   ——*frampold*——] This word I have never seen elsewhere, except in Dr. Hacket's *Life of Archbishop Williams,* where a *frampul* man signifies a peevish troublesome fellow.   JOHNSON.

In *The Roaring Girl,* a comedy, 1611, I meet with a word,

5

a word, which, though differently spelt, appears to be the same.

Lax. " Coachman.

Coach. " Anon, sir!

Lax. " Are we fitted with good *phrampell* jades?"

Ray, among his *South* and *East* country words, says that *frampald*, or *frampard*, signifies *fretful, peevish, cross, froward.* As *froward* (he adds) comes from *from*, so may *frampard*.

Nash, in his *Praise of the Red Herring*, 1599, speaking of Leander, says ; " the churlish *frampold* waves gave him his belly full of fish-broth."

So, in *The Inner Temple Masque*, by Middleton 1619 : ——" 'tis so *frampole*, the puritans will never yield to it." So, in *The Blind Beggar of Bethnal Green*, by John Day :

" I think the fellow's *frample*," &c.
So, in Beaumont and Fletcher's *Wit at several Weapons:*

" Is Pompey grown so malapert, so *frample?*"

STEEVENS.

Thus, in the *Isle of Gulls*—" What a goodyer aile your mother, are you *frampull*, know you not your own daughter?"   HENLEY.

345.—— *to send her your little page, of all loves :*—] *Of all loves*, is an adjuration only, and signifies no more, than if she had said, desires you to send him *by all means.*

It is used in Decker's *Honest Whore*, Part I. 1635 : —" conjuring his wife, *of all loves*, to prepare cheer
F ij   fitting,"

fitting," &c. Again, in Holinshed's *Chronicle,* p. 1064 : " Mrs. Arden desired him, *of all loves,* to come back againe." STEEVENS.

358. a *nay word,*——] i. e. a *watch word.* So in a subsequent scene : "—We have a *nay-word* to know one another," &c. STEEVENS.

369. *This* PINK *is one of Cupid's carriers :*

Clap on more sails ; pursue ; up with your fights ;

Give fire, she is my prize ;] A *pink* is a vessel of the small crafts employed as a *carrier* (and so called) for merchants. Fletcher uses the word in his *Tamer Tamed :*

" This PINK, this painted foist, this cockle-boat,

" To hang her *fights* out, and defy me, friends!

" A well known man of war."——

As to the word *fights,* both in the the text and in the quotation, it was then, and, for aught I know, may be now, a common sea-term. Sir Richard Hawkins, in his Voyages, p. 66, says : " For once we cleared her deck, and had we been able to have spared but a dozen men, doubtless we had done with her what we would ; for she had no close FIGHTS," i. e. if I understand it right, *no small arms.* So that by *fights* is meant any manner of defence, either small arms or cannon. So, Dryden, in his tragedy of *Amboyna :*

" Up with your FIGHTS,

" And your *nettings* prepare," &c.

But, not considering this, I led the Oxford editor into

a silly

a silly conjecture, which he has done me the honour of putting into *his* text, which is indeed a proper place for it.

"Up with YOND FRIGAT."   WARBURTON.

So, in *The Ladies Privilege*, 1640: "These gentle-men know better to cut a caper than a cable, or board a *pink* in the Bordells, than a pinnace at sea." A small salmon is called a salmon-*pink*.

Dr. Farmer, however, observes, that the word *punk* has been unnecessarily altered to *pink*. In Ben Johnson's *Bartholomew Fair*, justice Overdo says of the pig-woman; " She hath been before me, *punk*, *pin-nace*, and bawd, any time these two and twenty years."

STEEVENS.

The quotation from Dryden might at least have raised a suspicion, that *fights* were neither *small arms* nor *cannon*. *Fights* and *nettings* are properly joined. *Fights*, I find, are *cloaths* hung round the ship to conceal the men from the enemy, and *close-fights* are *bulk-heads*, or any other shelter that the fabrick of a ship affords.

JOHNSON.

So, in Heywood and Rowley's comedy, called *For-tune by Land and Sea* :——" display'd their ensigns, *up with all their feights*, their matches in their cocks," &c. So, in the *Christian turned Turk*, 1612: " Lace the netting, and let down the *fights*, make ready the shot," &c. Again, in the *Fair Maid of the West*, 1615:

" Then now *up with your fights*, and let your
      ensigns,
" Blest with St. George's cross, play with the
      winds."

F iij

Again

Again, in Beaumont and Fletcher's *Valentinian :*

   " ——while I were able to endure a tempest,

   " And bear my *fights* out bravely, till my tackle

   " Whistled i' th' wind."——

384. ——*go to :* via :] This cant phrase of exultation is common in the old plays. So, in *Blurt
Master Constable :*

   " *Via* for fate ! Fortune, lo ! this is all."

STEEVENS.

Markham uses this word as one of the vocal helps
necessary for reviving a horse's spirits in galloping
large rings when he grows slothful. Hence this cant
phrase (perhaps from the Italian, *via)* may be used
on other occasions to quicken or pluck up courage.

TOLLET.

395. ——*not to charge you ;*—] That is, not with
a purpose of putting you to expence, or *being burthen-
some.*   JOHNSON.

434. —— *meed,*——] i. e. rewards.   STEEVENS.

457. of *great admittance,*—] *i. e.* admitted into all,
or the greatest companies.   STEEVENS.

458. —— generally *allowed*——] *Allowed* is ap-
proved. So in *K. Lear.*

   " —— if your sweet sway

   " *Allow* obedience," &c.   STEEVENS.

464. —— *to lay an* amiable siege—] *i. e.* a siege of
love.   MALONE.

473. —— *She is too bright to be look'd against.*]

   " Nimium lubricus aspici." *Hor.*   MALONE.

475

475.   ——instance *and argument*——] *Instance* is *example.*   JOHNSON.

477.   —— the *ward* of her purity,——] *i.e.* The
defence of it.   STEEVENS.

512.   —— *and I will aggravate his* stile ;—] *Stile* is
a phrase from the Herald's office. Falstaff means,
that *he will add more titles to those he already enjoys.* So,
in Heywood's *Golden Age,* 1611 :
    " I will create lord of a greater *style.*"
Again, in Spenser's *Faery Queen,* b. v. c. 2.
    " As to abandon that which doth contain
    " Your honour's *stile,* that is, your warlike
        shield."   STEEVENS.

524.   —— *Amaimon—Barbason,*——] The reader who is curious to know any particulars concerning
these dæmons, may find them in Reginald Scott's *In-
ventorie of the Names, Shapes, Powers, Government, and
Effects of Devils and Spirits, of their several Seignories
and Degrees, a strange Discourse worth the reading,*
p. 377, &c. From hence it appears that *Amaimon* was
king of the East, and *Barbatos* a great *countie or earl.*
                                             STEEVENS.

531.   —— an *Irishman* with my *aqua vitæ* bottle,—]
Heywood, in his *Challenge for Beauty,* 1636, men-
tions the love of *aqua vitæ* as characteristick of the
Irish :
    " The Briton he metheglin quaffs,
    " The *Irish, aqua vitæ.*"
By *aqua vitæ,* was, I believe, understood, not
                                             brandy

brandy but *usquebaugh*, for which the Irish have been long celebrated. So, in Marston's *Malecontent*, 1604:

> " The Dutchman for a Drunkard,
> " The Dane for golden locks,
> " The *Irishman* for *usquebaugh*,
> " The Frenchman for the———." MALONE.

Dericke in *The Image of Irelande*, 1581, Sign. F 2. mentions *Uskebeaghe*, and in a note explains it to mean *aqua vitæ*.   REED.

537. ——— *Eleven o'Clock* —] Ford should rather have said *ten o'clock :* the time was between ten and eleven ; and his impatient suspicion was not likely to stay beyond the time.   JOHNSON.

565. ———to see thee *foin*,———] To *foin*, I believe, was the ancient term for making .. thrust in fencing, or tilting. So, in *The wise Woman of Hogsdon*, 1638 :

> " I had my wards, and *foins* and quarter blows."

Again, in the *Devils Charter*, 1607:

> " ——— suppose my duellist
> " Should falsify the *foine* upon me thus,
> " Here will I take him."

Spenser, in his *Faery Queen*, often uses the word *foin*. So in b. ii. c. 8.

> " And strook and *foyn'd*, and lash'd outrageously."

Again, in Holinshed, p. 833. " First six *foines* with hand-speares," &c.   STEEVENS.

567. ——— thy *stock*,—] *Stock* is a corruption of
stocata,

stocata, Italian, from which language the technical term that follow are likewise adopted.   STEEVENS.

570.   — *my heart of elder ?*—] It should be remember'd, to make this joke relish, that the *elder* tree has *no heart*. I suppose this expression was made use of in opposition to the common one, *heart of oak*.

STEEVENS.

571. —— bully *Stale ?*——] The reason why Caius is called bully *Stale*, and afterwards *Urinal*, must be sufficiently obvious to every reader, and especially to those whose credulity and weakness have enrolled them among the patients of the present *German* empiric, who calls himself *Doctor* Alexander Mayersbach.   STEEVENS.

574. —— *Castilian*——] *Castilian* and *Ethiopian*, like *Cataian*, appear in our author's time to have been cant terms. I have met with them in more than one of the old comedies. So, in a description of the *Armada* introduced in the *Stately Moral of the Three Lords of London*, 1590:

> " To carry as it were a careless regard
> " Of these *Castilians*, and their accustomed bravado."

Again :—" To parly with the proud *Castilians*."
I suppose *Castilian* was the cant term for *Spaniard* in general.   STEEVENS.

" Thou art a *Castilian king*, Urinal !" quoth mine host to Dr. Caius. I believe this was a popular slur upon the Spaniards, who were held in great contempt after the business of the *Armada*. Thus we

have

have a *Treatise Parænetical, wherein is shewed the right way to resist the* Castilian king: and a sonnet, prefixed to *Lea's Answer to the Untruths published in Spain, in gloric of their supposed Victory atchieved against our English Navie,* begins,

" 'Thou fond *Castilian king!*" and so in other places.   FARMER.

Dr. Farmer's observation is just. Don Philip the Second affected the title of King of Spain ; but the realms of Spain would not agree to it, and only styled him king of *Castile* and Leon, and so he wrote himself. His cruelty and ambitious views upon other states rendered him universally detested. The *Castilians* being descended chiefly from Jews and Moors, were deemed to be of a malign and perverse disposition ; and hence, perhaps, the term *Castilian* became opprobrious. I have extracted this note from an old pamphlet, called *The Spanish Pilgrime,* which I have reason to suppose is the same discourse with the *Treatise Parænetical,* mentioned by Dr. Farmer.

                                        TOLLET.

581. —— against the *hair,* &c.] This phrase is proverbial, and taken from stroking the *hair* of animals a contrary way to that in which it grows—We now say, against the *grain.*   STEEVENS.

599. ——*mock-water.*] The host means, I believe, to reflect on the inspection of urine, which made a considerable part of practical physick in that time ; yet I do not well see the meaning of *mock-water.*   JOHNSON.

Perhaps

Perhaps by *mock-water* is meant—*counterfeit.* The *water* of a gem is a technical term. So in *Timon*, act i. sc. i.

"——here is a *water*, look you."
Mock-water may therefore signify *a thing of a counterfeit lustre.* To *mock*, however, in *Antony and Cleopatra*, undoubtedly signifies to *play with.* Shakspere may therefore chuse to represent *Caius* as one to whom a *urinal* was a play-thing.

Dr. Farmer proposes to read *muck-water, i. e.* the drain of a dunghill.   STEEVENS.

626.   In old editions,

——*I will bring thee where Anne Page is, at a farm-house a feasting ; and thou shalt woo her:* CRY'D GAME, *said I well?*] We yet say, in colloquial language, that such a one is——*game*——or *game to the back.* *Cry'd game* might mean—a *profess'd buck*, one who as was well known by the report of his gallantry; as he could have been by *proclamation.* Thus, in *Troilus and Cressida:*

  " On whose bright crest, fame, with her loud'st
    " O yes,
  " *Cries*, this is he."
Again, in *All's well that ends well,* act ii.
  " ——find what you seek,
  " That fame may *cry you loud.*"
Again, in Ford's *Lover's Melancholy,* 1629:
  " A gull, an arrant gull *by proclamation.*"
Again, in *King Lear:*
  " ——A *proclaim'd* prize."

Again,

Again, in *Troilus and Cressida:*

    " Thou art *proclaim'd* a fool, I think."

Cock of the game is found in Warner's *Albion's England,* 1602, b. xii. c. 74. " This *cocke of game,* and (as might seem) this *hen* of the *same fether."* Again, in the *Martial Maid,* by Beaumont and Fletcher:

    " On craven chicken of a *cock o' th' game."*

And in many other places.   STEEVENS.

ACT III.

Line 5.——THE Pitty-wary,——] The old editions read, the *Pittie-ward,* the modern editors the *Pitty-wary.* There is now no place that answers to either name at Windsor. The author might possibly have written the *City-ward, i. e.* towards London. *Petty-ward* might, however, signify some small district in the town which is now forgotten.   STEEVENS.

    16. *By shallow rivers,* &c.] This is part of a beautiful little poem of the author's; which poem, and the answer to it, the reader will not be displeased to find here.

The Passionate Shepherd to his Love.

COME live with me, and be my love,
And we will all the pleasures prove
That hills and vallies, dale and field,
And all the craggy mountains yield.

                 There

There will we sit upon the rocks,
And see the Shepherds feed their flocks,
By shallow rivers, by whose falls
Melodious birds sing madrigals:
There will I make thee beds of roses,
With a thousand fragrant posies,
A cap of flowers, and a kirtle
Embroider'd all with leaves of myrtle;
A gown made of the finest wool,
Which from our pretty lambs we pull;
Fair lined slippers for the cold,
With buckles of the purest gold:
A belt of straw, and ivy buds,
With coral clasps, and amber studs:
And if these pleasures may thee move,
Come live with me, and be my love.
Thy silver dishes for thy meat,
As precious as the gods do eat,
Shall on an ivory table be
Prepar'd each day for thee and me.
The shepherd swains shall dance and sing,
For thy delight each May morning:
If these delights thy mind may move*,
Then live with me, and be my love.

---

* The conclusion of this and the following poem, seems to have furnished Milton with the hint for the last lines both of his *Allegro* and *Penseroso*.   STEEVENS.

The *Nymph's Reply to the Shepherd.*

IF that the world and love were young,
And truth in every shepherd's tongue,
These pretty pleasures might me move
To live with thee and be thy love.
But time drives flocks from field to fold,
When rivers rage, and rocks grow cold,
And Philomel becometh dumb,
And all complain of cares to come:
The flowers do fade, and wanton fields
To wayward winter reckoning yields:
A honey tongue, a heart of gall,
Is fancy's spring, but sorrow's fall.
Thy gowns, thy shoes, thy beds of roses,
Thy cap, thy kirtle, and thy posies,
Soon break, soon wither, soon forgotten,
In folly ripe, in reason rotten.
Thy belt of straw, and ivy buds,
Thy coral clasps, and amber studs;
All these in me no means can move
To come to thee, and be thy love.
What should we talk of dainties then,
Of better meat than's fit for men?
These are but vain: that's only good
Which God hath bless'd, and sent for food.
But could youth last, and love still breed,
Had joys no date, and age no need;
Then these delights my mind might move
To live with thee, and be thy love.

These

These two poems, which Dr. Warburton gives to Shakspere, are, by writers nearer that time, disposed of, one to Marlow, the other to Raleigh. They are read in different copies with great variations.

JOHNSON.

In *England's Helicon*, a collection of love-verses printed in Shakspere's life-time, viz. in 1600, the first of them is given to Marlow, the second to a person unknown: and Dr. Piercy, in the first volume of his *Reliques of Ancient English Poetry*, observes, that there is good reason to believe that (not Shakspere, but) Christopher Marlow wrote the song, and sir Walter Raleigh the *Nymph's Reply*; for so we are positively assured by Isaac Walton, a writer of some credit, who has inserted them both in his *Compleat Angler*, under the character of " That smooth song which was made by *Kit Marlow*, now at least fifty years ago; and an *Answer* to it, which was made by sir Walter Raleigh in his younger days . . . . . Old fashioned poetry, but choicely good." See the *Reliques*, &c. vol. I. p. 218. 221, third edit.

In Shakspere's sonnets, printed by Jaggard, 1599, this poem is attributed to Shakspere. Mr. Malone, however, observes, that, " What seems to ascertain it to be Marlowe's, is, that one of the lines is found (and not as a quotation) in a play of his—*The Jew of Malta*; which, though, not printed till 1633, must have been written before 1593, as he died in that year. '

" Thou in those groves, by Dis above,

" *Shalt live with me, and be my love.*" STEEVENS.

G ij   The

The tune to which the former was sung, I have lately discovered in a MS. as old as Shakspere's time, and it is as follows:

Sir J. Hawkins.

23. *When as I sat in Babylon——*] This line is from the old version of the 137th psalm:

> " *When we did sit in Babylon,*
>> " *The rivers round about,*
> " Then in remembrance for Sion,
> " The tears for grief burst out."

The word *rivers*, in the second line, may be supposed to have been brought to sir Hugh's thoughts by

the

the line of Marlowe's Madrigal, that he has just repeated; and in his fright he blends the sacred and
prophane song together.   The old quarto has——
" There liv'd a man *in Babylon*,"——which was the
first line of an old song, mentioned in *Twelfth Night:*
but the other line is more in character.   MALONE.

84.   ——*for missing your meetings and appointments.*]
These words, which are not in the folio, were recovered from the early quarto, by Mr. Pope.

MALONE.

91.   *Peace, I say*, Gallia *and* Gaul, *French* and
Welch,——] Possibly *Gallia* and *Guallia*.   FARMER.
Thus, in *K. Henry IV. Gualtier* for *Walter*.

STEEVENS.

The quarto, 1602, confirms Dr. Farmer's conjecture.   It reads——Peace I say, *Gawle* and *Gawlia*,
French and Welch, &c.   MALONE.

110.   ——make-a de *set* of us?]   *Sot* in French,
signifies *a fool*.   MALONE.

114.   ——scald, *scurvy*,]——*Scall* was an old word
of reproach, as *scab* was afterwards.   Chaucer impre-
cates on his *scrivener:*

" Under thy longe lockes mayest thou have the
    scalle."   JOHNSON.

Scall, as Dr. Johnson interprets it, is a scab break-
ing out in the hair, and approaching nearly to the le-
prosy.   It is used by other writers of Shakspere's
time.   You will find what was to be done by persons
afflicted with it by looking into Leviticus, ch. xiii.
30, 31, &c.   WHALLEY.

159.   ——so *seeming* mistress Page,——] *seeming* is *specious.*   So, in *K. Lear,*

  " If aught within that little *seeming* substance."
STEEVENS.

162.   ——shall *cry aim.*] *i. e.* shall *encourage.* The phrase is taken from archery.   See a note in *K. John,* act ii.
STEEVENS.

174.   *We have linger'd*——] They have not linger'd very long.   The match was proposed by sir *Hugh* but the day before.
JOHNSON.

Shallow represents the affair as having been *long in hand,* that he may better excuse himself and *Slender* from accepting *Ford's* invitation on the day when it was to be concluded.
STEEVENS.

184.   ——*he writes verses, he speaks holy-day,*——] *i. e.* in an high-flown, fustian style.   It was called *a holy-day style,* from the old custom of acting their farces of the *mysteries* and *moralities,* which were turgid and bombast, on *holy-days.*   So, in *Much ado about Nothing,*

  " I cannot woo in *festival terms.*"
And again, in *The Merchant of Venice,*

  " Thou spend'st such *high-day wit* in praising
      him."
WARBURTON.

——he speaks *holy-day,*——]   So, in *K. Henry IV.* Part I.

  " With many *holiday* and lady terms."
STEEVENS.

186.   ——*'tis in his* buttons;]   Alluding to an ancient custom among the country fellows, of trying whether
whether

whether they should succeed with their mistresses, by carrying the *batchelor's buttons* (a plant of the *Lychnis* kind, whose flowers resemble a coat button in form) in their pockets. And they judged of their good or bad success by their growing, or their not growing there.   SMITH.

Green mentions these *batchelor's buttons* in his *Quip for an upstart Courtier:*————" I saw the *batchelor's-buttons,* whose virtue is to make wanton maidens weep, when they have worne them forty weeks under their aprons." &c.

The same expression occurs in Heywood's *Fair Maid of the West,* 1631:

" He wears *batchelor's buttons,* does he not?"
Again, in *The Constant Maid,* by Shirley, 1640:

" I am a *batchelor.*

" I pray, let me be one of your *buttons* still then."
Again, in *A Fair Quarrel,* by Middleton and Rowley, 1617:

" I'll wear my *batchelor's buttons* still."
Again, in *A Woman never Vex'd,* comedy by Rowley, 1632:

" Go, go and rest on Venus' violets; shew her

" A dozen of *batchelor's buttons,* boy."
Again, in *Westward Hoe,* 1606: " Here's my husband, and no *batchelor's buttons* are at his doublet."

                                        STEEVENS.

What can Mr. Smith mean by the flowers *growing* in the pockets of those who carry them?   ★ ★ ★

189. ———*of no* having :———] *Having* is the same as *estate* or *fortune.*   JOHNSON.

So, in *Macbeth,*
    " Of noble *having,* and of royal hope."
Again, *Twelft Night,*
    " ———My *having* is not much,
    " I'll make division of my present store,
    " Hold, there is half my coffer."   STEEVENS.

204. Host. *Farewel, my hearts: I will to my honest knight Falstaff, and drink away canary with him.*

Ford. [Aside.] *I think, I shall drink* IN PIPE-*wine first with him : I'll make him dance.*———] To *drink in pipe-wine* is a phrase which I cannot understand. May we not suppose that Shakspere rather wrote, *I think I shall drink* HORN-PIPE *wine first with him : I'll make him dance ?*

Canary is the name of a *dance,* as well as of a *wine.* Ford lays hold of both senses; but, for an obvious reason, makes the dance a *horn-pipe.* It has been already remarked, that Shakspere has frequent allusions to a *cuckold's horns.*   TYRWHITT.

Pipe is known to be a vessel of wine, now containing two hogsheads. *Pipe*-wine is therefore wine, not from the *bottle,* but the *pipe;* and the jest consists in the ambiguity of the word, which signifies both a cask of wine, and a musical instrument.   JOHNSON.

The phrase,—" to drink *in* pipe-wine"—always appeared to me a very strange one, till I met with the following passage in King James's first speech to his parliament, in 1604; by which it appears that " to
                                              drink

drink *in*" was the phraseology of the time : " —who
either being old have retained their first drunken-*in*
liquor upon a certain shame-facedness," &c.

MALONE.

230. *How now, my* eyas-musket ?——] *Eyas* is a
young unfledg'd hawk; I suppose from the Italian
Niaso, which originally signified any young bird taken
from the nest unfledg'd, afterwards a young hawk. The
French, from hence, took their *niais*, and used it in both
those significations; to which they added a third, metaphorically *a silly fellow*; *un garçon fort niais, un niais*.
Musket signifies a *sparrow hawk*, or the smallest species
of hawks. This too is from the Italian *Muschetto*, a small
hawk, as appears from the original signification of the
word, namely, *a troublesome stinging fly*. So that the
humour of calling the little page an *eyas-musket* is very
intelligible.   WARBURTON.

So, in Greene's *Card of Fancy*, 1608 : " —no hawk
so haggard but will stoop to the lure : no *niesse* so ra-
mage but will be reclaimed to the lunes." *Eyas-musket*
is the same as *infant Lilliputian*.   Again, in Spenser's
Faery Queen, b. i. c. ——

    " ——youthful gay
    " Like *eyas-hauke*, up mounts into the skies,
    " His newly budded pinions to essay."

In the *Booke of Haukyng*, &c. commonly called the
Book of St. Albans, bl. l. no date, is the following derivation of the word ; but whether true or erroneous,
is not for me to determine : " An hauk is called an
eyesse from her *eyne*. For an hauke that is brought up
                                         under

under a bussarde or puttock, as many ben, have watry eyen," &c.   STEEVENS.

234. ——*Jack-a-lent,*——] A *Jack o' lent* was a puppet thrown at in Lent, like shrove-cocks. So, in *The Weakest goes to the Wall,* 1618:

  " A mere anatomy, a *Jack of Lent*."
Again, in the *Four Prentices of London,* 1632:

  " Now you old *Jack of Lent,* six weeks and up-
      wards."
Again, in Greene's *Tu Quoque,* 1599: "——for if a boy, that is throwing at his *Jack o' Lent,* chance to hit me on the shins, &c." See a note on the last scene of this comedy.   STEEVENS.

249. ——from *jays.*] So, in *Cymbeline,*

  " ——some *jay* of Italy,

  " Whose mother was her painting," &c.

          STEEVENS.

250. *Have I caught thee, my heavenly jewel?*] This is the first line of the second song in Sidney's *Astrophel and Stella.*   TOLLET.

251. ——*Why, now let me die; for I have lived long enough;*——] This sentiment, which is of sacred origin, is here indecently introduced. It appears again, with somewhat less of profaneness, in the *Winter's Tale,* act iv. and in *Othello,* act ii.   STEEVENS.

262. ——arched *bent*——] Thus the quartos 1602, and 1619. The folio reads——arched beauty.

          STEEVENS.

263. ——*that becomes the* ship-tire, *the* tire-VALI-
ANT, *or any* Venetian attire.] The old quarto reads,
          tire-

tire-vellet, and the old folio reads, *or any tire of Venetian admittance*. So that the true reading of the whole is this, *that becomes the ship-tire, the tire-*VALIANT, *or any tire of Venetian admittance*. The speaker tells his mistress, she had a face that would become all the head-dresses in fashion. The *ship-tire* was an open head-dress, with a kind of scarf depending from behind. Its name of *ship-tire* was, I presume, from its giving the wearer some resemblance of *a ship* (as Shakspere says) *in all her trim:* with all her pennants out, and flags and streamers flying. Thus Milton, in *Samson Agonistes*, paints Dalila:

    " But who is this, that thing of sea or land?
    " Female of sex it seems,
    " That so bedeck'd, ornate and gay,
    " Comes this way sailing
    " Like a stately ship
    " Of Tarsus, bound for the isles
    " Of Javan or Gadier,
    " With all her bravery on, and *tackle trim,*
    " Sails fill'd, and streamers waving,
    " Courted by all the winds that hold them play."

This was an image familiar with the poets of that time. Thus Beaumont and Fletcher, in their play of *Wit without Money:*——" She spreads sattens as the king's ships do canvas every where, she may space her misen," &c. This will direct us to reform the following word of *tire-valiant*, which I suspect to be corrupt, *valiant* being a very incongruous epithet for a woman's head-dress: I suppose Shakspere wrote *tire-vailant.*

vailant. As the *ship-tire* was an *open* head-dress, so the *tire vailant* was a *close* one ; in which the head and breast were covered as with a *veil.* And these were, in fact, the two different head-dresses then in fashion, as we may see by the pictures of that time : One of which was so open, that the whole neck, breasts, and shoulders, were opened to view : the other, so securely inclosed in kerchiefs, &c. that nothing could be seen above the eyes, or below the chin.

WARBURTON.

—— *or any Venetian* attire.] This is a wrong reading, as appears from the impropriety of the word *attire* here used for a woman's *head-dress:* whereas it signifies the dress of any part. We should read, therefore, *or any* tire *of Venetian admittance.* For the word *attire,* reduced by the aphæresis, to *'tire,* takes a new signification, and means only the head-dress. Hence *tire-woman,* for a dresser of the head. As to the meaning of the latter part of the sentence this may be seen by a paraphrase of the whole speech.— Your face is so good, says the speaker, that it would become any head-dress worn at court, either the open or the close, or indeed any rich and fashionable one worth adorning with Venetian point, or *which will admit to be adorned.* [Of Venetian admittance.] The fashionable lace, at that time was *Venetian point.*

WARBURTON.

This note is plausible, except in the explanation of *Venetian admittance :* but I am afraid this whole system of dress is unsupported by evidence. JOHNSON.

4

—— *of*

—— *of Venetian admittance.*] *i. e.* of a fashion received from Venice. So, in *Westward Hoe,* 1606,
by Decker and Webster : " —now she's in that Italian *head-tire* you sent her." Dr. Farmer proposes
to read—" of *Venetian remittance.*" Dr. Warburton might have found the same reading in the quarto,
1630. Instead of *tire-valiant,* I would read *tire-
volant.* Stubbs, who describes most minutely every
article of female-dress, has mentioned none of these
terms, but speaks of vails depending from the top of
the head, and flying behind in loose folds. The
word *volant* was in use before the age of Shakspere.
I find it in *Wilfride Holmes's Fall and evil Successe of
Rebellion,* 1537 :

" high *volant* in any thing divine."

Tire vellet, in the old 4to, may be printed, as Mr.
Tollet observes, by mistake, for tire-*velvet.* We
know that *velvet-hoods* were worn in the age of Shakspere.   STEEVENS.

Among the presents sent by the Queen of Spain to
the Queen of England, in April 1606, was a *velvet*
cap with gold buttons.   MALONE.

267. —— a *traitor*——] *i. e.* to thy own merit.

STEEVENS.

The folio reads : thou art a *tyrant* to say so.

MALONE.

271. *fortune thy foe.*] " Was the beginning of an
old ballad, in which were enumerated all the
misfortunes that fall upon mankind, through the caprice of fortune." See note on *The Custom of the*
H   *Country,*

Country, A 1. S 1. by Mr. Theobald, who observes, that this ballad is mentioned again in a comedy by John Tatham, printed 1660, called *The Rump, or Mirror of the Times*, wherein a Frenchman is introduced at the bonfire made for the burning of the rumps, and catching hold of Priscilla, will oblige her to dance, and orders the music to play *Fortune my Foe*. See also *Lingua*, Vol. V. Dodsley's collection of Old Plays, p. 188; and *Tom Essence*, 1667, p. 37.

REED.

This tune is the identical air now known by the song of *Death and the Lady*, to which the metrical lamentations of extraordinary criminals have been usually chanted for upwards of these two hundred years.   REMARKS.

The first and second folio read :—*I see what thou wert if Fortune thy foe were not Nature thy friend.* The passage is not in the early quarto.

——*like Bucklers-bury*, &c.] *Bucklers-bury*, in the time of Shakspere, was chiefly inhabited by druggists, who sold all kind of herbs, green as well as dry.

STEEVENS.

So, in Decker's *Westward Hoe*, a comedy, 1607 : " Go into *Bucklers-bury*, and fetch me two ounces of *preserved melounes*, look there be no tobacco taken in the shop when he weighs it." Again, in the same play : " Run into *Bucklers-bury*, and fetch me two ounces of *dragon-water*, some *spermaceti*, and *treacle*."

MALONE.

317. *speak louder*——] *i. e.* that Falstaff who

is

is retired may hear. This passage is only found in
the two elder quartos.   STEEVENS.

346. *I love thee—and none but thee;*] The words
printed in italicks, which are characteristick, and
spoken aside, deserve to be restored from the old quarto. He had used the same words before to Mrs. Ford.
      MALONE.

352. *——how you drumble:——*] The reverend
Mr. Lamb, the editor of the antient metrical history
of the *Battle of Floddon*, observes that—*look how you
drumble*, means—*how confused you are*; and that in the
North, *drumbled ale* is *muddy, disturbed ale*. Thus, a
Scottish proverb in Ray's collection:
" It is good fishing in *drumbling* waters."
Again, in *Have with you to Saffron Walden, or Gabriel
Harvey's hunt is up*, this word occurs: " —gray-beard
drumbling over a discourse." Again: " —your fly
in a box is but a *drumble*-bee in comparison of it."
Again: " —this *drumbling* course."   STEEVENS.

To *drumble*, in Devonshire, signifies to mutter in a
sullen and inarticulate voice. No other sense of the
word will either explain this interrogation, or the
passages adduced in Mr. Steevens's note. *To drumble
and drone* are often used in connexion.   HENLEY.

A *drumble drone*, signifies a drone or humble-bee.
      MALONE.

363. *——and of the season too it shall appear.*] I
would point differently.
      And of the season too;——it shall appear.
Ford seems to allude to the cuckold's horns. So
      H ij   afterwards:

afterwards : " And so buffets himself on the fore-head, crying, *peer* out, *peer* out."   MALONE.

I am satisfied with the old punctuation. In the *Rape of Lucrece,* our poet makes his heroine compare herself to an " *unseasonable doe;*" and, in Blunt's *Customs of Manors,* p. 168, is the same phrase employed by Ford :—" A bukke delivered him *of seyssone,* by the woodmaster and keepers of Need-woode."   STEEVENS.

368. ——*So now uncape.*] So the folio of 1623 reads, and rightly. It is a term in fox-hunting, which signifies to dig out the fox when earth'd.

                   WARBURTON.

The allusion in the foregoing sentence is to the stopping every hole at which a fox could enter, before they *uncape* or turn him out of the bag in which he was brought. I suppose every one has heard of a *bag-fox.*   STEEVENS.

440. ——*In your teeth :*——] This dirty restoration was made by Mr. Theobald. Evans's application of the doctor's words is not in the folio.

                   STEEVENS.

460. ——*father's wealth*] Some light may be given to those who shall endeavour to calculate the increase of English wealth, by observing, that Latymer, in the time of Edward VI. mentions it as a proof of his father's prosperity. *That though but a yeoman, he gave his daughters five pounds each for her portion.* At the latter end of Elizabeth, seven hundred pounds were such a temptation to courtship, as made all

                         other

other motives suspected. Congreve makes twelve thousand pounds more than a counterbalance to the affectation of Belinda. No poet would now fly his favourite character at less than fifty thousand.

JOHNSON.

468. *If opportunity and humblest suit*] Dr. Thirlby imagines, that our author with more propriety wrote,

If importunity *and humblest suit.*

I have not ventur'd to disturb the text, because it may mean, "If the frequent opportunities you find of solliciting my father, and your obsequiousness to him, cannot get him over to your party," &c. THEOBALD.

472. *I'll make a shaft or bolt on't:*] *To make a bolt or a shaft of a thing* is enumerated by *Ray*, in his collection of proverbial phrases.   REED.

494. ——come *cut* and *long tail,*——] *i. e.* come *poor*, or *rich*, to offer himself as my rival. The following is the origin of the phrase. According to the forest laws, the dog of a man, who had no right to the privilege of chace, was obliged to cut, or *law* his dog, among other modes of disabling him, by depriving him of his tail. A dog so cut was called *a cut,* or *curt-tail,* and by contraction *cur*. *Cut and long tail* therefore signified the dog of a clown, and the dog of a gentleman.

Again, in *The first Part of the Eighth liberal Science, entituled Ars Adulandi, &c. devised and compiled by Ulpian Fulwell,* 1576:—"yea, even their very *dogs,* Rug, Rig, and Risbie, yea, *cut and long taile,* they shall be welcome."   STEEVENS.

——come *cut* and *long tail*,—] I can see no meaning
in this phrase. Slender promises to make his mistress
a gentlewoman, and probably means to say, he will
deck her in a gown of the *court-cut*, and with a *long*
train or *tail.* In the comedy of *Eastward Hoe*, is
this passage : " The one must be ladyfied forsooth,
and be attired just to the *court cut* and *long tayle*;"
which seems to justify our reading—*Court* cut and long
tail.   SIR J. HAWKINS.

——*Come cut and long-tail*,—] This phrase is often
found in old plays, and seldom, if ever, with any
variation. The change therefore proposed by Sir
John Hawkins cannot be received without great violence to the text. Whenever the words occur, they
always bear the same meaning, and that meaning is
obvious enough without any explanation. The origin
of the phrase may however admit of some dispute,
and it is by no means certain that the account of it, ·
here adopted by Mr. Steevens from Doctor Johnson,
is well founded. That there ever existed such a mode
of disqualifying dogs by the laws of the forest as is
here asserted, cannot be acknowledged without evidence, and no authority is quoted to prove that such
a custom at any time prevailed. The writers on this
subject are totally silent as far as they have come to
my knowledge. *Manhood* who wrote on the Forest
Laws before they were entirely disused, mentions
expeditation or cutting off three claws of the fore-foot,
as the *only* manner of lawing dogs ; and with his account the *Charter of the Forest* seems to agree. Were
                                              I to

I to offer a conjecture, I should suppose that the phrase originally referred to horses, which might be denominated *cut and long-tail*, as they were curtailed of this part of their body, or allowed to enjoy its full growth ; and this might be practised according to the difference of their value, or the uses to which they were put. In this view, *cut and long-tail* would include the whole species of horses good and bad. In support of this opinion it may be added, that formerly a *cut* was a word of reproach in vulgar colloquial abuse, and I believe is never to be found applied to horses but to those of the worst kind. After all, i any authority can be produced to countenance Dr Johnson's explanation, I shall be very ready to retract every thing that is here said. See also note on *the Match at Midnight*. Dodsley's Collection of Old Plays, Vol. VII. p. 424. Edit. 1780.   REED.

The last conversation I had the honour to enjoy with Sir William Blackstone was on this subject ; and by a series of accurate references to the whole collection of ancient *Forest Laws*, he convinced me of our repeated error, *expeditation* and *genuscission*, being the only established and technical modes ever used for disabling the canine species. Part of the *tails* of spaniels indeed are generally *cut off (ornamenti gratia)* while they are puppies, so that (admitting a loose description) every kind of dog is comprehended in the phrase of *cut and long-tail*, and every rank of people in the same expression, if metaphorically used.

STEEVENS.

513. ——*happy man be his dole!*——] a proverbial expression. See Ray's collection, p. 116. edit.
1737.   STEEVENS.

536. Anne. *Alas, I had rather be set quick i' the
earth,*

And bowl'd to death with turnips.] Can
we think the speaker would thus ridicule her own im-
precation? We may be sure the last line should be
given to the procuress, Quickly, who would mock the
young woman's aversion for her master the doctor.

WARBURTON.

——*be set quick i' the earth,*

And bowl'd to death with turnips.] This is a
common proverb in the southern counties. I find almost the same expression in Ben Johnson's *Bartholomew Fair:* " Would I had been *set in the ground,* all
but the head of me, and had *my brains bowl'd at.*"

COLLINS.

547. ——*fool and a physician?*] I should read *fool*
or a *physician,* meaning Slender and Cains.

JOHNSON.

Sir Tho. Hanmer reads according to Dr. Johnson's
conjecture. This may be right.—Or my Dame
Quickly may allude to the proverb, a man of *forty* is
either a *fool* or a *physician;* but she asserts her master
to be both.   FARMER.

Mr. Dennis, of irascible memory, who altered this
play, and brought it on the stage, in the year 1702,
under the title of *The Comical Gallant,* (when, thanks
to the alterer, it was fairly damn'd) has introduced
the

the proverb at which Mrs. Quickly's allusion appears to be pointed.   STEEVENS.

——*once* to-night——] i. e. *sometime* to-night. So in a letter from the sixth earl of Northumberland (quoted in the notes on the household book of the fifth earl of that name); "——notwithstanding I trust. to be able *ons* to set up a chapell off mine owne."

STEEVENS.

557. ——*speciously*——] She means to say *specially*.   STEEVENS.

569. In former copies :—*as they would have drown'd a* blind bitch's *puppies,*——] I have ventured to transpose the adjective here, against the authority of the printed copies. I know, in horses, a colt from a blind stallion loses much of the value it might otherwise have ; but are *puppies* ever drown'd the sooner, for coming from a *blind bitch ?* The author certainly wrote, *as they would have drown'd a blind bitch's puppies.*

THEOBALD.

The transposition may be justified from the following passage in the *Two Gentlemen of Verona :* "——one that I saved from drowning, when three or four of his *blind* brothers and sisters went to it."   STEEVENS.

644. *Yea,* a buck basket——] The old quarto has,——*By the lord,* a buck-basket, which surely ought to be restored. The editor of the first folio, to avoid the penalty of the statute of King James I. reads——*Yea* &c. and the editor of the second, which has been followed by the moderns, has made Falstaff desert his own character, and assume the language of a Puritan   MALONE.

662.

662.   ——*several deaths:*] Thus the folio and the most correct of the quartos.   The first quarto reads ——*egregious deaths.*   STEEVENS.

663.   ——*detected* with——] Thus the old copies. *With* was sometimes used for *of.*   So, a little after,

   " I sooner will suspect the sun *with* cold."

Detected *of* a jealous, &c.] would have been the common grammar of the times.   The modern editors read *by.*   STEEVENS.

665.   ——*bilbo,*——] A *bilbo* is a Spanish blade, of which the excellence is flexibleness and elasticity.

          JOHNSON.

——*bilbo,* from *Bilboa,* a city of Biscay, where the best blades are made.   STEEVENS.

669.   ——*kidney.*——] *Kidney* in this phrase now signifies *kind* or *qualities,* but Falstaff means, *a man whose kidnies are as fat as mine.*   JOHNSON.

686.   ——*address me*——] *i. e.* make myself ready.   So in *K. Henry* V.

   " To-morrow for our march we are *addrest.*"

          STEEVENS.

705.   ——*I'll be horn-mad.*] There is no image which our author appears so fond of, as that of cuck-old's horns.   Scarcely a light character is introduced that does not endeavour to produce merriment by some allusion to horned husbands.   As he wrote his plays for the stage rather than the press, he perhaps reviewed them seldom, and did not observe this re-petition; or finding the jest, however frequent still successfull, did not think correction necessary.

          JOHNSON.

          This

This is a very trifling scene, of no use to the plot, and I should think of no great delight to the audience; but Shakspere best knew what would please.

JOHNSON.

We may suppose this scene to have been a very entertaining one to the audience for which it was written. Many of the old plays exhibit pedants instructing their scholars. Marston has a very long one in his *What you will*, between a schoolmaster, and *Holofernes Nathaniel*, &c. his pupils. The title of this play was perhaps borrowed by Shakspere, to join to that of *Twelfth Night*. *What you Will* appeared in 1607. *Twelfth Night*, in 1623.   STEEVENS.

ACT IV.

Line 57.—— HORUM, *harum, horum.*] Taylor, the water-poet, has borrowed this jest, such as it is, in his character of a strumpet:

  " And come to *horum harum whorum*, then
  " She proves a great proficient among men."

STEEVENS.

62.   ——*to hick and to hack*——] Sir William Blackstone thought that this, in Dame Quickly's language, signifies " to stammer or hesitate, as boys do, in saying their lessons;" but Mr. Steevens, with more

more probability, supposes that it signifies, in her dialect, *to do mischief.*   MALONE.

70. ——you must be *preeches.*] Sir Hugh means
to say——you must be *breech'd, i. e.* flogg'd. To
breech is to *flog.*   STEEVENS.

78. ——*sprag*——] I am told that this word is
still used by the common people in the neighbourhood
of Bath, where it signifies *ready, alert, sprightly,* and
is pronounced as if it was written—*sprack.* STEEVENS.

101. ——*lunes*——] *i. e.* lunacy, frenzy. See a
note on the *Winter's Tale.* The quarto 1630, and the
folio, read *lines,* instead of *lunes.* The elder quartos
—his old *vaine* again.   STEEVENS.

101. ——*he so takes on*——] *To take on,* which is
now used for *to grieve,* seems to be used by our author
for *to rage.* Perhaps it was applied to any passion.

JOHNSON.

It is likewise used for *to rage,* by Nashe, in *Pierce
Pennylesse his supplication,* &c. 1592 : " Some will
take on like a madman, if they see a pig come to table."

MALONE.

105. ——*peer out*——] That is, *appear horns.*
Shakspere is at his old lunes.   JOHNSON.

And buffets himself on the forehead, crying, peer out,
peer out !] Shakspere here refers to the practice of
children, when they call on a snail to push forth his
horns :

    " Peer out, peer out, peer out of your hole.
    " Or else I beat you black as a coal." HENLEY.

132.

132. *But what make you here?*] An obsolete expression for *what do you here.*   MALONE.

140. ——*an abstract*——] *i. e.* that is a list, an inventory.   STEEVENS.

——*an abstract.*——] *i. e.* a short note or description.
So, in *Hamlet,*

      " The *abstract,* and brief chronicle of the times."
                MALONE.

156. ——her *thrum* hat, and her *muffler* too :——
The *thrum* is the end of a weaver's warp, and we may
suppose, was used for the purpose of making coarse
hats.   In the *Midsummer Night's Dream.*

      " O fates, come, come,
      " Cut thread and *thrum.*"
A muffler was some part of dress that covered the
face.   So, in the *Cobler's Prophecy,* 1594 :

      " Now is she bare-fac'd to be seen :——strait on
          her *Muffler goes.*"
Again, in Laneham's account of Queen Elizabeth's
entertainment at Kenelworth castle, 1575 : "——his
mother lent him a nu *mufflar* for a napkin, that was
ty'd to his gyrdl for lozyng."   STEEVENS.

196. *You youth*] This is the reading of the old
quarto, and in my opinion preferable to that of the
folio, which only has——" Youth in a basket !"
                MALONE.

202. ——this *passes!*——] The force of the phrase
I did not understand when our former impression of
Shakspere was prepared ; and therefore gave these
two words as part of an imperfect sentence.   One of
the obsolete senses of the verb, *to pass,* is, *to go beyond*

I   *bounds*

bounds. So, in *Sir Clyomon, &c. knight of the Golden Shield*, 1599 :

> " I have such a deal of substance here when Bri-
>   tan's men are slaine,
> " That it *passeth*.   O that I had while to stay !"

Again, in the translation of the *Menæchmi*, 1595 :
" This *passeth*, that I meet with none, but thus they vexe me with strange speeches."   STEEVENS.

232. ——*this wrongs you.*] This is below your cha-
racter, unworthy of your understanding, injurious to your honour. So, in *The Taming of the Shrew*, Bianca, being ill-treated by her rugged sister, says,

> " You *wrong* me much, indeed you *wrong* your-
>   self."   JOHNSON.

242. ——his wife's *leman.*——] *Leman*, i. e. *lover*, is derived from *leef*, Dutch, *beloved*, and *man.*

STEEVENS.

254. *She works by charms, &c.*] Concerning some *old woman of Brentford*, there are several ballads ; among the rest, *Julian of Brentford's last Will and Testament*, 1599.   STEEVENS.

This, without doubt, was the person alluded to : for in the early quarto Mrs. Ford says, " my maid's aunt, *Gillian* of Brentford, hath a gown above."

So also, in *Westward Hoe*, 1607 : " I doubt that old hag, *Gillian* of Brainford, has bewitched me," &c.

MALONE.

Mr. Steevens perhaps, has been misled by the vague expression of the Stationers book, *Iyl of Breyntford's Testament*, to which he seems to allude, was written by Robert, and printed by William Copland, long before
1599.

1599. But this the only publication it is believed concerning the above lady at present known, is certainly
no ballad.   REMARKS.

Iulian of Brainford's testament, is mentioned by
Laneham in his letter from *Killingwoorth Castle,*
1575, amongst many other works of established noto-
riety.   HENLEY.

255.   ———such *daubery*———] *Dauberies* are *disguises.*
So, in *K. Lear,* Edgar says,
     " I cannot *daub* it further."   STEEVENS.

264.   ———*ronyon!*———] *Ronyon,* applied to a woman, means, as far as can be traced, much the same
with *scall* or *scab* spoken of a man.   JOHNSON.

So, in *Macbeth,*
     " Aroint thee witch, the rump-fed *ronyon* cries."
From *Regneux,* Fr. So, again : " The *roynish* clown,"
in *As You Like it.*   STEEVENS.

272.   ———a great *peard*;] One of the marks of a
supposed witch was a *beard.*

So, in the *Duke's Mistress,* 1638:
     " ———a chin, without all controversy, good
     " To go a fishing with a *witches beard* on't."

                                                 STEEVENS.
273.———*I spy a great peard under her muffler,*] As the
second stratagem, by which Falstaff escapes is much
the grosser of the two, I wish it had been practised
first. It is very unlikely that Ford, having been so
deceived before, and knowing that he had been deceived, would suffer him to escape in so slight a disguise.   JOHNSON.

276.   ———*cry out thus upon no trail*———,] The ex-

pression is taken from the hunters. *Trail* is the scent
left by the passage of the game. *To cry out,* is to
open or *bark.*   JOHNSON.

So, in *Hamlet,*

" How chearfully on the false *trail* they *cry:*

" Oh this is counter, ye false Danish *dogs!*"
                                       STEEVENS.

291. ——*in the way of waste, attempt us again.*] i. e.
he will not make further attempts to ruin us, by cor-
rupting our virtue, and destroying our reputation.
                                       STEEVENS.

300. ——*no period*—] Shakspere seems, by no period, to mean, *no proper catastrophe.* Of this Hanmer
was so well persuaded, that he thinks it nesessary to
read—no *right* period.   STEEVENS.

314. ——*they must come off ;*——] *To come off,* is
to pay. In this sense it is used by Massinger, in *The
Unnatural Combat,* act IV. sc. ii. where a wench, de-
manding money of the father to keep his bastard,
says, " *Will you come off, sir?*" Again, in Decker's
If this be not a good Play the Devil is in it, 1612 :

" Do not your gallants *come off* roundly then ?"
                                       STEEVENS.

321. *I rather will suspect the sun with cold,*] Thus
the modern editions.—The old ones read—with *gold,*
which may mean, I rather will suspect the sun can be
a thief, or be *corrupted by a bribe,* than thy honour
can be betrayed to wantonness. Mr. Rowe silently
made the change, which succeeding editors have as
silently adopted. A thought of a similar kind occurs
in *Hen.* IV. *Part* I.

                                       " Shall

" Shall the blessed *sun* of heaven prove a *mucker?*"
I have not, however, displaced Mr. Rowe's emendation; as a zeal to preserve old readings without distinction, may sometimes prove as injurious to the
author's reputation, as a desire to introduce new ones,
without attention to the quaintness of phraseology
then in use.   STEEVENS.

The examples here adduced by Mr. Steevens are,
I fear, scarcely in point; for in every one of them the
TO rather coalesces with ALL, than with the respec-
tive verb which follows it.   An instance more to his
purpose occurs in *Comus*, v. 366.

> " I do not think my sister so *to-seek*,
> " Or so unprincipled in virtue's book——"

At the same time it may be remarked that *all-to*, in
the sense of *altogether* (which Mr. Warton has judiciously restored) is used in the same context;

> " She plumes her feathers, and lets grow her
>   wings,
> " That in the various bustle of resort
> " Were *all-to* ruffled——"

In *North's Plutarch* is a passage which will confirm
the observation above:——" setting forth our cittie,
like a glorious woman, *all to be gawded* [all-to be-
gauded] with gold and precious stones." E. 174.——
Perhaps the line in *K. John*, should be thus printed:

> " Is *all-to* wanton, and too full of gauds——"

HENLEY.

347.   ——*and takes the cattle;*]   To *take*, in Shak-

spere, signifies to seize or strike with a disease, to blast.   So, in *Lear:*

"————Strike her young bones,

" **Ye** *taking* airs, with lameness."   JOHNSON.

So, in Markham's *Treatise of Horses*, 1595, chap. 8. " Of a horse that is *taken*.   A horse that is bereft of his feeling, mooving or styrring, is said to be *taken*, and in sooth so hee is, in that he is arrested by so villainous a disease, yet some farriors, not well understanding the ground of the disease, conster the word *taken*, to be striken by some planet or evil-spirit, which is false," &c.   Thus our poet:

"————No planets *strike*, no fairy *takes*."

TOLLET.

351.   ————idle-headed *eld*]   *Eld* seems to be used here, for what our poets call in *Macbeth*—the *olden time*. It is employed in *Measure for Measure*, to express *age* and *decrepitude*,

" ————doth beg the alms

" Of palsied *eld*."   .   STEEVENS.

360.   *Disguis'd like Herne, with huge* horns on his head.]   This line, which is not in the folio, was restored from the old quarto by Mr. Theobald.   He at the same time introduced another from the same copy —" We'll send him word to meet us in the field"———— which is clearly unnecessary, and indeed improper; for the word *field* relates to two preceding lines of the quarto, which have not been introduced:

" Now, for that Falstaff has been so deceiv'd,

" As

" As that he dares not meet us in the *house*,

" We'll send him word to meet us in the *field*."

MALONE.

367. ——*urchins, ouphes,*——] The primitive signification of *urchin* is a hedge-hog. In this sense it is used in the *Tempest*. Hence it comes to signify any thing little and dwarfish. *Ouph* is the Teutonick word for a *fairy* or *goblin*.   STEEVENS.

372. *With some diffused song :——*] A *diffused song* signifies a song that strikes out into wild sentiments beyond the bounds of nature, such as those whose subject is fairy land.   WARBURTON.

Diffused may mean *confused.* So in Stowe's *Chronicle*, p. 553. " Rice, quoth he, (*i. e.* Cardinal Wolsey,) speak you Welch to them : I doubt not but thy speech shall be more *diffuse* to him, than his French shall be to thee."   TOLLET.

By *diffused song*, Shakspere may mean such irregular songs as mad people sing. Kent, in *K. Lear*, when he has determined to assume the appearance of a travelling lunatick, declares his resolution to *diffuse his speech, i. e.* to give it the turn peculiar to madness.

STEEVENS.

375. *And, fairy-like,* TO *pinch the unclean knight ;*] The grammar requires us to read :

" *And, fairy-like* TOO, *pinch the unclean knight.*"

WARBURTON.

This should perhaps be written *to-pinch*, as one word. This use of *to*, in composition with verbs, is very common in Gower and Chaucer, but must have been

rather

rather antiquated in the time of Shakspere. See,
Gower, *De Confessione Amantis*, B. iv. fol. 7.

.   " All *to-tore* is myn araie."
And Chaucer, *Reeve's Tale*, 1169:

      " ——mouth and nose *to-broke*."
The construction will otherwise be very hard.

                                        TYRWHITT.

I add a few more instances, to shew that this use of
the preposition *to* was not entirely antiquated.   Spenser's *Faery Queen*, b. iv. c. 7.

      " With briers and bushes all *to-rent* and scrat-
            ched."
Again, b. v. c. 8.

      " With locks all loose, and raiment all *to-tore*."
Again, b. v. c. 9.

      " Made of strange stuffe, but all *to-worne* and
            ragged,
      " And underneath the breech was all *to-torne* and
            jagged."
Again, in the *Three Lords of London*, 1590:

      " The post at which he runs, and all *to-burns it*."
Again, in *Arden of Feversham*, 1592:

      " watchet sattin doublet, all *to-torn*." STEEVENS.

380.   ——pinch him *sound*,] i. e. *soundly*. The adjective used as an adverb.   STEEVENS.

394.   *That silk will I go buy; and, in that time*] Mr.
Theobald, referring *that time* to the time of buying
the silk, alters it to *tire*. But there is no need of any
change; *that time* evidently relating to the time of the
mask with which Falstaff was to be entertained, and
                                        which

which makes the whole subject of this dialogue.
Therefore the common reading is right.

WARBURTON.

399.   ——*properties*] *Properties* are little incidental
necessaries to a theatre, exclusive of scenes and dres
ses.   STEEVENS.

400.   ——*tricking* for our fairies.] To *trick*, is to
dress out.   So, in *Milton :*

  " No *trick'd* and frounc'd as she was wont,

  " With the Attic boy to hunt ;

  " But kirchief'd in a homely cloud." STEEVENS.

413.   ——what *thick-skin ?*——] I meet with this
term of abuse in Warner's *Albion's England*, 1602,
book vi. chap. 30.

  " That he so foul a *thick-skin* should so fair a
          lady catch."   STEEVENS.

418.   ——*standing-bed, and truckle-bed ;*——] The
usual furniture of chambers in that time was a standing-bed, under which was a *trockle*, *truckle*, or *running*
bed.   In the standing-bed lay the master, and in the
truckle-bed the servant.   So, in Hall's *Account of a
Servile Tutor :*

  " He lieth in the *truckle-bed*,

  " While his young master lieth o'er his head."

JOHNSON

So, in the *Return from Parnassus*, 1606 :

  " When I lay in a *trundle-bed* under my tutor."

And here the tutor has the upper bed.   Again, in
Heywood's *Royal King*, &c. 1637 : " ——shew these

gen-

gentlemen into a close room with a *standing-bed* in't,
and a *truckle* too."   STEEVENS.

420. ——*Anthropophaginian*] *i. e.* a canibal. See
Othello, act i. It is here used as a sounding word to
astonish *Simple*. *Ephesian*, which follows, has no more
meaning.   STEEVENS.

430. ——*Bohemian-Tartar*——] The French call
a *Bohemian* what we call a *Gypsey*; but I believe the Host
means nothing more than, by a wild appellation, to
insinuate that *Simple* makes a strange appearance.

        JOHNSON.

In Germany there were several companies of va-
gabonds, &c. called *Tartars* and *Zigens.* " These
were the same in my opinion," says Mezeray, " as
those the French call *Bohemians*, and the English Gyp-
sies." Bulteel's *Translation of Mezeray's History of
France*, under the year 1417.   TOLLET.

436. ——*wise woman*——] In our author's time
female dealers in palmistry and fortune-telling were
usually denominated *wise women*. So the person from
whom Heywood's play of *The Wise Woman of Hogsden*,
1638, takes its title, is employed in answering many
such questions as are the objects of *Simple*'s enquiry.

        REED.

438. ——*mussel-shell;*——] He calls poor *Simple
mussel-shell*, because he stands with his mouth open.
        JOHNSON

454. *I may not* conceal *them, sir,*
        Conceal *them or thou dy'st*] In both these
                                instances,

instances, Dr. Farmer thinks we should read, *reveal.*

STEEVENS.

467.   ——*clerkly,*——] *i. e.* scholar-like. So, in the
Two Gentlemen of Verona,

"   ——'Tis very *clerkly* done."   STEEVENS.

471.   ——I *paid* nothing for it neither, but was
paid for my learning]   He alludes to the beating which
he had just received.   The same play on words occurs
in *Cymbeline,* act v.

"   ——sorry you have *paid* too much, and sorry

"   that you are *paid* too much."   STEEVENS.

479.   ——three *German* devils, three *Doctor Fau-*
stuses.]   *John Faust,* commonly called *Doctor Faustus,*
was a *German.*   STEEVENS.

511.   ——*Primero*——]   A game at cards.

JOHNSON.

——since I foreswore myself at *Primero.*]   *Primero*
was, in Shakspere's time the fashionable game. In the
earl of Northumberland's letters about the powder
plot, Josc. Percy was playing at *Primero* on Sunday,
when his uncle, the conspirator, called on him at
Essex House.   This game is again mentioned in our
author's *Henry VIII.*   PERCY.

572.   ——*to say my prayers,*]   These words are
restored from the early quarto.   They were probably
omitted in the folio, on account of the stat. 3 Jac. I.
c. 21.   MALONE.

528.   ——*action of an old woman,*——]   The text
must certainly be restor'd *a wood* woman, a crazy,
frantick woman; one too wild, and silly, and unmean-

ing,

ing, to have either the malice, or mischievous subtlety of a witch in her.   THEOBALD.

The reading of the old copy is fully supported by what Falstaff says to Ford:

" I went to her, Master Brook, as you see, like a poor old man; but I came from her, Master Brook, like a poor *old* woman."   MALONE.

534.   ——*what adoe is here to bring you together!*——]
The great fault of this play is the frequency of expressions so profane, that no necessity of preserving character can justify them.   There are laws of higher authority than those of criticism.   JOHNSON.

552.   Fat *Sir John* Falstaff——]   The words——
Sir John,——which are not in the first folio, were arbitrarily inserted in the second, to supply the metre. The corresponding passage in the early quarto,

" *Whereon* fat Falstaffe hath a mighty *scarre*,"
[a misprint for scene], renders it highly probable that the omitted word was that above printed in Italicks. I would therefore read,

        ——Without the shew of both; *wherein* fat Falstaff
        Hath a great scene;——   MALONE.

        " ————————*Sir John Falstaff*
        " *Hath a great scene; the image of the jest*
        " *I'll shew you at large.*"

A similar allusion to a custom still in use of hanging out painted representations of shows, occurs in *Bussy d'Ambois:*

        " The witch policy makes him like a monster
        " Kept only to shew men for goddesse money:
    5   " That

    " That false hagge oftens paints him in her cloth

    " Ten times more monstrous than he is in troth."

                                 HENLEY.

553. ——the *image* of the jest] *Image* is *represen-tation.* So, in *K. Richard III.*

    " And looking on his *images.*"   STEEVENS.

557. ——is *here;*——] *i. e.* in the letter.

                               STEEVENS.

558. ——*are somewhat rank on foot.*] *i. e.* while they are hotly pursuing other merriment of their own.

                               STEEVENS.

562. ——*even* strong against that match] Thus the old copies. The modern editors read *ever,* but perhaps without necessity. *Even* strong, is *as strong, with a similar degree of strength.* So, in *Hamlet,*

    " ——*even* christian."

is, *fellow* christian.   STEEVENS.

565. ——*tasking* of their minds,] So, in another play of our author:

    " ——some things of weight

    " That *task* our thoughts concerning us and

        France."   STEEVENS.

574. ——to *devote*——] We might read—*denote.* So afterwards :

    " ——the white will *decipher* her well enough."

                             STEEVENS.

    Surely we not only may, but ought, to read—*denote*] In the folio 1623, the word is exhibited thus:—deuote. It is highly probable that the *u* was reversed at the

                 K   press.

press.   So, in *Much ado about Nothing*, we meet:
" He is *turn'd* orthographer"——instead of *turn'd*.
Again, in *The Winter's Tale:*

    " *Louely apart*——" for " *Lonely* apart."
Again, in *Hamlet*, quarto, 1605, we meet this very
word put by an error of the press for *denote:*

    " Together with all forms, modes, ships of grief
    " That can *deuote* me truly."
Again, in *Othello:* " —to the contemplation, mark and
denotcment of parts"—instead of *denotement.* Again, in
All's Well that Ends Well, act i. "—the mystery of your
loueliness" instead of *loneliness.*   Again, in *K. John:*
" This *expeditiou's* charge."   Again, ib. " *involuerable,*"
for—" *involnerable.*"   Again, in *K. Henry V.* act iii.
sc. vi.   " *Leuity* and cruelty," for " for *Lenity* and
cruelty."   MALONE.

    576.   ——*quaint* in green,] ——may mean fantas-
tically drest in green.   So, in Milton's *Masque at Lud-
low Castle:*

    " ——lest the place,
    " And this *quaint* habit breed astonishment."
Quaintness, however, was anciently used to signify
gracefulness.   So, in Green's *Dialogue between a He and
a She Coney-catcher*, 1592: " I began to think what a
handsome man he was, and wished that he would
come and take a night's lodging with me, sitting in a
dump to think of the *quaintness* of his personage."
In the *Two Gentlemen of Verona*, act iii. *quaintly* is used
for *ingeniously:*

                                " —ladder

"———ladder *quaintly* made of cords."

STEEVENS.

In *Daniel's Sonnets*, 1594, it is used for *fantastick.*

" Prayers prevail not with a *quaint* disdayne."

MALONE.

ACT V.

Line 8. ———*HOLD up your head, and* mince.] To *mince* is to walk with affected delicacy. So, in the *Merchant of Venice,*

" ———turn two *mincing* steps

" Into a manly stride."   STEEVENS.

36. ———*a nay-word*———] *i. e.* a watch-word. Mrs. Quickly has already used it in this sense. STEEVENS.

43. ———*No* MAN *means evil but the devil,*———] This is a double blunder; for some, of whom this was spoke, were women. We should read them, *No* ONE *means.*   WARBURTON.

There is no blunder. In the ancient interludes and moralities, the beings of supreme power, excellence, or depravity, are occasionally styled *men.* So, in *Much ado about Nothing,* Dogberry says: " God's a good man." Again, in an Epitaph, part of which has been borrowed as an absurd one, by Mr. Pope and his associates, who were not very well acquainted with ancient phraseology:

K ij " Do

" Do all we can,

" Death is a *man*

" That never spareth none."

Again, in *Jeronimo, or the First Part of the Spanish Tragedy,* 1605 :

" You're the last *man* I thought on, save the *devil.*"

STEEVENS.

57.   ——*and the Welch devil Evans?*]   The former impression, *and the Welch devil Herne?*   But Falstaff was to represent Herne, and he was on Welchman. Where was the attention or sagacity of our editors, not to observe that Mrs. Ford is inquiring for *Evans* by the name of the *Welch devil?* Dr. Thirlby likewise discover'd the blunder of this passage.   THEOBALD.

I suppose only the letter *H.* was set down in the MS; and therefore, instead of *Hugh* (which seems to be the true reading), the editors substitued *Herne.*

STEEVENS.

58.   ——*in a pit* hard by *Herne's oak,*——] An *oak,* which may be that alluded to by Shakspere, is still standing close to a *pit* in Windsor forest.   It is yet shewn as the *oak of Herne.*   STEEVENS.

85.   *When gods have hot backs, what shall poor men do?*] Shakspere had perhaps in his thoughts the argument which Cherea employed in a similar situation.   *Ter. Eun.* act iii. sc. v.

" ——————Quia consimilem luserat

" Jam olim ille ludum, impendio magis animus
        gaudebat mihi,

" Deum

" Deum sese in hominem convertisse, atque per
    alienas tegulas

" Venisse clanculum per impluvium, fucum fac-
    tum mulieri.

" At quem deum? qui templa cœli summa sonit
    concutit.

" *Ego homuncio hoc non facerem?* Ego illud vero ita
    feci, ac lubens."

A translation of Terence was published in 1598.

MALONE.

87. ——*Send me a cool rut-time, Jove, or who can
blame me to* piss my tallow ?——] This, I find, is technical. In Tuberville's *Booke of Hunting*, 1575 : " During the time of their rut, the rats live with small sus-
tenance.—The red mushroome helpeth well to make
them *pysse their greace*, they are then in so vehement
heate," &c.   FARMER.

In Ray's *Collection of Proverbs*, the phrase is yet further explained : " *He has piss'd his tallow.* This is
spoken of bucks who grow lean after rut ng-time,
and may be applied to men."   STEEVENS.

92. ——rain *potatoes ;*——] *Potatoes,* when they
were first introduced in England, were supposed to be
strong provocatives. See Mr. Collins's note on a passage in *Troilus and Cressida*, act v.   STEEVENS.

94. ——*kissing-comfits,*——] These were sugar-
plums, perfumed to make the breath sweet. So, in
Webster's *Dutchess of Malfy*, 1623 :

K iij

"—Sure

" ———Sure your pistol holds

" Nothing but perfumes or *kissing-comfits.*"

In *Sweetman Arraign'd*, 1620, these confections are called———" *kissing-causes.*"   " Their very breath is sophisticated with amberpellets, and *kissing-causes.*"
Again, in *The Siege*, or *Love's Convert*, by Cartwright:

" ———kept *mush-plumbs* continually in my mouth," &c.

Again in *A Very Woman*, by Massinger:

" *Comfits* of ambergris to help our *kisses.*"

For eating these, queen Mab may be said, in *Romeo and Juliet*, to *plague their lips with blisters.*   STEEVENS.

94.   ———*eringoes.*] So, in *Drayton's Polyolbion*,

" Whose root th' Eringo is, the reines that doth
      inflame,

" So strongly to performe the Cytherean game."
                                        HENDERSON.

100.   ———*fellow of this walk,*———] Who the *fellow* is, or why he keeps his shoulders for him, I do not understand.   JOHNSON.

To the keeper the *shoulders* and *humbles* belong as a perquisite.   GREY.

So, in *Friar Bacon* and *Friar Bungay*, 1599,

" Butter and cheese, and *humbles* of a deer,

" Such as poor keepers have within their lodge."

So, in Holinshed, 1586, vol. I. p. 204: " The keeper, by a custom———hath the skin, head, *umbles*, chine and *shoulders.*"

Holinshed informs us, that in the year 1583, for the entertainment of prince Alasco, was performed " a

verie

verie statelie tragedie named *Dido*, wherein the queen's banquet (with Eneas narration of the destruction of Troie) was livelie described in a marchpaine patterne, —*the tempest wherein it hailed small confects, rained rosewater, and shew an artificial kind of snow*, all strange, marvellous and abundant." On this circumstance very probably Shakspere was thinking, when he put the words quoted above into the mouth of Falstaff.

STEEVENS.

A *walk*, is that district in a forest, to which the jurisdiction of a particular keeper extends. So, in *Ledge's Rosalynd:*

" Tell me, forester, under whom maintainest
thou thy *walks?*"

Again, *ibid.* " Thus, for two or three days he walked up and down with his brother, to shew him all the commodities that belonged to his *walke.*"   MALONE.

104. *You* ORPHAN *heirs of fix'd destiny,*] But why *orphan heirs?* Destiny, whom they succeeded, was yet in being.   Doubtless the poet wrote:

You OUPHEN *heirs of fix'd destiny,*

i. e. you *elves*, who minister, and succeed in some of the works of destiny.   They are called, in this play, both before and afterwards, *ouphes*; here *ouphen*; *en* being the plural termination of Saxon nouns.   For the word is from the Saxon Alrenne, *lamiæ, dæmones.* Or it may be understood to be an adjective, as *wooden, woollen, golden,* &c.   WARBURTON.

Dr. Warburton corrects *orphan* to *ouphen*; and not

without

without plausibility, as the word *ouphes* occurs both before and afterwards. But I fancy, in acquiescence to the vulgar doctrine, the address in this line is to a part of the *troop*, as mortals by birth, but adopted by the fairies: *orphans* in respect of their real parents, and now only dependant on *destiny* herself. A few lines from Spenser will sufficiently illustrate this passage :

> " The man whom *heavens* have *ordaynd* to bee
>   " The spouse of *Britomart* is *Arthegall*,
> " He wonneth in the land of *Faycree*,
>   " Yet is no *Fary* borne, ne sib at all,
> " To elfes, but sprong of seed terrestriall,
>   " And whilome by false *Faries* stolen away,
> " While yet in infant cradle he did crall." &c.

Edit. 1590. b. iii. st. 26.

FARMER.

The old orthography of *elf* is thus, elphe and phayrie. See *Middleton's Family of Love*, 1602. Might we not read *elphen?*   HENDERSON.

116. *Crier Hobgoblin, make the fairy o-yes.*

Eva. Elves, list your names; silence, you airy toys.] These two lines were certainly intended to rhime together, as the preceding and subsequent couplets do; and accordingly, in the old editions, the final words of each line are printed, *oyes* and *toyes*. This, therefore, is a striking instance of the inconvenience which has arisen from modernizing the orthography of Shakspere.   TYRWHITT.

117.

117. *Elves list your names, &c.*] The modern editors, without any authority, have given these lines to *Sir Hugh*. But in the only authenthick antient copy, the first folio, they are attributed to *Pistol*; and ought to be restored to him. Neither he, indeed, nor Mrs. Quickly, seem to have been introduced with much propriety here; nor are they named by Ford in a former scene, where the intended plot against Falstaff is mentioned. It is highly probable, as the modern editor has observed, that the same performers, who had represented *Pistol* and *Quickly*, were afterwards from necessity employed as fairies. Their names thus crept into the copies.   MALONE.

120. ——as *bilberry*.] The *bilberry* is the *whortleberry*. Fairies were always supposed to have a strong aversion to sluttery. Thus, in the old song of *Robin Good Fellow*. See Dr. Percy's *Reliques*,

" When house or hearth doth sluttish lye,

" I pinch'd the maidens black and blue," &c.

     STEEVENS.

126. REIN *up the organs of her fantasy*;] i. e. *curb* them, that she be no more disturbed by irregular imaginations, than children in their sleep. For he adds immediately:

Sleep she as sound as careless infancy.

So, in *The Tempest:*

" Give not dalliance too much the REIN."

And, in *Measure for Measure:*

" I give my sensual race the REIN."

T

To give the rein, being just the contrary *to rein up.* The same thought he has again in *Macbeth:*

" ———— Merciful powers!

" Restrain in me the cursed thoughts that na-
      ture

" Gives way to in repose."   WARBURTON.

This is highly plausible; and yet, *Raise up the organs of her fantasy,* may mean, *elevate her ideas above
sensuality, exalt them to the noblest contemplation.*

STEEVENS.

Bede is enjoined, wherever he finds a maid, *though*
she, after having prayed to the deity, should sleep in
consequence of her innocence, as soundly as an infant,
to *elevate* her fancy, and amuse her mind with some
delightful vision.—A comma should, I think, be placed
after *fantasy,* and a semicolon after *infancy.* *Sleep she*
—has the force of—*though* she sleep.   MALONE.

134. *In* state *as wholesome,*————] The Oxford editor, not knowing the meaning of *wholesome,* has altered
it to,

In site as *wholesom,*

and so has made the wish a most absurd one. For the
site or situation must needs be what it is, till the general destruction. But *wholsom* here signifies *integer.*
He wishes the castle may stand in its present state of
perfection, which the following words plainly shew;

————as in state 'tis fit.   WARBURTON.

136. *The several chairs of order, look you scour with
juice of balm,* &c.] It was an article of our ancient
luxury, to rub tables, &c. with aromatick herbs.

Pliny

Pliny informs us, that the Romans did the same to
drive away evil spirits.   STEEVENS.

148. ——*charactery.*] For the matter with which
they make letters.   JOHNSON.

So, in another of our author's plays:

" All the *charactery* of my sad brows."

i. e. all that seems to be written on them.

STEEVENS.

155. ——*of middle earth.*] Spirits are supposed
to inhabit the ethereal regions, and fairies to dwell under ground; men therefore are in a middle station.

JOHNSON.

So, in the antient metrical romance of *Syr Guy of
Warwick*, bl. l. no date :

" Thou mayst them flea with dint of swearde,

" And win the fayrest mayde *of middle erde.*"

Again :

" ——————— the best knight

" That ever was *in middle earde.*"

Again, in Gower, *De Confessione Amantis*, fol. 26.

" Adam for pride lost his price

" In *mydell erth.*"

Again in an ancient alliterative ode, quoted by Mr.
Warton, in his *History of English Poetry :*

" *Middle-erd* for mon was made."

Again, the MSS. called *William and the Werwolf* in
the library of King's College, Cambridge, p. 15.

" And seide God that madest man and all *middle*

erthe."   STEEVENS.

The

The phrase signifies neither more nor less, than the *earth* or *world*, from its imaginary situation in the *midst* or *middle* of the Ptolemaic system, and has not the least reference to either spirits or fairies.

REMARKS.

158. *Vile worm*, thou wast o'er-look'd even in thy birth.] The old copy reads—*vild*. That *vild*, which so often occurs in these plays, was not an error of the press, but the pronunciation of the time, appears from these lines of Heywood, in his *Pleasant Dialogues and Dramas*, 1637 :

> " EARTH.   What goddess, or how *styl'd ?*
> " AGE.   *Age* am I call'd
> " EARTH.   Hence false virago *vild*."

MALONE.

159. *With trial-fire*, &c.] So Beaumont and Fletcher, in the *Faithful Shepherdess :*

> " In this flame his finger thrust,
> " Which will burn him if he lust ;
> " But if not, away will turn,
> " As loth unspotted flesh to burn." STEEVENS.

169. Eva. *It is right indeed,———*] This short speech, which is very much in character for sir Hugh, I have inserted from the old quarto, 1619.

THEOBALD.

172. *———and luxury !*] *Luxury* is here used for *incontinence.* So, in *K. Lear*, " To't *luxury* pell-mell, for I lack soldiers." STEEVENS.

173. *Lust is but a* bloody *fire*,] A *bloody fire,*
means

means *a fire in the blood.*   In *The Second Part of Hen. IV.* act iv. the same expression occurs:

" Led on by *bloody* youth," &c.

i. e. sanguine youth.   STEEVENS.

Again in *the Tempest,* we have the very expression of the text:

——— " the strongest oaths are straw,

" To the *fire i' the blood.*"

And in *Othello:* " It is merely a lust in the blood."

MALONE.

181. *During this song,*—] This direction I thought proper to insert from the old quartos.   THEOBALD.

——*they pinch him.*]   So, in Lylly's *Endymion,* 1591: " The fairies dance, and with a song, *pinch him.*"   And, in his *Maid's Metamorphosis,* 1600, they threaten the same punishment.   STEEVENS.

207. ———*how wit may be made a Jack-a-lent,*———] A Jack o'Lent appears to have been some puppet which was thrown at in Lent, like Shrove-tide cocks.

So, in the old comedy of *Lady Alimony,* 1659:

" ———throwing cudgels

" At *Jack-a-lents,* or Shrove-cocks."

Again, in Beaumont and Fletcher's *Tamer Tamed:*

" ———if I forfeit,

" Make me a *Jack o' Lent,* and break my shins

" For untagg'd points and counters."———

Again, in Ben Jonson's *Tale of a Tub:*

" ———on an Ash-Wednesday,

" Where thou didst stand six weeks the *Jack o' Lent,*

L   " For

" For boys to hurl three throws a penny at thee."
STEEVENS.

218. ———*a coxcomb of Frize ?*] *i. e.* a fool's cap made out of Welch materials. Wales was famous for this cloth. So, in *K. Edward* I. 1599 : " Enter Lluellin, alias Prince of Wales, &c. with swords and bucklers, and *frieze* jerkins." Again : " Enter Sussex, &c. with a mantle of *frieze*." "—my boy shall weare a mantle of this country's weaving, to keep him warm."
STEEVENS.

243.   ———the Welch *flannel* ;—] The very word is derived from a *Welch* one, so that it is almost unnecessary to add that *flannel* was originally the manufacture of Wales. In the old play of *K. Edward* I. 1599 : " Enter Hugh ap David, Guenthian his wench in *flannel*, and Jack his novice." Again :

" Here's a wholesome Welch wench,

" Lapt in her *flannel* as warm as wool."
STEEVENS.

243. ——— *ignorance itself is a plummet o'er me:———*] Though this be perhaps not unintelligible, yet it is an odd way of confessing his dejection. I should wish to read :

———*ignorance itself has a plume o' me:*

That is, I am so depressed, that ignorance itself plucks me, and decks itself with the spoils of my weakness. Of the present reading, which is probably right, the meaning may be, I am so enfeebled, that *ignorance itself* weighs me down and oppresses me.
JOHNSON.

" Ignorance

" Ignorance itself, says Falstaff, is a *plummet* o'er me." If any alteration be necessary, I think, "Ig- norance itself is a *planet* o'er me," would have a chance to be right. Thus Bobadil excuses his cowar- dice : " Sure I was struck with a *planet*, for I had no power to touch my *weapon*."   FARMER.

Dr. Farmer might have supported his conjecture by a passage in *K. Henry* VI. where Queen Margaret says, that Suffolk's face,

> "————rul'd like a wandering *planet over* me."
> STEEVENS.

Perhaps Falstaff's meaning may be this: "Igno- rance itself is a plummet *o'er me:* i. e. *above me;*" ignorance itself is not so low as I am, by the length of a *plummet-line*.   TYRWHITT.

A passage in our author's 78th *Sonnet* adds some support to the emendation proposed by Dr. Johnson :

> " Thine eyes, that taught the dumb on high to
>   sing,
> " And *heavy ignorance aloft to fly*————."

If *plume* be the true reading, Falstaff, I suppose meant to say, that even ignorance, however heavy, could *soar* above him.   MALONE.

Ignorance *itself is a* plummet *o'er me—i. e.* serves to point out my obliquities. This is said in conse- quence of Evans's last speech. The allusion is to the examination of a carpenter's work by the *plum- line* held over it ; of which line Sir Hugh is here re- presented as the *lead*.   HENLEY.

250. Mrs. Ford. *Nay, husband*——] This and the following little speech I have inserted from the old quartos. The retrenchment, I presume, was by the players. Sir John Falstaff is sufficiently punished, in being disappointed and exposed. The expectation of his being prosecuted for the twenty pounds, gives the conclusion too tragical a turn: Besides, it is *poetical justice* that Ford should sustain this loss, as a fine for his unreasonable jealousy.   THEOBALD.

255. ——*laugh at my wife*——] The two plots are excellently connected, and the transition very artfully made in this speech.   JOHNSON.

282. ——*marry boys ?*]This and the next speech are likewise restorations from the old quarto.

STEEVENS.

321. Page. *Well, what remedy?*] In the first sketch of this play, which, as Mr. Pope observes, is much inferior to the latter performance, the only sentiment of which I regret the omission, occurs at this critical time. When Fenton brings in his wife, there is this dialogue.

" Mrs. Ford. *Come Mrs. Page, I must be bold with you,*

'Tis pity to part love that is so true

Mrs. Page. [Aside.] *Although that I have missed in my intent, Yet I am glad my husband's match is cross'd.*

——*Here Fenton, take her.*——

Eva. *Come, master Page, you must needs agree.*

Ford.

Ford. *I' faith, Sir, come, you see your wife is pleas'd.*

Page. *I cannot tell, and yet my heart is eas'd;*
And yet it doth me good the doctor miss'd.
Come hither Fenton, and come hither daughter."

JOHNSON.

THE END.

Bell's Edition.

MUCH ADO ABOUT NOTHING,

BY

WILL. SHAKSPERE:

Printed Complete from the TEXT of

SAM. JOHNSON and GEO. STEEVENS,

And revised from the last Editions.

Passages omitted in Representation, are distinguished by inverted Commas, thus "

When Learning's triumph o'er her barb'rous foes
First rear'd the Stage, immortal *SHAKSPERE* rose ;
Each change of many-colour'd life he drew,
Exhausted worlds, and then imagin'd new :
Existence saw him spurn her bounded reign,
And panting Time toil'd after him in vain :
His pow'rful strokes presiding Truth confess'd,
And unresisted Passion storm'd the breast.

DR. SAMUEL JOHNSON.

LONDON:

Printed for, and under the direction of

JOHN BELL, British-Library, STRAND,

MDCCLXXXV.

IT is true, as Mr. Pope has observed, that somewhat resembling the story of this play, is to be found in the fifth book of the *Orlando Furioso*. In Spenser's *Fairy Queen*, b. ii. c. 4. as remote an original may be traced. A novel, however, of *Belleforest*, copied from another of *Bandello*, seems to have furnished Shakspere with his fable, as it approaches nearer, in all its particulars, to the play before us, than any other performance known to be extant. I have seen so many versions from this once popular collection, that I entertain no doubt but that the great majority of the tales it comprehends, have made their appearance in an English dress. Of that particular story which I have just mentioned, viz. the eighteenth history in the third volume, no translation has hitherto been met with.

This play may be justly said to contain two of the most sprightly characters that Shakspere ever drew. The wit, the humourist, the gentleman, and the soldier, are combined in Benedick. It is to be lamented, indeed, that the first and most splendid of these distinctions, is disgraced by unnecessary profaneness; for the goodness of his heart is hardly sufficient to atone for the licence of his tongue. The too sarcastic levity, which flashes out in the conversation of Beatrice, may be excused on account of the steadiness and friendship so apparent in her behaviour, when she urges her lover to risque his life by a challenge to Claudio. In the conduct of the fable, however, there is an imperfection similar to that which

Dr. Johnson has pointed out in the *Merry Wives of Windsor.*— The second contrivance is less ingenious than the first : or, to speak more plainly, the same incident is become stale by repetition. I wish some other method had been found to entrap Beatrice, than that very one which before had been successfully practised on Benedick.

Much ado about Nothing (as I understand from one of Mr. Vertue's MSS.) formerly paſſed under the title of Benedick and Beatrix. Heming, the player, received on the 20th of May, 1613, the sum of forty pounds, and twenty pounds more, as his majesty's gratuity for exhibiting ſix plays at Hampton-Court, among which was this comedy.

STEEVENS.

Dramatis Perſonae.

MEN.

Don PEDRO, *Prince of Arragon.*
LEONATO, *Governor of Meſſina.*
Don JOHN, *Bastard Brother to Don Pedro.*
CLAUDIO, *a young Lord of Florence, Favourite to Don Pedro.*
BENEDICK, *a young Lord of Padua, favoured likewise by Don Pedro.*
BALTHAZAR, *Servant to Don Pedro.*
ANTONIO, *Brother to Leonato.*
BORACHIO, *Confident to Don John.*
CONRADE, *Friend to Borachio.*
DOGBERRY, }
VERGES, } *two fooliſh Officers.*

WOMEN.

HERO, *Daughter to Leonato.*
BEATRICE, *Niece to Leonato.*
MARGARET, }
URSULA, } *two Gentlewomen attending on Hero.*

A Friar, Messenger, Watch, Town-Clerk, Sexton, and Attendants.

SCENE Meſſina in Sicily.

MUCH ADO ABOUT NOTHING.

ACT I. SCENE I.

Before LEONATO's *House. Enter* LEONATO, HERO, *and* BEATRICE, *with a Meſſenger.*

Leonato.

I LEARN in this letter that Don Pedro of Arragon comes this night to Messina.

Mess. He is very near by this; he was not three leagues off when I left him.

Leon. How many gentlemen have you lost in this action?

Mess. But few of any sort, and none of name.

Leon. A victory is twice itself, when the atchiever brings home full numbers. I find here, that Don Pedro hath bestowed much honour on a young Florentine, call'd Claudio.

11

A iij

Mess.

Mess. Much deserv'd on his part, and equally remembered by Don Pedro: He hath borne himself beyond the promise of his age; doing, in the figure of a lamb, the feats of a lion: " he hath, indeed, " better better'd expectation, than you must expect " of me to tell you how."

Leon. He hath an uncle here in Messina will be very much glad of it.   19

Mess. I have already delivered him letters; and there appears much joy in him; even so much, that joy could not shew itself modest enough without a badge of bitterness.

Leon. Did he break out into tears?

Mess. In great measure.

Leon. A kind overflow of kindness: There are no faces truer than those that are so wash'd. " How " much better is it to weep at joy, than to joy at " weeping!"   29

Beat. I pray you, is signior Montanto return'd from the wars, " or no"?

Mess. I know none of that name, lady; there was none such in the army of any sort.

Leon. What is he that you ask for, niece?

Hero. My cousin means signior Benedick of Padua.

Mess. O, he's return'd; and as pleasant as ever he was.   37

Beat. " He set up his bills here in Messina, and " challenged Cupid at the flight; and my uncle's " fool, reading the challenge, subscrib'd for Cupid, " and challenged him at the bird-bolt."—I pray you,

you, how many hath he kill'd and eaten in these wars? But how many hath he kill'd? for, indeed, I promis'd to eat all of his killing.

Leon. Faith, niece, you tax signior Benedick too much; but he'll be meet with you, I doubt it not.

Mess. He hath done good service, lady, in these wars.   48

Beat. You had musty victual, and he hath holp to eat it: he's a very valiant trencher-man, he hath an excellent stomach.

Mess. And a good soldier too, lady.

Beat. And a good soldier to a lady;—But what is he to a lord?

" *Mess.* A lord to a lord, a man to a man; stuff'd " with all honourable virtues.

" *Beat.* It is so, indeed; he is no less than a " stuff'd man: but for the stuffing,—well, we are " all mortal."   59

Leon. You must not, sir, mistake my niece: there is a kind of merry war betwixt signior Benedick and her: they never meet, but there's a skirmish of wit between them.

Beat. Alas, he gets nothing by that. In our last conflict, four of his five wits went halting off, and now is the whole man govern'd with one: so that if he have wit enough to keep himself warm, let him bear it for a difference between himself and his horse; for it is all the wealth that he hath left, to be known a reasonable creature.—Who is his companion now? he hath every month a new sworn brother.

Mess. Is it possible?

Beat. Very easily possible: he wears his faith but as the fashion of his hat, it ever changes with the next block.

Mess. I see, lady, the gentleman is not in your books.

Beat. No: an he were, I would burn my study. But, I pray you, who is his companion? " Is there " no young squarer now, that will make a voyage " with him to the devil ?"

Mess. He is most in the company of the right noble Claudio.

Beat. O lord! He will hang upon him like a disease: he is sooner caught than the pestilence, and the taker runs presently mad. God help the noble Claudio! if he have caught the Benedick, it will cost him a thousand pounds ere he be cur'd.

" *Mess.* I will hold friends with you, lady.   90
" *Beat.* Do, good friend."

Leon. You'll ne'er run mad, niece.

Beat. No, not 'till a hot January.

Mess. Don Pedro is approach'd.

Enter Don PEDRO, CLAUDIO, BENEDICK, BALTHAZAR, *and Don* JOHN.

Pedro. Good signior Leonato, you are come to meet your trouble: the fashion of the world is to avoid cost, and you encounter it.

Leon. Never came trouble to my house in the likeness of your grace: for trouble being gone, comfort
should

should remain ; but, when you depart from me, sorrow abides, and happiness takes his leave.   101

Pedro. You embrace your charge too willingly.—I think, this is your daughter.

Leon. Her mother hath many times told me so.

Bene. Were you in doubt, sir, that you ask'd her ?

Leon. Signior Benedick, no ; for then were you a child.   108

Pedro. You have it full, Benedick : we may guess by this what you are, being a man. Truly, the lady fathers herself :—Be happy, lady ! for you are like an honourable father.

Bene. If Signior Leonato be her father, she would not have his head on her shoulders for all Messina, as like him as she is.

Beat. I wonder, that you will still be talking, signior Benedick ; no body marks you.

Bene. What, my dear lady Disdain ! are you yet living ?   119

Beat. Is it possible, disdain should die, while she hath such meet food to feed it, as signior Benedick ? Courtesy itself must convert to disdain, if you come in her presence.

Bene. Then is courtesy a turn-coat :—But it is certain, I am lov'd of all ladies, only you excepted : and I would I could find in my heart that I had not a hard heart ; for truly, I love none.   127

Beat. A dear happiness to women : they would else have been troubled with a pernicious suitor. I thank

God,

God, and my cold blood, I am of your humour for that; I had rather hear my dog bark at a crow, than a man swear he loves me.

Bene. God keep you ladyship still in that mind! so some gentleman or other shall 'scape a predestinate scratch'd face.

Beat. Scratching could not make it worse, an 'twere such a face as your's "were."

Bene. Well, you are a rare parrot-teacher.

Beat. A bird of my tongue, is better than a beast of yours.   140

Bene. I would, my horse had the speed of your tongue; and so good a continuer: But keep your way o'God's name; I have done.

Beat. You always end with a jade's trick; I know you of old.

Pedro. This is the sum of all: Leonato,—Signior Claudio, and signior Benedick,—my dear friend Leonato hath invited you all. I tell him, we shall stay here at the least a month; and he heartily prays, some occasion may detain us longer: I dare swear he is no hypocrite, but prays from his heart.   151

Leon. If you swear, my lord, you shall not be forsworn.—Let me bid you welcome, my lord; being reconciled to the prince your brother, I owe you all duty.

John. I thank you: I am not of many words, but I thank you.

Leon. Please it your grace lead on?   158

Pedro. Your hand, Leonato; we will go together.

[*Exeunt all but* BENEDICK *and* CLAUDIO.

Claud.

Claud. Benedick, didst thou note the daughter of Signior Leonato?

Bene. I noted her not; but I look'd on her.

Claud. Is she not a modest young lady?

Bene. Do you question me, as an honest man should do, for my simple true judgment? or would you have me speak after my custom, as being a professed tyrant to their sex?

Claud. No, I pray thee, speak in sober judgment.   169

Bene. Why, i'faith, methinks she is too low for a high praise, too brown for a fair praise, and too little for a great praise: only this commendation I can afford her; that were she other than she is, she were unhandsome; and being no other but as she is, I do not like her.

Claud. Thou think'st, I am in sport; I pray thee, tell me truly how thou lik'st her?

Bene. Would you buy her, that you enquire after her?   179

Claud. Can the world buy such a jewel?

Bene. Yea, and a case to put it into. But speak you this with a sad brow? or do you play the flouting Jack; " to tell us Cupid is a good hare-finder, " and Vulcan a rare carpenter?" Come, in what key shall a man take you, " to go in the song"?

Claud. In mine eye, she is the sweetest lady that I ever looked on.   187

Bene. I can see yet without spectacles, and I see no such matter; there's her cousin, an she were not possess'd possess'd with a fury, exceeds her as much in beauty, as the first of May doth the last of December. But I hope, you have no intent to turn husband; have you?

Claud. I would scarce trust myself, though I had sworn the contrary, if Hero would be my wife.

Bene. Is't come to this, i'faith? Hath not the world one man, but he will wear his cap with suspicion? Shall I never see a bachelor of threescore again? Go to, i'faith; an thou wilt needs thrust thy neck into a yoke, wear the print of it, and sigh away Sundays. Look, Don Pedro is return'd to seek you.   202

Re-enter Don PEDRO.

Pedro. What secret hath held you here, that you follow'd not to Leonato's?

Bene. I would, your grace would constrain me to tell.

Pedro. I charge thee on thy allegiance.

Bene. 'You hear count Claudio: I can be secret as a dumb man, I would have you think so; but on my allegiance,—mark you this, on my allegiance.— He is in love. With who?—now that is your grace's part.—Mark, how short his answer is:—With Hero, Leonato's short daughter.   213

Claud. If this were so, so were it uttered.

Bene. Like the old tale, my lord: it is not so, nor 'twas not so; but, indeed, God forbid it should be so.

Claud.

Claud. If my passion change not shortly, God forbid it should be otherwise.   219

Pedro. Amen, if you love her, for the lady is very
well worthy.

Claud. You speak this to fetch me in, my lord.

Pedro. By my troth, I speak my thought.

Claud. And, in faith, my lord, I spoke mine.

Bene. And, by my two faiths and troths, my lord,
I speak mine.

Claud. That I love her, I feel.

Pedro. That she is worthy, I know.   228

Bene. That I neither feel how she should be loved,
nor know how she should be worthy, is the opinion
that fire cannot melt out of me; I will die in it at
the stake.

Pedro. Thou wast ever an obstinate heretick in the
despight of beauty.

Claud. And never could maintain his part, but in
the force of his will.

Bene. That a woman conceived me, I thank her;
that she brought me up, I likewise give her most
humble thanks: but that I will have a recheat
winded in my forehead, " or hang my bugle in an
" invisible baldrick," all women shall pardon me :
Because I will not do them the wrong to mistrust any,
I will do myself the right to trust none ; and the fine
is (for the which I may go the finer), I will live a
bachelor.   245

Pedro. I shall see thee, ere I die, look pale with
love.

B

Beat.

Bene. With anger, with sickness, or with hunger, my lord ; not with love:. prove, that ever I lose more blood with love, than I will get again with drinking, pick out mine eyes with a ballad-maker's pen, and hang me up at the door of a brothel-house for the sign of blind Cupid. .   253

Pedro. Well, if ever thou dost fall from this faith, thou wilt prove a notable argument.

Pedro. If I do, hang me in a bottle like a cat, and shoot at me ; " and he that hits me, let him be clap'd " on the shoulder, and call'd Adam."

. *Pedro.* Well, as time shall try :

In time the savage bull doth bear the yoke.   263

-- *Bene.* The savage bull may ; but if ever the sensible Benedick bear it, pluck off the bull's horns, and set them in my forehead: and let me be vilely painted ; and in such great letters as they write, *Here is good horse to hire*, let them signify under my sign,—*Here you may see Benedick the marry'd man.*

" *Claud.* If this should ever happen, thou would'st " be horn-mad."

Pedro. Nay, if Cupid hath not spent all his quiver in Venice, thou wilt quake for this shortly.   270

Bene. I look for an earthquake too then.

Pedro. Well, you will temporize with the hours. In the mean time, good signior Benedick, repair to Leonato's ; commend me to him, and tell him, I will not fail him at supper ; for, indeed, he hath made great preparation.

Bene.

Bene. I have almost matter enough in me for such an embassage; and so I commit you—

Claud. To the tuition of God; from my house (if I had it),—   280

Pedro. The sixth of July; your loving friend, Bedick.

Bene. Nay, mock not, mock not: The body of your discourse is sometime guarded with fragments, and the guards are but slightly basted on neither: ere you flout old ends any further, examine your conscience; and so I leave you.   [*Exit.*

Claud. My liege, your highness now may do me good.   289

Pedro. My love is thine to teach; teach it but how,
And thou shalt see how apt it is to learn
Any hard lesson that may do thee good.

Claud. Hath Leonato any son, my lord?

Pedro. No child but Hero, she's his only heir:
Dost thou affect her Claudio?

Claud. O my lord,
When you went onward on this ended action,
I look'd upon her with a soldier's eye,
That lik'd, but had a rougher task in hand
Than to drive liking to the name of love: 300
But now I am return'd, and that war-thoughts
Have left their places vacant, in their rooms
Come thronging soft and delicate desires,
All prompting me how fair young Hero is,
Saying, I lik'd her ere I went to wars.

Pedro. Thou wilt be like a lover presently,

B i j   And

And tire the hearer with a book of words:
If thou dost love fair Hero, cherish it;
And I will break with her "and with her father, 309
" And thou shalt have her:" Was't not to this end,
That thou began'st to twist so fine a story?

 Claud. How sweetly do you minister to love,
That know love's grief by his complection!
But lest my liking might too sudden seem,
I would have salv'd it with a longer treatise.

 Pedro. What need the bridge much broader than
   the flood?
The fairest grant is the necessity:
Look, what will serve, is fit: 'tis once, thou lov'st;
And I will fit thee with the remedy.
I know we shall have revelling to night;   320
I will assume thy part in some disguise,
And tell fair Hero I am Claudio;
And in her bosom I'll unclasp my heart,
And take her hearing prisoner with the force
And strong encounter of my amorous tale:
Then, after, to her father will I break;
And, the conclusion is, she shall be thine:
In practice let us put it presently.   [*Exeunt.*

SCENE II.

" *A Room in* LEONATO'S *House. Enter* LEONATO *and*
ANTONIO.

 " *Leo.* How now, brother? Where is my cousin,
" your son? Hath he provided this musick?   330
:   " *Ant.*

Ant. He is very busy about it. But, brother, I
" can tell you news that you yet dream'd not of.

" *Leon.* Are they good ?

" *Ant.* As the event stamps them ; but they have
" a good cover, they show well outward. The prince
" and count Claudio, walking in a thick-pleached
" alley in my orchard, were thus overheard by a
" man of mine : The prince discover'd to Claudio,
" that he lov'd my niece your daughter, and meant
" to acknowledge it this evening in a dance ; nay,
" if he found her accordant, he meant to take the
" present time by the top, and instantly break with
" you of it.   343

" *Leon.* Hath the fellow any wit that told you
" this ?

" *Ant.* A good sharp fellow ; I will send for him,
" and question him yourself.

" *Leon.* No, no ; we will hold it as a dream, till it
" appear itself :—but I will acquaint my daughter
" withal, that she may be the better prepared for an
" answer, if peradventure this be true : Go you, and
" tell her of it. [*Several Servants cross the stage here.*]
" Cousin, you know what you have to do.—O, I
" cry you mercy, friend ; go you with me, and I will
" use your skill : Good cousin, have a care this busy
" time."   [*Exeunt.*

B iij

SCENE

SCENE III.

Another Apartment in Leonato's *House.* Enter *Don* John *and* Conrade.

Conr. What the good-jer, my lord! why are you thus out of measure sad?

John. There is no measure in the occasion that breeds it, therefore the sadness is without limit. 360

Conr. You should hear reason.

John. And when I have heard it, what blessing bringeth it?

Conr. If not a present remedy, yet a patient sufferance.

John. I wonder, that thou being (as thou say'st thou art) born under Saturn, goest about to apply a moral medicine to a mortifying mischief. I cannot hide what I am: I must be sad when I have cause, and smile at no man's jests; eat when I have stomach, and wait for no man's leisure; sleep when I am drowsy, and tend on no man's business; laugh when I am merry, and claw no man in his humour. 374

Conr. Yea, but you must not make the full show of this, till you may do it without controulment. You have of late stood out against your brother, and he hath ta'en you newly into his grace; where it is impossible you should take root, but by the fair weather that you make yourself: it is needful that you frame the season for your own harvest. 381

John.

John. I had rather be a canker in a hedge, than a rose in his grace; and it better fits my blood to be disdain'd of all, than to fashion a carriage to rob love from any: in this, though I cannot be said to be a flattering honest man, it must not be deny'd but I am a plain-dealing villain. I am trusted with a muzzle, and infranchised with a clog; therefore I have decreed not to sing in my cage: If I had my mouth, I would bite; if I had my liberty, I would do my liking: in the mean time, let me be that I am, and seek not to alter me. 393

Conr. Can you make no use of your discontent?

John. I make all use of it, for I use it only. Who comes here? what news, Borachio?

Enter BORACHIO.

Bora. I came yonder from a great supper; the prince, your brother, is royally entertain'd by Leonato; and I can give you intelligence of an intended marriage. 400

John. Will it serve for any model to build mischief on? What is he, for a fool, that betroths himself to unquietness?

Bora. Marry, it is your brother's right hand.

John. Who? the most exquisite Claudio?

Bora. Even he!

John. A proper squire! and who, and who? which way looks he?

Bora.

Bora. Marry, on Hero, the daughter and heir of Leonato.   410

John. A very forward March-chick! " How come " you to know this?

" *Bora.* Being entertain'd for a perfumer, as I was " smoaking a musty room, comes me the prince, " and Claudio, hand in hand, in sad conference: I " whipt me behind the arras; and there heard it " agreed upon, that the prince should woo Hero for " himself, and having obtained her, give her to " count Claudio.   419

" *John.*" Come, come, let us thither; this may prove food to my displeasure: that young start-up hath all the glory of my overthrow; if I can cross him any way, I bless myself every way: You are both sure, and will assist me.

Conr. To the death, my lord.

John. Let us to the great supper; their cheer is the greater, that I am subdu'd: 'Would the cook were of my mind!—" Shall we go prove what's to " be done?

" *Bora.* We'll wait upon your lordship."   430

[*Exeunt.*

ACT II. SCENE I.

A Hall in LEONATO'S *House.   Enter* LEONATO,
ANTONIO, HERO, BEATRICE, MARGARET, *and*
URSULA.

Leonato.

WAS not count John here at supper?

Ant. I saw him not.

Beat. How tartly that gentleman looks! I never
can see him, but I am heart-burn'd an hour after.

Hero. He is of a very melancholy disposition.

Beat. He were an excellent man, that were made
just in the mid-way between him and Benedick:
the one is too like an image, and says nothing; and
the other, too like my lady's eldest son, evermore
tattling.   10

Leon. Then half signior Benedick's tongue in
count John's mouth; and half count John's melancholy in signior Benedick's face,—

Beat. With a good leg, and a good foot, uncle,
and money enough in his purse, such a man would
win any woman in the world,—if he could get her
good will.

Leon. By my troth, niece, thou wilt never get thee
a husband, if thou be'st so shrewd of thy tongue.

" *Ant.* In faith, she's too curst.   20

" *Beat.* Too curst is more than curst: I shall lessen
" God's sending that way: for it is said, *God sends a*
" *curst cow short horns*; but to a cow too curst he
" sends none.

" *Leon.*

" *Leon.* So, by being too curst, God will send you
" no horns.

" *Beat.* Just, if he send me no husband;" for the
which blessing, I am at him upon my knees every
morning and evening: Lord! I could not endure a
husband with a beard on his face: I had rather lie in
woollen.   31

Leon. You may light upon a husband, that hath no
beard.

Beat. What should I do with him? dress him in
my apparel, and make him my waiting-gentlewoman?
He that hath a beard, is more than a youth; and he
that hath no beard, is less than a man: and he that
is more than a youth, is not for me; and he that is
less than a man, I am not for him: Therefore I will
even take six-pence in earnest of the bear-herd, and
lead his apes into hell.

Leon. Well, then, go you into hell?

Beat. No; but to the gate: and there will the devil meet me, like an old cuckold, with horns on his
head, and say, *Get you to heaven, Beatrice, get you to
heaven; here's no place for you maids:* so deliver I up
my apes, and away to saint Peter for the heavens;
" he shews me" where the bachelors sit, and there
live we as merry as the day is long.   49

Ant. Well, niece, I trust, you will be rul'd by
your father.   [*To Hero.*

Beat. Yes, faith; it is my cousin's duty to make
a curtsy, and say, *Father, as it please you:*—but yet
for all that, cousin, let him be a handsome fellow,

                                                            O

or else make another curtsy, and say, *Father, as it
please me.*

Leon. Well, niece, I hope to see you one day
fitted with a husband.   58

Beat. Not till God make men of some other metal
than earth. Would it not grieve a woman to be
over-master'd with a piece of valiant dust? to make
account of her life to a clod of wayward marle? No,
uncle, I'll none: Adam's sons are my brethren, and
truly, I hold it a sin to match in my kindred.

Leon. Daughter, remember what I told you: if
the prince do solicit you in that kind, you know your
answer.   67

Beat. The fault will be in the musick, cousin, if
you be not woo'd in good time: if the prince be too
important, tell him, there is measure in every thing,
and so dance out the answer. For hear me, Hero,
Wooing, wedding, and repenting, is as a Scotch jig,
a measure, and a cinque-pace: the first suit is hot
and hasty, like a Scotch jig, and full as fantastical;
the wedding, mannerly modest, as a measure full of
state and ancientry; and then comes repentance, and,
with his bad legs, falls into the cinque-pace faster
and faster, 'till he sink into his grave.

Leon. Cousin, you apprehend passing shrewdly.

Beat. I have a good eye, uncle; I can see a church
by day-light.   81

Leon. The revellers are entring; brother, make
good room.

Enter

Enter Don PEDRO, CLAUDIO, BENEDICK, BAL-
THAZAR; *Don* JOHN, BORACHIO, MARGARET,
URSULA, *and others mask'd.*

Pedro. Lady, will you walk about with your
friend?

Hero. So you walk softly, and look sweetly, and
say nothing, I am yours for the walk; and, especially, when I walk away.

Pedro. With me in your company?

Hero. I may say so, when I please.   60

Pedro. And when please you to say so?

Hero. When I like your favour; for God defend,
the lute should be like the case!

Pedro. My visor is Philemon's roof; within the
house is Jove.

Hero. Why, then your visor should be thatch'd.

Pedro. Speak low, if you speak love.

Balth. Well, I would you did like me.

Marg. So would not I, for your own sake; for I
have many ill qualities.   100

Balth. Which is one?

Marg. I say my prayers aloud.

Balth. I love you the better; the hearers may cry
amen.

Marg. God match me with a good dancer!

Balth. Amen.

Marg. And God keep him out of my sight when
the dance is done!—Answer, clerk.

Balth.

Balth. No more words; the clerk is answer'd.

" *Urs.* I know you well enough; you are Signior " Antonio.   111

" *Ant.* At a word I am not.

" *Urs.* I know you by the wagling of your head.

" *Ant.* To tell you true I counterfeit him.

" *Urs.* You could never do him so ill-well, unless " you were the very man; Here's his dry hand up " and down; you are he, you are he.

" *Ant.* At a word, I am not.

" *Urs.* Come, come; do you think, I do not know " you by your excellent wit? Can virtue hide itself? " Go to, mum, you are he: graces will appear, and " there's an end."   122

Beat. Will you not tell me who told you so?

Bene. No, you shall pardon me.

Beat. Nor will you not tell me who you are?

Bene. Not now.

Beat. That I was disdainful—and that I had my good wit out of the *Hundred merry Tales*;—Well, this was signior Benedick that said so.

Bene. What's he?   130

Beat. I am sure, you know him well enough.

Bene. Not I, believe me.

Beat. Did he never make you laugh?

Bene. I pray you, what is he?

Beat. Why, he is the prince's jester: a very dull fool; only his gift is in devising impossible slanders: none but libertines delight in him; and the commendation is not in his wit, but in his villainy; for he

C

both

both pleaseth men, and angers them, and then they laugh at him, and beat him : I am sure, he is in the fleet; I would he had boarded me.   141

Bene. When I know the gentleman, I'll tell him what you say.

Beat. Do, do : he'll but break a comparison or two on me; which, peradventure, not mark'd, or not laugh'd at, strikes him into melancholy; and then there's a partridge wing sav'd, for the fool will eat no supper that night.   We must follow the leaders.

[Music within.

Bene. In every good thing.

Beat. Nay, if they lead to any ill, I will leave them at the next turning.   131

Manent JOHN, BORACHIO, *and* CLAUDIO.

John. Sure, my brother is amorous on Hero, and hath withdrawn her father to break with him about it : The ladies follow her, and but one visor remains.

Bora. And that is Claudio : I know him by his bearing.

John. Are you not signior Benedick?

Claud. You know me well; I am he.   159

John. Signior, you are very near my brother in his love : he is enamour'd on Hero ; I pray you, dissuade him from her, she is no equal for his birth : you may do the part of an honest man in it.

Claud. How know you he loves her?

John. I heard him swear his affection.

4

Bora.

Bora. So did I too; and he swore he would marry her to night.

John. Come let us to the banquet.

[*Exeunt* JOHN *and* BORA.

Claud. Thus answer I in name of Benedick,   169
But hear these ill news with the ears of Claudio.—
'Tis certain so:—The prince wooes for himself.
Friendship is constant in all other things,
Save in the office and affairs of love:
Therefore, all hearts in love use their own tongues:
Let ev'ry eye negotiate for itself,
And trust no agent: for beauty is a witch,
Against whose charms faith melteth into blood.
This is an accident of hourly proof,
Which I mistrusted not: Farewel, therefore, Hero.

Re-enter BENEDICK.

Bene. Count Claudio?
Claud. Yea, the same.   180
Bene. Come, will you go with me?
Claud. Whither?
Bene. Even to the next willow, about your own business, count. What fashion will you wear the garland of? About your neck, like an usurer's chain? or under your arm, like a lieutenant's scarf? You must wear it one way, for the prince hath got your Hero.

Claud. I wish him joy of her.   189
Bene. Why, that's spoken like an honest drover;

so they sell bullocks. But did you think, the prince would have served you thus?

Claud. I pray you leave me.

. *Bene.* Ho! now you strike like the blind man; 'twas the boy that stole your meat, and you'll beat the post.

Claud. If it will not be, I'll leave you.   [*Exit.*

Bene. Alas, poor hurt fowl! Now will he creep into sedges.——But, that my lady Beatrice should know me, and not know me! The prince's fool!— Ha? it may be, I go under that title, because I am merry.—Yea; but so; I am apt to do myself wrong: I am not so reputed: it is the base, though bitter disposition of Beatrice, that puts the world into her person, and so gives me out. Well, I'll be reveng'd as I may.

Re-enter Don PEDRO.

Pedro. Now, Signior, where's the Count? Did you see him?

Bene. Troth, my lord, I have play'd the part of lady Fame. I found him here as melancholy as a lodge in a warren; I told him, and, I think, I told him true, that your grace had got the good will of this young lady; and I offered him my company to a willow tree, either to make him a garland, as being forsaken, or to bind him up a rod, as being worthy to be whipt.

Pedro. To be whipt! What's his fault?

Bene.

Bene. The flat transgression of a school-boy ; who, being overjoy'd with finding a bird's nest, shews it his companion, and he steals it.   220

Pedro. Wilt thou make a trust a transgression? The transgression is in the stealer.

Bene. Yet it had not been amiss, the rod had been made, and the garland too; for the garland he might have worn himself; and the rod he might have bestow'd on you, who, as I take it, have stol'n his bird's nest.

Pedro. I will but teach them to sing, and restore them to the owner.   229

Bene. If their singing answer your saying, by my faith, you say honestly.

Pedro. The lady Beatrice hath a quarrel to you ; the gentleman, that danc'd with her, told her, she is much wrong'd by you.   234

Bene. O, she misus'd me past the endurance of a block; an oak, but with one green leaf on it, would have answer'd her; my very visor began to assume life, and scold with her: She told me, not thinking I had been myself, that I was the prince's jester; and that I was duller than a great thaw; huddling jest upon jest, with such impossible conveyance, upon me, that I stood like a man at a mark, with a whole army shooting at me: She speaks poniards, and every word stabs: if her breath were as terrible as her terminations, there were no living near her; she would infect to the north star. I would not marry her, though she were endowed with all that Adam had

C iij

left

left him before he transgress'd : she would have made Hercules have turn'd spit ; yea, and have cleft his club to make the fire too. " Come, talk not of her ; " you shall find her the infernal Até in good apparel." I would to God, some scholar would conjure her : for, certainly, while she is here, a man may live as quiet in hell, as in a sanctuary ; and people sin upon purpose, because they would go thither : so, indeed, all disquiet, horror, and perturbation follow her.   257

Enter CLAUDIO, BEATRICE, LEONATO, *and* HERO.

Pedro. Look, here she comes.

Bene. Will your grace command me any service to the world's end ? I will go on the slightest errand now to the Antipodes, that you can devise to send me on ; I will fetch you a tooth-picker now from the farthest inch of Asia ; bring you the length of prester John's foot ; fetch you a hair off the great Cham's beard ; do you any embassage to the Pigmies, rather than hold three words conference with this harpy : You have no employment for me ?   267

Pedro. None but to desire your good company.

Bene. O God, sir, here's a dish I love not ; I cannot endure my lady's Tongue.   270

Pedro. Come, lady, come ; you have lost the heart of signior Benedick.

" *Beat.* Indeed, my lord, he lent it me awhile ; and " I gave him use for it, a double heart for a single " one : marry, once before he won it of me with false
                                                        " dice,

" dice, therefore your grace may well say, I have
" lost it.

" *Pedro.*" You have put him down, lady, you
have put him down.   -

Beat. So I would not he should do me, my lord,
lest I should prove the mother of fools. I have
brought count Claudio, whom you sent me to
seek.   283

Pedro. Why, how now, count? wherefore are you
sad ?

Claud. Not sad, my lord.

Pedro. How then ? Sick ?

Claud. Neither, my lord.

Beat. The count is neither sad, nor sick, nor merry, nor well : but civil, count; civil as an orange,
and something of that jealous complection.   291

Pedro. I'faith, lady, I think your blazon to be,
true; though, I'll be sworn, if he be so, his conceit
is false. Here, Claudio, I have wooed in thy name,
and fair Hero is won ; I have broke with her father,
and his good will obtained : name the day of marriage, and God give thee joy !

Leon. Count, take of me my daughter, and with
her my fortunes : his grace hath made the match,
and all grace say amen to it !   300

Beat. Speak, count, 'tis your cue.

Claud. Silence is the perfectest herald of joy : I
were but little happy, if I could say how much.—
Lady, as you are mine, I am yours : I give away
myself for you, and doat upon the exchange.

3

Bene.

Beat. Speak, cousin ; or, if you cannot, stop his mouth with a kiss, and let him not speak neither.

Pedro. In faith, lady, you have a merry heart.

Beat. Yea, my lord ; I thank it, poor fool, it keeps on the windy side of care:—My cousin tells him in his ear, that he is in her heart.   312

Claud. And so she doth, cousin.

Beat. Good lord, for alliance!—Thus goes every one to the world but I, and I am sun-burn'd ; I may sit in a corner, and cry heigh ho! for a husband.

Pedro. Lady Beatrice, I will get you one.   318

Beat. I would rather have one of your father's getting : Hath your grace ne'er a brother like you ? Your father got excellent husbands, if a maid could come by them.

Pedro. Will you have me, lady ?

Beat. No, my lord, unless I might have another for working days ; your grace is too costly to wear every day :—But, I beseech your grace, pardon me ; I was born to speak all mirth, and no matter.

Pedro. Your silence most offends me, and to be merry best becomes you ; for, out of question, you were born in a merry hour.   330

Beat. No, sure, my lord, my mother cry'd ; but then there was a star danc'd, and under that I was born.—Cousins, God give you joy.

Leon. Niece, will you look to those things I told you of ?

Beat.

Beat. I cry you mercy, uncle.—By your grace's
pardon.   [*Exit Beatrice.*

Pedro. By my troth, a pleasant-spirited lady. 338

" *Leon.* There's little of the melancholy element in
" her, my lord: she is never sad, but when she
" sleeps: and not ever sad then; for I have heard
" my daughter say, she hath often dream'd of un-
" happiness, and wak'd herself with laughing.

" *Pedro.* She cannot endure to hear tell of a hus-
" band.

" *Leon.* O, by no means; she mocks all her
" wooers out of suit.

" *Pedro.* She were an excellent wife for Benedick.

" *Leon.* O Lord, my lord, if they were but a week
" marry'd, they would talk themselves mad.

" *Pedro.*" Count Claudio, when mean you to go
to church ?   .   352

Claud. To-morrow, my lord: Time goes on
crutches, till love have all his rites.

Leon. Not till Monday, my dear son, " which is
" hence a just seven-night;" and a time too brief
too, to have all things answer my mind.

Pedro. Come, you shake the head at so long a
breathing; but, I warrant thee, Claudio, the time
shall not go dully by us : I will, in the interim, undertake one of Hercules' labours; which is, to bring
signior Benedick, and the lady Beatrice, into a mountain of affection, the one with the other. I would
fain have it a match; and I doubt not to fashion it,

                                                   if

if you three will but minister such assistance as I shall give you direction.

Leon. My lord, I am for you, though it cost me ten nights watchings.

Claud. And I, my lord.

Pedro. And you too, gentle Hero?   370

Hero. I will do any modest office, my lord, to help my cousin to a good husband.

Pedro. And Benedick is not the unhopefullest husband that I know: thus far I can praise him; he is of a noble strain, of approv'd valour, and confirm'd honesty. I will teach you how to humour your cousin, that she shall fall in love with Benedick:—and I, with your two helps, will so practise on Benedick, that, in despight of his quick wit and his queasy stomach, he shall fall in love with Beatrice. If we can do this, Cupid is no longer an archer; his glory shall be ours, for we are the only love-gods. Go in with me, and I will tell you my drift.   [*Exeunt.*

SCENE II.

Another Apartment in LEONATO'S *House. Enter Don* JOHN *and* BORACHIO.

John. It is so; the count Claudio shall marry the daughter of Leonato.   385

Bora. Yea, my lord; but I can cross it.

                                   John.

John. Any bar, any cross, any impediment will be medicinal to me : I am sick in displeasure to him ; and whatsoever comes athwart his affection, ranges evenly with mine. How canst thou cross this marriage ?   391

Bora. Not honestly, my lord ; but so covertly that no dishonesty shall appear in me.

John. Shew me briefly how.

Bora. I think, I told your lordship, a year since, how much I am in the favour of Margaret, the waiting gentlewoman to Hero.

John. I remember.

Bora. I can, at any unseasonable instant of the night, appoint her to look out at her lady's chamber-window.   401

John. What life is in that, to be the death of this marriage ?

Bora. The poison of that lies in you to temper. Go you to the prince your brother ; spare not to tell him, that he hath wrong'd his honour in marrying the renown'd Claudio, (whose estimation do you mightily hold up) to a contaminated stale, such a one as Hero.   406

John. What proof shall I make of that ?

Bora. Proof enough to misuse the prince, to vex Claudio, to undo Hero, and kill Leonato : Look you for any other issue ?

John. Only to despite them, I will endeavour any thing.   415

Bora.

Bora. Go then, find me a meet hour to draw Don Pedro, and the count Claudio, alone : tell them that you know, Hero loves me; intend a kind of zeal both to the prince and Claudio, as—in a love of your brother's honour who hath made this match; and his friend's reputation, who is thus like to be cozen'd with the semblance of a maid,—that you have discover'd thus. They will scarcely believe this without trial: offer them instances; which shall bear no less likelihood, than to see me at her chamber window; hear me call Margaret, Hero; hear Margaret term me Claudio; and bring them to see this, the very night before the intended wedding: for, in the mean time, I will so fashion the matter, that Hero shall be absent; and there shall appear such seeming truth of Hero's disloyalty, that jealousy shall be call'd assurance, and all the preparation overthrown.

John. Grow this to what adverse issue it can, I will put it in practice: Be cunning in the working this, and thy fee is a thousand ducats.

Bora. Be thou constant in the accusation, and my cunning shall not shame me.

John. I will presently go learn their day of marriage.   [*Exeunt.*   440

<hr>

SCENE III.

LEONATO'S *Orchard. Enter* BENEDICK *" and a Boy."*

" *Bene.* Boy,—

" *Boy.* Signior.

" *Bene.* In my chamber-window lies a book; bring
" it hither to me in the orchard.

" *Boy.* I am here already, sir." 445

Bene. " I know that ;—but I would have thee
" hence, and here again. [*Exit Boy.*]"—I do much
wonder, that one man, seeing how much another
man is a fool when he dedicates his behaviours to love,
will, after he hath laugh'd at such shallow follies in
others, become the argument of his own scorn, by
falling in love : And such a man is Claudio. I have
known, when there was no musick with him but the
drum and the fife ; and now had he rather hear the
tabor and the pipe : I have known, when he would
have walk'd ten mile afoot, to see a good armour;
and now will he lye ten nights awake, carving the
fashion of a new doublet. He was wont to speak
plain, and to the purpose, like an honest man, and
a soldier : and now is he turn'd orthographer ; his
words are a very fantastical banquet, just so many
strange dishes. May I be so converted, and see with
these eyes ? I cannot tell ; I think not : I will not be
sworn, but love may transform me to an oyster ; but
I'll take my oath on it, till he have made an oyster

of

of me, he shall never make me such a fool. One
woman is fair; yet I am well: another is wise; yet
I am well: another virtuous; yet I am well: but till
all graces be in one woman, one woman shall not
come in my grace. Rich she shall be, that's certain;
wise, or I'll none; virtuous, or I'll never cheapen
her; fair, or I'il never look on her; mild, or come
not near me; noble, or not I for an angel; of
good discourse, an excellent musician, and her hair
shall be of what colour it please God. Ha! the prince
and monsieur Love! I will hide me in the ar-
bour.   [*Withdraws*.

Enter Don PEDRO, LEONATO, CLAUDIO, *and* BAL-
THAZAR.

Pedro. Come, shall we hear this musick?   4-8

Claud. Yea, my good lord :—how still the evening is,
As hush'd on purpose to grace harmony!

Pedro. See you where Benedick hath hid himself?

" *Claud.* O very well, my lord: the music ended,
" We'll fit the kid-fox with a penny-worth.

" *Pedro.*" Come, Balthazar, we'll hear that song
again.

Balth. O good my lord, tax not so bad a voice
To slander musick any more than once.

Pedro. It is the witness still of excellency,
To put a strange face on his own perfection :—
I pray thee sing, and let me woo no more.   490

" *Balth.* Because you talk of wooing, I will sing:
" Since many a wooer doth commence his suit
" To her he thinks not worthy; yet he wooes;

                                          " Yet

" Yet will he swear, he loves.

 " *Pedro.* Nay, pray thee, come :

" Or, if thou wilt hold longer argument,

" Do it in notes.

 " *Balth.* Note this before my notes,

" There's not a note of mine, that's worth the
   noting.   500

 " *Pedro.* Why these are very crotchets that he
   speaks ;

" Note, notes, forsooth, and noting !"

 Bene. Now, *Divine air !* now is his soul ravish'd !—
Is it not strange, that sheeps guts should hale souls
out of men's bodies ?—Well, a horn for my money,
when all's done.

S O N G.

Sigh no more, ladies, sigh no more,
 Men were deceivers ever ;
One foot in sea, and one on shore ;
 To one thing constant never :
  Then sigh not so,
  But let them go,
And be you blith and bonny ;
Converting all your sounds of woe
 Into, Hey nonny, nonny.   515
Sing no more ditties, sing no mo
 Of dumps so dull and heavy ;
The frauds of men were ever so,
 Since summer first was leavy.
  Then sigh not so, &c.

D ij

Pedro.

Pedro. By my troth, a good song.

Balth. And an ill singer, my lord.

" *Pedro.* Ha? no; no, faith; thou sing'st well
" enough for a shift."

Bene. [*Aside.*] An he had been a dog, that should
have howl'd thus, they would have hang'd him : and,
I pray God, his bad voice bode no mischief! I had
as lief have heard the night-raven, " come what
plague could have come after it."   530

Pedro. " Yea, marry ;"—Dost thou hear, Balthazar? I pray thee, get us some excellent musick; for
to-morrow night we would have it at the lady Hero's
chamber-window.

Balth. The best I can, my lord.

[Exit BALTHAZAR.

Pedro. Do so : farewel. Come hither, Leonato;
What was it you told me of to-day, that your niece
Beatrice was in love with signior Benedick?

Claud. O, ay ;—Stalk on, stalk on, the fowl sits.
[*Aside to Pedro.*] I did never think that lady would
have loved any man.   541

Leon. No, nor I neither; but most wonderful,
that she should so dote· on signior Benedick, whom
she hath in all outward behaviours seem'd ever to
abhor.

Bene. Is't possible? Sits the wind in that corner?

[*Aside.*

Leon. By my troth, my lord, I cannot tell what to
think of it, but that she loves him with an enraged
affection :—it is past the infinite of thought.

Pedro.

Pedro. May be, she doth but counterfeit.   550

Claud. Faith, like enough.

Leon. O God! counterfeit! There never was counterfeit of passion came so near the life of passion, as she discovers it.

Pedro. Why, what effects of passion shews she?

Claud. Bait the hook well: this fish will bite.

             [*Aside.*

Leon. What effects, my lord! She will sit you,—You heard my daughter tell you how.

Claud. She did, indeed.

Pedro. How, how, I pray you? You amaze me: I would have thought her spirit had been invincible against all assaults of affection.   560

Leon. I would have sworn it had, my lord; especially against Benedick.

Bene. [*Aside.*] I should think this a gull, but that the white-bearded fellow speaks it: knavery cannot, sure, hide himself in such reverence.

Claud. He hath ta'en the infection; hold it up.

             [*Aside.*

Pedro. Hath she made her affection known to Benedick?   570

Leon. No; and swears she never will: that's her torment.

" *Claud.* 'Tis true, indeed; so your daughter
" says: *Shall I,* says she, *that have so oft encounter'd*
" *him with scorn, write to him that I love him?*

" *Leon.* This says she now when she is beginning
" to write to him: for she'll be up twenty times a
      D i i j   " night;

" night; and there she will sit in her smock, 'till
" she have writ a sheet of paper :—my daughter
" tells us all.   580

" *Claud.* Now you talk of a sheet of paper, I re-
" member a pretty jest your daughter told us of.

" *Leon.* Oh,—When she had writ it, and was
" reading it over, she found Benedick and Beatrice
" between the sheet ?—

" *Claud.* That.

" *Leon.* O, she tore the letter into a thousand half-
" pence ; rail'd at herself, that she should be so
" immodest to write to one that she knew would flout
" her : *I measure him*, says she, *by my own spirit; for,*
" *I should flout him, if he writ to me ; yea, though I love*
" *him, I should,*   592

" *Claud.* Then down upon her knees she falls,
" weeps, sobs, beats her heart, tears her hair, prays,
" curses ;—*O sweet Benedick ! God give me patience.*

" *Leon.* She doth indeed ; my daughter says so :"
and the ecstacy hath so much overborne her, that my
daughter is sometime afraid she will do desperate
outrage to herself; " It is very true."

Pedro. It were good, that Benedick knew of it by
some other, if she will not discover it,   601

" *Claud.* To what end ? He would but make a
" sport of it, and torment the poor lady worse.

" *Pedro.* An he should, it were an alms to hang
" him : She's an excellent sweet lady ; and, out of
" all suspicion, she is virtuous.

" *Claud.* And she is exceeding wise,

                                   " *Pedro.*

" *Pedro.* In every thing, but in loving Bene-
" dick.

" *Leon.* O my lord, wisdom and blood combating
" in so tender a body, we have ten proofs to one,
" that blood hath the victory. I am sorry for her, as
" I have just cause, being her uncle and her guardian.

" *Pedro.* I would, she had bestowed this dotage on
" me; I would have daff'd all other respects, and
" made her half myself:" I pray you tell Benedick
of it, and hear what he will say.

Leon. Were it good, think you?   618

" *Claud.* Hero thinks surely, she will die : for she
" says, she will die if he love her not; and she will
" die ere she make her love known; and she will die
" if he woo her, rather than she will bate one breath
" of her accustom'd crossness."   623

Pedro. " She doth well : if she should make tender
" of her love," 'tis very possible, he'll scorn it; for
the man, as you know all, hath a contemptible
spirit.

" *Claud.* He is a very proper man.

" *Pedro.* He hath, indeed, a good outward happi-
" ness.

" *Claud.* 'Fore God, and in my mind, very wise.

" *Pedro.* He doth, indeed, shew some sparks that
" are like wit,   633

" *Leon.* And I take him to be valiant.

" *Pedro.* As Hector, I assure you : and in the
" managing of quarrels you may say he is wise; for
                    3   " either

" either he avoids them with great discretion, or
" undertakes them with a christian-like fear. .

 " *Leon.* If he do fear God, he must necessarily
" keep peace ; if he break the peace, he ought to
" enter into a quarrel with fear and trembling.

 " *Pedro.* And so will he do ; for the man doth
" fear God, howsoever it seems not in him, by some
" large jests he will make.   Well, I am sorry for
" your niece : Shall we go seek Benedick, and tell
" him of her love ?"   646

Claud. Never tell him, my lord ; let her wear it
out with good counsel.

Leon. Nay, that's impossible ; she may wear her
heart out first.

Pedro. Well, we will hear further of it by your
daughter ; let it cool the while.   I love Benedick
well ; and I could wish he would modestly examine
himself, to see how much he is unworthy to have so
good a lady.   655

Leon. My lord, will you walk ? dinner is ready.

Claud. If he do not dote on her upon this, I will
never trust my expectation.   [*Aside.*

Pedro. Let there be the same net spread for her,
and that must your daughter and her gentlewoman
carry.   The sport will be, when they hold an opinion
of one another's dotage, and no such matter ; that's
the scene that I would see, " which will be merely
" a dumb show." Let us send her to call him to
dinner.   [*Aside*] [*Exeunt.*

BENEDICK.

BENEDICK *advances from the arbour.*

Bene. This can be no trick : The conference was sadly borne.—They have the truth of this from Hero. They seem to pity the lady; it seems, her affections have the full bent. Love me! why, it must be requited. I hear how I am censur'd : they say, I will bear myself proudly, if I perceive the love come from her; they say too, that she will rather die than give any sign of affection.—I did never think to marry :—I must not seem proud :—happy are they that hear their detractions, and can put them to mending. They say, the lady is fair; 'tis a truth, I can bear them witness : and virtuous;—'tis so, I cannot reprove it : and wise—but for loving me :—By my troth it is no addition to her wit ;—nor no great argument of her folly, for I will be horribly in love with her.—I may chance have some odd quirks and remnants of wit broken on me, because I have rail'd so long against marriage : But doth not the appetite alter ? A man loves the meat in his youth, that he cannot endure in his age :—Shall quips, and sentences, and these paper bullets of the brain, awe a man from the career of his humour ? No : the world must be peopled. When I said, I would die a bachelor, I did not think I should live till I were marry'd.—Here comes Beatrice : By this day, she's a fair lady : I do spy some marks of love in her. 691

Enter

Enter BEATRICE.

Beat. Against my will, I am sent to bid you come in to dinner.

Bene. Fair Beatrice, I thank you for your pains.

Beat. I took no more pains for those thanks, than you take pains to thank me; if it had been painful, I would not have come.

Bene. You take pleasure then in the message? 699

Beat. Yea, just as much as you may take upon a knife's point, and choak a daw withal :—You have no stomach, signior; fare you well.   [*Exit.*

Bene. Ha! *Against my will I am sent to bid you come in to dinner*—there's a double meaning in that. *I took no more pains for those thanks, than you take pains to thank me*—that's as much as to say, Any pains that I take for you is as easy as thanks :—If I do not take pity of her, I am a villain; if I do not love her, I am a Jew : I will go get her picture.   [*Exit.* 709

ACT III. SCENE I.

Continues in the Orchard.   Enter HERO, MARGARET, *and* URSULA.

Hero.

GOOD Margaret, run thee into the parlour;
There shalt thou find my cousin Beatrice
" Proposing with the prince and Claudio:"

Whisper

Whisper her ear, and tell her, I and Ursula
Walk in the orchard, and our whole discourse
Is all of her; say, that thou overheard'st us;
And bid her steal into the pleached bower,
" Where honey-suckles, ripen'd by the sun,
" Forbid the sun to enter;—like favourites,
" Made proud by princes, that advance their pride   10
" Against that power that bred it:—there will she hide her,"
To listen our purpose: This is thy office,
Bear thee well in it, and leave us alone.

Marg. I'll make her come, I warrant you, presently.   [*Exit.*

Hero. Now, Ursula, when Beatrice doth come,
As we do trace this alley up and down,
Our talk must only be of Benedick:
When I do name him, let it be thy part
To praise him more than ever man did merit: 20
My talk to thee must be, how Benedick
Is sick in love with Beatrice: Of this matter
Is little Cupid's crafty arrow made,
That only wounds by hear-say. Now begin.

Enter BEATRICE, *behind.*

For look where Beatrice, like a lapwing, runs
Close by the ground, to hear our conference.

Urs. The pleasant'st angling is to see the fish
Cut with her golden oars the silver stream,
And greedily devour the treacherous bait:

So angle we for Beatrice; who even now   30
Is couched in the woodbine coverture :
Fear you not my part of the dialogue.

Hero. Then go we near her, that her ear lose nothing
Of the false sweet bait that we lay for it.—

      [*They advance to the bower.*

No, truly, Ursula, she is too disdainful;
I know, her spirits are as coy and wild
As haggards of the rock.

 Urs. But are you sure,
That Benedick loves Beatrice so entirely?

 Hero. So says the prince, and my new-trothed
  lord.   40
 " *Urs.* And did they bid you tell her of it, madam ?
 " *Hero.*" They did intreat me to acquaint her
  of it :
But I persuaded them, if they lov'd Benedick,
To wish him wrestle with affection,
And never to let Beatrice know of it.

 Urs. Why did you so ? Doth not the gentleman
Deserve as full, as fortunate a bed,
As ever Beatrice shall couch upon ?

 Hero. O God of love! I know, he doth deserve
As much as may be yielded to a man :   50
But nature never fram'd a woman's heart
Of prouder stuff than that of Beatrice ;
Disdain and scorn ride sparkling in her eyes,
Misprising what they look on ; and her wit
Values itself so highly, that to her

         All

All matter else seems weak: she cannot love,
Nor take no shape nor project of affection,
She is so self-endeared.
   Urs. Sure, I think so;
And therefore, certainly, it were not good   60
She knew his love, lest she make sport at it.
   Hero. Why, you speak truth: I never yet saw man,
How wise, how noble, young, how rarely featur'd,
But she would spell him backward: if fair-fac'd,
She'd swear, the gentleman should be her sister;
If black, why, nature, drawing of an antick,
Made a foul blot: if tall, a lance ill-headed;
If low, an aglet very vilely cut:
If speaking, why, a vane blown with all winds;
If silent, why, a block moved with none.   70
So turns she every man the wrong side out;
And never gives to truth and virtue, that
Which simpleness and merit purchaseth.
   Urs. Sure, sure, such carping is not commendable.
   Hero. "No; not to be so odd, and from all fashions,
" As Beatrice is, cannot be commendable:"
But who dare tell her so? If I should speak,
She'd mock me into air; O, she would laugh me
Out of myself, press me to death with wit.
Therefore let Benedick, like cover'd fire,   80
Consume away in sighs, waste inwardly:
It were a better death than die with mocks;
" Which is as bad as die with tickling."

E

Urs.

Urs. Yet tell her of it ; hear what she will say.

Hero. No ; rather I will go to Benedick,
And counsel him to fight against his passion :
And, truly, I'll devise some honest slanders
To stain my cousin with ; one doth not know,
How much an ill word may empoison liking.

Urs. O, do not do your cousin such a wrong. 90
She cannot be so much without true judgment,
(Having so swift and excellent a wit,
As she is priz'd to have) as to refuse
So rare a gentleman as signior Benedick.
" *Hero.* He is the only man of Italy,
" Always excepted my dear Claudio.
" *Urs.* I pray you, be not angry with me, madam,
" Speaking my fancy ; signior Benedick,
" For shape, for bearing, argument and valour,
" Goes foremost in report through Italy."   100
Hero. Indeed, he hath an excellent good name.
Urs. His excellence did earn it, ere he had it.—
When are you marry'd, madam ?
Hero. Why, every day ;—to-morrow : Come, go
          in,
I'll shew thee some attires : and have thy counsel,
Which is the best to furnish me to-morrow.
Urs. She's lim'd, I warrant you ; we have caught
          her, madam.
Hero. If it prove so, then loving goes by haps :
Some Cupid kills with arrows, some with traps. 109
          [*Exeunt.*

                              BEATRICE

BEATRICE *advancing.*

Beat. What fire is in mine ears? Can this be true?
    Stand I condemn'd for pride and scorn so
        much?
Contempt, farewel! and maiden pride, adieu!
    No glory lives behind the back of such.
And, Benedick, love on, I will requite thee;
    Taming my wild heart to thy loving hand;
If thou dost love, my kindness shall incite thee
    To bind our loves up in a holy band:
For others say, thou dost deserve; and I
Believe it better than reportingly.   [*Exit.*

SCENE II.

LEONATO's *House.   Enter Don* PEDRO, CLAUDIO,
        BENEDICK, *and* LEONATO.

Pedro. I do but stay till your marriage be con-
summate, and then go I toward Arragon.   121

Claud. I'll bring you thither, my lord, if you'll
vouchsafe me.

Pedro. Nay, " that would be as great a soil in the
" new gloss of your marriage, as to shew a child his
" new coat, and forbid him to wear it."   I will only
be bold with Benedick for his company; for, from
the crown of his head to the sole of his foot, he is all
mirth; he hath twice or thrice cut Cupid's bow-
string, and the little hangman dare not shoot at him:

he hath a heart as sound as a bell, and his tongue is
the clapper; for what his heart thinks, his tongue
speaks.   133

Bene. Gallants, I am not as I have been.

Leon. So say I; methinks, you are sadder.

Claud. I hope, he be in love.

Pedro. Hang him, truant; there's no true drop
of blood in him, to be truly touch'd with love: if
he be sad, he wants money.

Bene. I have the tooth-ach.   140

Pedro. Draw it.

Bene. Hang it.

" *Claud.* You must hang it first, and draw it after-
" wards."

Pedro. What? sigh for the tooth-ach?

Leon. Where is but a humour, or a worm?

Bene. Well, Every one can master a grief, but he
that has it.

Claud. Yet say I, he is in love.   149

" *Pedro.* There is no appearance of fancy in him,
" unless it be a fancy that he hath to strange disguises;
" as to be a Dutch man to-day; a French man to-
" morrow; or in the shape of two countries at once;
" as a German from the waist downward, all slops;
" and a Spaniard from the hip upward, no doublet:
" Unless he have a fancy to this foolery, as it appears
" he hath, he is no fool for fancy, as you would
" have it to appear he is.

" *Claud,*" If he be not in love with some woman,
                                                    there

there is no believing old signs : he brushes his hat o'
mornings : What should that bode?   161

" *Pedro.* Hath any man seen him at the barber's?

" *Claud.* No, but the barber's man hath been seen
" with him ; and the old ornament of his cheek hath
" already stuff'd tennis-balls.

" *Leon.* Indeed, he looks younger than he did, by
" the loss of a beard."

Pedro. Nay, he rubs himself with civet : Can you
smell him out by that?

Claud. That's as much as to say, The sweet youth's
in love.   171

Pedro. The greatest note of it, is his melancholy.

." *Claud.* And when was he wont to wash his face?

" *Pedro.* Yea, or to paint himself? for the which,
" I hear, what they say of him."

Claud. Nay, but his jesting spirit ; which is now
crept into a lute-string, " and now govern'd by
" stops."

Pedro. Indeed, that tells a heavy tale for him :
Conclude, conclude he is in love.   180

Claud. Nay, but I know who loves him.

Pedro. That would I know too ; I warrant, one
that knows him not.

Claud. Yes, and his ill conditions ; and, in despight
of all, dies for him.

Pedro. She shall be buried with her face upwards.

Bene. Yet is this no charm for the tooth-ach.—Old
signior, walk aside with me ; I have studied eight

or nine wise words to speak to you, which these
hobby-horses must not hear.   190
      [*Exeunt* BENEDICK *and* LEONATO.

Pedro. For my life, to break with him about
Beatrice.

Claud. 'Tis even so: Hero and Margaret have by
this time play'd their parts with Beatrice; and then
the two bears will not bite one another, when
they meet.

Enter Don JOHN.

John. My lord and brother, God save you.

Pedro. Good den, brother.

John. If your leisure serv'd, I would speak with
you.   200

Pedro. In private?

John. If it please you:—yet count Claudio may
hear; for what I would speak of, concerns him.

Pedro. What's the matter?

John. Means your lordship to be marry'd to-morrow?   [*To* CLAUDIO.

Pedro. You know, he does.

John. I know not that, when he knows what I
know.

Claud. If there be any impediment, I pray you,
discover it.   211

John. You may think, I love you not; let that
appear hereafter, and aim better at me by that I now
will manifest: For my brother, I think, he holds you
well; and in dearness of heart hath holp to effect
             your

your ensuing marriage: surely, suit ill-spent, and labour ill-bestow'd!

Pedro. Why, what's the matter?

John. I came hither to tell you, and circumstances shorten'd (for she hath been too long a talking of), the lady is disloyal.   221

Claud. Who? Hero?

John. Even she; Leonato's Hero, your Hero, every man's Hero.

Claud. Disloyal?

John. The word is too good to paint out her wickedness; I could say, she were worse; think you of a worse title, and I will fit her to it. Wonder not till further warrant: go but with me to-night, you shall see her chamber-window enter'd; even the night before her wedding-day: if you love her then, to-morrow wed her; but it would better fit your honour to change your mind.   233

Claud. May this be so?

Pedro. I will not think it.—

John. If you dare not trust that you see, confess not that you know: If you will follow me, I will shew you enough: and when you have seen more, and heard more, proceed accordingly.   239

Claud. If I see any thing to-night why I should not marry her; to-morrow, in the congregation, where I should wed, there will I shame her.

Pedro. And, as I wooed for thee to obtain her, I will join with thee to disgrace her.

John. I will disparage her no farther, till you are

my

my witnesses: bear it coldly but till midnight, and let the issue shew itself.

" *Pedro.* O day untowardly turned!

" *Claud.* O mischief strangely thwarting!

" *John.* O plague right well prevented!   250

" So you will say, when you have seen the sequel."

[*Exeunt.*

SCENE III.

The Street.   Enter DOGBERRY *and* VERGES, *with the Watch.*

Dogb. Are you good men and true?

Verg. Yea, or else it were pity but they should suffer salvation, body and soul.

Dogb. Nay that were a punishment too good for them, if they should have any allegiance in them, being chosen for the prince's watch.

Verg. Well, give them their charge, neighbour Dogberry.

Dogb. First, who think you the most desartless man to be constable?   261

1 *Watch.* Hugh Oatcake, sir, or George Seacoal; for they can write and read.

Dogb. Come hither, neighbour Seacoal: God hath bless'd you with a good name: to be a well-favour'd man is the gift of fortune; but to write and read comes by nature.

2 *Watch.*

2 *Watch.* Both which, master constable,—— 268

Dogb. You have; I knew it would be your answer. Well, for your favour, sir, why, give God thanks, and make no boast of it; and for your writing and reading, let that appear when there is no need of such vanity. You are thought here to be the most senseless and fit man for the constable of the watch; therefore bear you the lantern: This is your charge; you shall comprehend all vagrom men; you are to bid any man stand, in the prince's name.

2 *Watch.* How if he will not stand?

Dogb. Why then, take no note of him, but let him go; and presently call the rest of the watch together, and thank God you are rid of a knave. 282

Verg. If he will not stand when he is bidden, he is none of the prince's subjects.

Dogb. True, and they are to meddle with none but the prince's subjects:—You shall also make no noise in the streets; for, for the watch to babble and talk, is most tolerable and not to be endur'd.

2 *Watch.* We will rather sleep than talk; we know what belongs to a watch. 290

Dogb. Why, you speak like an ancient and most quiet watchman; for I cannot see how sleeping should offend: only, have a care that your bills be not stolen!—Well, you are to call at all the ale-houses, and bid them that are drunk get them to bed.

2 *Watch.* How if they will not?

Dogb. Why then, let them alone till they are sober;

if

if they make you not then the better answer, you may say, they are not the men you took them for.

2 Watch. Well, sir.   300

Dogb. If you meet a thief, you may suspect him, by virtue of your office, to be no true man; and, for such kind of men, the less you meddle or make with them, why the more is for your honesty.

2 Watch. If we know him to be a thief, shall we not lay hands on him?

Dogb. Truly, by your office you may; but I think, they that touch pitch will be defil'd: the most peaceable way for you, if you do take a thief, is, to let him shew himself what he is, and steal out of your company.   311

Verg. You have always been call'd a merciful man, partner.

Dogb. Truly, I would not hang a dog by my will; much more a man who hath any honesty in him.

Verg. If you hear a child cry in the night, you must call to the nurse, and bid her still it.

2 Watch. How if the nurse be asleep, and will not hear us?   320

Dogb. Why then, depart in peace, and let the child wake her with crying: for the ewe that will not hear her lamb when it baes, will never answer a calf when he bleats.

Verg. 'Tis very true.

Dogb. This is the end of the charge.. You, con-stable, are to present the prince's own person; if

you

you meet the prince in the night, you may stay him.

Verg. Nay, by'rlady, that, I think, he cannot. 329

Dogb. Five shillings to one on't, with any man that knows the statues, he may stay him : marry, not without the prince be willing : for, indeed, the watch ought to offend no man ; and it is an offence to stay a man against his will.

Verg. By'rlady, I think, it be so.

Dogb. Ha, ha, ha! Well, masters, good night : an there be any matter of weight chances, call up me : keep your fellows' counsels and your own, d good night.—Come, neighbour. 339

2 *Watch.* Well, masters, we hear our charge : let us go sit here upon the church-bench till two, and then all to bed.

Dogb. One word more, honest neighbours : I pray you, watch about signior Leonato's door; for the wedding being there to-morrow, there is a great coil to-night : Adieu, be vigilant, I beseech you.

[*Exeunt* DOGBERRY *and* VERGES.

Enter BORACHIO *and* CONRADE.

Bora. What! Conrade,—

Watch. Peace, stir not. [*Aside.*

Bora. Conrade, I say!

Conr. Here man, I am at thy elbow. 350

Bora. Mass, and my elbow itch'd; I thought, there would a scab follow.

" *Conr.* I will owe thee an answer for that ; and " now forward with thy tale.

" *Bora.*"

" *Bora.*" Stand thee close then under this pent-house, for it drizzles rain; and I will, like a true drunkard, utter all to thee.

Watch. [*Aside.*] Some treason, masters; yet stand close.

Bora. Therefore know, I have earned of Don John a thousand ducats.   361

Conr. Is it possible that any villainy should be so dear?

Bora. Thou should'st rather ask, if it were possible any villainy should be so rich: for when rich villains have need of poor ones, poor ones may make what price they will.

Conr. I wonder at it.

Bora. That shews, thou art unconfirm'd: Thou knowest, that the fashion of a doublet, or a hat, or a cloak, is nothing to a man.   371

Conr. Yes, it is apparel.

Bora. I mean, the fashion.

Conr. Yes, the fashion is the fashion.

Bora. Tush! I may as well say, the fool's the fool. But see'st thou not, what a deformed thief this fashion is?

Watch. I know that Deformed; he has been a vile thief these seven year; he goes up and down like a gentleman: I remember his name.   380

Bora. Didst thou not hear some body?

Conr. No; 'twas the vane on the house.

Bora. Seest thou not, I say, what a deformed thief this fashion is? how giddily he turns about all the

hot

hot bloods, between fourteen and five and thirty?
" sometime, fashioning them like Pharaoh's soldiers
" in the reechy painting; sometime, like god Bel's
" priests in the old church window; sometime, like
" the shaven Hercules in the smirch'd worm-eaten
" tapestry, where his cod-piece seems as massy as his
" club?"   391

Conr. " All this I see; and see, that the fashion
" wears out more apparel than the man: But" art
not thou thyself giddy with the fashion too, that thou
hast shifted out of thy tale into telling me of the
fashion?

Bora. Not so neither: but know, that I have to-
night wooed Margaret, the lady Hero's gentlewoman,
by the name of Hero; she leans me out at her
mistress's chamber-window, bids me a thousand times
good night—I tell this tale vilely:—I should first tell
thee, how the prince, Claudio, and my master,
planted and placed, and possessed by my master Don
John, saw afar off in the orchard this amiable encounter.   403

Conr. And thought they, Margaret was Hero?

Bora. Two of them did, the prince and Claudio;
but the devil my master knew she was Margaret;
" and partly by his oaths, which first possess'd them,
" partly by the dark night, which did deceive them,
" but chiefly by my villainy, which did confirm any
" slander that Don John had made," away went
Claudio enraged; swore he would meet her, as he was
appointed, next morning at the temple, and there,

F

before

before the whole congregation, shame her with what he saw o'er night, and send her home again without a husband.

1 Watch. We charge you in the prince's name, stand.   419

2 Watch. Call up the right master constable: We have here recovered the most dangerous piece of lechery that ever was known in the common-wealth.

1 Watch. And one Deformed is one of them; I know him, he wears a lock.

Conr. Masters, masters.—

2 Watch. You'll be made bring Deformed forth, I warrant you.

Conr. Masters,—

1 Watch. Never speak; we charge you, let us obey you to go with us.   431

Bora. We are like to prove a goodly commodity, being taken up of these men's bills.

" *Conr.* A commodity in question, I warrant you. Come, we'll obey you."   [*Exeunt.*

SCENE IV.

An Apartment in LEONATO'S *House. Enter* HERO, MARGARET, *and* URSULA.

" *Hero.* Good Ursula, wake my cousin Beatrice, " and desire her to rise.

" *Urs.* I will, lady.

" *Hero.*

" *Hero.* And bid her come hither.

" *Urs.* Well." 		[*Exit* URSULA. 		440

Marg. Troth, I think, your other rabato were better.

Hero. No, pray thee, good Meg, I'll wear this.

Marg. By my troth, it's not so good ; and I warrant, your cousin will say so.

Hero. My cousin's a .fool, and thou art another ; I'll wear none but this.

Marg. I like the new tire within excellently, " if " the hair were a thought browner ;" and your gown's a most rare fashion, i'faith. I saw the dutchess of Milan's gown, that they praise so.   451

" *Hero.* O, that exceeds, they say.

" *Marg.* By my troth, it's but a night-gown in " respect of yours : Cloth of gold, and cuts, and " lac'd with silver ; set with pearls, down sleeves, " side sleeves, and skirts round, underborne with a " blueish tinsel :" but for a fine, quaint, graceful, and excellent fashion, yours is worth ten on't.

Hero. God give me joy to wear it, for my heart is exceeding heavy !

Marg. 'Twill be heavier soon, by the weight of a man.

Hero. Fie upon thee ! art not asham'd ?

" *Marg.* Of what, lady ? of speaking honour- " ably ? Is not marriage honourable in a beggar ? Is " not your lord honourable without marriage ? I " think you would have me say, saving your reve- " rence,—*a husband :* an bad thinking do not wrest

F i j			" true

" true speaking, I'll offend no body : Is there any harm
" in—*the heavier for a husband ?* None, I think, an it
" be the right husband, and the right wife ; other-
" wise, 'tis light, and not heavy : Ask my lady
" Beatrice else, here she comes."   473

Enter BEATRICE.

Hero. Good morrow, coz.

Beat. Good morrow, sweet Hero.

Hero. Why, how now! do you speak in the sick
tune ?

Beat. I am out of all other tune, methinks.

" *Marg.* Clap us into *Light o' Love* ; that goes
" without a burden ; do you sing it, and I'll dance
" it.   481

" *Beat.* Yea, *Light o' Love*, with your heels !—then
" if your husband have stables enough, you'll look he
" shall lack no barns.

" *Marg.* O illegitimate construction ! I scorn that
" —with my heels.

" *Beat.*" 'Tis almost five o'clock, cousin ; 'tis time
you were ready.   By my troth, I am exceeding ill :—
hey ho !

Marg. For a hawk, a horse, or a husband ?   490

" *Beat.* For the letter that begins them all, H.

" *Marg.* Well, an you be not turn'd Turk, there's
" no more sailing by the star

" *Beat.* What means the fool, trow ?

" *Marg.* Nothing I ; but God send every one their
" heart's desire !   ●

" *Hero.*

" *Hero.* These gloves the count sent me, they are
" an excellent perfume.

" *Beat.* I am stuff'd, cousin, I cannot smell.

" *Marg.* A maid, and stuff'd! there's goodly catch-
" ing of cold.　　　　　　　　　　　　　　501

" *Beat.* O, God help me! God help me! how long
" have you profess'd apprehension?

" *Marg.* Ever since you left it; Doth not my wit
" become me rarely?"

　Beat. " It is not seen enough, you should wear it
" in your cap."—By my troth, I am sick.

Marg. Get you some of this distill'd Carduus Benedictus, and lay it to your heart; it is the only
thing for a qualm.　　　　　　　　　　510

" *Hero.* There thou prick'st her with a thistle."

Beat. Benedictus! why Benedictus? you have
some moral in this Benedictus.

　Marg. Moral? no by my troth, I have no moral
meaning; I meant, plain holy-thistle. You may
think, perchance, that I think you are in love: nay,
by'rlady, I am not such a fool to think what I list;
nor I list not to think what I can; nor, indeed, I
cannot think, if I would think my heart out o' thinking, that you are in love, or that you will be in
love, or that you can be in love: yet Benedick was
such another, and now is he become a man: he swore
he would never marry; and yet now, in despight of
his heart, he eats his meat without grudging: and
how you may be converted, I know not: but,
　　　　　　　　　F i i j　　　　　　methinks,

methinks, you look with your eyes as other women do.

Beat. What pace is this that thy tongue keeps ?

Marg. Not a false gallop.   529

Re-enter URSULA.

Urs. Madam, withdraw ; the prince, the count, signior Benedick, Don John, and all the gallants of the town, are come to fetch you to church.

Hero. Help to dress me, good coz, good Meg, good Ursula.   [*Exeunt.*

SCENE V.

Another Apartment in LEONATO'S *House.*   Enter LEONATO, *with* DOGBERRY *and* VERGES.

Leon. What would you have with me, honest neighbour ?

Dogb. Marry, sir, I would have some confidence with you, that decerns you nearly.

Leon. Brief, I pray you ; for you see, 'tis a busy time with me.   540

Dogb. Marry, this it is, sir.

Verg. Yes, in truth it is, sir.

Leon. What is it, my good friends ?

Dogb. Goodman Verges, sir, speaks a little of the matter : an old man, sir, and his wits are not so blunt, as, God help, I would desire they were ; but, in faith, honest, as the skin between his brows.

Verg.

Verg. Yes, I thank God, I am as honest as any man living, that is an old man, and no honester than I. 550

Dogb. Comparisons are odorous : *palabras*, neighbour Verges.

Leon. Neighbours, you are tedious.

Dogb. It pleases your worship to say so, but we are the poor duke's officers; but, truly, for mine own part, if I were as tedious as a king, I could find in my heart to bestow it all of your worship.

Leon. All thy tediousness on me ! ha ! 558

Dogb. Yea, and 'twere a thousand times more than 'tis : for I hear as good exclamation on your worship, as of any man in the city ; and though I be but a poor man, I am glad to hear it.

Verg. And so am I.

Leon. I would fain know what you have to say.

Verg. Marry, sir, our watch to-night, excepting your worship's presence, hath ta'en a couple of as arrant knaves as any in Messina.

Dogb. A good old man, sir ; he will be talking ; as they say, When the age is in, the wit is out ; God help us ! it is a world to see!—Well said, i'faith, neighbour Verges :—well, God's a good man ; an two men ride of a horse, one must ride behind :—An honest soul, i'faith, sir ; by my troth he is, as ever broke bread : but, God is to be worshipp'd ; All men are not alike ; alas good neighbour ! 575

Leon. Indeed, neighbour, he comes too short of you.

Dogb.

Dogb. Gifts, that God gives.

Leon. I must leave you.

Dogb. One word, sir: our watch have, indeed, comprehended two aspicious persons, and we would have them this morning examin'd before your worship.

Leon. Take their examination yourself, and bring it me; I am now in great haste, as may appear unto you.

Dogb. It shall be suffigance.

Leon. Drink some wine ere you go: fare you well.   589

" *Enter a Messenger.*

" *Mess.* My lord, they stay for you to give your
" daughter to her husband.

"*Leon.* I will wait upon them; I am ready."

[*Exit* LEONATO.

Dogb. Go, good partner, go, get you to Francis Seacoal, bid him bring his pen and inkhorn to the jail; we are now to examination these men.

Verg. And we must do it wisely.

Dogb. We will spare for no wit, I warrant you; here's that [*touching his forehead*] shall drive some of them to a *non-com*: only get the learned writer to set down our excommunication, and meet me at the jail.   [*Exeunt.*   601

ACT

ACT IV.   SCENE I.

A Church.   Enter Don PEDRO, *Don* JOHN, LEONATO,
Friar, CLAUDIO, BENEDICK, HERO, *and* BEA-
TRICE.

Leon.

COME, friar Francis, be brief; only to the plain
form of marriage, and you shall recount their particular duties afterwards.

Friar. You come hither, my lord, to marry this
lady ?

Claud. No.

Leon. To be marry'd to her, friar; you come to
marry her.

Friar. Lady, you come hither to be marry'd to this
count ?   10

Hero. I do.

Friar. If either of you know any inward impediment why you should not be conjoined, I charge you,
on your souls, to utter it.

Claud. Know you any, Hero ?

Hero. None, my lord.

Friar. Know you any, count ?

Leon. I dare make his answer, none.

Claud. O what men dare do! what men may do!
        what
Men daily do! " not knowing what they do!"   20

Bene. How now! Interjections ? " Why, then
" some be of laughing, as, ha! ha! he!"

Claud.

Claud. Stand thee by, friar :—Father, by your
    leave ;
Will you with free and unconstrained soul
Give me this maid your daughter ?
    Leon. As freely, son, as God did give her me.
    Claud. And what have I to give you back, whose
    worth
May counterpoise this rich and precious gift ?
    Pedro. Nothing, unless you render her again.
    Claud. Sweet prince, you learn me noble thankful-
    ness.—   30
There, Leonato, take her back again ;
" Give not this rotten orange to your friend :"
She's but the sign and semblance of her honour :—
Behold, how like a maid she blushes here :
O, what authority and shew of truth
Can cunning sin cover itself withal !
" Comes not that blood, as modest evidence,
" To witness simple virtue ? Would you not swear,
" All you that see her, that she were a maid,
" By these exterior shews ? But she is none :"   40
She knows the heat of a luxurious bed :
Her blush is guiltiness, not modesty.
    Leon. What do you mean, my lord ?
    Claud. Not to be marry'd, not knit my soul
To an approv'd wanton.
    Leon. Dear my lord,
If you in your own proof,
Have vanquish'd the resistance of her youth,
And made defeat of her virginity,——

                                  Claud.

Claud. " I know what you would say ; if I have
    known her,   50
" You'll say, she did embrace me as a husband,
" And so extenuate the forehand sin :"
No, Leonato,
I never tempted her with word too large ;
But, as a brother to his sister, shew'd
Bashful sincerity and comely love.

  Hero. And seem'd I ever otherwise to you ?

  Claud. Out on thy seeming ! I will write against it :
You seem to me as Dian in her orb ;
As chaste as is the bud ere it be blown ;   60
But you are more intemperate in your blood
Than Venus, or those pamper'd animals
That rage in savage sensuality.

  Hero. Is my lord well, that he doth speak so wide ?

  Leon. Sweet prince, why speak not you ?

  Pedro. What should I speak ?
I stand dishonour'd, that have gone about
To link my dear friend to a common stale.

  Leon. Are these things spoken, or do I but
    dream ?

  John. Sir, they are spoken, and these things are
    true.   70

  Bene. This looks not like a nuptial.

  Hero. True, O God !

  Claud. Leonato, stand I here ?
Is this the prince ? Is this the prince's brother ?
Is this face Hero's ? Are our eyes our own ?

  Leon. All this is so ; But what of this, my lord ?

Claud.

 Claud. Let me but move one question to your
   daughter ;
And, by that fatherly and kindly power
That you have in her, bid her answer truly. 79
 Leon. I charge thee do so, as thou art my child.
 Hero. O God defend me ! how I am beset !—
What kind of catechizing call you this ?
 Claud. To make you answer truly to your name.
 Hero. Is it not Hero ? Who can blot that name
With any just reproach ?
 Claud. Marry, that can Hero ;
Hero itself can blot out Hero's virtue.
What man was he talk'd with you yesternight
Out at your window, betwixt twelve and one ?
Now, if you are a maid, answer to this. 90
 Hero. I talk'd with no man at that hour, my lord.
 Pedro. " Why, then you are no maiden."—
   Leonato,
I am sorry, you must hear ; Upon mine honour,
Myself, my brother, and this grieved count,
Did see her, hear her, at that hour last night,
Talk with a ruffian at her chamber window ;
Who hath, indeed, most like a liberal villain,
Confess'd the vile encounters they have had
A thousand times in secret.
 John. Fie, fie ! they are 100
Not to be nam'd, my lord, not to be spoke of ;
There is not chastity enough in language,
Without offence, to utter them : Thus, pretty lady,
I am sorry for thy much misgovernment.
       Claud.

Printed for J Bell, British Library, Strand, London, Nov.r 16th 1784

Claud. O Hero! what a Hero hadst thou been
If half thy outward graces had been plac'd
About the thoughts and counsels of thy heart!
But, fare thee well, most foul, most fair! farewel,
" Thou pure impiety, and impious purity !"
For thee I'll lock up all the gates of love,   110
And on my eye-lids shall conjecture hang,
To turn all beauty into thoughts of harm,
And never shall it more be gracious.

  Leon. Hath no man's dagger here a point for me ?

  Beat. Why, how now, cousin, wherefore sink you
down ?   [HERO *swoons*.

  John. Come, let us go : these things, come thus to
light,
Smother her spirits up.

    [*Exeunt Don* PEDRO, *Don* JOHN, *and* CLAUDIO.

  Bene. How doth the lady ?

  Beat. Dead, I think ;—Help, uncle ;—
Hero! why, Hero !—uncle !—Signior Benedick !—
friar !   120

  Leon. O fate! take not away thy heavy hand !
Death is the fairest cover for her shame,
That may be wish'd for.

  Beat. How now, cousin Hero ?

  Friar. Have comfort, lady.

  Leon. Dost thou look up ?

  Friar. Yea; Wherefore should she not ?

  Leon. Wherefore ? Why, doth not every earthly
thing
Cry shame upon her ? Could she here deny

G

Th

The story that is printed in her blood?—   130
" Do not live, Hero; do not ope thine eyes:
" For did I think, thou would'st not quickly die,
" Thought I, thy spirits were stronger than thy
        shames,
" Myself would, on the rearward of reproaches,
" Strike at thy life."   Griev'd I, I had but one?
Chid I for that at frugal nature's frame?
O, one too much by thee! " Why had I one?
" Why ever wast thou lovely in my eyes?
" Why had I not, with charitable hand,
" Took up a beggar's issue at my gates;   140
" Who smeared thus, and mir'd with infamy,
" I might have said, *No part of it is mine,*
" *This shame derives itself from unknown loins?*
" But mine, and mine I lov'd, and mine I prais'd,
" And mine that I was proud on; mine so much,
" That I myself was to myself not mine,
" Valuing of her; why, she"—O, she, is fallen
Into a pit of ink! that the wide sea
Hath drops too few to wash her clean again;
" And salt too little, which may season give   150
" To her foul tainted flesh!"
        Bene. Sir, sir, be patient:
For my part, I am so attir'd in wonder,
I know not what to say.
        Beat. O, on my soul, my cousin is bely'd!
        Bene. Lady, were you her bedfellow last night?
        Beat. No, truly, not; although, until last night,
I have this twelvemonth been her bedfellow.

4.

Leon.

Leon. Confirm'd, confirm'd! O, that is stronger made,
Which was before barr'd up with ribs of iron !   160
Would the two princes lie ? and Claudio lie ?
Who lov'd her so, that, speaking of her foulness,
Wash'd it with tears ? Hence from her; let her die.

Friar. Hear me a little ;
For I have only been silent so long,
And given way unto this course of fortune,
By noting of the lady ; I have mark'd
A thousand blushing apparitions
To start into her face ; a thousand innocent shames
In angel whiteness bear away those blushes ;   170
And in her eye there hath appear'd a fire,
To burn the errors that these princes hold
Against her maiden truth :—Call me a fool;
Trust not my reading, nor my observation,
" Which with experimental seal doth warrant
" The tenour of my book; trust not my age,"
My reverence, calling, nor divinity,
If this sweet lady lie not guiltless here
Under some biting error.

Leon. Friar, it cannot be :   180
Thou seest, that all the grace that she hath left,
Is, that she will not add to her damnation
A sin of perjury; she not denies it :
Why seek'st thou then to cover with excuse
That, which appears in proper nakedness ?

Friar. Lady, what man is he you are accus'd of ?

G i j

Here.

Hero. They know, that do accuse me; I know
   none :
If I know more of any man alive,
Than that which maiden modesty doth warrant,
Let all my sins lack mercy!—O my father,   190
Prove you that any man with me convers'd
At hours unmeet, or that I yesternight
Maintain'd the change of words with any creature,
Refuse me, hate me, torture me to death.
  Friar. There is some strange misprision in the
   princes.
  Bene. Two of them have the very bent of honour;
And if their wisdoms be misled in this,
The practice of it lives in John the bastard,
Whose spirits toil in frames of villainies.   199
  Leon. I know not; If they speak but truth of her,
These hands shall tear her; if they wrong her ho-
   nour,
The proudest of them shall well hear of it.
" Time hath not yet so dry'd this blood of mine,
" Nor age so eat up my invention,
" Nor fortune made such havock of my means,
" Nor my bad life reft me so much of friends,
" But they shall find, awak'd in such a kind,
" Both strength of limb, and policy of mind,
" Ability in means, and choice of friends,
" To quit me of them throughly."   210
  Friar. Pause awhile,
And let my counsel sway you in this case.
Your daughter here the princes left for dead;

             Let

Let her awhile be secretly kept in,
And publish it, that she is dead indeed:
" Maintain a mourning ostentation;
" And on your family's old monument
" Hang mournful epitaphs, and do all rites
" That appertain unto a burial."
   Leon. What shall become of this? What will this
      do?   220
   Friar. Marry, this, well carry'd, shall on her be-
      half
Change slander to remorse; " that is some good:"
But not for that, dream I on this strange course,
But on this travail look for greater birth.
She dying, as it must be so maintain'd,
Upon the instant that she was accus'd,
Shall be lamented, pity'd, and excus'd,
Of every hearer: " For it so falls out,
" That what we have we prize not to the worth,
" Whiles we enjoy it; but being lack'd and lost, 230
" Why, then we rack the value; then we find
" The virtue, that possession would not shew us
" Whiles it was ours:—So will it fare with Claudio:
" When he shall hear she dy'd upon his words,
" The idea of her life shall sweetly creep
" Into his study of imagination;
" And every lovely organ of her life
" Shall come apparel'd in more precious habit,
" More moving, delicate, and full of life,
" Into the eye and prospect of his soul,   240
" Than when she liv'd indeed:—then shall he mourn
         G i i j   " (If

" (If ever love had interest in his liver),
" And wish he had not so accused her;
" No, though he thought his accusation true.
" Let this be so, and doubt not but success
" Will fashion the event in better shape
" Than I can lay it down in likelihood.
" But if all aim but this be levell'd false,
" The supposition of the lady's death
" Will quench the wonder of her infamy: 250
" And, if it sort not well, you may conceal her
" (As best befits her wounded reputation)
" In some reclusive and religious life,
" Out of all-eyes, tongues, minds, and injuries."
   Bene. Signior Leonato, let the friar advise you:
And though, you know my inwardness and love
Is very much into the prince and Claudio,
Yet, by mine honour, I will deal in this
As secretly, and justly, as your soul
Should with your body.   260
   Leon. Being that I flow in grief,
The smallest twine may lead me.
   Friar. 'Tis well consented; presently away;
    " For to strange sores strangely they strain the
       cure—"
Come, lady, die to live: this wedding day,
    Perhaps, is but prolong'd; have patience, and
     endure.   [*Exeunt.*

                               Manent

Manent BENEDICK *and* BEATRICE.

Bene. Lady Beatrice, have you wept all this while?

Beat. Yea, and I will weep a while longer.

Bene. I will not desire that.

Beat. You have no reason, I do it freely.   270

Bene. Surely, I do believe your fair cousin is
wrong'd.

Beat. Ah, how much might the man deserve of me,
that would right her!

Bene. Is there any way to shew such friendship?

Beat. A very even way, but no such friend.

Bene. May a man do it?

Beat. It is a man's office, but not yours.

Bene. I do love nothing in the world so well as you:
Is not that strange?   279

Beat. As strange as the thing I know not: It were
as possible for me to say, I loved nothing so well as
you: but believe me not; and yet I lie not; I confess nothing, nor I deny nothing:—I am sorry for my
cousin.

Bene. By my sword, Beatrice, thou lov'st me.

Beat. Do not swear by it, and eat it.

Bene. I will swear by it, that you love me; and I
will make him eat it, that says, I love not you.

Beat. Will you not eat your word?

Bene. With no sauce that can be devis'd to it: I
protest I love thee.   291

Beat. Why then, God forgive me!

Bene. What offence, sweet Beatrice?

Beat. You have staid me in a happy hour; I was about to protest I lov'd you.

Bene. And do it with all thy heart.

Beat. I love you with so much of my heart, that none is left to protest.

Bene. Come, bid me do any thing for thee.

Beat. Kill Claudio.   300

Bene. Ha! not for the wide world.

Beat. You kill me to deny it: Farewel.

Bene. Tarry, sweet Beatrice.

Beat. I am gone, though I am here;—There is no love in you:—nay, I pray you, let me go.

Bene. Beatrice,—

Beat. In faith, I will go.

Bene. We'll be friends first.

Beat. You dare easier be friends with me, than fight with mine enemy.   310

Bene. Is Claudio thine enemy?

Beat. Is he not approv'd in the height a villain, that hath slander'd, scorn'd, dishonour'd my kinswoman? —O, that I were a man!—What, bear her in hand until they come to take hands; and then with public accusation, uncover'd slander, unmitigated rancour, —O God, that I were a man! I would eat his heart in the market-place.

Bene. Hear me, Beatrice.

Beat. Talk with a man out at a window?—a proper saying!   321

Bene. Nay, but Beatrice;—

Beat.

Beat. Sweet Hero!—she is wrong'd, she is slander'd, she is undone.

Bene. Beat—

Beat. Princes and counties! Surely, a princely testimony, a goodly count-comfect; a sweet gallant, surely! O that I were a man for his sake! or that I had any friend would be a man for my sake! But manhood is melted into courtesies, valour into compliment, and men are only turned into tongue, and trim ones too: he is now as valiant as Hercules, that only tells a lye, and swears it:—I cannot be a man with wishing, therefore I will die a woman with grieving.   335

Bene. Tarry, good Beatrice: By this hand, I love thee.

Beat. Use it for my love some other way than swearing by it.

Bene. Think you in your soul, the count Claudio hath wrong'd Hero?   341

Beat. Yea, as sure as I have a thought, or a soul.

Bene. Enough, I am engag'd, I will challenge him; I will kiss your hand, and so leave you: By this hand, Claudio shall render me a dear account: As you hear of me, so think of me. Go comfort your cousin: I must say, she is dead; and so farewel.

[*Exeunt.*

SCENE

SCENE II.

A Prison. Enter DOGBERRY, VERGES, BORACHIO, CONRADE, *the Town-Clerk and Sexton in gowns.*

Dogb. Is our whole dissembly appear'd?

Verg. O, a stool and cushion for the sexton!

Sexton. Which be the malefaĉtors?   350

Dogb. Marry, that am I and my partner.

Verg. Nay, that's certain; we have the exhibition to examine.

Sexton. But which are the offenders that are to be examin'd? let them come before master constable.

Dogb. Yea, marry, let them come before me.— What is your name, friend?

Bora. Borachio.

Dogb. Pray, write down — Borachio. — Yours,   sirrah?   360

Conr. I am a gentleman, sir, and my name is Conrade.

Dogb. Write down—master gentleman Conrade.— Masters, do you serve God?

Both. Yea, sir, we hope.

Dogb. Write down—that they hope they serve God:—and write God first; for God defend but God should go before such villains!—Masters, it is proved already that you are little better than false knaves, and it will go near to be thought so shortly. How answer you for yourselves?   371

Conr. Marry, sir, we say, we are none.

Dogb.

Dogb. A marvellous witty fellow, I assure you; but I will go about with him.—Come you hither, sirrah; a word in your ear, sir; I say to you, it is thought you are false knaves.

Bora. Sir, I say to you, we are none.

Dogb. Well, stand aside.—'Fore God, they are both in a tale:—Have you writ down—that hey are none?   380

Sexton. Master constable, you go not the way to examine; you must call the watch that are their accusers.

Dogb. Yea, marry, that's the eftest way:—Let the watch come forth:—Masters, I charge you in the prince's name accuse these men.

Enter Watchmen.

1 *Watch.* This man said, sir, that Don John, the prince's brother, was a villain.

Dogb. Write down—Prince John a villain:—Why this is flat perjury, to call a Prince's brother—villain.

Bora. Master constable,—   391

Dogb. Pray thee, fellow, peace; I do not like thy look, I promise thee.

Sexton. What heard you him say else?

2 *Watch.* Marry, that he had receiv'd a thousand ducats of Don John, for accusing the lady Hero wrongfully.

Dogb. Flat burglary, as ever was committed.

Verg. Yea, by the mass, that it is.

Sexton.

Sexton. What else, fellow ?   400

1 *Watch.* And that Count Claudio did mean, upon his words, to disgrace Hero before the whole assembly, and not marry her.

Dogb. O villain ! thou wilt be condemned into everlasting redemption for this.

Sexton. What else ?

2 *Watch.* This is all.

Sexton. And this is more, masters, than you can deny. Prince John is this morning secretly stolen away; Hero was in this manner accus'd, in this very manner refus'd, and upon the grief of this, suddenly dy'd.—Master constable, let these men be bound, and brought to Leonato's ; I will go before, and shew him their examination.   [*Exit.*

Dogb. Come, let them be opinion'd.

 " *Verg.* Let them be in hand.

 " *Conr.* Off, coxcomb !

 " *Dogb.* God's my life ! where's the sexton ? let him " write down—the prince's officer, coxcomb."— Come, bind them :—Thou naughty varlet ! 420

Conr. Away ! you are an ass, you are an ass.

Dogb. Dost thou not suspect my place ? Dost thou not suspect my years ?—O that he were here to write me down—an ass !—but, masters, remember, that I am an ass ; though it be not written down, yet forget not that I am an ass :—No, thou villain, thou art full of piety, as shall be proved upon thee by good witness : I am a wise fellow ; and, which is more, an officer ; and, which is more, an housholder ; and,

which

which is more, as pretty a piece of flesh as any is in
Messina; and one that knows the law, go to; and a
rich fellow enough, go to; and a fellow that hath
had losses; and one that hath two gowns, and every
thing handsome about him :—Bring him away. O,
that I had been writ down—an ass !— 435
[*Exeunt.*

ACT V. SCENE I.

Before LEONATO'S *House. Enter* LEONATO *and*
ANTONIO.

Antonio.

IF you go on thus, you will kill yourself;
And 'tis not wisdom, thus to second grief
Against yourself.
   Leon. I pray thee, cease thy counsel,
Which falls into mine ears as profitless
As water in a sieve : give not me counsel;
Nor let no comforter delight mine ear,
But such a one whose wrongs do suit with mine.
Bring me a father, that so lov'd his child,
Whose joy of her is overwhelm'd like mine, 10
And bid him speak of patience ;
" Measure his woe the length and breadth of mine,
" And let it answer every strain for strain ;
" As thus for thus, and such a grief for such,
" In every lineament, branch, shape, and form :
H " If

" If such a one will smile, and stroke his beard ;
" In sorrow wag! cry hem, when he should groan ;
" Patch grief with proverbs ; make misfortune drunk
" With candle-wasters ; bring him yet to me,
" And I of him will gather patience.   20
" But there is no such man : For, brother, men
" Can counsel, and give comfort to that grief
" Which they themselves not feel ; but tasting it,
" Their counsel turns to passion, which before
" Would give preceptial medicine to rage,
" Fetter strong madness in a silken thread,
" Charm ach with air, and agony with words :"
No, no ; 'tis all men's office to speak patience
To those that wring under the load of sorrow ;
But no man's virtue, nor sufficiency   30
To be so moral, when he shall endure
The like himself : therefore give me no counsel ;
" My griefs cry louder than advertisement."

   Ant. Therein do men from children nothing differ.

   Leon. I pray thee, peace ; I will be flesh and blood ;
For there was never yet philosopher,
That could endure the tooth-ach patiently ;
Howeyer they have writ the style of gods,
And made a pish at chance and sufferance.

   Ant. Yet bend not all the harm upon yourself ; 40
Make those, that do offend you, suffer too.

   Leon. There thou speak'st reason : nay, I will do
       so :
My soul doth tell me, Hero is bely'd ;

                      And

And that shall Claudio know, so shall the prince
And all of them that thus dishonour her.

Enter Don PEDRO *and* CLAUDIO.

Ant. Here comes the prince, and Claudio, hastily.
Pedro. Good den, good den.
Claud. Good day to both of you.
Leon. Hear you, my lords,—
Pedro. We have some haste, Leonato.　　50
Leon. Some haste, my lord ?—well, fare you well,
　　　my lord :—
Are you so hasty now ?—well, all is one.
Pedro. Nay, do not quarrel with us, good old man.
Ant. If he could right himself with quarrelling,
Some of us would lye low.
Claud. Who wrongs him ?
Leon. Marry, thou dost wrong me, thou dissembler,
　　　thou !
Nay, never lay thy hand upon thy sword,
I fear thee not.
Claud. Marry, beshrew my hand,　　60
If it should give your age such cause of fear :
In faith, my hand meant nothing to my sword.
Leon. Tush, tush, man, never fleer and jest at me;
I speak not like a dotard, nor a fool ;
As, under privilege of age, to brag
What I have done being young, or what would do,
Were I not old : Know, Claudio, to thy head,
Thou hast so wrong'd my innocent child, and me,
That I am forc'd to lay my reverence by ;

H ij

And,

And, with grey hairs, and bruise of many days,   70
Do challenge thee to tryal of a man.
I say, thou hast bely'd mine innocent child,
Thy slander hath gone through and through her
        heart,
And she lies bury'd with her ancestors:
O, in a tomb where scandal never slept,
Save this of hers, fram'd by thy villainy!
  Claud. My villainy?
  Leon. Thine, Claudio; thine I say.
  Pedro. You say not right, old man.
  Leon. My lord, my lord,   80
I'll prove it on his body, if he dare;
Despight his nice fence, and his active practice,
His May of youth, and bloom of lustyhood.
  Claud. Away, I will not have to do with you.
  Leon. Canst thou so daffe me? Thou hast kill'd my
        child;
If thou kill'st me, boy, thou shalt kill a man.
  Ant. He shall kill two of us, and men indeed:
But that's no matter; let him kill one first;—
Win me and wear me,—let him answer me:—   89
Come, follow me, boy; come, sir boy, follow me;
Sir, boy, I'll whip you from your foining fence
Nay, as I am a gentleman, I will.
  Leon. Brother,—
  Ant. Content yourself: God knows, I lov'd my
        niece;
And she is dead, slander'd to death by villains
That dare as well answer a man, indeed,

                                As

As I dare take a serpent by the tongue :
Boys, apes, braggarts, jacks, milksops!—
   Leon. Brother Anthony,—
   Ant. Hold you content; What, man? I know
     them, yea,   100
And what they weigh, even to the utmost scruple :
Scambling, out-facing, fashion-mong'ring boys,
That lye, and cog, and flout, deprave and slander,
" Go antickly, and show outward hideousness,"
And speak off half a dozen dangerous words,
How they might hurt their enemies, if they durst,
And this is all.
   Leon. But, brother Anthony,—
   Ant. Come, 'tis no matter ;
Do not you meddle, let me deal in this.   110
   Pedro. Gentlemen both, we will not wake your
     patience.
My heart is sorry for your daughter's death ;
But on my honour, she was charg'd with nothing
But what was true, and very full of proof.
   Leon. My lord, my lord,—
   Pedro. I will not hear you.
   Leon. No ?
Come, brother, away :—I will be heard ;—
   Ant. And shall,
Or some of us will smart for it.   120
                 [*Exeunt ambo.*
        Enter BENEDICK.
   Pedro. See, see,
Here comes the man we went to seek.
           H i i j   *Claud.*

Claud. Now, signior!
What news?

Bene Good day, my lord.

Pedro. Welcome signior:
You are almost come to part almost a fray.

Claud. We had like to have had our two noses
snapt off with two old men without teeth.   129

Pedro. Leonato and his brother: What think'st
thou? had we fought, I doubt, we should have been
too young for them.

Bene. In a false quarrel there is no true valour.
I came to seek you both.

Claud. We have been up and down to seek thee;
for we are high-proof melancholy, and would fain
have it beaten away: Wilt thou use thy wit?

Bene. It is in my scabbard; shall I draw it?

" *Pedro.* Dost thou wear thy wit by thy side?"

Claud. " Never any did so, though very many have
been beside their wit."—I will bid thee draw, as we
do the minstrels; draw, to pleasure us.   142

Pedro. As I am an honest man, he looks pale :—
Art thou sick or angry?

Claud. What! courage, man! What though care
kill'd a cat, thou hast mettle enough in thee to kill
care.

. *Bene.* Sir, I shall meet your wit in the career, if
you charge it against me :—I pray you, chuse another
subject.

" *Claud.* Nay, then give him another staff; this
" last was broke cross."   152

Pedro.

Pedro. By this light, he changes more and more; I think, he be angry indeed.

Claud. If he be, he knows how to turn his girdle.

Bene. Shall I speak a word in your ear?

Claud. God bless me from a challenge!

Bene. You are a villain;—I jest not:—I will make it good how you dare, with what you dare, and when you dare:—Do me right, or I will protest your cowardice. You have kill'd a sweet lady, and her death shall fall heavy on you:—Let me hear from you.   163

Claud. Well, I will meet you, so I may have good cheer.

Pedro. What, a feast? a feast?

Claud. I'faith, I thank him; he hath bid me to a calves-head and a capon; the which if I do not carve most curiously, say my knife's naught. Shall I not find a woodcock too?

Bene. Sir, your wit ambles well; it goes easily.

" *Pedro.* I'll tell thee, how Beatrice prais'd thy
" wit the other day : I said, thou had'st a fine wit;
" *True,* says she, *a fine little one*; *No,* said I, *a great*
" *wit*; *Right,* said she, *a great gross one*; *Nay,* said I, *a*
" *good wit*; *Just,* says she, *it hurts nobody*; *Nay,* said
" I, *the gentleman is wise*; *Certain,* said she, *a wise*
" *gentleman*; *Nay,* said I, *he hath the tongues*; *That I*
" *believe,* said she, *for he swore a thing to me on Monday*
" *night, which he forswore on Tuesday morning*; *there's*
" *a double tongue, there's two tongues.* Thus did she,
" an hour together, trans-shape thy particular virtues :
                                                        " yet

" yet at last, she concluded with a sigh, thou wast
" the properest man in Italy.

" *Claud.* For the which she wept heartily, and said,
" she car'd not.

" *Pedro.* Yea, that she did; but yet, for all that,
" an if she did not hate him deadly, she would love him
" dearly; the old man's daughter told us all.   189

" *Claud.* All, all; and moreover, *God saw him when*
" *he was hid in the garden.*"

Pedro. But when shall we set the savage bull's
horns on the sensible Benedick's head?

Claud. Yea, and text underneath, *Here dwells Benedick the married man?*

Bene. Fare you well, boy; you know my mind; I
will leave you now to your gossip-like humour: you
break jests as braggarts do their blades, which, God
be thanked, hurt not.   My lord, for your many
courtesies I thank you; I must discontinue your
company: your brother, the bastard, is fled from
Messina; you have, among you, kill'd a sweet and
innocent lady: For my lord lack-beard there, he and
I shall meet; and till then, peace be with him!

[*Exit* BENEDICK.

Pedro. He is in earnest.

Claud. In most profound earnest; and, I'll warrant
you, for the love of Beatrice.

Pedro. And hath challeng'd thee?

Claud. Most sincerely.   209

Pedro. What a pretty thing man is, when he goes
in his doublet and hose, and leaves off his wit!

Enter

Enter DOGBERRY, VERGES, CONRADE *and* BORA-
CHIO *guarded.*

" *Claud.* He is then a giant to an ape : but then is
an ape a doctor to such a man.

" *Pedro.*" But, soft you, let be ; " pluck up my
" heart, and be sad :" Did he not say, my brother was
fled ?

Dogb. Come, you, sir ; if justice cannot tame you,
she shall ne'er weigh more reasons in her balance :
nay, an you be a cursing hypocrite once, you must
be look'd to.   220

Pedro. How now, two of my brother's men bound !
Borachio, one !

Claud. Hearken after their offence, my lord !

Pedro. Officers, what offence have these men done ?

Dogb. Marry, sir, they have committed false report ; moreover, they have spoken untruths ; secon-
darily, they are slanders ; sixth and lastly, they have
bely'd a lady ; thirdly, they have verify'd unjust
things : and, to conclude, they are lying knaves. 229

Pedro. First, I ask thee what they have done ;
thirdly, I ask thee what's their offence ; sixth and
lastly, why they are committed ; and, to conclude,
what you lay to their charge ?

Claud. Rightly reason'd, and in his own division ;
" and, by my truth, there's one meaning well suited."

Pedro. Whom have you offended, masters, that
you are thus bound to your answer ? this learned constable is too cunning to be understood : what's your
offence ?   239

Bora.

Bora. Sweet prince, let me go no further to mine answer; do you hear me, and let this count kill me. I have deceived even your very eyes: what your wisdoms could not discover, these shallow fools have brought to light; who, in the night, overheard me confessing to this man, how Don John your brother incens'd me to slander the lady Hero; how you were brought into the orchard, and saw me court Margaret in Hero's garments; how you disgrac'd her, when you should marry her: my villainy they have upon record; which I had rather seal with my death, than repeat over to my shame: the lady is dead upon mine and my master's false accusation; and briefly, I desire nothing but the reward of a villain.   253

Pedro. Runs not this speech like iron through your
  blood?

Claud. I have drunk poison, whiles he utter'd it.

Pedro. But did my brother set thee on to this?

Bora. Yea, and paid me richly for the practice of
  it.

Pedro. He is compos'd and fram'd of treachery:—
And fled he is upon this villainy.

Claud. Sweet Hero! now thy image doth appear
In the rare semblance that I lov'd it first.   261

Dogb. Come bring away the plaintiffs; by this time our sexton hath reform'd signior Leonato of the matter: And masters do not forget to specify, when time and place shall serve, that I am an ass.

Verg. Here, here comes master Signior Leonato, and the sexton too.

Re-enter

Re-enter LEONATO *and* ANTONIO, *with the Sexton.*

Leon. Which is the villain ? Let me see his eyes ;
That when I note another man like him,
I may avoid him : which of these is he ?   270
  Bora. If you would know your wronger, look on
          me.
  Leon. Art thou the slave, that with thy breath hast
          kill'd
Mine innocent child ?
  Bora. Yea, even I alone.
  Leon. No, not so villain ; thou bely'st thyself ;
Here stand a pair of honourable men,
A third is fled, that had a hand in it :—
I thank you, princes, for my daughter's death ;
Record it with your high and worthy deeds ;
'Twas bravely done, if you bethink you of it.   280
  Claud. I know not how to pray your patience,
Yet I must speak : Chuse your revenge yourself ;
Impose me to what penance your invention
Can lay upon my sin : yet sinn'd I not,
But in mistaking.
  Pedro. By my soul, nor I ;
And yet, to satisfy this good old man,
I would bend under any heavy weight
That he'll enjoin me to.
  Leon. I cannot bid you bid my daughter live,   290
That were impossible ; but, I pray you both,
Possess the people in Messina here
How innocent she dy'd : " and, if your love

                              " Can

" Can labour aught in sad invention,
" Hang her an epitaph upon her tomb,
" And sing it to her bones ; sing it to-night" :
To-morrow morning come you to my house ;
And since you could not be my son-in-law,
Be yet my nephew : my brother hath a daughter,
Almost the copy of my child that's dead, 300
And she alone is heir to both of us ;
Give her the right you should have given her cousin,
And so dies my revenge.

 Claud. O noble sir,
Your over-kindness doth wring tears from me !
I do embrace your offer ; and dispose
For henceforth of poor Claudio.

 Leon. To-morrow then I will expect your coming ;
To-night I take my leave. This naughty man
Shall face to face be brought to Margaret, 310
Who, I believe, was pack'd in all this wrong,
Hir'd to it by your brother.

 Bora. No, by my soul, she was not ;
Nor knew not what she did, when she spoke to me ;
But always hath been just and virtuous,
In any thing that I do know by her.

 Dogb. Moreover, sir (which, indeed, is not under
white and black), this plaintiff here, the offender, did
call me ass : I beseech you, let it be remembred in
his punishment : And also, the watch heard them talk
of one Deformed : " they say, he wears a key in his
" ear, and a lock hanging by it ; and borrows money
" in God's name ; the which he hath us'd so long, and

" never

" never paid, that now men grow hard-hearted, and
" will lend nothing for God's sake :" Pray you, examine him upon that point.

Leon. I thank thee for thy care and honest pains.

Dogb. Your worship speaks like a most thankful
and reverend youth ; and I praise God for you.

Leon. There's for thy pains.   330

Dogb. God save the foundation !

Leon. Go, I discharge thee of thy prisoner, and I
thank thee.

Dogb. I leave an errant knave with your worship ;
which, I beseech your worship, to correct yourself,
for the example of others.   God keep your worship ;
I wish your worship well ; God restore you to health :
I humbly give you leave to depart ; and if a merry
meeting may be wish'd, God prohibit it.—Come,
neighbour.   [*Exeunt.*   340

" *Leon.* Until to-morrow morning, lords, farewel.

" *Ant.* Farewel, my lords ; we look for you to-
morrow.

Pedro. We will not fail.

" *Claud.* To-night I'll mourn with Hero."

Leon. Bring you these fellows on ; we'll talk with
Margaret,
How her acquaintance grew with this lewd fellow.

[*Exeunt severally.*

---

1   *SCENE*

SCENE II.

A Room in LEONATO'S *House.   Enter* BENEDICK, *and* MARGARET, *meeting.*

Bene. Pray thee, sweet mistress Margaret, deserve well at my hands, by helping me to the speech of Beatrice.

Marg. Will you then write me a sonnet in praise of my beauty?

Bene. In so high a style, Margaret, that no man living shall come over it; for, in most comely truth, thou deservest it.

Marg. To have no man come over me? why, shall I always keep below stairs?

Bene. Thy wit is as quick as the greyhound's mouth, it catches.

Marg. And your's as blunt as the fencer's foils, which hit, but hurt not.   360

Bene. A most manly wit, Margaret, it will not hurt a woman; and so, I pray thee, call Beatrice: " I give thee the bucklers."

" *Marg.* Give us the swords, we have bucklers of " our own.

" *Bene.* If you use them, Margaret, you must put " in the pikes with a vice; and they are dangerous " weapons for maids."

Marg. Well, I will call Beatrice to you, " who I " think hath legs."   [*Exit* MARGARET.   370

Bene. " And therefore will come."   [*Sings.*]

The

> *The god of love,*
> *That sits above,*
> *" And knows me, and knows me,"*
> *" How pitiful I deserve,—"*

I mean in singing; but in loving, Leander the good swimmer, Troilus the first employer of pandars, and a whole book full of these quondam carpet-mongers, whose names yet run smoothly in the even road of a blank verse, why, they were never so truly turn'd over and over, as my poor self, in love: Marry, I cannot shew it in rhime; I have try'd; I can find out no rhime to *lady* but *baby*, an inno cent rhime; for *scorn*, *horn*, a hard rhime; for *school*, *fool*, a babbling rhime; very ominous endings: No, I was not born under a rhiming planet, for I cannot woo in festival terms.—

Enter BEATRICE.

Sweet Beatrice, would'st thou come when I call thee?

Beat. Yea, signior, and depart when you bid me.

Bene. O, stay but till then!   390

Beat. Then, is spoken; fare you well now:—and yet ere I go, let me go with that I came for, which is, with knowing what hath past between you and Claudio.

Bene. Only foul words; and thereupon I will kiss thee.

Beat. Foul words are but foul wind, and foul wind

is but foul breath, and foul breath is noisome ; therefore I will depart unkiss'd.

Bene. Thou hast frighted the word out of its right sense, so forcible is thy wit : But, I must tell thee plainly, Claudio undergoes my challenge ; and either I must shortly hear from him, or I will subscribe him a coward. And, I pray thee now, tell me, for which of my bad parts didst thou first fall in love with me ?

Beat. For them all together ; which maintain'd so politick a state of evil, that they will not admit any good part to intermingle with them. But for which of my good parts did you first suffer love for me ?

Bene. Suffer love ; a good epithet! I do suffer love, indeed, for I love thee against my will.

Beat. In spight of your heart, I think ; alas! poor heart ! If you spight it for my sake, I will spight it for yours ; for I will never love that, which my friend hates.

Bene. Thou and I are too wise to woo peaceably.

Beat. It appears not in this confession ; there's not one wise man among twenty, that will praise himself.   420

Bene. An old, an old instance, Beatrice, that liv'd in the time of good neighbours : if a man do not erect in this age his own tomb ere he dies, he shall live no longer in monument, than the bell rings, and the widow weeps.

Beat And how long is that, think you ?

Bene. Question ? — Why, an hour in clamour,

and

and a quarter in rheum: Therefore it is most expe-
dient for the wise (if don Worm, his conscience,
find no impediment to the contrary), to be the trum-
pet of his own virtues, as I am to myself: So much
for praising myself (who, I myself will bear witness
is praise-worthy), and now tell me, How doth your
cousin ? .

Beat. Very ill   435
Bene. And how do you ?
Beat. Very ill too.
Bene. Serve God, love me, and mend: there will
I leave you too, for here comes one in haste

Enter URSULA.

Urs. Madam, you must come to your uncle; " yon-
" der's old coil at home:" it is proved, my lady Hero
hath been falsely accus'd, the prince and Claudio
mightily abus'd; and Don John is the author of all,
who is fled and gone: " Will you come presently?"

Beat. Will you go hear this news, signior?

Bene. I will live in thy heart, die in thy lap, and be
bury'd in thy eyes; and, moreover, I will go with
thee to thy uncle.   [*Exeunt.*

SCENE III.

" *A Church.   Enter Don* PEDRO, CLAUDIO, *and*
" *Attendants with Music and Tapers.*

" *Claud.* Is this the monument of Leonato?
" *Atten.* It is, my lord.   450

I i i j   " CLAUDIO

" CLAUDIO reads.

" Done to death by slanderous tongues
 " Was the Hero, that here lies:
" Death, in guerdon of her wrongs,
 " Gives her fame which never dies:
" So the life, that dy'd with shame,
 " Lives in death with glorious fame.

" Hang thou there upon the tomb,
" Praising her when I am dumb.—
" Now musick sound, and sing your solemn hymn.

" S   O   N   G.

" Pardon, Goddess of the night,   460
" Those that slew thy virgin knight;
" For the which, with songs of woe,
" Round about her tomb they go.
 " Midnight, assist our moan;
 " Help us to sigh and groan,
  " Heavily, heavily:
" Graves yawn and yield your dead,
" Till death be uttered,
  " Heavily, heavily.

" Claud. Now, unto thy bones good night!   470
" Yearly will I do this rite.
 " Pedro. Good morrow, masters; put your torches
  out :
 " The wolves have prey'd; and look, the gentle
  day

" Befor-

“ Before the wheels of Phœbus, round about
    “ Dapples the drowsy east with spots of grey :
“ Thanks to you all, and leave us ; fare you well.
   “ *Claud.* Good morrow, masters ; each his several
      way.
   “ *Pedro.* Come, let us hence, and put on other
      weeds ;
“ And then to Leonato's we will go.   479
   “ *Claud.* And Hymen now with luckier issue
      speeds,
“ Than this, for whom we render'd up this woe !
[*Exeunt.*”

SCENE IV.

LEONATO's *House.*   *Enter* LEONATO, BENEDICK,
MARGARET, URSULA, ANTONIO, *Friar and* HERO.

   Friar. Did not I tell you she was innocent?
   Leon. So are the prince and Claudio, who accus'd
      her,
Upon the error that you heard debated :
But Margaret was in some fault for this ;
Although against her will, as it appears
“ In the true course of all the question.”
   Ant. Well, I am glad that all things sort so well.
   Bene. And so am I, being else by faith enforc'd
To call young Claudio to a reckoning for it.   492
   Leon. Well, daughter, and you gentlewomen all,
Withdraw into a chamber by yourselves ;
And,

And, when I send for you, come hither mask'd;
The prince and Claudio promis'd by this hour
To visit me :—You know your office, brother;
You must be father to your brother's daughter,
And give her to young Claudio.   [*Exeunt Ladies.*

   Ant. Which I will do with confirm'd countenance.
   Bene. Friar, I must entreat your pains, I think.
   Friar. To do what, signior ?   500
   Bene. To bind me, or undo me, one of them.—
Signior Leonato, truth it is, good signior,
Your niece regards me with an eye of favour.
   Leon. That eye my daughter lent her; 'tis most
       true,
   Bene. And I do with an eye of love requite her.
   Leon. The sight whereof, I think, you had from
       me,
From Claudio and the prince ; But what's your will ?
   Bene. Your answer, sir, is enigmatical :
But, for my will, my will is, your good will
May stand with ours, this day to be conjoin'd   510
In the estate of honourable marriage ;—
In which, good friar, I shall desire your help.
   Leon. My heart is with your liking.
   Friar. And my help.
" Here comes the prince, and Claudio."

Enter Don PEDRO *and* CLAUDIO, *with Attendants.*

   Pedro. Good morrow to this fair assembly.
   Leon. " Good morrow, prince ; good morrow,
      " Claudio ;"
                  We

We here attend you ; Are you yet determined
To-day to marry with my brother's daughter?
   Claud. I'll hold my mind, were she an Ethiope. 525
   Leon. Call her forth, brother, here's the friar ready.
                      [*Exit* ANTONIO.
   Pedro. Good morrow, Benedick : Why, what's the
     matter,
That you have such a February face,
So full of frost, of storm, and cloudiness ?
   Claud. I think, he thinks upon the savage bull :-
Tush, fear not, man, we'll tip thy horns with gold,
And all Europa shall rejoice at thee ;
As once Europa did at lusty Jove,
When he would play the noble beast in love.
   Bene. Bull Jove, sir, had an amiable low ;   530
And some such strange bull leapt your father's cow,
And got a calf in that same noble feat,
Much like to you, for you have just his bleat.

Re-enter ANTONIO, *with* HERO, BEATRICE, MAR-
     GARET, *and* URSULA, *mask'd.*

   " *Claud.* For this I owe you : here come other
     reck'nings."
Which is the lady I must seize upon ?
   Ant. This same is she, and I do give you her.
   Claud. Why then she's mine ; Sweet, let me see
     your face.
   Leon. No, that you shall not, till you take her
     hand
Before this friar, and swear to marry her.
                         Claud.

Claud. Give me your hand before this holy friar;
I am your husband, if you like of me.   550

   Hero. And when I liv'd, I was your other wife:
                                        [*Unmasking.*
And when you lov'd, you were my other husband.

   Claud. Another Hero?

   Hero. Nothing certainer:
One Hero dy'd defil'd; but I do live,
And, surely as I live, I am a maid.

   Pedro. The former Hero! Hero, that is dead!

   Leon. She dy'd, my lord, but whiles her slander liv'd.

   Friar. All this amazement can I qualify;   550
When, after that the holy rites are ended,
I'll tell you largely of fair Hero's death:
Mean time let wonder seem familiar,
And to the chapel let us presently.

   Bene. Soft and fair, friar.—Which is Beatrice?

   Beat. I answer to that name; What is your will?

   Bene. Do not you love me?

   Beat. Why, no, no more than reason.

   Bene. Why then your uncle, and the prince, and
          Claudio
Have been deceived; they swore you did.   560

   Beat. Do not you love me?

   Bene. Troth, no, no more than reason.

   Beat. Why, then my cousin, Margaret, and Ursula,
Are much deceiv'd; for they did swear you did.

   Bene. They swore, that you were almost sick for me.

   Beat. They swore, that you were well-nigh dead
          for me.
                                        Bene.

Bene. 'Tis no such matter:—Then, you do not
    love me?

Beat. No, truly, but in friendly recompence.

Leon. Come, cousin, I am sure you love the gen-
    tleman.

Claud. And I'll be sworn upon't, that he loves her;
For here's a paper, written in his hand,   571
A halting sonnet of his own pure brain,
Fashion'd to Beatrice.

. *Hero.* And here's another,
Writ in my cousin's hand, stolen from her pocket,   ,
Containing her affection unto Benedick.

. *Bene.* A miracle! here's our own hands against our
hearts!—Come, I will have thee; but, by this light,
I take thee for pity.   579

Beat. I would not deny you;—but, by this good
day, I yield upon great persuasion; and, partly, to save
your life, for I was told, you were in a consumption.

. *Bene.* Peace, I will stop your mouth.—   583
                                        [*Kissing her.*

. *Pedro.* How dost thou, Benedick the married man?

Bene. I'll tell thee what, prince; a college of wit-
crackers cannot flout. me out of my humour: Dost
thou think, I care for a satire, or an epigram? No:
if a man will be beaten with brains, he shall wear
nothing handsome about him: In brief, since I do
purpose to marry, I will think nothing to any purpose
that the world can say against it; and therefore never
flout at me for what I have said against it; for man is
a giddy thing, and this is my conclusion.—For thy
                                                    part,

part, Claudio, I did think to have beaten thee; but
in that thou art like to be my kinsman, live unbruis'd,
and love my cousin.   596

Claud. I had well hoped, thou would'st have denied
Beatrice, that I might have cudgell'd thee " out of
" thy single life, to make thee a double dealer; which,
" out of question, thou wilt be, if my cousin do not
" look exceeding narrowly to thee."   601

Bene. Come, come, we are friends :—let's have a
dance ere we are marry'd, that we may lighten our
own hearts, and our wives' heels.

Leon. We'll have dancing afterwards.

Bene. First, o' my word; therefore, play, musick.—
Prince, thou art sad; get thee a wife, get thee a wife:
there is no staff more reverend than one tipt with horn.

Enter Messenger.

Mess. My lord, your brother John is ta'en in flight,
And brought with armed men back to Messina. 610

Bene. Think not on him till to-morrow : I'll devise
thee brave punishments for him.—Strike up, pipers.

      Dance. [*Exeunt omnes.*

THE END.

ANNOTATIONS

BY

SAM. JOHNSON & GEO. STEEVENS,

A N D

THE VARIOUS COMMENTATORS

U P O N

MUCH ADO ABOUT NOTHING,

WRITTEN BY

WILL. SHAKSPERE.

——SIC ITUR AD ASTRA.

VIRG.

LONDON:

Printed for, and under the Direction of,

JOHN BELL, British-Library, STRAND,

Bookseller to His Royal Highness the PRINCE of WALES.

M DCC LXXXVII.

ANNOTATIONS

UPON

MUCH ADO ABOUT NOTHING.

ACT I.

Much Ado about Nothing.] *INNOGEN* (the mother of Hero), in the oldest quarto that I have seen of this play, printed in 1600, is mentioned to enter in two several scenes. The succeeding editions have all continued her name in the Dramatis Personæ. But I have ventured to expunge it; there being no mention of her through the play, no one speech address'd to her, nor one syllable spoken by her. Neither is there any one passage, from which we have any reason to determine that Hero's mother was living. It seems, as if the poet had in his first plan design'd such a character : which, on a survey of it, he found would be superfluous ; and therefore he left it out.

THEOBALD.

A ij

Line

Line 7.   ——*of any* sort,—] *Sort* is rank.   So, in Chapman's version of the 16th book of *Homer's Odyssey :*

" A ship, and in her many a man of *sort.*"

STEVEENS.

Sort is rather *distinction.*   HENLEY.

22.   ——*joy could not shew itself* modest *enough without a* badge *of bitterness.*] This is judiciously express'd. Of all the transports of joy, that which is attended with tears is least offensive ; because, carrying with it this mark of pain, it allays the envy that usually attends another's happiness.   This he finely calls a *modest* joy, such a one as did not insult the observer by an indication of happiness unmixed with pain.

WARBURTON.

Such another expression occurs in Chapman's version of the tenth book of the Odyssey :

" ————our eyes wore

" The same wet *badge* of weak humanity."

This is an idea which Shakspere seems to have been delighted to introduce.   It occurs again in *Macbeth :*

" ————*my plenteous joys*

" *Wanton in fullness, seek to hide themselves*

" *In drops of sorrow.*"   STEEVENS.

27.   ——*no faces truer*] That is, none *honester,* none *more sincere.*   .   JOHNSON.

30.   —*is signior Montanto return'd—*] *Montante,* in Spanish, is a *huge two-handed sword,* given, with much
humour,

humour, to one the speaker would represent as a boaster or bravado. WARBURTON.

Montanto was one of the ancient terms of the fencing-school. So, in *Every Man in his Humour :* " —your punto, your reverso, your stoccata, your imbrocata, your passada, your *montanto*," &c. Again, in the *Merry Wives of Windsor :*

" ————thy reverse, thy distance, thy *montant*."
STEEVENS.

32. *—there was none such in the army of any* sort.] Not meaning there was none such of *any order or degree whatever,* but that there was none such of *any quality above the common.* WARBURTON.

38. *He set up his bills,* &c.] In Ben Jonson's *Every Man out of his Humour,* Shift says :

" This is rare, I have set up my *bills* without
discovery."

Again, in *Swetnam Arraign'd,* 1620:

" I have bought foils already, *set up bills,*

" Hung up my two-hand sword," &c.

Again, in Nash's *Have with you to Saffron-Walden,* &c. 1596:

" *—setting up bills* like a bearward or fencer, what fights we shall have, and what weapons she will meet me at."

The following account of one of these challenges, taken from an ancient MS. of which some account is given in a note on the first act and first scene of the *Merry Wives of Windsor,* may not be unacceptable to

the

the inquisitive reader. " Item, a challenge playde before the King's majestie (Edward VI.) at Westminster,
by three maisters, Willym Pascall, Robert Greene,
and W. Browne, at seven kynde of weapons. That
is to saye, the axe, the pike, the rapier and target,
the rapier and cloke, and with two swords, against all
alyens and strangers, being borne without the King's
dominions, of what countrie so ever he or they were,
geving them a warninge by theyr *bills set up* by the
three maisters, the space of eight weeks before the
sayd challenge was playde; and it was holden four
severall Sundayes, one after another." It appears
from the same work that all challenges " to any
maister within the realme of Englande being an Eng-
lishe man," were against the statutes of the " Noble
science of Defence."

Beatrice means, that Benedick published a general
challenge, like a prize-fighter.   STEEVENS.

39.   —*challenged Cupid at the flight;*—] To challenge
at the *flight*, was a challenge to shoot with an *arrow.*
Flight means an arrow, as may be proved from the
following lines in Beaumont and Fletcher's *Bonduca :*

" ———— *not the quick rack swifter :*
" *The virgin from the hated ravisher*
" *Not half so fearful : not a* flight *drawn home,*
" *A round stone from a sling.*"————

But it is apparent from the following passage in the
Civil Wars of Daniel, B. VIII. st. 15. that a *flight* was
not used to signify an *arrow in general,* but some
particular

particular kind of arrow ; I believe one of an unusual length :

> " —————— ——— and assign'd
> " The archers their *flight*-shafts to shoot away ;
> " Which th' adverse side (with sleet and dimness blind,
> " Mistaken in the distance of the way),
> " Answer with their *sheaf-arrows*, that came short
> " Of their intended aim, and did no hurt."

Holinshed makes the same distinction in his account of the same occurrence, and adds, that these *flights* were provided on purpose. Again, in Holinshed, p. 649,—" He caused the soldiers to shoot their *flights* towards the lord Audlies company."

Mr. Tollet observes, that the length of a *flight-shot* seems ascertained by a passage in Leland's Itinerary, 1769, Vol. IV. p. 44. " The passage into it at ful se is a *flite-shot* over, as much as the Tamise is above the bridge."—It were easy to know the length of London-Bridge ; and Stowe's Survey may inform the curious reader whether the river has been narrowed by embanking since the days of Leland.

The *bird-bolt* is a short thick arrow without point, and spreading at the extremity so much, as to leave a flat surface, about the breadth of a shilling. Such are to this day in use to kill rooks with, and are shot from a cross-bow. So, in Marston's *What You Will*, 1607 :

> " —ignorance

" ————ignorance should shoot
" His gross-knobb'd *bird bolt.*——"

Again, in *Love in a Maze*, 1632:

" ————Cupid,
" Pox of his *bird-bolt !* Venus,
" Speak to thy boy to fetch his *arrow* back,
" Or strike her with a *sharp one !*"

STEEVENS.

He challenged Cupid at the flight, *and my uncle's fool challenged him at the* bird-bolt.] The flight was an arrow of a particular kind :—In the Harleian Catalogue of MSS. Vol. I. n. 69. is " a challenge of the lady *Maice*'s servants to all comers, to be performed at *Greenwiche*—to shoot standart arrow, or *flight.*" I find the title-page of an old pamphlet still more explicit : " A new *post*—a marke exceeding necessary for all men's arrows : whether the great man's *flight*, the gallant's *rover*, the wise man's *pricke-shaft*, the poor man's *but-shaft*, or the fool's *bird-bolt.*"

FARMER.

The *flight*, which in the Latin of the middle ages was called *flecta*, was a fleet arrow with narrow feathers, usually employed against rovers. See *Blount's Ancient Tenures*, 1679.

A *bolt* seems to have been a general term for an *arrow*. So, in Shirley's *Love's Cruelty :* " When the keepers are none of the wisest, their *bolts* are sooner shot."

There the *bolt* is supposed to be employed against
deer-

deer-stealers. The word is still used in the common proverb: *A fool's bolt is soon shot.*

That particular species of arrow which was employed in killing birds, appears to have been called a *bird*-bolt.   MALONE.

An *arrow* employed in war was never termed a *bolt.* *Bolt*, therefore, could not have been a *general* term for an *arrow.*   STEEVENS.

46. ————*he'll be meet with you,*————] This is a very common expression in the midland counties, and signifies, *he'll be your match, he'll be even with you.*

So, in TEXNOΓAMIA, by B. Holiday, 1618:

" Go meet her, or else she'll *be meet* with me."

55. ————Stuff'd *with all honourable virtues.*] *Stuff'd*, in this first instance, has no ridiculous meaning. Mr. Edwards observes that *Mede* in his *Discourses on Scripture,* speaking of Adam, says, " —he whom God had *stuffed* with so many excellent qualities "
                Edwards's MS.

Again, in *The Winter's Tale :*

" ————whom you know

" Of *stuff'd sufficiency.*"

Un homme bien *etoffe,* signifies, in French, *a man in good circumstances.*   STEEVENS.

57. —*he is no less than a* stuff'd *man : but for the* stuffing—*well, we are all mortal.*] Mr. Theobald plumed himself much on the pointing of this passage; which, by the way, he might learn from Davenant: but he says not a word, nor any one else that I know of, about the reason of this abruption. The truth is,

B

Beatrice

Beatrice starts an idea at the words *stuff'd man*; and prudently checks herself in the pursuit of it. A *stuff'd man* was one of the many cant phrases for a *cuckold*. In *Lilly's Midas*, we have an inventory of *Motto's moveables.*—" Item, says Petulus, one paire of hornes in the bride-chamber on the *bed's head.*—The *beast's* head, observes Licio; for *Motto* is *stuff'd in the head*, and these are among *unmoveable goods.*"   FARMER.

65.   ——*four of his five wits*——] In our author's time *wit* was the general term for intellectual powers. So, *Davies on the Soul :*

" Wit, *seeking truth, from cause to cause ascends,*
 " *And never rests till it the first attain* ;
" Will, *seeking good, finds many middle ends,*
 " *But never stays till it the last do gain.*"

And, in another part :

" *But, if a phrenzy do possess the brain,*
 " *It so disturbs and blots the form of things,*
" *As fantasy proves altogether vain,*
 " *And to the* wit *no true relation brings.*
" *Then doth the* wit, *admitting all for true,*
 " *Build fond conclusions on those idle grounds.*"—

The *wits* seem to have been reckoned five, by analogy to the five senses, or the five inlets of ideas.
          JOHNSON.

67.   ——*wit enough to keep himself* WARM, &c.] *Such a one has wit enough to keep himself warm,* is a proverbial expression.

So, in the *Wise Woman of Hogsden,* 1638 : " You are the wise woman, are you? and have *wit to keep*

          yourself

yourself warm enough, I warrant you." To bear any thing for a *difference*, is a term in heraldry. So, in *Hamlet*, Ophelia says:

"——you may wear yours with a *difference*."
STEEVENS.

74. ——*he wears his* faith——] Not religious profession, but *profession of friendship*; for the speaker gives it as the reason of her asking, *who was now his companion?* that *he had every month a new sworn brother.*
WARBURTON.

75. ——*with the next* block] A *block* is the mould on which a hat is formed. So, in Decker's *Satiromastix :*

" Of what fashion is this knight's wit? of what
    block ?"

See a note on *K. Lear*, act iv. sc. 6.

The old writers sometimes use the word *block* for the hat itself.
STEEVENS.

77. ——————*the gentleman is not in your books.*] This is a phrase used, I believe, by more than understand it. *To be in one's books, is to be in one's* codicils *or* will, *to be among friends set down for legacies.* JOHNSON.

I rather think that the *books* alluded to, are memorandum books, like the visiting-books of the present age: so, in Decker's *Honest Whore*, Part II. 1630:

" I am sure her name was in my *Table-Book*
    once."

Or, perhaps, the allusion is to matriculation at the university.

So, in *Aristippus*, or the *Jovial Philosopher*, 1630:
B ij

" You

·" You must be matriculated, and have your name recorded *in Albo Academiæ*."

Again,—" What, have you enrolled him *in Albo?* Have you fully admitted him into the Society ?—to be a member of the body academick ?"

Again, " And if I be not entered, and have my name admitted into some of their *books*, let," &c.

And yet I think the following passage in the *Maid's Revenge*, by Shirley, 1639, will sufficiently support my first supposition :

" Pox of your compliment, you were best not write in her *Table-Books*."

It appears to have been anciently the custom to *chronicle the small beer* of every occurrence, whether literary or domestick, in these *Table-Books*.
So, in the play last quoted :

" Devolve itself!—that word is not in my *Table-Books* "
Hamlet, likewise has,—" my *tables*," &c.
Again, in the *Whore of Babylon*, 1607:
　　　" ———— Campeius !—Babylon
　　" His name hath *in her Tables*."
Again, in *Acolastus*, a comedy, 1540.
" —We weyl haunse thee, or set thy name into our *felowship boke*, with clappynge of handes," &c.

I know not exactly to what custom this last quoted passage refers, unless to the *album :* for just after, the same expression occurs again: that " —from henceforthe thou may'st have a place worthy for thee in our
whyte ;

whyte: from hence thou may'st have thy name written in our *boke*."

It should seem, from the following passage in the *Taming of a Shrew*, that this phrase might have originated from the *Herald's Office :*

" A herald, Kate! oh, put me *in thy books !*"
After all, the following note in one of the Harleian MSS. No. 847, may be the best illustration:

" W. C. to Henry Fradsham, Gent. the owner of this book :

  " Some write their fantasies in verse

  " *In theire bookes* where they friendshippe shewe,

  " Wherein oft tymes they doe rehearse

  " The great good will that they doe owe," &c.

STEEVENS.

The gentleman is not in your books.] This phrase has not been exactly interpreted. *To be in a man's books,* originally meant to be in the list of his *retainers.* Sir John Mandevile tells us, " alle the mynstrelles that comen before the great Chan ben witholden with him, as of his houshold, and entred in his *bookes,* as for his own men." FARMER.

This expression, I make no doubt, took its rise from the custom mentioned by Dr. Farmer, That in all great families, the names of the servants of the household were written in *books* kept for that purpose, appears from the following passage in *A new Trick to cheat the Devil,* a comedy, 1639 : " See, master Treatwell, that his name be *enrolled* among my other

B iij

servants—

servants—Let my *steward* receive such notice from you."

A *servant* and a *lover* were in Cupid's Vocabulary, synonymous.   Thus, in Marston's *Malecontent*, 1604: " Is not Marshal *Makeroom*, my *servant* in reversion, a proper gentleman?"

Hence the phrase—*to be in a person's books*—was applied equally to the *lover* and the *menial attendant.*

MALONE.

81.   —*young squarer*——] A *squarer* I take to be a cholerick, quarrelsome fellow, for in this sense Shakspere uses the word to *square*.   So, in the *Midsummer Night's Dream*, it is said of Oberon and Titania, that *they never meet but they* square.   So the sense may be, *Is there no* hot-blooded *youth that will keep him company through all his mad pranks?*   JOHNSON.

102.   *You embrace your charge*——] That is, your *burden*, your *incumbrance.*   JOHNSON.

121.   ——*such food to feed it, as signior Benedick?*] A kindred thought occurs in *Coriolanus*, act ii. scene 1.

" Our very priests must become *mockers*, if they encounter such ridiculous subjects as you are."

STEEVENS.

156.   *I thank you:*——] The poet has judiciously marked the gloominess of Don John's character, by making him averse to the common forms of civility.

SIR J. HAWKINS.

183.   ——*to tell us, Cupid is a good hare-finder,* &c.] I know not whether I conceive the jest here intended.

tended. ' Claudio hints his love of Hero. Benedick asks, whether he is serious, or whether he only means to jest, and tell them that *Cupid is a good hare-finder, and Vulcan a rare carpenter.* A man praising a pretty lady in jest, may shew the quick sight of Cupid, but what has it to do with the *carpentry* of Vulcan ? Perhaps the thought lies no deeper than this, *Do you mean to tell us as new what we all know already ?*

JOHNSON.

I believe no more is meant by those ludicrous expressions than this—Do you mean, says Benedick, to amuse us with improbable stories?

An ingenious correspondent, whose signature is R. W. explains the passage in the same sense, but more amply : " Do you mean to tell us that love is not blind, and that fire will not consume what is combustible?"——for both these propositions are implied in making Cupid *a good hare-finder,* and Vulcan (the God of fire) *a good carpenter.* In other words, *would you convince me, whose opinion on this head is well-known, that you can be in love without being blind, and can play with the flame of beauty without being scorched.*

STEEVENS.

. I explain the passage thus : *Do you scoff and mock in telling us that Cupid, who is blind, is a good hare-finder, which requires a quick eye-sight; and that Vulcan, a blacksmith, is a rare carpenter ?*   TOLLET.

185. ——*to go in the song ?*] *i. e.* to join with you in your song—to strike in with you in the song.

STEEVENS.

197.

197.   *wear his cap with suspicion?*] That is, subject his head to the disquiet of jealousy.

JOHNSON.

In the *Palace of Pleasure*, p. 233, we have the following passage : " Al they that *weare hornes* be pardoned to weare their *capps* upon their heads."

HENDERSON.

200. ————*sigh away Sundays.*] This expression most probably alludes to the strict manner in which the Sabbath was observed by the *Puritans*, who usually spent that day in *sighs* and *gruntings*, and other hypocritical marks of devotion.   STEEVENS.

214. Claud. *If this were so, so were it uttered.*] Claudio, evading at first a confession of his passion, says ; if I had really confided such a secret to him, yet he would have blabbed it in this manner. In his next speech, he thinks proper to avow his love ; and when Benedick says, *God forbid it should be so,* i. e. God forbid he should even wish to marry her ; Claudio replies—God forbid I should not wish it. STEEVENS.

235. ————*but in the force of his will.*] Alluding to the definition of a heretick in the schools.

WARBURTON.

239. ————*but that I will have a recheat winded in my forehead,*] That is, *I will wear a horn on my forehead, which the huntsman may blow.* A *recheate* is the sound by which dogs are called back. Shakspere had no mercy upon the poor cuckold, his *horn* is an inexhaustible subject of merriment.   JOHNSON.

So, in the *Return from Parnassus :*

" —When

" ——When you blow the death of your fox in the field or covert, then you must sound three notes, with three winds; and *recheat*, mark you, sir, upon the same three winds."

" Now, sir, when you come to your stately gate, as you sounded the *recheat* before, so now you must sound the relief three times."

Again, in the *Book of Huntynge*, &c. bl. let. no date, " Blow the whole *rechate* with three wyndes, the first wynde one longe and six shorte. The seconde wynde two shorte and one longe. The thred wynde one longe and two shorte."

Among Bagford's Collections relative to Typography, in the British Museum, 1044, c. ii. in an engraved half sheet, containing the ancient Hunting Notes of England, &c. Among these, I find, Single, Double, and Treble *Recheats*, Running *Recheat*, Warbling *Recheat*, another *Recheat* with the tongue very hard, another smoother *Recheat*, and another warbling *Recheat*. The musical notes are affixed to them all.   STEEVENS.

A *recheate* is a particular lesson upon the horn, to call dogs back from the scent : from the old French word *recet*, which was used in the same sense as *retraite*.   HANMER.

240. ——*hang my bugle in an invisible baldrick,*] *Bugle*, i. e. bugle-horn or hunting-horn. The meaning seems to be—or that I should be compelled to carry any horn that I must wish to remain invisible,

and

and that I should be ashamed to hang openly in my belt or baldrick.

It is still said of the mercenary cuckold, that he *carries his horns in his pockets.*   STEEVENS.

255.   ——*notable argument.*] An eminent subject for satire.   JOHNSON.

256.   ——*in a bottle like a cat,*——] As to *the cat and bottle,* I can procure no better information than the following, which does not exactly suit with the text:

In some counties of England, a cat was formerly closed up with a quantity of soot in a wooden bottle (such as that in which shepherds carry their liquor), and was suspended on a line.   He who beat out the bottom as he ran under it, and was nimble enough to escape its contents, was regarded as the hero of this inhuman diversion.   STEEVENS.

257.   ——*and he that hits me, let him be clap'd on the shoulder, and call'd* Adam.] But why should he therefore be call'd *Adam?* Perhaps, by a quotation or two we may be able to trace the poet's allusion here.   In *Law-Tricks,* or, *Who would have thought it* (a comedy written by John Day, and printed in 1608), I find this speech: *Adam Bell, a substantial outlaw, and a passing good* archer, *yet no tobacconist.*   By this it appears, that Adam Bell, at that time of day, was of reputation for his skill at the bow.   I find him again mentioned in a burlesque poem of Sir William Davenant's, called, *The Long Vacation in London.*   THEOBALD.

Adam

Adam Bell, Clym of the Clough, and William of Cloudesly, were, says Dr. Percy, three noted outlaws, whose skill in Archery rendered them formerly as famous in the North of England, as Robin Hood and his fellows were in the midland Counties. Their place of residence was in the forest of Englewood, not far from Carlisle. At what time they lived does not appear. The author of the common ballads on *The Pedigree, Education, and Marriage of Robin Hood*, makes them contemporary with Robin Hood's father, in order to give him the honour of beating them. See *Reliques of ancient Poetry*, Vol. I. p. 143, where the ballad on these outlaws is preserved.   STEEVENS.

260. *In time the savage bull doth bear the yoke.*] This line is taken from the *Spanish Tragedy*, or *Hieronymo*, &c. 1605, which itself, with a slight variation, is taken from Watson's Sonnets, 4to. bl. let. printed about 1580. See Note on the last Edition of Dodsley's Old Plays, Vol. XII. p. 387.   STEEVENS.

269. ——*if Cupid hath not spent all his quiver in Venice,*] All modern writers agree in representing Venice in the same light as the ancients did Cyprus. And it is this character of the people that is here alluded to.

WARBURTON.

284. ——guarded *with fragments,*] *Guards* were ornamental lace or borders. So, in the *Merchant of Venice :*

       " ——give him a livery
       " More *guarded* than his fellows."
Again, in *Henry* IV. Part I.

              " —velvet

" ——velvet *guards* and Sunday citizens."

STEEVENS.

286. ——*ere you flout old ends*, &c.] The ridicule here is to the formal conclusions of Epistles dedicatory, and Letters. Barnaby Googe thus ends his dedication to the first edition of Palengenius, 12mo. 1560 : "And thus *committyng* your Ladiship with all yours to the *tuicion* of the moste mercifull *God*, I ende. From Staple Inne at London, the eighte and twenty of March." REED.

317. *The fairest* grant *is the necessity :*] *i. e.* no one can have a better reason for granting a request than the necessity of its being granted. WARBURTON.

Mr. Hayley with great acuteness proposes to read,

The fairest grant is to necessity. STEEVENS.

336. ——*a* thick-pleached *alley*] *Thick-pleached* is thickly interwoven. In *Antony and Cleopatra :*

" ——with *pleached* arms, bending down

" His corrigible neck." STEEVENS.

353. *Cousin,* you know—(and afterwards) *good cousin——*] Surely, *brother* and *cousin* never could have had the same meaning : yet, as this passage stands at present, Leonato appears to address himself to Antonio (or as he is styled in the first folio, *the old man*), his *brother*, whom he is made to call *cousin.*

It appears that several persons, I suppose Leonato's *kinsmen,* are at this time crossing the stage, to whom he here addresses himself. Accordingly, the old copy reads, not *cousin*, but——

" *Cousins,* you know what you have to do."

You

You all know your several offices; take care to assist in making preparations at this busy time for my new guests.

I would therefore read *cousins* in both places.

MALONE.

357.   Don *John*] The folio has *Sir* John. MALONE.
What, the good jer, *my lord!*]   We should read, *goujere.*

STEEVENS.

368.   ————*I cannot hide what I am:*] This is one of our author's natural touches.   An envious and un-social mind, too proud to give pleasure, and too sullen to receive it, always endeavours to hide its malignity from the world and from itself, under the plainness of simple honesty, or the dignity of haughty independence.

JOHNSON.

373.   ————claw *no man in his humour.*] To *claw* is to flatter.   So *the pope's claw-backs*, in bishop Jewel, are the pope's *flatterers.*   The sense is the same in the proverb, *Mulus mulum scabit.*

JOHNSON.

In *Wylsen on Usury*, 1571, p. 141.

"————therefore I will *clawe* him, and saye well might he fare, and Godd's blessing have he too."

REED.

382.   *I had rather be a* canker *in a hedge, than a* rose *in his* grace;] A *canker* is the *canker* rose, *dog rose, cynosbatus,* or *hip.*

JOHNSON.

So, in Heywood's *Love's Mistress*, 1636 :

"A rose, a lily, a blew-bottle, and a *canker*
        flower."

Again, in Shakspere's 54th *Sonnet :*

C

"The

" The *canker* blooms have full as deep a die

" As the perfumed tincture of the rose."

I think no change is necessary.   STEEVENS.

The former speech, in my apprehension, shews clearly that the old copy is right. Conrade had said : " He hath ta'en you new into his *grace,* where it is impossible that you should take *root* but by the fair weather that you make yourself." To this Don John replies, with critical correctness : " I had rather be a *canker* in a hedge, than a *rose* in his *grace.*" We meet a kindred expression in *Macbeth :*

" ————Welcome hither :

" I have begun to *plant* thee, and will labour

" To make thee full of *growing.*"

Again, in *K. Henry VI.* Part III.

" I'll *plant* Plantaganet, *root* him up who dares."

MALONE.

415. ——*in* sad *conference ;*] *Sad* in this, as in other instances, signifies *serious.*   STEEVENS.

424. *both* sure,——] *i. e.* to be depended on. .

STEEVENS.

ACT II.

Line 4. ——*HEART-BURN'D an hour after.*] The pain commonly called the *heart-burn,* proceeds

from

from an *acid* humour in the stomach, and is there-fore properly enough imputed to *tart* looks.

JOHNSON.

30. ——*in* woollen.] Thus the modern editors. The old copies read——*in* the woollen.   STEEVENS.

69. —*if the prince be too* important,] *Important* here, and in many other places, is *importunate.*

JOHNSON.

84. *Balthazar,*] The quarto and folio add—*or dumb John.*   STEEVENS.

or dumb John.] Here is another proof, that when the first copies of our author's plays were prepared for the press, the transcript was made out by the ear. If the MS. had lain before the transcriber, it is very unlikely that he should have mistaken *Don* for *dumb:* but, by an inarticulate speaker, or inattentive hearer, they might easily be confounded.   MALONE.

In answer to this remark, it is well observed by Mr. Reed, that Don John's taciturnity has been already no-ticed.   It seems therefore not improbable, that the author himself might have occasionally applied the epithet *dumb* to him.   HENLEY.

97. Pedro. *Speak low,* &c.] This speech, which is given to Pedro, should be given to Margaret.

REVISAL.

98. Balth. *Well, I would you did like me.*] This, and the two following little speeches, which I have placed to Balthazar, are in all the printed copies given to Benedick. But, 'tis clear, the dialogue here ought to be betwixt Balthazar and Margaret: Bene-

C ij

dick,

dick, a little lower, converses with Beatrice: and so every man talks with his woman once round.

THEOBALD.

104. *amen.*] I do not concur with Theobald in his arbitrary disposition of these speeches. Balthazar is called in the old copies *dumb John*, as I have already observed; and therefore it should seem, that he was meant to speak but little. When Benedick says, *the hearers may cry, amen*, we must suppose that he leaves Margaret and goes in search of some other sport. Margaret, utters a wish for a good partner. Balthazar, who is represented as a man of the fewest words, repeats Benedick's *Amen*, and leads her off, desiring, as he says in the following short speech, to put himself to no greater expence of breath.

STEEVENS.

This whole note is, I apprehend, founded on a mistake; *or*, in the stage-direction in the old copy, at the beginning of this scene, was, I believe, an accidental repetition; and *dumb*, I suspect, was written instead of *Don*, through the mistake of the transcriber, whose ear deceived him.

I think it extremely probable, that the regulation proposed by Theobald, and the author of the *Revisal*, is right.

MALONE.

115. ——*his* dry *hand*——] A *dry* hand was anciently regarded as the sign of a cold constitution. To this Maria, in *Twelfth Night*, alludes, act i. sc. 3.

STEEVENS.

128. ——*Hundred merry Tales*;——] The book, to which Shakspere alludes, was an old translation of

Les

Les cent Nouvelles Nouvelles. The original was published at Paris, in the black letter, before the year
1500, and is said to have been written by some of the
royal family of France. Ames mentions a translation
of it prior to the time of Shakspere.

In the *London Chaunticleres*, 1659, this work, among
others, is cry'd for sale by a ballad-man. " The
Seven Wise Men of Gotham ; a *Hundred Merry Tales ;*
Scoggin's Jests," &c.

Again, in the *Nice Valour*, &c. by Beaumont and
Fletcher :

" —————the Almanacks,

" The *Hundred Novels*, and the Books of Cookery."

Of this collection there are frequent entries in the
register of the Stationers' Company. The first I met
with was in January 1581. 　　STEEVENS.

This Book was certainly printed before the year
1575, and in much repute, as appears from the mention of it in Langham's Letter. Again, in *The English Courtier and the Cuntrey Gentleman*, bl. let. 1586.
Sign. H. 4. " ——wee want not also pleasant mad-
headed knaves that bee properly learned and well
reade in diverse pleasant bookes and good authors.
As Sir Guy of Warwicke, the Foure Sonnes of Amon,
the Ship of Fooles, the Budget of Demaundes, *the
Hundredth Merry Tales*, the Booke of Ryddles, and
many other excellent writers both witty and pleasaunt."
It has been suggested to me, that there is no other
reason than the word *hundred* to suppose this book a
translation of the *Cent Nouvelles Nouvelles.* 　　REED.

C iij

136. ——*his gift is in devising* impossible *slanders :*]
Impossible slanders are, I suppose, such slanders as,
from their absurdity and impossibility, bring their own
confutation with them.   JOHNSON.

138. ——*his villany;*——] By which she means
his malice and impiety. By his impious jests, she in-
sinuates, he *pleased* libertines; and by his *devising*
slanders of them, he angred them.   WARBURTON.

156. ——*his* bearing.] *i. e.* his carriage, his de-
meanour. So, in *Measure for Measure :*
   " How I may formally in person *bear* me."
                                          STEEVENS.

174. *Therefore, &c.*] *Let,* which is found in the
next line, is understood here.   MALONE.

176. ————*beauty is a witch,*

   Against whose charms faith melteth into blood.]
i. e. as wax, when opposed to the fire kindled by a
witch, no longer preserves the figure of the person
whom it was designed to represent, but flows into a
shapeless lump; so fidelity, when confronted with
beauty, dissolves into our ruling passion, and is lost
there like a drop of water in the sea.   STEEVENS.

185. ——*usurer's chain ?*] *Chains* of gold in our
author's time, usually worn by wealthy citizens, in the
same manner as they now are by the aldermen of
London. See *The Puritan, or Widow of Watling-*
Street, act iii. sc. 3. *Albumazar,* act i. sc. 7. &c. REED.

Usury seems about this time to have been a common
topick of invective. I have three or four dialogues,
pasquils, and discourses on the subject, printed before
                                               the

the year 1600. From every one of these it appears, that the merchants were the chief usurers of the age.

STEEVENS.

203. —*it is the base*, though *bitter disposition of Beatrice, that puts the world into her person,*] That is, It is the disposition of Beatrice, who takes upon her to personate the world, and therefore represents the world as saying what she only says herself.

Base, though bitter. I do not understand how *base* and *bitter* are inconsistent, or why what is *bitter* should not be *base*. I believe, we may safely read, *It is the base*, the *bitter* disposition. JOHNSON.

The *base* though *bitter*, may mean the *ill-natur'd* though *witty*. STEEVENS.

210. ——*as melancholy as a lodge in a warren;*] A parallel thought occurs in the first chapter of Isaiah, where the prophet, describing the desolation of Judah, says: " The daughter of Zion is left as a cottage in a vineyard, as a *lodge* in a garden of cucumbers," &c. I am informed, that near Aleppo, these lonely buildings are still made use of, it being necessary, that the fields where water-melons, cucumbers, &c. are raised, should be regularly watched. I learn from Thomas Newton's *Herball to the Bible*, 8vo. 1587, that " so soone as the cucumbers, &c. be gathered, these lodges are abandoned of the watchmen and keepers, and no more frequented." From these forsaken buildings, it should seem, the prophet takes his comparison. STEEVENS.

Lodges

Lodges were formerly common in our *warrens*, and in many of them they may still be seen ; so that Shakspere need not have gone for this to a cucumber-garden in Judæa.   HENLEY.

212. —*of this young lady* ;] Benedick speaks of Hero as if she were on the stage. Perhaps, both she and Leonato, were meant to make their entrance with Don Pedro. When Beatrice enters, she is spoken of as coming in with only Claudio.

STEEVENS.

241. ——*such* impossible *conveyance,*——] *Impossible* may be licentiously used for *unaccountable*. Beatrice has already said, that Benedick invents *impossible* slanders.

. So, in the *Fair maid of the Inn*, by Beaumont and Fletcher :

"You would look for some most *impossible* antick."

Again, in *The Roman Actor*, by Massinger :

" ——to lose

" Ourselves, by building on *impossible* hopes."

I believe the meaning is——*with a rapidity equal to that of* jugglers, *who appear to perform* impossibilities.

Conveyance was the common term in our author's time for *slight of hand.*   MALONE.

Dr. Warburton reads *impassable*, and this agrees with what follows—" that I stood like a man at a mark, with a whole army shooting at me."   * * *.

263. —*bring you the length of prester John's foot ; fetch you a hair off the great Cham's beard ;*] *i. e.* I will under-

undertake the hardest task, rather than have any conversation with lady Beatrice. Alluding to the difficulty of access to either of those monarchs, but more particularly to the former.

So Cartwright, in his comedy call'd *The Siege, or Love's Convert*, 1641:

" ——bid me take the Parthian king by the beard: or draw an eye-tooth from the jaw royal of the Persian monarch."   STEEVENS.

270. ——my *lady's Tongue.*] Thus the quarto 1600. The folio reads——*this* lady tongue.

STEEVENS.

290. ——*civil* as an *orange.*] This conceit occurs likewise in *Nash's four Letters confuted*, 1592. " For the order of my life it is as *civil* as an *orange.*"

STEEVENS.

291. ——*of* that *jealous complexion.*] Thus the quarto 1600. The folio reads, *of* a *jealous complexion.*

STEEVENS.

314. *Thus goes every one to the world but I, and I am sun-burn'd ;*] What is it, *to go to the world?* perhaps, to enter by marriage into a settled state ; but why is the unmarry'd lady *sun-burnt?* I believe we should read, *Thus goes every one to the* wood *but I, and I am sun-burnt.* Thus does every one but I find a shelter, and I am left exposed to wind and *sun. The nearest way to the* wood, is a phrase for the readiest means to any end. It is said of a woman, who accepts a worse match than those which she had refused, that she has passed through the *wood,* and at last taken a crooked stick.

stick.   But conjectural criticism has always something
to abate its confidence.   Shakspere, in *All's Well that
End's Well*, uses the phrase, *to go to the world*, for
marriage.   So that my emendation depends only on the
opposition of *wood* to *sun-burnt*.   JOHNSON.

I am *sun-burnt*, may mean, I have lost my beauty,
and am consequently no longer such an object as can
tempt a man to marry.   STEEVENS.

342.   —— *she hath often dream'd of* unhappiness,]
Thus Beaumont and Fletcher, in their comedy of the
Maid of the Mill:

> " —— *My* dreams *are like my thoughts, honest and*
>   *innocent:*

> " *Yours are* unhappy."

i. e. wild, wanton, unlucky.   WARBURTON.

361.   —— *to bring signior Benedick, and the lady
Beatrice, into a mountain of affection, the one with the
other.*]   *A mountain of affection with one another* is a
strange expression, yet I know not well how to change
it.   Perhaps it was originally written, *to bring Benedick and Beatrice into a* mooting *of affection*; to bring
them not to any more *mootings* of contention, but to a
mooting or conversation of love.   This reading is confirmed by the prepostion *with*; *a mountain with each
other*, or *affection with each other*, cannot be used, but
a mooting with each other is proper and regular.

          JOHNSON.

Uncommon as the word proposed by Dr. Johnson
may appear, it is used in several of the old plays.
So, in *Glapthorne's Wit in a Constable*, 1639:

                              " —— one

    " ————————one who never
    " Had *mooted* in the hall, or seen the revels
    " Kept in the house at Christmas."
Again, in the *Return from Parnassus*, 1606:
    " It is a plain case whereon I *mooted* in our
       temple."
Again, "—at a *mooting* in our temple."   Ibid.

And yet all that I believe is meant by a *mountain of
affection*, is *a great deal of affection.*

In one of *Stanyhurst*'s poems, is the following phrase
to denote a large quantity of love:
    " *Lumps* of love promist, nothing perform'd," &c.
Again, in the *Renegado*, by Massinger:
    " ————————'tis but parting with
    " A *mountain* of vexation."

Thus in *K. Henry VIII.* "a *sea* of glory."   In *Hamlet*,
" a *sea* of trouble."   Again, in Howel's *History of
Venice:* " though they see *mountains* of miseries heaped
on one's back."   Again, in Bacon's *History of King
Henry VII.* " Perkin sought to corrupt the servants to
the lieutenant of the tower by *mountains* of promises."
Again, in the *Comedy of Errors:* " —the *mountain* of
mad flesh that claims marriage of me."   Little can
be inferr'd from Shakspere's offence against grammar.

Mr. Malone observes, that, " Shakspere has many
phrases equally harsh.   He who would hazard such
expressions as *a storm of fortunes, a vale of years,* and
a tempest of provocation, would not scruple to write *a
mountain of affection.*"   STEEVENS.
                           375.

375.   ——*a noble* strain,——] *i. e* descent, lineage.
So, in the *Fairy Queen,* B. IV. c. viii. s. 33.

> " Sprung from the auncient stocke of prince's
>   *straine.*"

Again, B. V. c. ix. s. 32.

> " Sate goodly temperaunce in garments clene,
> " And sacred reverence yborne of heavenly
>   *strene* "

416.   Bora. *Go then, find me a meet hour to draw
Don Pedro, and the count Claudio, alone: tell them that
you know Hero loves me;—Offer them instances, which
shall bear no less likelihood than to see* me *at her chamber-
window; hear me call Margaret, Hero; hear Margaret
term me* Claudio; *and bring them to see this, the very
night before the intended wedding:*] Thus the whole
stream of the editions from the first quarto downwards.
I am obliged here to give a short account of the plot
depending, that the emendation I have made may
appear the more clear and unquestionable. The business stands thus: Claudio, a favourite of the Arragon prince, is by his intercessions with her father,
to be married to fair Hero; Don John, natural brother of the prince, and a hater of Claudio, is in his
spleen zealous to disappoint the match. Borachio, a
rascally dependant on Don John, offers his assistance,
and engages to break off the marriage by this stratagem. " Tell the prince and Claudio (says he) that
Hero is in love with *me*; they won't believe it: offer
them proofs, as, that they shall see me converse with
her in her chamber-window. I am in the good graces
                                                    of

of her waiting-woman, Margaret; and I'll prevail with Margaret, at a dead hour of night, to personate her mistress Hero; do you then bring the prince and Claudio to overhear our discourse; and they shall have the torment to hear *me* address Margaret by the name of Hero; and her say sweet things to me by the name of Claudio."——This is the substance of Borachio's device to make Hero suspected of disloyalty, and to break off her match with Claudio. But, in the name of common sense, could it displease Claudio, to hear his mistress making use of *his* name tenderly? If he saw another man with her, and heard her call him Claudio, he might reasonably think her betrayed, but not have the same reason to accuse her of disloyalty. Besides, how could her naming Claudio, make the prince and Claudio believe that she lov'd Borachio, as he desires Don John to insinuate to them that she did? The circumstances weighed, there is no doubt but the passage ought to be reformed, as I have settled in the text—*hear me call Margaret, Hero; hear Margaret term me* Borachio.   THEOBALD.

I am not convinced that this exchange is necessary. *Claudio* would naturally resent the circumstance of hearing another called by his own name; because, in that case, baseness of treachery would appear to be aggravated by wantonness of insult; and, at the same time he would imagine the person so distinguished to be *Borachio*, because *Don John* was previously to have informed both him and *Don Pedro*, that *Borachio* was the favoured lover.   STEEVENS.

457.   ——*carving the fashion of a new doublet.*] This folly, so conspicuous in the gallants of former ages, is laughed at by all our comick writers. So in Greene's *Farewell to Folly*, 1617: "——We are almost as fantastick as the English gentleman that is painted naked, with a pair of sheers in his hand, as not being resolved after what fashion to have his coat cut."

STEEVENS.

The English gentleman in the above extract alludes to a plate in Borde's Introduction.   REED.

460.   ——*orthographer;*——] The old copies read —*orthography.*   STEEVENS.

474.   ——*and her hair shall be of what colour it please,* &c.] Perhaps *Benedick* alludes to a fashion, very common in the time of Skakspere, that of *dying the hair.*

Stubbs, in his *Anatomy of Abuses*, 1595, speaking of the attires of women's heads, says : "*If any have haire of her owne naturall growing, which is not faire ynough, then will they die it in divers collours.*"

STEEVENS.

481. Pedro. *See where Benedick hath hid himself?*
Claudio. *O, very well, my lord: the musick ended, we'll fit the* kid-fox *with a penny-worth.*] *i. e.* we will be even with the fox now discovered. So the word *kid,* or *hidde,* signifies in Chaucer:

"The soothfastness that now is hid,
" Without coverture shall be *kid*
" When I undoen have this dreming."

Romaunt of the Rose, 2171, &c.
" Perceiv'd

" Perceiv'd or shew'd.
" He *kidde* anon his bone was not broken."
                    Troilus and Cresseide, lib. i. 208.
" With that anon sterte out daungere,
" Out of the place where he was hidde;
" His malice in his cheere was *kidde*."
                    Romaunt of the Rose, 2130.
                                        GREY.

It is not impossible but that Shakspere chose, on this occasion, to employ an antiquated word; and yet, if any future editor should choose to read—*hid* fox, he may observe that Hamlet has said—" *Hide* fox and all after."
                                        STEEVENS.

A *kid-fox* seems to be no more than a *young fox* or *cub.*   REMARKS.

539.   ——*Stalk on, stalk on, the fowl sits.*] This is an allusion to the *stalking-horse*; a horse either real or factitious, by which the fowler anciently shelter'd himself from the sight of the game.

So, in the *Honest Lawyer*, 1616:
    " Lye there thou happy warranted case
    " Of any villain. Thou hast been my *stalking-
        horse*
    " Now these ten months."
Again, in the 25th Song of Drayton's *Polyolbion*:
    " One underneath his *horse* to get a shoot doth
        stalk."
Again, in his *Muses Elysium*:
    " Then underneath my horse, I *stalk* my game
        to strike."   STEEVENS.

D ij   Again,

Again, in *New Shreds of the Old Snare*, by John Gee, quarto, p. 23.

"————Methinks I behold the cunning fowler, such as I have knowne in the fenne countries and elswhere, that doe shoot at woodcockes, snipes, and wilde fowle by sneaking behind a painted cloth which they carrey before them, having pictured in it the *shape of a horse*; which, while the silly fowle gazeth on, is knockt downe with hale shot, and so put in the fowler's budget." Mr. Reed, in addition to this quotation, might have referred to the *Aviceptologie Françoise*; where the author, after giving directions for a similar contrivance, observes:—c'est dans ce moment, où la *vache artificielle* devient aux animaux ce que, d'après *Virgile*, fut aux TROYENS le fameux cheval de bois.

HENLEY.

548. ————*but that she loves him with an enraged affection:—it is past the* infinite *of thought.*] The sense is, *I know not what to think* otherwise, *but that she loves him with* an enraged *affection: It* (this affection) is past the infinite of thought. *Infinite* is used by most careful writers for *indefinite:* the speaker means, that *thought,* though in itself *unbounded,* cannot reach or estimate the degree of her passion.   JOHNSON.

The meaning I think is————*but with what an enraged affection she loves him, it is beyond the power of thought to conceive.*   MALONE.

576. *This says she now when she is beginning to write to him: for she'll be up twenty times a* night; *and* there she'll sit in her smock, 'till she have writ a sheet of

paper :]

paper :] Shakspere has more than once availed himself of such incidents as occurred to him from history,
&c. to compliment the princes before whom his pieces
were performed. A striking instance of flattery to
James occurs in Macbeth ; perhaps the passage here
quoted was not less grateful to Elizabeth, as it apparently alludes to an extraordinary trait in one of the
letters pretended to have been written by the hated
Mary to Bothwell :

" I am *nakit*, and ganging to sleep, and zit I cease
not to scribble all this paper, in so meikle as rest is
thairof." *That is*, I am naked, and going to sleepe,
and yet I cease not to scribble to the end of my paper,
much of it as remains unwritten.   HENLEY.

587.   *O, she tore the letter into a thousand* half-pence ;]
A *farthing* and perhaps a *halfpenny*, was used to signify any small particle or division. So, in the character of the *Prioress* in *Chaucer :*

     " That in hire cuppe was no *ferthing* sene
     " Of grese, whan she dronken haddle hire
         draught."
               Prol. to the Cant. Tales, late edit. v. 135.
                              STEEVENS.

615.   ——*have* daff'd——] To *daff* is the same as
to *duff*, to *do off*, to put aside. So in *Macbeth :*
     " ———————to *doff* their dire distresses."
                              STEEVENS.

626.   ——*contemptible spirit*.] That is, a temper in-
clined to scorn and contempt. It has been before remarked, that our author uses his verbal adjective
                  D iij   with

with great licence. There is, therefore, no need of changing the word with sir T. Hanmer to *contemptuous.*

JOHNSON.

In the *argument* to *Darius,* a tragedy, by lord Ster-line, 1603, it is said, that Darius wrote to *Alexander* " in a proud and *contemptible* manner." In this place, *contemptible* certainly means *contemptuous.*

Again, Drayton, in the 24th Song of his *Polyolbion,* speaking in praise of a hermit, says, that he,

" The mad tumultuous world *contemptibly* forsook,
" And to his quiet cell by Crowland him betook."

STEEVENS.

626. ——*was sadly borne.*] *i. e.* was seriously car-ried on.   STEEVENS.

ACT III.

Line 3. PROPOSING *with the prince and Claudio :*] *Proposing* is conversing, from the French word—*pro-pos,* discourse, talk.   STEEVENS.

37. *As haggards of the rock.*] *Turbervile,* in his book of *Falconry,* 1575, tells us, that " the *haggard* doth come from foreign parts a stranger and a passenger;" and *Latham,* who wrote after him, says, that " she keeps in subjection the most part of all the fowl that fly, insomuch, that the tassel gentle, her natural and chiefest companion, dares not come near that coast where she useth, nor sit by the place where she stand-eth.

eth. Such is the greatness of her spirit, *she will not admit of any society*, until such a time as nature work-eth," &c. So, in *The tragical history of Didaco and Violenta*, 1576:

> " Perchaunce she's not of *haggard*'s kind,
> " Nor heart so hard to bend," &c.
>
> STEEVENS.

44. *To* wish *him——*] i. e. *recommend* or *desire.* So in *The Honest Whore*, 1604 :

> " Go *wish* the surgeon to have great respect."
>
> REED.'

47. *——as* full, *&c.*] A *full* bed means a *rich* wife. So in *Othello :*

> " What a *full* fortune doth the thick-lips owe ?"
> &c.   STEEVENS.

· 54. *Misprising——*] Despising, contemning.

> JOHNSON.

To *misprise* is to *undervalue*, or take in a wrong light.   STEEVENS.

64. *——spell him backward :——*] Alluding to the practice of witches in uttering prayers.

The following passages containing a similar train of thought, are from Lilly's *Anatomy of Wit*, 1581.

" If one be hard in conceiving, they pronounce him a dowlte : if given to studie, they proclaim him a dunce : if merry, a jester : if sad, a saint : if full of words, a sot : if without speech, a cypher : if one argue with him boldly, then is he impudent : if coldly, an innocent : if there be reasoning of divinitie, they cry, Quæ supra nos, nihil ad nos : if of humanitie, sententias loquitur carnifex."

Again, p. 44. b. " —if he be cleanly, they [wo‐men] term him proude; if meene in apparel, a slo‐ven : if tall, a lungis : if short, a dwarfe : if bold, blunt : if shame-fac'd, a cowarde, &c. P. 55. If she be well set, then call her a bosse : if slender, a hasill twig : if nut brown, black as a coal : if well colour'd, a painted wall : if she be pleasant, then is she wan‐ton : if sullen, a clowne : if honest, then is she coye."

STEEVENS.

66.   *If* black, *why, nature, drawing of an* antick,
       Made a foul blot: ———————] The *antick* was a buffoon character in the old English farces, with a *blacked face*, and a *patch-work habit*. What I would observe from hence is, that the name of *antick* or *an‐tique*, given to this character, shews that the people had some traditional ideas of its being borrowed from the *ancient mimes*, who are thus described by Apu‐leius, " *Mimi centunculo, fuligine faciem obducti.*"

WARBURTON.

69.   This comparison might have been borrowed from an ancient bl. let. ballad, entitled, *A Comparison of the Life of Man.*

     " I may compare a *man* againe
     " Even like unto a *twining vane,*
     " That changeth even as doth the wind;
     " Indeed so is man's fickle mind."   STEEVENS.

79.   —*press me to death*—] The allusion is to an ancient punishment of our law, called *peine fort et dure,*
which

which was formerly infl.æted on those persons, who, being indicted, refused to plead. In consequence of their silence, they were pressed to death by an heavy weight laid upon their stomach. This punishment the good sense and humanity of the legislature have within these few years abolished.   MALONE.

83. *Which is as bad as die with* tickling.] The author meant that *tickling* should be pronounced as a trisyllable, *tickeling*. So, in Spenser, B. II. Canto 12.

" The while sweet Zephirus loud *whisteled*
" His treble, a strange kind of harmony;
" Which Gayon's senses softly *tickeled*," &c.

MALONE.

99. ——*argument*——] This word seems here to signify *discourse*, or, the *powers* of reasoning.

JOHNSON.

107. *She's lim'd,*——] She is ensnared and entangled as a sparrow with *birdlime*.   JOHNSON.

So, in the *Spanish Tragedy:*

" Which sweet conceits are *lim'd* with sly deceits."
The folio reads——She's *ta'en*.   STEEVENS.

110. *What fire is in mine ears?*——] Alluding to a proverbial saying of the common people, that their ears burn, when others are talking of them.

WARBURTON.

The opinion from whence this proverbial saying is derived, is of great antiquity, being thus mentioned by Pliny : " Moreover is not this an opinion generally received, That when our *ears do glow and tingle,*
some

some there be that in our absence do talke of us."
Philemon Holland's Translation, **B.** XXVIII. p. 297,
and *Brown's Vulgar Errors.*   REED.

115.   *Taming my wild heart to thy loving hand ;*] This
image is taken from falconry.   She had been charged
with being as wild as *haggards of the rock ;* she therefore says, that *wild* as her *heart* is, she will *tame* it *to
the hand.*   JOHNSON.

124.   *Nay, that would be as great a soil in the new
gloss of your marriage, as* to shew a child his new
coat, and forbid him to wear it.]   So, in *Romeo and
Juliet :*

  " As is the night before some festival,

  " To an impatient child, that hath new robes,

  " And may not wear them."   STEEVENS.

130.   ——*the little hangman dare not shoot at him :*]
This character of Cupid came from the *Arcadia* of sir
Philip Sidney :

  " Millions of yeares this old drivell Cupid
      lives ;

  " While still more wretch, more wicked he doth
      prove :

  " 'Till now at length that Jove him office gives,

  " (At Juno's suite who much did Argus love)

  " In this our world a *hangman* for to be

  " Of all those fooles that will have all they
      see." **B. II.** ch. 14.   FARMER.

131.   ——*as a bell, and his tongue is the clapper ;*
&c.] A covert allusion to the old proverb :

          " As

" As the fool thinketh

" So the bell clinketh."   STEEVENS.

150.   *There is no appearance of* fancy, *&c.*] Here is
a play upon the word *fancy*, which Shakspere uses for
love, as well as for *humour, caprice,* or *affectation.*

JOHNSON.

154.   —*all* slops.] *Slops* are large loose *breeches* or
trowsers, worn only by sailors at present. They are
mentioned by Jonson, in his Alchymist:

" ————six great *slops*

" Bigger than three *Dutch hoys.*"

Again, in *Ram Alley, or Merry Tricks,* 1611:

" ————three pounds in gold

" These *slops* contain."   STEEVENS.

164.   —*and the old ornament of his cheek hath already*
stuff'd tennis-balls.] So, in *A wonderful, strange, and
miraculous astrological Prognostication for this Year of
our Lord* 1591; written by Nashe, in ridicule of
Richard Harvey: " —they may sell their haire by
the pound to *stuffe tennice balles.*"   STEEVENS.

Again, in *Ram Alley, or Merry Tricks,* 1611.

" Thy *beard* shall serve to *stuff* those *balls* by which
I get me heat at Tenice."

Gentle Craft, 1600.

" He shave it off, and *stuffe* tenice balles with it."

HENDERSON.

186.   *She shall be buried with her face upwards.*]
Thus the whole set of editions; but what, is there any
way particular in this? Are not all men and women
buried so? Sure, the poet means, in opposition to

the

the general rule, and by way of distinction, with her *heels* upwards, or *face* downwards. I have chosen the first reading, because I find it the expression in vogue in our author's time.   THEOBALD.

This emendation, which appears to me very specious, is rejected by Dr. Warburton.   JOHNSON.

Theobald's conjecture may, however, be supported by a passage in *The Wild Goose Chace* of Beaumont and Fletcher:

"———love cannot starve me :

" For if I die o'th' first fit, I am unhappy,

" And worthy to be *buried with my heels upwards.*"

The passage, indeed, may mean only— *She shall be buried in her lover's arms.* So, in *The Winter's Tale :*

" *Flo.* What ? like a corse ?

" *Per.* No, like a bank for love to lie and
            play on ;

" Not like a corse :———or if,—not to be *buried,*

" *But quick and in my arms.*"   STEEVENS.

223. *Leonato's Hero, your Hero, every man's Hero.*]
Dryden has transplanted this sarcasm into his *All for Love:*

" Your Cleopatra ; Dolabella's Cleopatra ; every man's Cleopatra."   STEEVENS.

258. *Well, give them their charge,———*] To *charge* his fellows, seems to have been a regular part of the duty of the constable of the Watch. So, in *A New Trick to cheat the Devil,* 1639: " My watch is set— charge given—and all at peace." Again, in *The Insatiate Countess,* by Marston, 1603: " Come on, my
                                                    hearts ;

mentioned in *Much ado about Nothing.*

hearts; we are the city's security—I'll give you your charge. '   MALONE.

293. ———*bills be not stolen!*] A *bill* is still carried by the watchmen at Litchfield.   It was the old weapon of English infantry, which, says Temple, *gave the most ghastly and deplorable wounds.*   It may be called *securis falcata.*   JOHNSON.

These weapons are mentioned in Glapthorne's *Wit in a Constable,* 1639:

    "   ————Well said, neighbours;
    " You're chatting wisely o'er your *bills* and
            lanthorns,
    " As becomes watchmen of discretion."

Again, in *Arden of Feversham,* 1592:

    "   ————the watch
    " Are coming tow'rd our house with glaives and
            bills."

For examples of ancient *bills,* see the print.

                                        STEEVENS.

317. *If you hear a child cry,* &c] It is not impossible but that part of this scene was intended as a burlesque on *The Statute of the Streets,* imprinted by Wolfe, in 1595.   Among these I find the following:

22. " No man shall blowe any horne in the night, within this cittie, or whistle after the houre of nyne of the clock in the night, under the paine of imprisonment."

23. " No man shall use to goe with visoures, or disguised by night, under the like paine of imprisonment."

E

24.

24. " Made that night-walkers, and evisdropers, like punishment."

25. " No hammar-man, as a smith, a pewterer, a founder, and all artificers making great sound, shall not worke after the houre of nyne at night," &c.

30. " No man shall, after the hour of nyne at night, keepe any rule, whereby any such suddaine out-cry be made in the still of the night, as making any affray, or beating his wyfe, or servant, or singing, or revyling in his house, to the disturbaunce of his neigh-bours, under payne of iiis. iiiid." &c. &c.

Ben Jonson, however, appears to have ridiculed this scene in the Induction to his *Bartholomew-Fair :*

" And then a substantial *watch* to have stole in upon 'em, and taken them away with *mistaking words,* as the fashion is in the stage practice."   STEEVENS.

369. ——*thou art unconfirm'd :——*] *i. e.* un-practised in the ways of the world.   WARBURTON.

387. ——reechy *painting ;——*] Is painting stain'd by smoke. So, in *Han's Beer Pot's Invisible Comedy,* 1618 :

" ————he look'd so *reechily*

" Like bacon hanging on the chimney's roof."
From Recan, Anglo-Saxon, to *reek, fumare,* Lat.

STEEVENS.

388. ——*sometime, like the shaven Hercules, &c.*] *The shaven Hercules,* meant *Hercules when shaved to make him look like a woman,* while he remained in the service of Omphale, his Lydian mistress.   STEEVENS.

389.

389. ——*smirch'd*——] *Smirch'd* is soiled, obscured. So, in *As you Like It*, act i. sc. 3.

" And with a kind of umber *smirch* my face."

STEEVENS.

425. ——*wears a lock.*] So in the *Return from Parnassus*, 1600 :

" He whose thin fire dwells in a smoky roofe,

" Must take tobacco, and must wear *a lock.*"

See Dr. Warburton's Note, act v. sc. 1.   STEEVENS.

426. Conr. *Masters, Masters,* &c.] In former copies :

Conr. *Masters.*

2 Watch. *You'll be made bring Deformed forth, I warrant you.*

Conr. *Masters never speak, we charge you, let us obey you to go with us.*

The regulation which I have made in this last speech, though against the authority of all the printed copies, I flatter myself, carries its proof with it. Conrade and Borachio are not designed to talk absurd nonsense. It is evident, therefore, that Conrade is attempting his own justification ; but is interrupted in it by the impertinence of the men in office. THEOBALD.

441. ——*rabato*——] A neckband; a ruff. *Rabat*, French.   HANMER.

Rabato, an ornament for the neck, a collar-band, or kind of ruff. Fr. *Rabat*. Menage saith it comes from *rabattre* to put back, because it was at first nothing but the collar of the shirt or shift turn'd back towards the shoulders.   HAWKINS.

E ij

This

This article of dress is frequently mentioned by our ancient comick writers.

So, in the comedy of *Law Tricks*, &c. 1608:

"Broke broad jests upon her narrow heel,

"Pok'd her *rabatos*, and survey'd her *steel*."

Again, in Decker's *Satiromastix*, 1602:—"He would persuade me that love was a *rabato*, and his reason was, that a *rabato* was worn out with pinning," &c.

Again, in Decker's *Untrussing the Humourous Poet:* What a miserable thing it is to be a noble bride! There's such delays in rising, in fitting gowns, in pinning *rebatoes*, in *poaking*," &c.

The first and last of these passages will likewise serve for an additional explanation of the *poking-sticks of steel*, mentioned by Autolycus in the *Winter's Tale*.

STEEVENS.

479. ———*Light o'love;*———] This tune is mentioned in Beaumont and Fletcher's *Two Noble Kinsmen.* The gaoler's daughter, speaking of a horse, says,

"He gallops to the tune of *Light o'love*."

It is mentioned again in the *Two gentlemen of Verona*,

"Best sing it to the tune of *Light o'love*."

And in the *Noble gentleman* of Beaumont and Fletcher.

STEEVENS.

Light

Light o'love.] This is the name of an old dance tune which has occurred already in the *Two Gentlemen of Verona:* I have lately recovered it from an ancient MS. and it is as follows:

SIR JOHN HAWKINS.

484.   ——*no barns.*] A quibble between *barns*, repositories of corn, and *bairns*, the old word for children.   JOHNSON.

So, in the *Winter's Tale:* " Mercy on us, a *barn!* a very pretty *barn!*"   STEEVENS.

489. *Hey ho!*

Marg. For *a hawk, a horse, or* a husband?] " *Heigh ho for a husband,* or the willing maid's wants made
E i i j   known,"

known," is the title of an old ballad in the Pepysian Collection, in Magdalen-College, Cambridge.

MALONE.

491. *For the letter that begins them all, H.*] This is a poor jest, somewhat obscured, and not worth the trouble of elucidation.

Margaret asks Beatrice for what she cries, *hey ho*; Beatrice answers, for an *H*, that is for an *ache* or *pain*.

JOHNSON.

Heywood, among his Epigrams, published in 1566, has one on the letter H,

"H is worse among letters in the cross-row:
" For if thou find him either in thine elbow,
" In thine arm, or leg, in any degree;
" In thine head, or teeth, or toe, or knee;
" Into what place soever H may pike him,
" Wherever thou find *ache* thou shalt not like
    him."   STEEVENS.

492. ——*turn'd Turk*——] *i. e.* taken captive by love, and turned a renegado to his religion.

WARBURTON.

This interpretation is somewhat far-fetched, yet, perhaps, it is right.   JOHNSON.

Hamlet uses the same expression, and talks of his *fortune's turning Turk. To turn Turk* was a common phrase for a change of condition or opinion. So, in *The Honest Whore*, by Decker, 1616:

" If you *turn Turk* again," &c.   STEEVENS.

513. *some moral*——] That is, some secret meaning, like the *moral* of a fable.   JOHNSON.

4

A moral

A *moral* is the same as a *morality*, one of the earliest kinds of our dramatick performances. So, in Greene's *Groatsworth of Wit*, 1621: " —It was I that penned the *Moral of Man's Wit,* the *Dialogue of Dives,*" &c.

" The people make no estimation
" Of *morals,* teaching education."

A player, on this occasion, is the speaker, and these performances were full of double meanings and conceits. Again, in Decker's *Guls Hornbook,* 1609: " —bee it pastoral or comedy, *moral* or tragedy.—"
STEEVENS.

524. *——he eats his meat without grudging :——*] I do not see how this is a proof of Benedick's change of mind. It would afford more proof of amorousness to say, *he eats* not *his meat without grudging* ; but it is impossible to fix the meaning of proverbial expressions: perhaps, *to eat meat without grudging,* was the same as, *to do as others do*; and the meaning is, *he is content to live by eating like other mortals, and will be content, notwithstanding his boasts, like other mortals, to have a wife.*   JOHNSON.

547. *——honest as the skin between his brows.*] This is a proverbial expression.   STEEVENS.

So, in *Gammer Gurton's Needle,* 1575:
" I am as true, I would thou knew, as *skin between thy brows.*"   REED.

548. *——I am as honest as any man living, that is an old man, and no honester than I.*] There is much humour, and extreme good sense under the covering of this blundering expression. It is a sly insinuation,
that

that length of years, and the being much *hacknied in the ways of men*, as Shakspere expresses it, take off the gloss of virtue, and bring much defilement on the manners.   For, as a great wit says, *Youth is the season of virtue: corruptions grow with years, and I believe the oldest rogue in England is the greatest.*   WARBURTON.

Much of this is true, but I believe Shakspere did not intend to bestow all this reflection on the speaker.
                                            JOHNSON.

551.   ——*palabras,*——] So, in the *Taming the Shrew*, the Tinker says, *pocas pallabras*, i. e. few words.   A scrap of Spanish, which might once have been current among the vulgar.   STEEVENS.

It occurs likewise in the *Spanish Tragedy:*
   " *Pocas Palabras*, milde as the lambe."
                                            HENLEY.

570.   *It is a world to see!*] i. e. it is wonderful to see.   So, in *All for Money*, an old morality, 1594 : " *It is a world to see* how greedy they be of money." The same phrase often occurs, with the same meaning, in Holinshed.   STEEVENS.

571.   ——*well*, God's a good man ;] So, in the old Morality, or Interlude of *Lusty Juventus*, 1561, and again, in *A mery Geste of Robin Hoode*, bl. let. no date.
                                            STEEVENS.

572.   —*an two men ride*, &c.] This is not out of place, or without meaning.   Dogberry, in his vanity of superior parts, apologizing for his neighbour, observes, that *of two men on an horse, one must ride behind.*
                                            The

The *first* place of rank or understanding can belong
but to *one*, and that happy *one* ought not to despise his
inferior.   JOHNSON.

Shakspere might have caught this idea from the
common seal of the Knight's Templars; the device of
which was *two riding upon one horse*.   An engraving of
the seal is preserved at the end of Matt. Paris Hist.
Ang. 1640.   STEEVENS.

ACT IV.

Line 22. SOME *be of laughing,*——] This is a
quotation from the *Accidence*.   JOHNSON.

41. ————*luxurious bed :*] That is, *lascivious*.
Luxury is the confessor's term for unlawful pleasures
of the sex.   JOHNSON.

So, in *K. Lear :*
   "To't *luxury*, pell mell, for I lack soldiers."
                                           STEEVENS.

Again, in *Life and Death of Edward II.* p. 129.
   "*Luxurious* Queene this is thy foule desire."
                                           REED.

54. ————*word too large* ;] So he uses *large jests*
in this play, for *licentious, not restrained within due*
bounds.   JOHNSON.

58. ————*I will* write *against it :*] So, in *Cym-*
beline, Posthumus speaking of women, says,
                                           "I'll

    " I'll *write against them,*

    " Detest them, curse them."   STEEVENS.

    60. ————*chaste as the bud*————] Before the air has tasted its sweetness.   JOHNSON.

    78. ————*kindly power*] That is, *natural power. Kind* is *nature.*   JOHNSON.

    97. ————*liberal villain,*] *Liberal* here, as in many places of these plays, means, *frank beyond honesty* or *decency. Free of tongue.* Dr. Warburton unnecessarily reads, *illiberal.*   JOHNSON.

So, in the *Fair Maid of Bristow*, 1605 :

    " But Vallinger, most like a *liberal* villain,

    " Did give her scandalous ignoble terms."

Again, in *The Captain,* by Beaumont and Fletcher :

    " And give allowance to your *liberal* jests

    " Upon his person."   STEEVENS.

This sense of the word *liberal* is not peculiar to Shakspere. John Taylor, in his *Suite concerning Players,* complains of the " many aspersions very *liberally,* unmannerly, and ingratefully bestowed upon him."   FARMER.

    105. ————*What a Hero hadst thou been*] I am afraid here is intended a poor conceit upon the word *Hero.*   JOHNSON.

    111. ————*conjecture*————] Conjecture is here used for suspicion.   MALONE.

    114. *Hath no man's dagger here a point for me ?*]

    " A thousand daggers, all in honest hands !

    " And have not I a friend to stick one here?"

                       Venice Preserv'd.

                          STEEVENS.

                          130.

130. *The story that is printed in her blood?*] That is, the story which her blushes discover to be true. JOHNSON.

135. ————*Griev'd I, I had but one?*

    Chid I for that at frugal nature's frame?

    O, one too much by thee!————] *Frame* is contrivance, order, disposition of things. So, in the *Death of Robert Earl of Huntington,* 1603:

    " And therefore seek to set each thing in *frame.*"

Again, in Holinshed's *Chronicle,* p. 555. " —there was no man that studied to bring the unrulie to *frame.*"

Again, in Daniel's *Verses on Montaigne:*

    " ————extracts of men,

    " Though in a troubled *frame* confusedly set."

Again, in *Much Ado about Nothing :*

    " Whose spirits toil in *frame* of villanies."

STEEVENS.

144. *But mine, and mine I lov'd, and mine I prais'd,*

    And mine that I was proud on;————] The speaker utters his emotion abruptly, But *mine, and mine* that *I lov'd,* &c. by an ellipsis frequent, perhaps too frequent, both in verse and prose.

JOHNSON.

186. Friar. *Lady, what man is he you are accus'd of?*] The friar had just before boasted his great skill in fishing out the truth. And, indeed, he appears by this question to be no fool. He was by all the while at the accusation, and heard no names mentioned. Why then should he ask her what man she was accused of? But in this lay the subtilty of his examination.

nation. For, had Hero been guilty, it was very probable that in that hurry and confusion of spirits into
which the terrible insult of her lover had thrown her,
she would never have observed that the man's name
was not mentioned; and so, on this question, have
betrayed herself by naming the person she was
conscious of an affair with. The friar observed this,
and so concluded, that were she guilty, she would
probably fall into the trap he laid for her.——I only
take notice of this, to shew how admirably well
Shakspere knew how to sustain his characters.

WARBURTON.

196. ——bent *of honour*;] *Bent* is used by our
author for the utmost degree of any passion, or
mental quality. In this play before, Benedick says
of Beatrice, *her affection has its full bent.* The expression is derived from archery; the bow has its *bent*,
when it is drawn as far as it can be.   JOHNSON.

213. *Your daughter here the princes left for dead*;]
In former copies,

> *Your daughter here the* princess *left for dead;*

But how comes Hero to start up a princess here? We
have no intimation of her father being a prince; and
this is the first and only time she is complimented with
this dignity. The remotion of a single letter, and of
the parenthesis, will bring her to her own rank, and
the place to its true meaning :

> *Your daughter here the* princes *left for dead:*

i. e. Don Pedro, prince of Arragon; and his bastard
brother, who is likewise called a prince. THEOBALD.

216.

216. ——*ostentation*;] Show, appearance.

JOHNSON.

231. ————*we rack the value*;————] *i. e.* We exaggerate the value. The allusion is to *rack-rents.* The same kind of thought occurs in *Antony and Cleopatra :*

" What our contempts do often hurl from us,

" We wish it ours again." STEEVENS.

The following passage in the *Widow's Tears*, by Chapman, 1612, strengthens Mr. Steevens's interpretation :

" One joint of him I lost,—was much more worth

" Than the *rackt* value of thy entire body."

MALONE.

252. *The smallest twine may lead me.*] This is one of our author's observations upon life. Men overpowered with distress, eagerly listen to the first offers of relief, close with every scheme, and believe every promise. He that has no longer any confidence in himself, is glad to repose his trust in any other that will undertake to guide him. JOHNSON.

267. Manent *Benedick and Beatrice.*] The poet, in my opinion, has shewn a great deal of address in this scene. Beatrice here engages her lover to revenge the injury done her cousin Hero : and without this very natural incident, considering the character of Beatrice, and that the story of her passion for Benedick was all a fable, she could never have been easily or naturally brought to confess she loved him, notwithstanding all the foregoing preparation. And yet,

F

on

on this confession, in this very place, depended the whole success of the plot upon her and Benedick. For had she not owned her love here, they must have soon found out the trick, and then the design of bringing them together had been defeated; and she would never have owned a passion she had been only tricked into, had not her desire of revenging her cousin's wrong made her drop her capricious humour at once.

WARBURTON.

304. *I am gone, though I am here;——*] *i. e.* I am out of your mind already, though I remain here in person before you.   STEEVENS.

312. *——in the* height *a villain,—*] So in *Hen. VIII.* " He's traitor to the *height.*"

STEEVENS.

326. *——and* counties!——] *County* was the ancient general term for a *nobleman.* See a note on the *County* Paris in *Romeo and Juliet.*   STEEVENS.

327. *——a goodly* count-comfect;——] *i. e.* a specious nobleman made out of sugar.   STEEVENS.

331 *——and men are only turned into tongue, and trim ones too:*] The construction of the sentence is— not only men but trim ones, are turned into tongue, *i. e.* not only *common* but *clever* men, &c. STEEVENS.

348 *Scene II.*] The persons, throughout this scene, have been strangely confounded in the modern editions. The first error has been the introduction of a *Town-Clerk,* who is, indeed, mentioned in the stagedirection, prefixed to this scene in the old editions *(Enter the Constables, Borachio, and the Town-Clerke in gownes),*

gownes), but no where else; nor is there a single speech ascribed to him in those editions. The part, which he might reasonably have been expected to take upon this occasion, is performed by *the Sexton*; who assists at, or rather directs, the examinations; sets them down in writing, and reports them to Leonato. It is probable, therefore, I think, that *the Sexton* has been styled *the Town-Clerk*, in the stage-direction above mentioned, from his doing the duty of such an officer. But the editors, having brought *both Sexton and Town-Clerk* upon the stage, were unwilling, as it seems, that the latter should be a mute personage; and therefore they have put into his mouth *almost all the absurdities* which the poet certainly intended for his ignorant *constable*. To rectify this confusion, little more is necessary than to go back to the old editions, remembering that the names of *Kempe* and *Cowley*, two celebrated actors of the time, are put in this scene for the names of the persons represented; viz. *Kempe* for *Dogberry*, and *Cowley* for *Verges*.

TYRWHITT.

I have followed Mr. Tyrwhitt's regulation, which is undoubtedly just; but have left Mr. Theobald's notes as I found them.   STEEVENS.

365. Both. *Yea, sir, we hope.*

To. Cl. *Write down—that they hope they serve God:— and write God first; for God defend but God should go before such villains !——*] This short passage, which is truly humorous and in character, I have added from the old quarto. Besides, it supplies a defect: for

F ij

with-

without it, the Town-Clerk asks a question of the prisoners, and goes on without staying for any answer to it. THEOBALD.

The omission of this passage, since the edition of 1600, may be accounted for from the stat. 3 Jac. I. c. 21. the sacred name being jestingly used four times in one line. BLACKSTONE.

378. *'Fore God, they are both in a tale:*] This is an admirable stroke of humour: *Dogberry* says of the prisoners that they are false knaves, and from that denial of the charge, which one in his wits could not be supposed to make, he infers a communion of counsels, and records it in the examination as an evidence of their guilt. SIR J. HAWKINS.

If the learned annotator will amend his comment by omitting the word *guilt*, and inserting the word *innocency*, it will (except as to the supposed inference of a communication of counsels, which should likewise be omitted or corrected) be a just and pertinent remark. REMARKS.

384. To. Cl. *Yea, marry, that's the* easiest *way:*—*Let the watch come forth:*] This *easiest*, is a sophistication of our modern editors, who were at a loss to make out the corrupted reading of the old copies. The quarto in 1600, and the first and second editions in folio, all concur in reading; *Yea, marry, that's the* eftest *way*, &c. A letter happened to slip out at press in the first edition; and 'twas too hard a task for the subsequent editors to put it in, or guess at the word under this accidental depravation. There is no doubt but

but the author wrote, as I have restor'd the text ;
Yea, marry, that's the deftest *way*, &c. *i. e.* the
readiest, most *commodious* way.   THEOBALD.

Mr. Theobald might have recollected the word
deftly in *Macbeth :*

   " Thyself and office *deftly* show."
Shakspere, I suppose, design'd Dogberry to corrupt
this word as well as many others.   STEEVENS.

<hr>

ACT V.

Line 16. *I*F *such a one will smile* and *stroke his beard* ;

   In *sorrow wag !* cry hem, *when he should groan* ;]
And and *in,* hastily or indistinctly pronounced, might
easily have been confounded, supposing (what there
is great reason to believe) that these plays were copied
for the press by the ear.

By this reading a clear sense is given, and the latter
part of the line is a paraphrase on the former.

To *cry hem* was, as appears from the passage cited by
Mr. Tyrwhitt, a mark of festivity. So also from
Love's Cruelty, a tragedy by Shirley, 1640 :

 " Cannot he *laugh* and *hem* and kiss his bride,

 " But he must send me word ?"
Again, in *The Second Part of Henry IV.*

 " We have heard the bells chime at midnight——
That we have, that we have ;—our watch-word was,
hem, boys."

     F iij   On

On the other hand, *to cry woe*, was used to denote grief.

Thus, in the *Winter's Tale :*

"——but the last, O Lords,

" When I have said, *cry woe.*"

With respect to the word *wag*, the using it as a verb, in the sense of *to play the wag*, is entirely in Shakspere's manner. There is scarcely one of his plays in which we do not find substantives used as verbs. Thus we meet——to testimony, to buy, to couch, to grave, to bench, to voice, to paper, to page, to dram, to stage, to fever, to fool, to palate, to mountebank, to god, to virgin, to passion, to monster, to history, to fable, to wall, to period, to spaniel, to stranger, &c. &c.   MALONE.

I think our author would hardly have used *wag*, a verb in the sense recommended, lest his present sentiment should have been liable to misapprehension, he having employed the same verb, with its common signification, in many other places.   STEEVENS.

Here is a manifest corruption. The tenour of the context is undoubtedly this : " If a man in such melancholy circumstances will smile, stroke his beard with great complacency, and in the very depth of affliction cheerfully cry *hem* when he should groan," &c. I, therefore, with the least departure from the old copies, and in entire conformity to the acknowledged and obvious sense of the passage, venture to correct thus :

If

If such a one will smile and stroke his beard,

And *sorrowing* cry hem, when he should groan.
Sorrowing, to say no more, was a participle extremely common in our author's age. Rowe's emendation of this place is equally without meaning and without authority. *Sorrowing* was here, perhaps, originally written *Sorrowinge*, according to the old manner of spelling; which brings the correction I have proposed still nearer to the letters of the text in early editions.   WARTON.

To cry, *care away!* was once an expression of triumph. So, in *Acolastus*, a comedy, 1529: " I may nowe say, *Care awaye!*" Again, ibid. " Nowe grievous *sorrowe and care away!*"

Sorrow wagge! may be such another phrase of exultation.

What will be said of the conceit I shall now offer, I know not; let it, however, take its chance. We might read,

> If such a one will smile, and stroke his beard,
> And, *sorry wag!* cry hem! when he should
> groan.—

i. e *unfeeling humourist! to employ a note of festivity, when his sighs ought to express concern.* Both the words I would introduce, are used by Shakspere. Falstaff calls the prince, *sweet wag!* and the epithet *sorry* is applied, even at this time, to denote any moderate deviation from propriety or morality; as, for instance, *a sorry fellow. Othello* speaks of a salt and *sorry* rheum. The prince, in the *First Part of K. Henry IV.*

act

act ii. sc. 4. says   " —they *cry, hem !* and bid you play it off."   This sufficiently proves the exclamation to have been of a comick turn.   STEEVENS.

That all the conjectures on this difficult passage may be collected together, Mr. Reed adds that of the author of THE REMARKS, who proposes to read :

>   And, *sorrow waggery*, hem, when he should
>   groan.

i. e. sorrow becoming waggery ; or, converting sorrow into waggery, hem.   To this he subjoins : " I believe this will be at least as unsatisfactory as any of the preceding, and I confess that none of them bring conviction to my mind.   Against such as depend on an alteration of the text, I acknowledge myself prejudiced, being convinced, from a review of the conjectures of former criticks, on passages once as little understood as the present, but now clearly established, without varying from the old copies, that innovations are seldom necessary.   An explanation, I think, is only wanted, and the following is offered with much diffidence.   I would read :

>   And *sorrow wag; cry hem!* when he should
>   groan,

i. e. sorrow wag (*dismiss, shake off*), cry hem ! (*use a note of festivity*) when he should groan.   The difficulty seems to be only in the word *wag*, which may, without much violence, be presumed to be used in the sense I have affixed to it, by a writer of such licence as our author.   That it had not a ludicrous meaning formerly, may be proved from its frequent occurrence

in

in the translation of the scriptures. See particularly St. Matthew, ch. xxvii. ver. 39. and other places might be pointed out. I take this opportunity to observe, that the various and discordant opinions about this passage, should teach both the present and future race of commentators, to be less dogmatical than we frequently find them on a subject wherein there is so little certainty as that of conjectural criticism."

I believe nothing more is requisite to the recovery of the right reading, than a correction of the old punctuation :

> And, *sorrow wagge!* cry ;—hem, when he should
> groan ;—   HENLEY.

18. ———*make misfortune drunk*

With candle-wasters ;] This may mean, either wash away his sorrow among those who sit up all night to drink; and in that sense may be styled *wasters of candles* ; or overpower his misfortunes by swallowing flap-dragons in his glass, which are described by Falstaff as made of *candles' ends.*   STEEVENS.

This is a very difficult passage, and hath not, I think, been satisfactorily cleared up. The explanation I shall offer will give, I believe, as little satisfaction ; but I will, however, venture it. *Candle-wasters* is a term of contempt for scholars : thus Jonson, in *Cynthia's Revels,* act iii. sc. 2. " spoiled by a whoreson book-worm, a *candle-waster.*" In the *Antiquary,* act iii. is a like term of ridicule : " He should more catch your delicate court-ear, than all your head-scratchers, thumb-biters, *lamp-wasters* of them all."

all." The sense then, which I would assign to Shak-spere, is this: " If such a one will patch grief with proverbs—case or cover the wounds of his grief with proverbial sayings—make misfortune drunk with *candle-wasters*—stupify misfortune, or render himself insensible to the strokes of it, by the conversation or lucubrations of scholars; the production of the lamp, but not fitted to human nature. *Patch*, in the sense of mending a defect or breach, occurs in Hamlet, act v. scene 1.

> " O, that that earth, which kept the world in
>   awe,
> " Should *patch* a wall, to expel the winter's flaw."
>   WHALLEY.

33.   ——*than advertisement.*] That is, than *admonition*, than *moral instruction.*   JOHNSON.

38.   *However they have writ* the style of gods,] Sapiens *ille cum* Diis *ex pare vivit.* Senec. Ep. 59. *Jupiter quo antecedit virum bonum? diutius bonus est.* Sapiens *nihilo se minoris æstimat.*—Deus *non vincit* sapientem *felicitate.* Ep. 73.   WARBURTON.

By the *style of gods,* is meant an exalted language; such as we may suppose would be written by beings superior to human calamities, and therefore regarding them with neglect and coldness.

Beaumont and Fletcher have the same expression in the first of their *Four Plays in One :*

> " Athens doth make women philosophers,
> " And sure their children chat *the talk of gods.*"
>   STEEVENS.

39.

39. *And made a pish at* chance and sufferance.]
Alludes to the famous *apathy* of the stoics.

WARBURTON.

The old copies read *push.* Mr. Pope, I believe
made the change. MALONE.

85. *Canst thou so* daffe *me ?————*] To *daffe* and
doffe are synonymous terms, that mean, to *put off:*
which is the very sense required here, and what Leonato would reply upon Claudio's saying, he would
have nothing to do with him. THEOBALD.

Theobald has well interpreted the word. Shakspere uses it more than once:

" The nimble footed mad-cap prince of Wales,

" And his comrades that *daff'd* the world aside."
Again, " —I would have *daff'd* other respects," &c.
Again, in the *Lover's Complaint :*

" There my white stole of chastity I *daff'd.*"
It is perhaps of Scottish origin, as I find it in *Ane
verie excellent and deleÆabill Treatise intitulit* PHILOTUS,
&c. Edinburgh, 1603:

" Their *daffing* does us so undo." STEEVENS.

87. Ant. *He shall kill two of us,* &c.] This *brother
Anthony* is the truest picture imaginable of human
nature. He had assumed the character of a sage to
comfort his brother, o'erwhelmed with grief for his
only daughter's affront and dishonour ; and had
severely reproved him for not commanding his passion
better on so trying an occasion. Yet, immediately after
this, no sooner does he begin to suspect that his *age*
and *valour* are slighted, but he falls into the most
intemperate

intemperate fit of rage himself: and all he can do or say is not of power to pacify him. This is copying nature with a penetration and exactness of judgment peculiar to Shakspere. As to the expression, too, of his passion, nothing can be more highly painted.

WARBURTON.

102. *Scambling,—*] i. e. *scrambling.* The word is more than once used by Shakspere. See Dr. Percy's note on the first speech of the play of *K. Henry V.* and likewise the Scots proverb, "It is well ken'd your father's son was never a *scambler.*" A *scambler,* in its literal sense, is one who goes about among his friends to get a dinner; by the Irish call'd a *coskerer.*

STEEVENS.

111. *——we will not* wake *your patience.*] This conveys a sentiment that the speaker would by no means have implied. That the patience of the two old men was not exercised, but asleep, which up-braids them for insensibility under their wrong. Shak-spere must have wrote,

——we will not wrack*——*

i. e. destroy your patience by tantalizing you.

WARBURTON.

This emendation is very specious, and perhaps is right; yet the present reading may admit a congruous meaning with less difficulty than many other of Shak-spere's expressions.

The old men have been both very angry and outra-geous; the prince tells them that he and Claudio *will not* wake *their patience*; will not any longer force them

to .

to *endure* the presence of those whom, though they
look on them as enemies, they cannot resist.

JOHNSON.

Wake, I believe, is the original word. The fero-
city of wild beasts is overcome by not suffering them
to sleep. *We will not* wake *your patience,* therefore
means, we will forbear any further provocation.

HENLEY.

151. *Nay, then give him another staff,* &c.] An allusion to *tilting.* See note, *As You Like It,* act iii.
sc. 4.   WARBURTON.

155. ——*to turn his girdle.*] We have a proverbial
speech, *If he be angry, let him turn the buckle of his
girdle.* But I do not know its original or meaning.

JOHNSON.

A corresponding expression is used to this day in
Ireland—*If he be angry, let him tie up his brogues.*
Neither proverb, I believe, has any other meaning
than this: If he is in a bad humour, let him employ
himself till he is in a better.

Dr. Farmer furnishes me with an instance of this
proverbial expression as used by Claudio, from Winwood's Memorials, fol. edit. 1725, Vol. I. p. 453.
See letter from *Winwood* to *Cecyll,* from Paris, 1602,
about an affront he received there from *an Englishman :* " I said what I spake was not to make *him*
angry. He replied, if I were angry, *I might turn the
buckle of my girdle* behind me." So likewise Cowley,
On the Government of Oliver Cromwell : " —The next
month he swears by the living God, that he will turn
them out of doors, and he does so in his princely way

G

of

of threatening, bidding them, " *turne the buckles of their girdles* behind them."   STEEVENS.

A writer in the *Gentleman's Mag.* 1783, says, large belts were worn with the buckle before, but in wrestling the buckle was turned behind, to give the adversary a fair grasp at the belt; therefore turning the buckle behind was a challenge.   REED.

167. ——*bid*—] i. e. *asked.* Thus in *Titus Andronicus*, act i. sc. 2.

" I am not *bid* to wait upon this bride."——
And in the *New Testament :*

" —they that were *bidden* were not worthy."
                                                  * * *.

169. *Shall I not find a* woodcock *too ?*] A woodcock was a proverbial term for a foolish fellow. So in the *London Prodigal*, a comedy, 1605 : " *Woodcock o' my side!*" The same words also occur in *Law Tricks*, a comedy, by John Day, 1608.   MALONE.

177. ——*a wise gentleman ;*] This jest depending on the colloquial use of words is now obscure; perhaps we should read, *a wise gentleman*, or *a man wise enough to be a coward.* Perhaps *wise gentleman* was in that age used ironically, and always stood for *silly fellow.*   JOHNSON.

210. *What a pretty thing man is, when he goes in his doublet and hose, and leaves off his wit !*] It was esteemed a mark of levity and want of becoming gravity, at that time, *to go in the doublet and hose, and leave off the cloak*, to which this well-turned *expression* alludes. The *thought* is, that love makes a man as ridiculous,

and exposes him as naked, as being in the doublet and hose without a cloak.   WARBURTON.

214.   *But, soft you, let be;*——] The first folio reads :

But soft you; let *me* be ; pluck, &c.
The second folio reads :

But soft you let *me see* ; pluck up, &c.
which is, I believe, the true reading.   MALONE.

Let be, is the true reading.   It means, *let things remain as they are.*   I have heard the phrase used by Dr. Johnson himself.   STEEVENS.

The same expression occurs in Matt. xxvii. 49.

HENLEY.

So, in *Henry VIII.* act i. sc. 1.
Again, *Winter's Tale,* act v. sc. 3.   REED.

235.   ——*one meaning well suited.*] That is, *one meaning is put into many different dresses;* the prince having asked the same question in four modes of speech.   JOHNSON.

301.   *And she alone is heir to both of us ;*] Shakspere seems to have forgot what he had made Leonato say, in the fifth scene of the first act to Antonio, *How now, brother; where is my cousin your son ? hath he provided the musick ?*   ANONYMOUS.

311.   *Who, I believe, was* pack'd *in all this wrong,*] *i. e.* combined ; an accomplice. So, in lord Bacon's Works, Vol. iv. p. 269. edit. 1740. " If the issue shall be this, that whatever shall be done for him, shall be thought to be done by a number of persons that shall be laboured and *packed*——."   MALONE.

G ij   So,

So, in *King Lear :*

" —snuffs and *packings* of the dukes."

STEEVENS.

355.   *To have no man come* over *me ? why, shall I always keep* below *stairs ?*] So, in Marston's *Insatiate
Countess,* 1603 :

" Alas! when we are once o'th falling hand,

" A man may easily *come over* us."   COLLINS.

363.   *I give thee the bucklers.*] I suppose that *to give
the bucklers* is, *to yield,* or to *lay by all thoughts of defence,* so *clypeum abjicere.* The rest deserves no comment.   JOHNSON.

Greene, in his Second Part of *Coney Catching,* 1592,
uses the same expression :—" At this his master
laught, and was glad, for further advantage, to *yield
the bucklers* to his prentise."

Again, in *A Woman never Vex'd,* a comedy by Rowley, 1632 :

"——into whose hands she thrusts the weapons first,
let him *take up the bucklers.*"

Again, in Decker's *Satiromastix :*

" Charge one of them to *take up the bucklers*

" Against that hair-monger Horace."

Again, in Chapman's *May-Day,* 1611 :

" And now I lay *the bucklers* at your feet."

Again, in *Every Woman in her Humour,* 1609 :

" —if you lay down *the bucklers,* you lose the
      victory."

Again, in P. Holland's translation of Pliny's *Nat.
Hist.* B. X. c. 21. "—it goeth against his stomach

(the

(the cock's) to yeeld the gantlet and *give the bucklers.*"
STEEVENS.

422. ——*in the time of good neighbours :*] *i. e.*
When men were not envious, but every one gave
another his due.   The reply is extremely humorous.
WARBURTON.

427.   Question?—*Why, an hour, &c.*] *i. e.* What a
question's there, or what a foolish question do you
ask ?
WARBURTON.

The phrase occurs frequently in Shakspere, and
means no more than—*you ask a question,* or *that is the
question.*
REMARKS.

451.   *Done to death*——] This obsolete phrase occurs frequently in our ancient writers.——Thus, in
Marlow's *Lust's Dominions,* 1657 :

    " His mother's hand shall stop thy breath,
    " Thinking her own son is *done to death.*"
MALONE.

461.   *Those that slew thy virgin knight;*] *Knight,* in
its original signification, means *follower* or *pupil,* and
in this sense may be feminine.   Helena, in *All's Well
that Ends Well,* uses *knight* in the same signification.
JOHNSON.

Virgin *knight* is virgin hero.   In the times of chi-
valry, a *virgin knight* was one who had as yet
achieved no adventure.   Hero had as yet achieved no
matrimonial one.   It may be added, that a *virgin
knight* wore no device on his shield, having no right
to any till he had deserved it.

So,

So, in the *History of Clyomon, Knight of the Golden Shield,* &c. 1599:

> " Then as thou seem'st in thy attire *a virgin knight*
>   to be,
> " Take thou this *shield* likewise *of white,*" &c.

It appears, however, from several passages in Spenser's *Faery Queen,* B. I. c. 7. that an *ideal order* of this name was supposed, as a compliment to queen Elizabeth's virginity :

> " Of doughtie knights whom faery land did raise
> " That noble order hight of *maidenhead.*"

Again, B. II. c. 2.

> " Order of *maidenhead* the most renown'd."

Again, B. II. c. 9.

> " And numbred be mongst knights of *maidenhead.*"

On the books of the Stationers-Company, in the year 1594, is entered, " ——Pheander the *mayden knight.*"

STEEVENS.

608. ——*no staff more reverend than one* tipt with horn.] This passage may admit of some explanation that I am unable to furnish. By accident I lost several instances I had collected for the purpose of throwing light on it. The following, however, may assist the future commentator.

MS. Sloan, 1691,

> " That a fellon may wage battaile, with th' order thereof."

> " ——by order of the lawe both the parties must at theire own charge be armed withoute any yron or long armoure, and theire heades bare and bare-headed and
>
> bare-

bare-footed, every one of them having a baston *horned* at ech ende of one length," &c.   STEEVENS.

So, in *Britton, Pleas of the Crown.* c. xxii. s. 18.— " Next let them go to combat armed without iron and without linen armour, their heads uncovered and their hands naked and on foot, with *two bastons tipped with horn* of equal length, and each of them a target of four corners, without any other armour, whereby any of them may annoy the other ; and if either of them have any other weapon concealed about him, and therewith annoy his adversary, let it be done as shall be mentioned amongst combats in a plea of land."

REED.

THE END.

www.ingramcontent.com/pod-product-compliance
Lightning Source LLC
Chambersburg PA
CBHW020900130726
47900CB00014B/1210